COFFIN MAN

"Charlie Moon looks into several puzzles that confound . . . in Doss's amusing . . . adventure featuring the Ute Indian part-time deputy and full-time rancher. Series fans will enjoy spending time with old friends." —*Publishers Weekly*

A DEAD MAN'S TALE

"Top-flight work from Doss . . . a droll fandango."
                                —*Kirkus Reviews* (starred review)

"Funny, even slapstick in places . . . memorable characters add zest."   —*Booklist*

THE WIDOW'S REVENGE

"Insanely good."   —*Kirkus Reviews* (starred review)

"It's Moon who stands tallest in *The Widow's Revenge* . . . a nonstop read [in] this solid series."   —*Booklist*

"Successfully evokes the mysticism of traditional Native American storytelling."   —*Publishers Weekly*

SNAKE DREAMS

"Outstanding. . . . The narrator clearly is having fun as he unveils his tale, liberally laced with Native American lore, character idiosyncrasies, comedic asides, and a plot that weaves and twists like a highway in the Rockies."

                                —*Library Journal* (starred review)

MORE . . .

"*Snake Dreams* is the thirteenth novel in this series, and since it's a very good one—funny, smart, and totally different—it's a great place for readers to discover Moon."

—*Globe and Mail* (Toronto)

THREE SISTERS

"One of his best yet!" —*Booklist*

Wild, authentic . . . and highly satisfying." —*Detroit Free Press*

"A finely cut gem." —*Publishers Weekly* (starred review)

"James D. Doss's novels about Charlie Moon . . . feel as if the author is sitting around a campfire, spinning a tall tale that engulfs a circle of listeners . . . Doss's tale is evocative of the area and of Indian lore, and his chatty, down-home style shines in *Three Sisters*." —*Florida Sun-Sentinel*

"Doss's trademark humor keeps Charlie and Scott wisecracking as the plot spins smartly along to an unpredictable ending . . . Moon mysteries still charm us with Western voices and ways." —*Rocky Mountain News*

STONE BUTTERFLY

"Style, pathos, enthusiasm, and humor to spare." —*Mystery Scene*

"A clever plot . . . will keep readers turning the pages." —*Publishers Weekly*

"The Moon series deftly blends traditional mystery elements with Native American mythology—a surefire read-alike for Hillerman fans." —*Booklist*

"Droll, crafty, upper-echelon reading." —*Kirkus Reviews* (starred review)

SHADOW MAN

"Doss likes to toss a little Native American spiritualism and a lot of local color into his mysteries. Fans of the series will be well pleased." —*Booklist*

"Fans of Daisy Perika, the 80-something shaman who brings much of the charm and supernatural thrill to James D. Doss's mystery series, should like *Shadow Man* . . . nice reading." —*Rocky Mountain News*

THE WITCH'S TONGUE

"With all the skill and timing of a master magician, Doss unfolds a meticulous plot laced with a delicious sense of humor and set against a vivid southern Colorado." —*Publishers Weekly*

"Doss's ear for Western voices is remarkable, his tone whimsical. . . . If you don't have time for the seven-hour drive from Denver to Pagosa, try *Witch's Tongue* for a taste of southern Colorado." —*Rocky Mountain News*

"A classy bit of storytelling that combines myth, dreams, and plot complications so wily they'll rattle your synapses and tweak your sense of humor." —*Kirkus Reviews*

DEAD SOUL

"Hillerman gets the most press, but Doss mixes an equally potent brew of crime and Native American spirituality." —*Booklist*

"Lyrical and he gets the sardonic, macho patter between men down cold. The finale is heartfelt and unexpected, and a final confrontation stuns with its violent and confessional precision." —*Providence Journal Bulletin*

ALSO BY JAMES D. DOSS

Coffin
Man

JAMES D. DOSS

St. Martin's Paperbacks

This is a work of fiction. All of the characters, organizations, and events portrayed in this novel are either products of the author's imagination or are used fictitiously.

COFFIN MAN

Copyright © 2011 by James D. Doss.
Excerpt from *The Old Gray Wolf* copyright © 2011 by James D. Doss.

For information address St. Martin's Press, 175 Fifth Avenue, New York, NY 10010.

Library of Congress Catalog Card Number: 2011026219

ISBN: 978-1-250-00855-8

Printed in the United States of America

Minotaur hardcover edition / November 2011
St. Martin's Paperbacks edition / August 2012

St. Martin's Paperbacks are published by St. Martin's Press, 175 Fifth Avenue, New York, NY 10010.

10 9 8 7 6 5 4 3 2

For the following nice folks in Taos County, New Mexico:

Art and Susan Bachrach
Dennis and Winnie Concha
Judy Morita
John and Jeannie Norris
Rick Smith
and
Tyrone and Jennifer Tsoodle

PROLOGUE

A Crusty Old Lady

By the gradual falling away of an increasingly frail competition, Daisy Perika has become the Southern Ute tribe's oldest member. It might reasonably be supposed that the current holder of this title has become feeble in mind and body, but that would be an unwarranted assumption—and a risky one.

As folks used to say in bygone days, Miss Daisy is *set in her ways*. And very firmly so. Like senior citizens the world over, the tribal elder is intent on doing things as she sees fit, particularly when in her own home—which modest domicile is located on the sparsely populated eastern edge of the reservation, and not so far north of Colorado's wilderness border with New Mexico. A universal proverb is: "Hard country makes hard people." Another, more parochial maxim whispered by those locals *in the know* is: "Don't Ever Cross Daisy Perika." Good advice.

Ask Charlie Moon, and he'll tell you that when his aunt wakes up in one of her better moods, she is pure hell-for-breakfast. On those mornings when Daisy greets the dawn with a flinty glint of fire in her eye—look out for the baddest woolly-booger west of the Pecos! Charlie claims that irate stepped-on rattlesnakes, snarling badgers, sting-you-just-for-fun scorpions, and foaming-at-the-mouth rabid packrats—all alike tip their little cowboy hats and step aside to yield the right-of-way to the cranky old lady. And it must be true because Daisy's Catholic nephew will swear to this testimony on an Anglican prayer book without cracking a grin, and there's not a hairy-chested hombre in Granite Creek County who'll call Mr. Moon a low-down, egg-sucking, yeller-dog liar or an habitual dissembler—not to Moon's face. Not if he wants to keep his teeth betwixt lips and tongue.

If Daisy had been aware of her relative's happy hyperbole, she would have dismissed Charlie Moon's boasts as faint praise. The old lady doesn't mind playing the heavy—a big, bad rep has its advantages. General nuisances and major troublemakers tend to steer clear of elderly civilians who are deemed emotionally unstable and inclined toward gratuitous violence. Especially when those potential malefactors toddle about armed with a stout oak walking stick and know how to use it and on who—and do.

On the downside, an eminent lady's social intercourse is somewhat restricted by the other party's expectation that a slight difference of opinion might result in an urgent visit to the nearest emergency room. As a consequence, the fractious old soul who is reputed to be the *meanest Ute woman ever to draw a breath* does not have a multitude of adoring pals who come calling for afternoon tea and crumpets. That's okay with Daisy, who comforts herself with the conviction that the few comrades she does have are absolutely first rate.

Right at the top of the list is her skinny, seven-foot-tall nephew. The part-time tribal investigator, occasional deputy to the Granite Creek chief of police, and full-time cattle rancher is (in Daisy's opinion) as good a man as walks the earth. But being the best of a sorry lot doesn't make Charlie Moon all that much to brag about. To put it in the words of this woman who has buried three troublesome husbands: "If I was to meet the finest porcupine that ever chewed the bark off a mulberry tree, I wouldn't invite him home for supper." Which brings us to the runner-up.

Despite the fact that she is only half Ute, nineteen-year-old Sarah Frank firmly occupies the number-two spot on Daisy's Friends' List. The willowy lass (as they also said in olden days) "has her cap set" on Charlie Moon, whose affections for the Ute-Papago orphan are of a fatherly nature.

The third member of Daisy's inner circle is Scott Parris—a beefy, pale-skinned, blue-eyed *matukach*. The Caucasian cop is Charlie Moon's best friend and the aforementioned chief of police.

Of the three, only Charlie Moon is her blood kin, but Daisy Perika considers the trio to be her *family*. From time to time, closely knit clans get together to share a meal at a mutually convenient table, and for this foursome such gatherings generally take place at a favorite local restaurant, the headquarters of Mr. Moon's Columbine Ranch, or at Daisy's remote reservation home.

One such reunion is currently under way at that latter location.

CHAPTER ONE

CAÑÓN DEL ESPÍRITU

Thursday Morning

Daisy Perika has resided at the mouth of Spirit Canyon for more bone-chilling winters than she cares to remember. Since the tribal elder now spends about nine days out of ten at her nephew's vast cattle ranch northwest of Granite Creek, her home has become a place to spend a day or two in now and then. During these occasional visits, Miss Daisy begins by making sure that nothing is amiss, such as an odorous skunk that has taken up residence under the hardwood floor, a pair of frisky squirrels raising a family in the attic, or a broken window where the dry west wind blows dust in. Charlie Moon can be counted on to deal with such problems forthwith, and when all has been made right, Daisy enjoys sleeping away a peaceful night in her own bed, cooking breakfast on her six-burner propane range, and taking long, soul-satisfying walks in her canyon.

Yes, *her* canyon.

It matters little that the shadowy space between miles-long Three Sisters Mesa and the lesser promontory known as Dogleg is owned by the tribe. As long as Daisy Perika has lived in this remote location, hardly anyone besides herself ever sets foot inside Spirit Canyon but those lonely haunts that *Cañón del Espíritu* is named for and the dwarfish *pitukupf* who allegedly resides therein.

But enough about local geography and Daisy's thousand-year-old neighbor, who will make his presence known if and when he is "of a mind to." What currently commands our attention (and excites our olfactory senses) are the tantalizing aromas drifting out of Daisy's kitchen. Ahhh . . . sniff a whiff of *that*!

(Nothing smells quite so appetizing as burning animal fat.)

On the left half of a massive Tennessee Forge skillet, plump pork sausages are sizzling deliciously. On the opposite side, strips of bacon pop grease hot enough to put out a bronze statue's eyeball.

And that's not all.

In a matching black cast-iron cooking implement, fresh eggs, sharp cheddar cheese, presautéed Vidalia onions, and Hatch green chili are being stirred by Sarah Frank into an exceedingly tasty scramble.

In a blue enameled pot, tar-black coffee percolates with seductive *plickity-plocks*. This high-octane concoction is guaranteed to knock off your socks.

In the top of the oven, Daisy's secret-recipe, made-from-scratch biscuits are slowly baking to a golden-brown perfection. On the shelf below that, a tray of delicious cinnamon-bun confections are swelling with justifiable pride.

One is tempted to drop in and tuck a napkin under the chin. Sadly, Daisy's dining table is set only for four.

Breakfast in Daisy's Kitchen

After busying herself importantly around the stove—where Sarah Frank was doing all the real work and graciously accepting sage advice from the tribal elder—Daisy Perika decided that her assistant was doing a fairly competent job for someone who was only half Ute. The senior cook took the coffeepot to the table and filled all four cups with steaming brew. This done, the lady of the house seated herself and waited for the girl to bring on the victuals. Daisy knew precisely what Sarah would put onto her plate: two strips of crispy bacon, one patty of sausage, one biscuit, and a just-so helping of scrambled eggs.

As the hungry fellows bellied up to the table, Sarah began to deliver the food on preheated stoneware platters.

Charlie Moon offered a heartfelt cowboy compliment: "That looks good enough to eat."

Nodding his agreement, Scott Parris upped the ante: "That and then some."

So much for original conversation when breaking fast; the taciturn menfolk got right at it with knife and fork.

Daisy buttered her biscuit, added a dab of Kroger strawberry preserves, and took a bite. *I can't hardly taste that.* But even an old body needed nourishment and . . . *I have to keep my strength up.* This being so, she chewed and dutifully choked it down. Being of an analytic and morbid inclination, the old soul reviewed the highlights of her decline. *First it was my hearing.* A second dab of jam on the biscuit. *Then my eyes started to get cloudy.* Another halfhearted bite, followed by feeble mastication. *Now I can't hardly taste anything I put in my mouth.* She supposed that aged people were much like rusty old pickup trucks or antique sewing machines: sooner or later, various parts were bound to wear out. Daisy figured her brain would go next. *Some morning soon, I'll wake up and wonder what my name is.* In search of something more pleasant to think about, she looked across the table at Sarah, who was gazing at Moon with big cow eyes. *Sooner or later Charlie'll have to tell this silly little half-Papago girl that he don't intend to marry her because he's old enough to be her daddy.* The senior member of the gathering helped herself to another mouthful of buttered biscuit and jam. *That tastes a little better— maybe my mouth just needs more practice.*

Scott Parris reached for a jar of Daisy's homemade damson-plum preserves. While spooning a generous helping of the fruity treat onto his second biscuit, he cast a glance at Sarah. "What classes are you taking at Rocky Mountain Polytechnic?"

"Computer Science, History of Western Civilization, and Statistical Analysis." The young woman, who had avoided both meats and the bread, pecked at her modest portion of scrambled eggs. "Oh, and Social Studies."

"That's a pretty heavy load," Moon observed.

"It keeps me busy." The slender little scholar shrugged under her blue polka-dot dress. "In Social Studies, I'll be doing a research project on indigent persons in Granite Creek."

His mouth full, Parris was obliged to suppress a snort. After swallowing, the stocky white cop offered this observation: "We got plenty of those characters hanging around town."

Sarah Frank took a sip of coffee. "My professor suggested that I find my subjects in U.S. Grant Park."

Taking on the role of a concerned uncle, the chief of police eyed the orphan sternly. "Don't you get caught in the park after dark. Most of those so-called 'indigent' folks are wild-eyed dope addicts, whiskey-soaked alcoholics, or flat-out howling-at-the-moon lunatics." He took a hard look at his biscuit. "Some are all three."

A smile played at the edges of the girl's lips. *He's so sweet.*

"Pay attention, Sarah." Charlie Moon used his Buck sheath knife to deftly slice a pork patty into four equal pieces. "Scott knows what he's talking about." He speared a quarter section with the tip of the blade. "Some of those unfortunate folks are downright dangerous."

"I'll be careful." Sarah flashed a pretty smile at Moon. "I'll do all of my research in the middle of the day."

The lawmen grunted their approval; even Daisy seemed pleased with the girl's prudence. And so it went. A delightful breakfast.

No one present could have imagined what was about to happen.

When the morning meal was completed, the eldest of the diners opened her mouth to let out a long, satisfying yawn. *I feel a nice nap coming on.* The tribal elder withdrew to her parlor without a word to her guests or the least concern about who would clean off the table, wash dishes, and so on and so forth. The sleepy woman wedged herself into a creaky old rocking chair and settled in there with her feet on the bricked hearth. A second yawn began to slip between Daisy Perika's lips. She was asleep before her mouth had time to close.

A brief siesta is generally beneficial after a meal, especially for those citizens who are older than eighty-foot-tall pink-barked ponderosas. This was not an appropriate time for a nightmare, but the morning's sweetest dream occasionally walks arm-in-arm with her sinister midnight sister.

CHAPTER TWO

THE OLD WOMAN'S VISION

As with so many misadventures, Daisy Perika's nap-dream began innocently enough.

Like a tender brown bean shelled from its dry hull, something forever young was set free from the prison of her old, tired body. As it slipped away into a velvety-soft twilight, this essence of her soul (or so it seemed) prepared to take flight. Her spirit floated effortlessly up from the rocking chair to pass through the beamed ceiling and into the attic. Daisy was intensely aware of every detail in that musty, dusty space. She counted eleven spiders on eleven webs, examined every knot in every pine two-by-six, frowned at a nail that an inept carpenter had bent, and spotted a hickory-handled Ace claw hammer the careless fellow had left behind. But the dreamer did not tarry there; she penetrated the roof as if that sturdy assembly of planks, plywood, and shiny red Pro-Panel was merely a misty figment of her Lower World imagination.

Up—up—up she rose, ever faster—and spread her strong young arms to soar among those proud hawks and eagles who ruled this airy underbelly of the earthly heavens. As if hours were minutes in this singular dimension, the cerulean sky began to darken with a ferocious rapidity. Roiling blue-black clouds inflated with explosive intent; thunder began to rumble over those big-shouldered mountains that would not be named after San Juan for centuries. Lifted by the sighing winds, Daisy drifted effortlessly over Three Sisters Mesa, gazing down at the sandstone remnants of those Pueblo women who had fled to escape the horror of a marauding band of painted-face, filed-tooth cannibal terrorists from the south. Though the atrocities had occurred more than a millennium ago, Daisy's dream-eyes witnessed the slaughter of the remnants of the Sisters' tribe—those unfortunates who had attempted to hide in the shadowy depths of Spirit Canyon.

But like her feathered comrades who drifted over the scene with serene indifference to the problems of wingless human beings, Daisy's heart was likewise hardened to the suffering and death unfolding below. Her experience was like watching a moving-picture show about the horrors of some long-ago calamity where nameless innocents were slain. The dreamer was so far removed from the carnage that it seemed more like lurid fiction than tragic history.

But, as so often happens with those of us who have no empathy for the suffering of others, the shaman's experience was about to become extremely personal—and take a sudden turn for the worse.

Though Daisy did not fall from the sky like a stone, her majestic, soaring form was abruptly diminished to something resembling a tiny, wing-flapping sparrow. No longer the peer of bald eagles and red-tailed hawks, the shaman darted a few yards over the floor of *Cañón del Espíritu*— pursued by a rapacious predator. The fleeing dreamer did not see the creature that was intent upon eating her alive, but her spirit eyes did perceive a huge owl shadow slipping quickly along the canyon's sandy bottom.

Daisy's Jarring Awakening

The kitchen now shipshape and squeaky clean, the men-folk and the Ute-Papago girl were almost ready to leave Aunt Daisy at home alone.

After taking a final swipe at the shining dining table, Sarah Frank withdrew to the guest bedroom that she used when staying overnight with Daisy Perika. She opened the closet door to take her dark-blue coat off a plastic hanger, reached up to a shelf for her nifty cowgirl hat—and during the process knocked off a shoe box, which fell to spill its contents onto the floor. The girl knelt to gather odd bits of this and that, which included the chubby snow-white leg of an antique china doll (a brown shoe was painted onto the tiny foot), a jet-black 1940s-era Sheaffer fountain pen with the nib broken off, a red plastic flower, and—something else that was folded in a piece of gauzy tissue paper.

Sarah picked it up, her smooth brow furrowing as she unwrapped it. *What's this?*

Hers was a rhetorical question.

The thing she held between finger and thumb was quite obviously a feather. And not a particularly distinguished member of that category of covering that had first sprouted on the nimble limbs of smallish proto-dinosaurs. Perhaps three inches long, its sorry excuse for color resided some-where in that dreary neighborhood between mouse brown and slate gray. The tip of the feather appeared to have been scorched, and a hint of odor remained that was similar to the unpleasant scent of burned hair. Sarah wrinkled her nose. *I wonder why Aunt Daisy is keeping this old thing?* She im-mediately smiled at her silly question. One might as well ask why the old woman had stashed away a doll's leg, a broken fountain pen, and a plastic rose. *They all mean something to her, I suppose.* Still, the girl was curious about the feather. *I'll ask her about it.* If there was not a good story behind this unlikely artifact, the tribal elder would feel obliged to make one up.

After restoring the other objects to the shoe box and returning it to the closet shelf, Sarah donned her coat and wide-brimmed hat. Entering the parlor, she gazed at the old woman who slept in the rocking chair. *It seems like a shame to wake her up.* She twirled the feather between finger and thumb. *But we can't just leave her here all alone and asleep without saying goodbye.* Not wanting to awaken the sleeper too abruptly, she whispered, "Aunt Daisy?"

No response.

Feeling more than a little whimsical—very nearly mischievous—Sarah thought: *I ought to use the feather to tickle her nose.* But for whatever reason, that was not precisely what she did. The girl stroked the feather ever so lightly over the old woman's left eyelid, the bridge of her nose, and across the other closed eye.

The sleeper shuddered; both eyes popped open to glare at Sarah. "What'd you do?"

Startled by the suddenness of the awakening, Sarah stuttered. "I . . . tick-tickled your . . ." By way of explanation, she showed the old woman the feather.

"Silly girl." Daisy snorted. "If you want to wake me up, just let out a big war whoop and tell me the 'Paches are riding in to massacre us all—or shoot off a big pistol by my ear!"

Relieved, the nervous youth giggled. "I'm sorry. It's just that we're about to leave, and—"

"We're about to leave?" Disoriented by her awakening, the old woman blinked. "Where're we going?"

Sarah Frank was saved from the pain of explaining when Charlie Moon and Scott Parris stomped into the parlor to announce their imminent departure.

Sarah offered the face tickler to Daisy, who waved it aside. "What would I want with *that!*"

Not knowing what else to do with the offending feather, Sarah stuck it into her hatband. "When do you want me to come back?"

The old woman frowned. "Come back for what?"

"To take you back to the Columbine."

"Oh . . . sometime next week, I guess." Rubbing the residue of sleep from her eyes, Daisy got a grip on her oak staff and pushed herself up from the rocking chair. "I'll call you when I'm ready." She followed Sarah and the men outside, where her small family commenced with the standard rituals of departure.

The old woman received a big hug from Charlie Moon and the usual suggestion that she should stay close to her house until Sarah returned. Which was Moon's way of advising his reckless relative to resist any temptation to stray alone into *Cañón del Espíritu*. A lot of good such advice from her nephew would do.

Scott Parris bear-hugged Daisy, too, and warned, "There's always black bears and hungry cougars and a few two-legged varmints roaming about, so you'd best be on the lookout." Breathless from these manly embraces, Daisy was unable to respond with her usual tart remark that if any furry varmints or wild-eyed outlaws came skulking around her place, it'd be *them* that'd need to be on the lookout because she had a double-barrel 12-gauge shotgun in the closet that was loaded with buckshot and she knew how to use it. But the white cop knew what Daisy was thinking and she knew that he knew and that Charlie Moon did too.

The final hug, a light embrace such as might be made by a fairy queen in a little girl's dream, was administered by Sarah Frank. This expression of affection was accompanied by a pair of surprises that quite took the old woman's breath away—two tender expressions that Charlie Moon's aunt had not experienced in decades.

The sweet girl whispered in Daisy's ear, "You're like a grandmother to me."

This was more than sufficient to strike the old woman dumb.

Sarah whispered again, "I love you." And kissed Daisy's wrinkled cheek.

Overkill.

If Daisy Perika was not literally bowled over by these tender endearments, they created a peculiar sense of disorientation. The woman with the barbed tongue and quick wit had not even the *urge* to make a sarcastic reply. Indeed, a salty tear appeared in the corner of her left eye. Daisy promptly blinked it away. *Now what did Sarah do that for?*

To those tender souls who appreciate occasional displays of fondness, Daisy's querulous query might seem peculiar. But the woman who had suffered multiple huggings—and even being *kissed*—felt like one who has been deprived of some essential strength. And not the mere weakening of muscle or intellect; it was as if the tribal elder had been robbed of some precious inner possession . . . an essential secret weapon.

Daisy Perika scowled at her departing friends as if one of them were a thief. *Or maybe it's all three.*

Any fair-minded person who is acquainted with Charlie Moon, Scott Parris, and Sarah Frank will be appalled and insist that Daisy's unspoken accusation is without the slightest justification. The old woman—always prone to unseemly excesses—has finally become completely unhinged.

That possibility cannot be ruled out.

But bizarre as Daisy Perika's conviction may seem, this much may be stated with absolute certainty—a vital arrow was suddenly missing from the shaman's quiver.

Even so, did someone really purloin the pointed projectile?

Despite Daisy's dark suspicions, a deliberate theft seems unlikely.

But it is equally improbable that the tribal elder has mislaid her treasured weapon—or that the missing arrow has bent a metaphoric bow and set *itself* aflame.

So what the dickens *is* going on here?

Those intrepid souls who raise such questions might be well advised to exercise a degree of caution. Ignorance, if not always bliss, is occasionally preferable to knowing what's going on.

CHAPTER THREE

CONCERNING THE VISUALIZATION OF DEAD PEOPLE AND THE PERCEPTION OF THEIR VOICES

As Scott Parris drove away in his aged red Volvo, Charlie Moon's Expedition was close behind. Sarah Frank waited in her freshly washed and waxed red F-150 pickup until the dust had settled, then waved at Daisy Perika as she left.

The very instant when the departing vehicles were out of sight, Charlie Moon's aunt locked the front door of her house, got a firm grip on her walking stick, and set her wrinkled face resolutely toward her intended destination. Within the minute, the canyon's gaping mouth had swallowed her whole.

As she trod along slowly, the tribal elder wondered how many times she had followed this sinuous deer path into the solitude of *Cañón del Espíritu*. A thousand? No. *More than I could count on the fingers of a thousand hands—and here I go again.* And she entered therein with the comfortable certainty that today's journey into this inner sanctum of her soul would be witnessed by a multitude of curious characters. Daisy could already *feel* the cunning animal eyes watching her from their various concealments. (Her observers included a pair of prairie rattlesnakes, several cottontail rabbits, a gray squirrel, and a harem of shy mule deer.) Daisy was confident that the gossipy raven would show her face, and that Delilah Darkwing would to bring her up-to-date on the latest gossip concerning the occupants of Spirit Canyon. Thus far, her feathered friend was nowhere to be seen. The feisty old woman particularly looked forward to a contentious conversation with the venerable *pitukupf*. She supposed that after a light breakfast of wild honey and piñon nuts, the dwarf was probably napping in his snug underground home. (He may have been; we have no reliable information on the Little Man's current whereabouts.)

But even if Daisy encountered neither her diminutive neighbor nor Delilah Darkwing, there was one constant in the Ute elder's pilgrimages into these shadowy spaces between the canyon's sandstone walls—the dead people who dwelled there. Like flitting bats who appeared with soft twilight and fuzzy moths drawn to flickering candlelight, the haunts were bound to show their faces—and several of these disembodied souls would bend Daisy's ear with pleas for one thing and another. Among the recently deceased, the most common request was for information about friends and relatives who remained among the living. Once in a while, a vindictive apparition would (with considerable relish) inquire whether old So-and-So had finally died yet, and express the hope that his death had been painful. Some long-dead phantoms would announce their presence with sinister grunts and horrible groanings, and one of these ancients might utter unintelligible mutterings in a language that had died ages ago with his long-forgotten tribe. Most of these dead folk were unpleasant to behold, but Daisy had grown accustomed to empty eye sockets, withered limbs showing gristle and bone, and skin that hung in tattered shreds. Unique among the residents of *Cañón del Espíritu* was an Apache skin-walker whom Daisy had (with malice aforethought) personally dispatched to his present condition. Evidently chagrined, her victim delighted in making dire threats against the Ute elder's person, to which the shaman would reply in like kind. The irascible old woman enjoyed such interactions, and most of her encounters with the ghosts of Spirit Canyon were stimulating social events. Though she would not have admitted it, the old woman looked forward to the hideous apparitions' predictable appearances.

To her dismay, on this day they did not.

Appear, that is.

Oh, the haunts were *there,* all right.

Daisy could hear the voices of several wandering souls. A recently dead quilt maker from Ignacio asked how her unmarried daughter was getting along. An Anasazi sorcerer who evidently considered the shaman a kindred spirit whispered urgently into Daisy's ear. She could not understand a single syllable of what the dead magician said. A lonely old prospector who'd panned the stream almost two centuries ago inquired about the current price of gold. An 1870s Fort Garland soldier who'd died within sight of Three Sisters Mesa pleaded with the old woman to find his resting place and see that he got a decent Christian burial.

Though she usually enjoyed conversing with the dead, the Ute elder did not utter one word in response.

Her Apache victim (presumably waiting at the end of the queue) muttered several obscenities. He also threatened to sneak into her bedroom some dark night, suck all the blood from her veins, and vomit it into her water well. This aggravation was sufficient to loosen her tongue. "Come right ahead," the feisty old woman said. "Try to put the bite on me and I'll sew your nasty lips shut so tight that you won't be able to say a four-letter word or suck sour stump water through a straw!" Under ordinary circumstances, this threat-counterthreat entertainment would have brightened up her morning. But not on this occasion.

Daisy was distracted by a totally unforeseen development. For the first time ever, the shaman could not *see* a single one of those dead people who hovered so closely about her.

It was unnerving.

So much so, that without a thought to the friendly raven who was gliding down to land on a nearby juniper, or the cantankerous *pitukupf* whom she assumed was napping in his underground den, Daisy Perika turned as abruptly as one of her advanced age can and set her haggard face toward the open end of *Cañón del Espíritu*. As she pegged her way back along the deer path with her sturdy oak walking stick, a dismal thought hovered about her like a noxious vapor rising from a fetid swamp: *I'm losing my powers.* From Daisy's unique perspective, this was equivalent to admitting that her vital life forces were ebbing. *Sure as snow melts in May and cottonwood leaves fall to the ground in November and rot right on the spot—I'm dying.*

Are Dr. Daisy's self-diagnosis and bleak prognosis accurate? Perhaps. The truth of the matter remains to be discerned.

But of this much we can be certain: even as the old soul trodeth steadfastly toward hearth and home, Charlie Moon's despondent aunty is not alone in this world of troubles. Other problems are always brewing in other pots, and one in particular is about to boil over that will—in one way or another—*scald every member of the tribal elder's inner circle.*

When and where?

Tomorrow morning in Granite Creek.

For those who hanker for a higher degree of specificity, the epicenter of this localized eruption will be—the Wanda Naranjo residence and its environs.

You've never heard of the place?

That lack of familiarity shall be immediately remedied.

CHAPTER FOUR

THE SHAKEDOWN

Granite Creek, Friday Morning

Bleak bouquets of black clouds were blossoming over the mountains like sooty roses when Michael Kauffmann arrived in his Jeep Wagoneer. Oblivious to the looming storm, he braked to a stop in Wanda Naranjo's cluttered yard, set the gearshift to Park, and cut the ignition. The long, thin face under his mop of red hair wore a wary expression—suggesting a famished coyote who'd spent the entire night on the prowl without making a kill. His ranging gaze took in an unpainted house with a rickety front porch. The dwelling was hatted with a rusted metal roof; at one end towered a mossy brick chimney where a hint of gray smoke curled up. On the porch were a pair of windows with paper shades lowered halfway; these lidded eyes looked back at him. Evading the disinterested gaze, Kauffmann glanced at the dilapidated one-window shack out back that leaned confidently against a rotting cottonwood. On the far side of a pathway through a weedy garden, a gnarly grape arbor made a tunnel to a weatherworn outhouse that served as a rustic backup when Wanda's septic tank got backed up. Kauffmann found the normalcy of the familiar setting reassuring, but his bloodshot eyes had also noticed what *wasn't* there—his lady friend's Toyota Tercel. *Wanda must be working overtime again.* Which reminded him that his main squeeze had nagged him yesterday about repairing something or other at the house before she returned home from her graveyard shift at Snyder Memorial Hospital. *But what was I supposed to fix?* Kauffmann's brow furrowed into a painfully strained frown. *I think it had something to do with water dripping.* A leaky roof? *No, that wasn't it.* The showerhead in the bathroom? *I don't think so.* He shrugged his scrawny shoulders. *Well, whatever it was, it can wait till after some breakfast.* Kauffmann's 'possum grin bared a set of yellowed teeth. *Wanda has a good memory and she won't forget to remind me.* As the part-time carpenter emerged from his old motor vehicle to amble across the yard, it occurred to him that she might not show up for a while. *I might have to wait for some eats.* His empty stomach growled in protest, reminding him that the absent woman had a teenage daughter. *If Betty ain't suffering from the morning sickness or some such thing, maybe I can talk her into breaking some eggs and perking a pot of coffee.* In Mr. Kauffmann's expert opinion, the daughter was every bit as good a cook as her mother. *One of 'em can boil water about as well as the other.*

Garbed in a tattered cotton bathrobe, her hands clasped around her protruding abdomen, Betty Naranjo watched her mother's boyfriend from a dirty window. When Michael Kauffmann began making his way to the porch, the impressively pregnant sixteen-year-old waddled across the shoddy parlor toward the door. The pine floor squeaked under her weight, which was now in excess of 140 pounds. She opened the door without a word of greeting and received the same in return.

Kauffmann hung his Wally Wordsworth's Woodworks billed cap on a cedar peg, tossed his denim jacket onto the floor, then ambled indolently over to the couch, where he plopped down and stretched out flat on his back. "I could eat a half-dozen fried eggs, a pound of greasy bacon, and chuga-lug a whole gallon of coffee." He closed his eyes. "Wake me up when breakfast is ready."

Betty's lip curled in an ugly sneer. "I wouldn't wake you up if the house was on fire!"

"Don't try sweet-talking me, youngster—I know you're just angling for a favor." Kauffmann cracked a wry eye long enough to wink it at his antagonist. "Besides, I like you better when you're downright mean—so see if you can think of something *really* nasty to say."

Searching vainly for another poisonous barb, Betty found her supply depleted. Defeated by the thick-skinned scoundrel, she withdrew into her bedroom. Seating herself before a dresser, she picked up a purple plastic comb and listlessly began to pull it through strands of straggly black hair. Pausing, the teenager stared in the mirror at a bloated face floating over a big belly. *Just a few months ago, I had a nice figure and was almost as pretty as some of those hotshot movie stars.* As if to remind her of its presence, the new life shifted behind her naval. It was depressing to have a baby that was going to come into the world in a couple of weeks without a daddy who'd admit to being the father. *But I guess I brought this on myself.* The young woman scowled at her homely behind-the-looking-glass counterpart, who faithfully returned the favor. *So it's up to me to take care of things.* She put the purple plastic comb into a white leatherette jewelry box that was filled with gaudy baubles and waddled back into the parlor. While considering her options, she stood by the sofa where her mother's boyfriend was pretending to nap. Betty fixed her myopic gaze on Mike Kauffmann's tightly closed eyelids. *What a faker.* She toyed with the notion of kicking his left foot, which was dangling off the couch, but decided that . . . *It'll be more fun to stare at him till he can't stand it anymore and opens his eyes.* And so she did.

The weasel-faced man with the unruly shock of red hair did his level best to reinforce the pretense that he was dozing. To that end, Kauffmann allowed his mouth to fall open. He also emitted a snorting snore. And frowned like a sleeper having a bad dream.

Betty waited, patient as a frozen figure in a photograph.

Having no other option, Kauffmann gamely continued the contest.

Another unconvincing snore. A shudder, as if a monster in his nightmare was about to put the grab on him. A pitiful moan.

The top-heavy girl smiled as the second hand on the wall clock touched the 12. *He won't hold out another minute.*

By and by, a muscle began to twitch nervously in his jaw. This was the real thing.

As the clock's slender sliver of silvered steel approached 4, Kauffmann pressed his lips hard together.

As the half minute was approaching, the lightweight threw in the towel.

Betty watched the fraud open his eyes, fake a yawn, and pretend to be wide-eyed in surprise at discovering her presence.

"Hello, Miss Mean-mouth." The part-time carpenter stretched his long, sinewy arms. "How long've you been standing there?"

"Give me twenty dollars." The girl had a way of getting right to the point.

This time, his surprise was genuine. "What for?"

"Because I asked you for it. And don't take all day; I've gotta catch the bus into town."

Mike Kauffmann raised his angular frame to a sitting position and planted both of his booted feet firmly on the floor. "I ain't worked in over a week, sugar dumplin', and the rent's due today so I don't have that much cash to spare—"

"Yes you do. Put it there." Betty extended her sweaty palm.

He shook his head. "No way."

"Momma's liable to show up any minute now." The pregnant girl cocked her head. "You don't give me twenty bucks, I'll tell your *older* girlfriend something you don't want her to know."

His weasel eyes narrowed. "Like what?"

The girl smirked. "Like who my baby's daddy is."

A flash of cloud-fire illuminated the parlor windows.

Crouching tensely on the couch like a cougar about to pounce, Kauffmann glared hatefully at his tormentor.

Three thumping heartbeats after the lightning, thunder rumbled.

For about four more, his eyes burned holes into the flaccid face that had been so attractive a few months ago. Finally, he said, "Hell, you don't even *know* who the father is."

"Maybe I do, maybe I don't." Betty reached out to flick a finger at his red hair. "But what if baby turns out to be a cute little carrot-top?" She laughed. "If I was to drop a hint to Momma that you was the daddy, she'd sharpen up her butcher knife and fix you so you'd never father another brat."

Kauffmann knew that Betty wasn't bluffing. The defeated man pulled a wallet from his hip pocket, removed a wrinkled greenback, and slapped it onto her hand. "That's my onliest twenty," he whined. "All I got left is six dollars."

"Tough cookies." Betty stuffed the take into her bathrobe pocket. "By this time next week, I'll be needing s'more cash money, so you'd better go over to the furniture factory and ask the boss man to scare up some work for you to do." She winked at her victim. "Maybe somebody died last night and they need a nice pine box to sleep in."

Mike Kauffmann's hands made fists as he muttered under his sour, beer-scented breath, "By this time next week, you might be needing—"

Might be needing *what*?

It is irritating, when awaiting the completion of a presumably witty riposte, to have the barbed end clipped off. But that is precisely what the thoughtless fellow has done.

The question is: "Why?"

The answer is: "Because."

Because even though the storm rumbling ominously over the mountains had drowned out the sound of Wanda Naranjo's arriving automobile, Michael Kauffmann heard Betty's mother climbing the squeaky porch steps and stomping across the loose boards to open the door to the parlor. Whatever the boyfriend thought Betty might be needing this time next week must remain his dark secret. We shall not fret about it; the knowledge is surely not a great loss. Though Mr. Kauffmann is a competent carpenter, he is not known among the hammer-and-nails set for his verbal virtuosity. His pithy comeback was probably something like: *By this time next week, you may be needing a new set of teeth.* If so, the fellow's attempt at a snappy comeback was far off the mark.

Seven days hence, Betty Naranjo would not be in the market for a single incisor, bicuspid, or molar.

CHAPTER FIVE

A ROUTINE DOMESTIC DISPUTE

Slamming the door behind her, Wanda Naranjo simulated a convincing shiver. "Before long, it's gonna be raining fuzzy cats and hairy dogs and fat toad-frogs." Receiving no greeting from either her taciturn boyfriend or her sulky daughter, the forty-eight-year-old nurse's aide dropped her purse onto a parlor armchair, pulled off her shabby coat and tossed it over the purse, strode into the kitchen—and screeched like an edgy banshee whose flank had been prodded with a red-hot branding iron: "Aiiieeee!"

Such gut-wrenching screams tend to raise the small hairs on bystanders' necks and make them wonder what the matter is. Hairs did bristle on the necks of Michael Kauffmann and Betty Naranjo, and both were perplexed about the cause that had produced this alarming effect. Had the lady of the house actually been branded with the Bar-Double-X logo by a whimsical cowboy who—mistaking the rear entrance of the Naranjo residence for Pinky Dan's Last Chance Saloon—had entered the premises in search of some wholesome entertainment? While the probability of this scenario could not be set at zero, the arrival of a prankster-cowpuncher armed with his brand-new DeWalt battery-operated branding iron seemed somewhat unlikely. It was deemed more plausible that Wanda had encountered a far more dangerous visitor in her kitchen. Betty imagined a nine-foot rattlesnake, coiled and ready to fang her unfortunate mother, swallow her corpse whole, and—with characteristic reptilian rudeness—burp up Momma's indigestible rubber-soled shoes. Mr. Kauffmann, who had viewed hundreds of excessively violent flicks, pictured a humongous, hairy, ski-masked gorilla who was about to decapitate his sweetheart with a samurai sword that was already stained with the blood of dozens of ill-fated nurses' aides. Though both daughter and boyfriend were perplexed and troubled about Wanda's distress, neither made a move to leave the parlor and investigate—much less lend a hand in the lady's defense.

Evidently sensing their curiosity and realizing that some kind of explanation was required of her, the horrified woman yelled, "There's water all over the floor!"

His memory triggered by this hint, the man in the parlor nodded. *Oh, right—the leak Wanda nagged me about was in the kitchen.* As the likely consequence of this circumstance occurred to him, Michael Kauffmann's long face dropped. *With the floor to mop, there's no telling when she'll get around to fixing me some breakfast.* Major bummer.

The furious woman in the mauve uniform surged back into the parlor to glare at her boyfriend. Mike was sitting on the couch, doing his best to look as innocent as a week-old pink-skinned infant who had never known sin. This deceitful ploy served only to further enrage his girlfriend. "I told you about it last night—so why didn't you fix it?"

About eleven men out of ten hate to admit to their shortcomings, such as a tendency to disremember odd jobs that need doing. This virtue conserves considerable energy, which they expend in making excuses. "I ain't got the right kinda tools to work on water pipes." The carpenter shrugged. "And even if I had some pipe wrenches and solder and whatnot—I ain't a qualified plumber."

"Well, you could have *called* one!"

Kauffmann countered this unkind assertion with a drawling whine: "It wasn't much of a leak when you left for work last night—just a little drip."

You're a big drip. Wanda gave him a look that would have curdled fresh milk.

Showing her a grimy palm, the clueless fellow yawned into the hairy side of his hand. "I figured it could wait till you got home."

"Oh you did, did you."

"Uh-huh. Anyway, I ain't got enough money to pay a plumber." Mike Kauffmann shot an accusing sideways glance at Betty, whose blackmail had reduced him from poverty to penury.

"Well, then—I guess I shouldn't have bothered you with my little problem." Wanda Naranjo's tone had softened to silky smooth, her lips curved into a smile. Dangerous signs.

But ones that did not register with the freckled-faced man whose intelligence quotient hovered a few notches below room temperature. *I knew she'd cool off.*

In a manner of speaking, she had. The cold water had soaked into the canvas seams of Wanda's blue rubber-soled shoes and was wetting the bottom of her white cotton stockings. Curling her chilly toes, she picked up a cordless telephone and carried it into the kitchen to make the call. After describing the location of the leak as well as she could, the bone-tired woman asked, "How soon can you get here?" She was wide-eyed with surprise. "That soon?" The man on the other end of the line assured Mrs. Naranjo that he wouldn't be late. But this sounded too good to be true. *I'll be lucky if the liar shows up tomorrow.* The destitute woman didn't dare ask how much the service call would cost. "Okay, I'll be looking for you." She returned the turquoise telephone to the parlor, laid it gently into the matching cradle as if it were her plastic baby. Taking no notice of her worthless boyfriend, Wanda spoke to her daughter: "What do you want for breakfast, honey?"

Betty shrugged. "I'm not all that hungry."

"Well, I am." Kauffmann patted his flat belly.

Wanda pointedly ignored the odious fellow. "Don't forget that you're eating for two."

"I know," Betty said. "I already made me a baloney and mustard sandwich to go."

Wanda's brow gathered itself into a frown. "To go where?"

"To see Dr. Whyte."

"That geeky shrink who works for the high school?"

"Dr. Whyte's my counselor." Betty felt a vigorous kick in her belly. "My appointment's for eleven o'clock."

"Soon as I get on some dry stockings and shoes, I'll make you some scrambled eggs." The weary woman groaned and rubbed at a stinging ache in the small of her back. "Then I'll drive you over to see the doc."

"No, Momma. You've worked all night at the hospital—you need to get some sleep." The girl gave her mother a hug. "I'll walk down to the road and catch that little bus."

Wanda Naranjo was surprised and pleased at this uncharacteristic display of affection and concern. "But it's going to rain."

"Not right away."

The mother's tone hinted of some suspicion. "You sure you don't mind?"

"I like to ride the bus." The girl glanced at her Walmart wristwatch. "It's free and it'll come along in about a half hour, so I'd better get my shower and get dressed."

"Well, I guess it'll be all right then." As Betty trod off to the bathroom and shut the door, Wanda realized that her daughter's shower bath would provide an opportunity to take care of some serious business. *I've been putting it off for weeks, and right now is the time to get it done.*

Getting Shut of an Egg-Sucking Dog

That's how they put it down in West Texas, where Wanda Naranjo had spent a few formative years in Pecos, Fort Stockton, and Alpine. She picked up her purse, hitched it over her shoulder. Taking a deep breath, she positioned herself halfway between the couch and the front door. The lonely woman experienced a slight twinge of regret for what had to be done. *Except for having a face like a rat, he's not all that bad-looking.* "Come over here, Mike."

After helping himself to a satisfying yawn, Michael Kauffmann eased his lanky frame off the couch and padded across the parlor to look down his long, pointy nose at the stocky little woman. *Wanda's always sorry after she mouths off. Now she'll want to kiss and make up.* Primed for puckering, his lips turned upward at the corners.

Wanda returned his Kewpie-doll smile. "I have something to say to you."

"Aw, you don't hafta 'pologize, sweetie peach."

Sweetie peach pointed at the door. "Hit the road, Jack." *Who's the hell's Jack?* He stared. "What?"

"And don't come back."

"But . . . I don't understand—"

"I'll try to dumb it down for you, moron." Wanda's smile was beginning to show some teeth. (The lady had a fine set of canines.) "Make tracks. Vamoose. Scram." The pointing finger of her left hand waggled. "Skedaddle. Make yourself scarce. Beat it."

Kauffmann was beginning to get the gist of it. "You want me to go somewheres?"

"That's right, Einstein." She told him where. Down there.

Well. That was a bit strong, and a man has his pride. "Now you listen here, woman—"

"Hush your mouth, Mike." Wanda's right hand reached into her purse, produced a .38 caliber revolver, and pointed it at his brass belt buckle. "I'll give you to the count of five. One—"

The startled boyfriend made a grab for his WWW gimme cap.

"Two." Betty's momma cocked her pistol.

On a dead run for the door, the natural athlete snatched his jacket off the floor.

"Three." She closed her left eye and raised her arm to

look down the short barrel. "Four." Wanda had the back of his cap lined up in the sights.

Kauffmann yanked the door almost off the hinges, bolted onto the porch—

"Five!" She pulled the trigger.

Ka-bam!

No. Wanda Naranjo did not shoot his head "clean off." Betty Naranjo's malicious little momma had a lot more horse sense than Michael Kauffmann and all the other jack-asses it would take to pull a wagonload of fool's gold over Slumgullion Pass. At the count of five, she had deliberately aimed high. But not *too* high.

The spinning slug passed six inches over his red hair. Or, as folks say in these parts, a *good* six inches. Indeed, these were the goodest half-dozen inches that Michael Kauffmann had ever been gifted with. Ignoring the steps, the nimble fellow made a gazelle-like leap from the porch, an admirable two-point landing on the earth, and in less time than it takes to tell about it was inside his rattletrap Jeep Wagoneer and tearing off down the lane toward the paved road like all the hungry grizzly bears in Alaska were nipping at his rear bumper.

Wanda Naranjo waved her pistol from the front porch and yelled, "Don't ever come back, you #*&$% lowlife—if I ever see you again I'll shoot you right between the eyes!" When it occurred to her that a head shot would probably not prove fatal, she giggled. But fun was fun and there was work to be done, so the lady returned the pistol to her purse and comforted herself with the assurance that . . . *Mike's gone and gone for good.*

But he was not. Not by a long or a short shot.

Barely aware of the damp breeze that was whipping up dead leaves and bits of trash in the yard, the woman went back inside. As she closed and latched the door, her freshly showered daughter turned off a noisy blow-dryer and called from the bathroom, "Did I hear gunshots?"

"Yeah." Wanda grinned. "I chased off a mangy old coyote."

Betty brayed a harsh laugh. "So we say goodbye to another boyfriend."

The moment Michael Kauffmann was out of pistol range, his gut-wrenching fear was replaced by a flood of relief. After bouncing down the rutted dirt lane and rolling onto the smooth blacktop, he made a hard left to head south out of town. *I'll crash for a few days at my little trailer.* But within half a block, he pulled into Big Moe's Stop 'N Shop and braked the Jeep to a lurching stop by one of a half-dozen Chevron pumps. This morning's double humiliation was really over the top. *First, Betty blackmails me out of my last twenty-dollar bill and then her nutty mother shoots at me because I forgot to fix a piddling little water leak!* As he seethed with a volatile mix of rage and shame, the carpenter's lanky body began to tremble. A prideful man can take only so much, and this one boiled over. Erupting with a string of obscenities, he banged his knobby fist on the steering wheel—very nearly shattering that inoffensive circle of plastic and steel. But by and by, the heat of his fury began to subside. Kauffmann stared straight ahead, hardly seeing the dirty concrete where isolated pellets of rain were making dark spots in the dust. As plump blobs of water began to thump the Wagoneer's hood and windshield, the driver's left hand automatically reached for the wiper switch. When he was a small boy in Yazoo City, Mississippi, the sound of rainfall on a steel roof had soothed him. It still did. He closed his eyes and took a series of long, deep breaths that swelled his thin chest . . . and enabled his racing heart to slow. By some mysterious melding of man and machine, Kauffmann's left and right ventricles became synchronized with the wipers.

Brrump . . . thrrump.

Ssswish . . . ssswipe.

Within a few dozen heartbeats, he was suspended in that

gray region between consciousness and trance. As he drifted in this twilight space, the hint of an impish smile began to appear on his face. Time seemed suspended. Later, the carpenter would be uncertain about how long he had parked his Wagoneer in front of the convenience store. It might have been for two minutes or twenty. But by the time he'd pulled away, Mr. Kauffmann was a man with a plan.

Betty pulled on her black raincoat and slipped a formidable sandwich into one of the rubber coat's big pockets. (A half-inch-thick slab of baloney, two slices of Velveeta, and a generous helping of French's Honey Dijon mustard, all on white bread.) Thus prepared and without so much as a good-bye to her mother, she walked out the front door, across the porch, and down the rickety steps.

As Wanda Naranjo watched the door close behind her daughter, she remembered the unpleasant task awaiting her in the kitchen. *I guess I might as well go mop the water off the floor.* But at the very thought of that dismal labor, an overpowering weariness settled onto her like the weight of a mountain. *Oh, I am so tired to the bone.* The nurse's aide also felt a dull pain in her lumbar region. *My poor back aches like all get-out.* And that wasn't all. *My feet are soaking wet and feel like they're going to freeze.* Betty's overworked mother eyed the tempting couch. *Before I do any hard work, I'll grab me a little catnap.*

Seating herself, Wanda untied her soggy shoes and pulled them off. *Oh, that feels soooo much better.* After removing her stockings, she stretched out on the couch. *I hope Mike drives his old jalopy into a big pine tree and gets smashed flatter than a tortilla.* No, an instant death was too good for the SOB. *I hope the bastard gets a really awful venereal disease*—her mouth gaped in a huge yawn—*and hangs on for years and years and slobbers all the time and the pain is really terrific. . . .*

Hopeful thoughts can be a remarkable soporific.

But there are always regrets. *I guess I should've given my silly daughter a ride to the bus stop.* (Big yawn.) *I could still get up and start the car and . . .*

But Betty knew how to take care of herself.

She don't need my help. And Mrs. Naranjo was terribly weary.

Unlike so many other bone-tired souls, Betty's mother did not tarry long in that gray borderland between Wide Awake and Dead to the World. Within three breaths and eight heartbeats, the woman who had worked all night was fathoms deep in a dreamless sleep. But not for long. Images of a forlorn Betty began to stumble across the sleeper's subconscious landscape where white-hot fire flashed from cloud to ground and torrents of icy rain pelted down. The distraught mother dreamed herself getting off the couch, pulling on her coat, slamming the door behind her, and running for the trusty Toyota. *If I don't get there in time, the poor thing's liable to drown in a flood or get struck down by lightning!*

Chapter Six

Betty's Unprecedented Experience

Only a few weeks ago, on her last walk from her home to the bus stop, Betty Naranjo had arrived at the paved road in six minutes flat. But on this morning, the very pregnant sixteen-year-old was slogging along the slight incline like an old woman ascending Pike's Peak with a bowling ball in her apron pocket. Every heavy step, each gasping breath, was pure punishment. But she tried to look on the bright side: *At least it's not raining hard.* Not yet. Betty was barely a hundred yards from the highway when bigger drops began to plop down here and there. *Well, that's not so bad.* But as sprinkles often are, this one was suddenly transformed into downpour.

The exhausted girl stopped to fasten the buttons on her black raincoat. Attending to that task with fumbling fingers, she made the best of it. *At least I've got some time to catch my breath.* After she had gotten some of her wind back, Betty began putting one foot in front of the other. She was making fair progress when the storm that had formed in the mountaintops came roaring over the foothills behind her. A gust of wind slapped the young woman's back with such force that she slipped on the muddy lane and tumbled flat onto her face. With an enormous effort of flabby muscles and raw willpower—her slip-sliding efforts punctuated by heartfelt oaths—the angry youth eventually managed to get back onto her feet. When she did, Betty was shocked to discover that the morning's misty daylight had been swallowed up by inky midnight. She could barely make out the sparse forest of juniper and piñon that lined and defined the lane. The befuddled pilgrim took a few tentative steps before pausing to pose a pertinent question: *Which way am I going?* Was she still trudging toward the paved road—or was she walking back home? This sudden disorientation was almost as alarming as the fall that had injured her pride. Her heart pounded hard.

Then came the dawning.

No, not as in the sense of realizing which direction she was headed.

Like an anemic moonrise glowing in a foggy-black sky, this dawning was a matter of actual light. Real, honest-to-goodness illumination—streams of countless photons registered fuzzy images on her retinas.

Betty Naranjo blinked at the increasing glow. *Whatever it is, it's getting bigger.* Or was it getting closer?

In the girl's bewildered state, this growing-approaching blurry-lights phenomenon was unnerving. The puzzled girl was trying to figure out what it was, when—*what it was* hit her.

A violent metaphor, and appropriately so.

LATER

Momma Naranjo Awakens from her Nap . . .

But ever so slowly. Demonic disfigured inhabitants of a horrible nightmare tugged at their victim with clawed hands, determined to hold on to the sleeper and drag her even deeper into the bowels of their hellish domain. Happily, it was a wasted effort. Wanda Naranjo's escape was as inevitable as the loss of memory that preserves a dreamer's sanity.

When the lady finally opened her eyes, she was surprised to discover that it was dark outside. Moreover, the wind was humming a funereal hymn in the eaves as a hard rain pelted on dirty windowpanes. The groggy woman stared at the ceiling. *Where am I?* Not in her bed, she decided. *I'm on a couch.* But not the feathery-soft sofa in the nurses' lounge at Snyder Memorial Hospital, where the nighttime aides occasionally caught a quick catnap. *It's my couch . . . in my house.* She wondered what time it was, and why she felt so completely alone in her home. Little by little, the morning's events began to come back to her. *I chased Mike off.* She smiled at the hazy recollection. *I don't remember what the argument was all about.* Nevertheless, she had no doubt that it served the no-good right. Her second yawn was interrupted with: *But where's my daughter?* That memory presented itself immediately. *Oh, right, Betty caught the bus into town to see that shrink.* Wanda forced herself to a sitting position, put her bare feet on the cold parlor floor, and immediately remembered the water leak in the kitchen. *Sure, that's what the fuss was all about. Mike should've fixed it but the lazy bum wouldn't lift a finger if my life depended on it.* Another yawn. *But I called somebody to come fix the leak and . . .* Uh-oh. *I wonder what time it is.* She switched on a floor lamp and squinted at her wristwatch. "Oh no!" *The plumber probably showed up while I was napping—but I didn't hear him knock, so he left.* She groaned. *The money-grubbing bastard will probably charge me for the call anyway.*

She checked her watch again. *Betty should be home by now.* The worried mother found the Granite Creek telephone book, looked up the number listed under Dr. Stuart Whyte, and punched the buttons. After seven droning rings, a lady's recorded voice crisply informed the caller that ". . . office hours are nine A.M. till noon and one P.M. to four P.M., Monday through Friday, except that Dr. Whyte's office is closed on the second Friday of every month. Please call during our normal hours." After a few other unhelpful comments, the caller was invited to leave a message after the beep, which piercing sound startled her. "Uh . . . This is Wanda Naranjo.

My daughter thought she had an eleven A.M. appointment with the doctor, but . . . I guess she must've been mixed up about what day it was for." She closed her eyes and tried to imagine her daughter walking through the front door. "Betty's awfully late getting home and I'm worried about her . . . but I guess I shouldn't be bothering you with my troubles." This was beginning to get embarrassing. "Sorry." She hung up.

Wanda was rattled, but she had gotten the recorded message loud and clear. *Today's the second Friday, so the shrink's office is closed.* Wide awake now, she began to analyze the situation. *Betty was either confused about her appointment—or she lied.* Given her daughter's talent in producing creative fiction, the latter possibility seemed far more likely. *So where did she go this morning?* The woman who leaned heavily on intuition thought she knew: *She's probably gone to visit the baby's father—whoever the hell he is.* Which brought the worried mother full circle to her original concern: *Why's my daughter so late coming home?* She shuddered. *I feel like something bad has happened to Betty.* This worry naturally summoned up another to haunt the hopeful grandmother: *Oh, God—I hope her baby is all right.*

As if dropping a malicious, sinister hint of calamity, the tempestuous wind tossed something against the window. Something small . . . that cracked and popped . . . like tiny twigs snapping.

Betty's fearful mother hugged herself. *It was just a dead cottonwood branch.*

Not so, her lurid imagination insisted. *That was a cluster of brittle little bones breaking.*

Wanda Naranjo glanced at the window, but only for an instant. Fearing that she might see something *looking back at her,* the woman averted her eyes from that dark portal into the unknown.

CHAPTER SEVEN

AN URGENT CONSULTATION

Southern Ute Reservation

Like Wanda Naranjo earlier in the day, Daisy Perika was taking a restful nap on her parlor couch. She was dreaming of a sunlit meadow of wildflowers and multicolored butterflies when . . . *brraaang,* the telephone rang. She awakened with a muttered expletive that shall be designated: "Dang!" Charlie Moon's aged auntie reached for the offending instrument and accidentally knocked it off her knotty pine coffee table. The grumpy woman fumbled around until she got hold of the corded receiver. She pressed it against her ear and said in a sugary-sweet tone, "If this is somebody who wants to sell me something, just leave your address—and I'll drop by some night with a gallon of kerosene and set your house afire."

From somewhere far away came a rattle of unintelligible words.

Sounds like some idiot foreigner who's dialed a wrong number. "Talk American, and louder so I can hear you!"

The distant voice increased in volume.

The caller was speaking English, and Daisy was able to pick up about every third word, but she caught the name. "Slow down, Wanda—I can't make out what you're trying to tell me." *Sounds like she's got her head in a tin bucket.*

Wanda Naranjo slowed.

"Oh, now I know what's wrong." *Ignorant Pueblo woman.* "You're not talking into my ear, Wanda—you're trying to talk into my mouth!" After Daisy swallowed another mouthful of the annoying woman's babbling, she shouted, "Try turning your telephone around!"

Wanda Naranjo shouted back.

Daisy Perika tasted every bitter word. The annoyed old woman was about to hang up when she realized that the cord was dangling over her ear. *Oh, my—I'm the one who's talking into the wrong end of the phone.* Chuckling, she reversed the instrument. "Sorry—but it's not my fault. You woke me up from a nice nap, and I got all bumfuzzled."

"I'm sorry, Daisy. But I'm worried sick. Betty left this morning and she's pregnant and hasn't come home and I don't know where she is and—"

"Hush."

Wanda hushed.

"That's better. First off, tell me who this Betty is." Daisy listened. "Your daughter?" *Oh, I remember little Betty now.* A film clip of a cute five-year-old with a Raggedy Ann doll flickered across the tribal elder's memory. "And you say she's missing?" She listened again, and puffed up with pride. "And you want my help?"

"No, I want your nephew's cell phone number."

"Oh." Daisy unpuffed. "Charlie Moon's a rancher now, Wanda." The deflated tribal elder explained what that meant: "He don't do that kind of work anymore—"

"But he's still a cop, and I want him to find my daughter."

"He's a big-shot tribal investigator who does some work for the Southern Ute chairman from time to time, but you're not a Ute so—"

"He also works with the police here in Granite Creek, Daisy."

"I know that!" A pause as Charlie's cantankerous relative tried to figure out how to get rid of this pest. "Why don't you call the Granite Creek cops?"

"Because . . ." The line went dead for a few heartbeats. "Because I don't want the whole damn town to know that Betty's run away from home."

"Listen, here's what you do. You call the police and tell them you won't talk to nobody but the boss."

Wanda made no attempt to conceal her doubts about this advice. "You want me to call the chief of police?"

"Sure. He's no big shot, and Scott Parris is Charlie's friend and mine, too. If that white cop gives you any static, you tell him *Daisy* said to come out to your place and to bring Charlie Moon with him."

The Ute elder's confidence was contagious. "D'you really think that'd work?"

"I flat-out guarantee it," Daisy snapped. "Make the call right now."

"Okay, I will. Thank you."

"You're welcome, goodbye." *And good riddance and don't call back for at least ten years after I'm dead and buried.* Pleased to hear the sharp click in her ear, the weary Ute elder settled back onto the couch and nestled her head on a blue velvet pillow embroidered with tiny sunflower blossoms. In hopes of picking up her pleasant dream where it had been so rudely disturbed, Daisy Perika helped herself to a satisfying yawn. As she drifted off toward sleep, her final waking thought was . . . *I ought to get me an unlisted telephone number and not tell anybody what it is. Except for Charlie Moon . . . and Sarah . . . and . . .*

When the hopeful dreamer returned to the meadow, the sky was overcast and gray, the acres of wildflowers had wilted, and the clouds of colorful butterflies had flitted away to a brighter place. Moreover, tombstones of every description had sprouted like weeds in the unsightly field, and the dreary space was filled with doleful souls of the dead. It seemed that all the wandering spirits were muttering about one thing and another.

Daisy Perika could hear every word they said. But, like her recent experience in the depths of *Cañón del Espíritu*—all of these dream haunts were invisible.

CHAPTER EIGHT

CHARLIE MOON'S RAINY AFTERNOON

Friday, 5:15 P.M.

It would be an exaggeration to say that mile-thick thunder-clouds covered Granite Creek and the town was dark and wet as the bottom of a Mississippi swamp—but not by much. This was the wettest, gloomiest day the locals had seen for months. It was time for wage earners to be heading home from work, but even among the hardy mountain folk inclement weather tends to attenuate rush-hour traffic. A mere trickle of shiny sedans, rusty pickups, and one big SUV beetled along the town's main artery. Who might this latter motorist be?

Charlie Moon. He was rolling along Copper Street in his blue Expedition, watching the flailing windshield wipers do their best to keep up with the heavy downpour. As a few ill-tempered drivers muttered impotent curses against the weather, the cattle rancher voiced no complaints. This Westerner who depended upon grass for his livelihood was sufficiently pleased with the rainfall to smile at the plopping drops. Moon had already placed a call to Columbine foreman Pete Bushman, who had provided the happy news that the massive storm had already watered the thirsty ranch's vast acreage with enough moisture to last a month—and if anything, the gully washer was picking up steam. The Indian who owned the Columbine was delighted to hear the good news. *This keeps up another forty days, I'll trade this old barge in on an ark that's 300 cubits long and 50 wide.* Which raised an idle thought: *How much would that be in good old American feet?* Moon, who tended to store peculiar odds and ends in his memory, recalled the conversion factor (1.5 feet per cubit) and performed the simple mental arithmetic. *That'd be 450 feet long by 75 wide.* A sizable vessel to float on a flooded valley. *I bet I could get all my cattle and horses and ranch hands aboard.* With plenty of elbow room for grumpy Aunt Daisy and a three-room suite for sweet little Sarah Frank. The part-time tribal investigator was wondering how many mating pairs of elephants, hippopotami, hippogriffs, moose, mice, elks, storks, reindeers, eagles, buffaloes, kangaroos, hummingbirds, cougars, penguins, and the like he could cram onto the huge vessel (no scorpions, fleas, lice, or fire ants need apply!) when something in the rearview mirror caught his eye.

Red and blue lights were winking at him. But not seductively.

Like any motorist you might bump fenders with, Charlie Moon instinctively glanced at his speedometer. The needle was hovering at a tad above thirty-five miles per hour, and the posted speed limit on the downtown section of Copper Street was twenty-five. If Sarah or Aunt Daisy had been in the car with him, the driver would've said, "Dang!" No ladies being present, he mouthed a mild expletive that would not have shocked any of the three most important women in his life. (The third, a potential wife, was pretty Patsy Poynter. The sweetheart he was working up the courage to pop the question to was a reference librarian and the girl singer in the Ute banjo plucker's Columbine Grass bluegrass band.)

Charlie Moon wondered which of the GCPD cops was behind him. If it was Officer Alicia Martin, the lenient lady would merely warn the lawbreaking deputy and send him on his way. *But with my luck, it'll be Eddie Knox and his sidekick E. C. Slocum.* Moon put the odds at five to one that the

Keystone Kops were about to put the big ticket on him. Good thing that he was wagering with himself. The compulsive gambler, who collected on about four bets out of five, would've had to pay up on this one.

So who was driving the black-and-white with flashing lights?

The Cop on Whose Desk the Buck
Stopped, That's Who

The John Law cruising along behind Charlie Moon on Copper Street was the senior member of the local constabulary; the very same fellow who had shared yesterday's breakfast with Charlie, Sarah, and Daisy.

Chief of Police Scott Parris tapped the siren switch and chuckled as the Expedition stopped. Protected from the late-afternoon waterfall by a hooded slicker, the happy cop emerged from his black-and-white and sidled up to Moon's Ford Motor Company motor machine to rap a knuckle on the driver's window.

The cattleman lowered the glass to eye his best friend's beefy red face. "That's just about the yellowest raincoat I ever laid eyes on." Moon blinked. "It hurts my eyes."

"Thank you. But don't think you can sweet-talk your way out of this one—I've got you red-handed."

"So what's the charge, Ossifer Canary—did I run over a catfish in the crosswalk?"

The man who was warm and dry under the rubber coat glared at the merry Ute. "You were doing thirty-seven miles an hour in a zone that's posted twenty-five."

"Thirty-six."

"Tell it to the judge," the stern-faced cop said.

"You really gonna put a ticket on me?"

"It's my duty. The fact that you're my best buddy don't make a smidgen of difference—you flat-out broke a local ordinance." Parris grinned with a mouthful of teeth. "But there might be a way out for you."

"I'd offer you a two-dollar bribe, but times are tough in the beef business."

"Sorry to hear it." The county's top cop looked this way and that as if to make sure no local was near enough to overhear this incriminating conversation. "I might be able to look the other way, if you was to volunteer a coupla hours to some worthy community service."

I should've known. Moon groaned. "Which is?"

"Assisting the chief of police with a minor little matter." Parris pointed at the curb, where a sizable stream was washing the gutter clean of cigarette butts, McDonald's paper cups, and miscellaneous other refuse, debris, and detritus. "Park your gas hog right there by the No Parking sign, get into my unit, and I'll tell you all about it."

Moon hesitated. "I really need to be getting home, pardner. Aunt Daisy and Sarah are expecting me for supper. Not only that, there's firewood to be chopped and hogs to be slopped and—"

Parris snorted at this unseemly display of domestic sentiment. "A peaceful home life is for sissies, Chucky." The ex-Chicago cop flashed his toothy grin again. "Come along with your carefree bachelor buddy and we'll have us a fine old time. Why, it might even turn out to be the beginning of a ripsnorting adventure."

"That's more or less what I'd like to avoid." But the speed-demon outlaw parked his car, pulled on a scuffed leather jacket, popped a black John B. Stetson lid onto his head, and sprinted to the GCPD unit, where a wide-open passenger-side door was ready to gobble him up.

As Scott Parris eased the gleaming black-and-white along Copper Street, Charlie Moon buckled himself in and settled his long, lanky frame into the form-fitting seat.

The GCPD chief of police, who should have known better, waited for his occasional deputy to ask, *What's this all about?*

Staring straight ahead through the rain-streaked windshield, the taciturn Indian watched the wiper smear an oily spot into a gossamer-thin film of rainbow sheen.

"So," Parris said with an expectant lift of his chin. "I bet you're wondering what this is all about." He thought he heard the Ute grunt.

Genuinely disinterested in whatever his friend had up his sleeve, Moon was trying to remember the process by which molecular films (whose thicknesses are comparable to the wavelengths of the visible spectrum) perform the magic of separating white light into its constituent colors. *Seems to me that the thinner parts of the oil film make purple light and the thicker parts red.* But that didn't help much because . . . *It's hard to tell which parts of the oil slick are thick and which are thin.*

The white cop tried again. "About half an hour ago, Clara took a call from a concerned citizen who insisted that I come see her, but the lady wouldn't say what the problem was."

Clara Tavishuts was, like Charlie Moon, a Southern Ute. She was also GCPD's senior dispatcher. With three hungry children and a sickly mother to support, the widow routinely worked two eight-hour shifts for the overtime pay.

The ardent angler baited his barbed hook and made another toss: "And get this—the caller said I should bring Charlie Moon with me."

Mr. Moon didn't bite.

Parris shot the dark, silent man a barbed glance. "Am I boring you, Charlie?"

"Not a bit, pardner." Moon's eye caught a glimpse of iridescent green on the greasy windshield. "I'm hanging on every word you say."

"Good." The chief of police switched on his emergency lights to startle an eighty-year-old lady who was creeping along at fifteen miles per hour. Expecting to be arrested and handcuffed for some obscure infraction, the alarmed senior citizen immediately pulled to the curb. She was enormously relieved when the blue-and-red lights were extinguished and the cop car zoomed past her.

Charlie Moon was sorely tempted to remind the driver

that flashing lights were to be used only when a GCPD unit was involved in bona fide police business. And on top of that, Scott Parris was now zipping along Arapaho Avenue at fifty miles per hour, which was fifteen notches in excess of the posted speed limit. In the interest of tact, he withheld comment. But the deputy did lean sideways to take a look at the speedometer.

They had been friends for a long time. "Don't say it, Charlie."

"My lips are stapled shut."

Parris slowed to thirty-five and exhaled a sigh that fogged his side of the windshield. He switched on the defroster. "Spit out the staples and ask me who the caller was."

"Okay." Moon lips came very near grinning. "Who the caller was, pard?"

"Wanda Naranjo."

The Indian's almost-grin was replaced with a thoughtful frown. "Am I supposed to know the lady?"

"She apparently knows you." Parris swerved to miss a potbellied beagle trailed by three fat puppies. "And that every once in a while, you act as my deputy."

Moon searched his memory. *There are some Naranjos in Ignacio, but I don't recall a Wanda.* "Did the caller say why she wanted you to bring me along?"

"Yes, she did." Parris turned onto Rodeo Road. "Mrs. Naranjo told Clara that us paleface Anglo cops are worth about as much a thimble full of lizard spit. Said she wanted Charlie Moon to come take care of things."

The Southern Ute tribal investigator was beginning to get a glimmer. "Was the caller an Indian?"

"Half Indian." Parris nodded at the dark ribbon of road ahead. "Clara tells me that Wanda Naranjo's mother was from one of those pueblos down in New Mexico." He tried to remember which one. *It wasn't Taos Pueblo . . . or Santa Clara.* "So, the citizen being half Indian *and* asking for you personally, I didn't know how I could say *no*."

"It's a simple single-syllable word, pard."

"So's *yes*," Parris shot back. "And I'm a positive kinda guy. So I phoned the Columbine and found out you was in town, picking up some nuts and bolts at ABC Hardware. But when I called ABC, they said you'd left almost an hour ago." When Moon didn't ask how Parris had tailed him to Copper Street, the copper told him. "Officer Martin spotted you leaving Fast Eddie's Barbershop, so I hit the street and was all over you like ugly on a warthog." To make way for some unpleasant news, he cleared his throat. "Turns out Wanda Naranjo has an interesting history."

Moon grinned at the euphemism. "So the lady's a troublemaker?"

"Only from time to time." Parris slowed to the speed limit. "A couple of years ago, Mrs. Naranjo drove over to Big Moe's Stop 'N Shop at about two A.M., barged in like Calamity Jane on a ripsnortin' rampage, banged her fist on the counter—and demanded a six-pack of RC Cola and a half-dozen MoonPies."

"Not my notion of an early breakfast, but it don't sound like an overly serious misdemeanor."

"She was not there to make a purchase, Charlie."

"You telling me she was holding up the joint for a post-midnight snack?"

"Not like any respectable felon—the lady wasn't toting a smokin' Saturday-night special or waving a bloody machete."

"I like it—tell me more, pard."

"Mrs. Naranjo was armed with a Bic cigarette lighter, which she flicked on and held under Big Moe's chin. She told him that if he didn't hand over the colas and sugar cakes *muy pronto* she'd set his beard afire."

"I don't like to step on another man's story, Scott—but this strikes me as highly unlikely. Unless my memory is on vacation, the proprietor of that convenience store don't have a hair anywhere on his face."

"You recollect correctly, Chuck. But that's the very threat Mrs. Naranjo made."

"Was the lady under the influence of some mind-bending substance?"

"Not so far as we know."

"So did Big Moe disarm the unruly customer?"

"Nope. The sensible proprietor called GCPD and in two minutes flat Eddie Knox and E. C. Slocum showed up, sized up the situation, and did their duty as sworn officers of the law."

Moon grinned. "Slocum cuffed the lady, and Eddie beat her senseless with his five-cell flashlight?"

The chief of police was about to chuckle when he recalled several of the Knox/Slocum team's previous misadventures. "My fearless GCPD boys in blue relieved the citizen of the potentially lethal cigarette lighter, took her home, and tucked her into bed. The next day when she came to retrieve her vehicle from the convenience store parking lot, Mrs. Naranjo apologized to Moe and swore on a stack of *TV Guides* that she couldn't recall a thing about what'd happened last night."

"Sounds like the lady's a certifiable somnambulist."

"She might be a registered Rosicrucian for all I know, but Big Moe and Eddie and E.C. concluded that she was sleepwalking when she showed up at the Stop 'N Shop."

"Now that you mention it, I guess that possibility can't be entirely ruled out."

"Point is, Charlie—the Naranjo woman has more than a few screws loose, so we'll need to take that factoid into account."

"Thanks for the heads-up, pard—I'll keep the lady's nighttime meanderings in mind—and if she pulls a cigarette lighter on me I'll be gone so fast I'll leave my shadow behind."

As they passed the fairgrounds, where the Granite Creek Rodeo put on a big show every time August rolled around, Charlie Moon could barely make out the grandstands overlooking the muddy arena where pretty cowgirls roped calves and flirted with hard-muscled young men who did their level best to stay on the backs of wild-eyed bucking horses and mean-as-hell Brahma bulls. The rancher interlaced his long fingers across a silver belt buckle he'd won in the Ignacio All-Indian Rodeo almost twenty years ago. In damp weather, like right now, he could still feel the soreness in his left ribs and hip joint where the piebald bronc had pitched him sky-high one second flat after the buzzer—and on his way down to the ground had said "howdy" with an iron-shod hoof. Moon figured the game had been worth the pain. *And if I was young and dumb enough, I'd do it all over again.*

CHAPTER NINE

A WOMAN WITH BIG TROUBLES

Slowing his black-and-white to a creep, Scott Parris switched on the spotlight and swept the beam along the sidewalk until it illuminated a sheltered bus stop that resembled an oversize telephone booth. "The driveway to the Naranjo residence is supposed to be a little ways down the road from here—hey, there it is!" He turned into the rutted, muddy lane just a tad too fast and gave the V-8 engine just a little too much gas. As the sleek police car began to slip and slide thisaway and thataway, he shifted down. But, like any red-blooded American male, the driver knew it wasn't *his* fault and was quick to make the point: "This dirt track needs a coupla truckloads of gravel." The instant the Chevy gave up fishtailing and began rolling along in a more or less straight line, Parris barreled ahead, kicking up mud and casting aspersions on "this so-called driveway." Braking to a sliding stop at the shabby house, the annoyed driver upped his gravel estimate to a dozen truckloads. "And that's just for filling the knee-deep mud holes!"

Charlie Moon held his tongue and enjoyed the minor episode.

Shrugging out of his yellow slicker, Parris donned his shiny black leather jacket and the cherished felt fedora his daddy had worn in the 1940s. The chief of police adjusted the rearview mirror, switched on the dome light, and eyed a ruddy face that grinned back at him. Rain or shine, a man wanted to look *fine* when meeting a lady. Especially a lady who figured he was worth a minuscule portion of lizard spit.

Whether or not Wanda Naranjo was a lady in the strictest sense of that descriptor, she did appreciate men, and she was delighted to see the cop car in her yard.

When Moon and Parris saw her short, stocky presence framed in the dimly lighted doorway, Betty's mother appeared to be dressed for a long walk in the chill, late-afternoon rain, but . . . put that on hold. We shall defer to the woman, who prefers to explain the situation herself. As she does, we hope that Scott Parris will listen carefully, and that Charlie Moon will show as much interest in Wanda's story as he does to oil smears on wet windshields. Experienced officers of the law are supposed to notice the most subtle hint of something amiss.

If Parris and Moon had paid *very* close attention to everything they would see during the following hour, and listened carefully to every word uttered by the distraught mother, the lawmen might have figured out what had happened right off the bat. But they wouldn't and didn't. Why? Like others of their prideful gender, these happy comrades hate to admit to the least shortcoming—and we are not in the finger-pointing business. Blame it on distractions.

Help Wanted:
Able-Bodied Man with Tool Box

Wanda Naranjo was outfitted in a black woolen overcoat, a scruffy navy-blue sock hat that was pulled down past her ears, and garish yellow galoshes that matched the slicker Scott Parris had left in the car. She admitted the lawmen without a word of greeting and slammed the door against the chill, damp air flooding in from the front porch. The atmosphere inside her home was almost as cold and definitely as humid.

As the western gentlemen removed their hats, Parris introduced himself and his part-time deputy.

Wanda eyed the tall, slender Ute. "I appreciate you coming all the way out here to help me." She shot a quick glance at the paleface chief of police. "Oh, and you too."

After Mr. Lizard Spit had shaken the rain off his old fedora, he took a look at the woman's coat, hat, and boots. "Been out in the rain?"

Betty Naranjo's mother shook her head. "If you fellas hadn't shown up, I guess I might have gone outside to look for . . ." But she wasn't quite ready to tell them about her missing daughter. Wanda would have to work her way up to that dismal task, and she hoped that before she did, Betty would come walking through the door with a big lie to explain her late return. The nurse's aide pointed at the kitchen. "I got home from work this morning to find out that Mike didn't fix the leak under the sink so we had an argument and he left." Wanda was sorely tempted to enlarge on the only bright spot in her miserable day, but thought it unwise to boast about how she had motivated Kauffmann's hasty departure.

Parris and Moon exchanged wary glances and shared identical thoughts: *Surely she didn't call us out here to fix her plumbing.* But both lawmen had answered far stranger calls than that.

"I called a plumber." She sighed. "The fella said he'd be here right away—but you know how those guys are."

The white cop responded in a soothing tone, "Plumber's minutes tend to stretch out into hours."

Wanda Naranjo seemed not to hear. "Not long after I made the call, I fell asleep on the couch. If the plumber did show up, he didn't knock hard enough on the door to wake me up."

"Forget about that no-show plumber." Moon flashed a hundred-kilowatt smile at the woman. "I'll take care of that water leak."

Afraid to hope, Wanda Naranjo stared in disbelief. "D'you think you might be able fix it?"

Feigning an injured expression, the amateur plumber looked down his nose. "With three hands and a foot tied behind my back."

The doubtful lady forced a smile. *He'll probably break a pipe and cause a flood that'd sink Noah's Ark.* But she liked a man who was sure of himself.

Scott Parris rolled his blue eyes. *Big show-off.* And that wasn't all that galled him. One way or another, Granite Creek's top cop always ended up playing his deputy's side-kick. *Here we go again, Charlie's the Lone Ranger and I'm Tonto.* The eye roller grinned. *But if a seasoned pro knows his role and plays it best as he can, someday maybe he'll get to be leading man.* "I'll go get the toolbox out of my unit."

Which he did, and did a fine job backing up the star of the minor melodrama.

While the chief of police knelt on the wet kitchen linoleum and aimed a skull-cracker flashlight to illuminate the damp situation, Charlie Moon managed to get the upper half of his skinny frame under Wanda Naranjo's double sink, which was almost as old as Aunt Daisy. For a dozen heartbeats, the Indian was dead silent. On beat number thirteen, he said, "Hand me the Vise-Grips, pard—and the adjustable wrench."

Scott Parris passed the specified tools to the hopeful plumber.

As the next several minutes passed irreversibly into that dark void we call history, Moon uttered a grunt or two. Maybe three. He also shifted himself into another position. Asked for the five-cell flashlight and got it.

"There," the repairman said.

Wanda clapped her hands. "Did you stop the water from dripping?"

"Yep. It was just a loose fitting." Moon came scooting out from under the sink, his face and new white shirt spotted with greasy goop. He gave the woman of the house an apologetic look. "It's not what you'd call a professional job, but it oughta hold for a little while." He added this helpful advice: "There's a lot of old, corroded pipes under there, ma'am—you'd better get a real plumber out here before one of 'em springs another leak."

Before he could get off the floor, the happy little woman embraced her hero, found a goop-free spot on his forehead, and kissed it. "Oh, you're so *sweet*." When all seven feet of the Ute had unfolded like a carpenter's rule and Moon was towering over her, Wanda added, "And you're a *real* handyman—I should've called you instead of the other guy." She winked. "Is your number in the book?"

"Sure it is." Parris snickered. "Just look under Columbine Ranch."

Neither the woman nor the white cop could see the blush on the Ute's dark face, but they knew it was there.

Wanda began to dab at Moon with a wet dishrag. *I bet this one's got a dozen girlfriends who'd like to keep house for him.*

The lonely rancher seemed oblivious to the filth.

She shook her head at his shirt. "That's probably ruined, but take it off and I'll throw it in the washing machine."

Mr. Moon demurred. "Oh, we won't be here long enough for that, ma'am."

"That's right," Parris said. "We showed up because you called 911 and insisted on seeing me and Charlie Moon." The cop's expression was deadly serious. *And if you called us all the way out here to fix your leaky pipes, I'll file charges against you so fast it'll make your silly head spin.* Then again . . . *That'd make great newspaper headlines.* Scott Parris knew he'd never live it down. *I'd get laughed right out of town.*

CHAPTER TEN

NOW, THE SERIOUS BUSINESS

Wanda Naranjo plopped onto a flimsy kitchen chair that creaked and threatened to collapse under her moderate weight. "In all the excitement about getting the leak fixed, I'd almost forgot about Betty." She looked up at the ceiling, as if expressing regret to the cracked plaster. "I guess I'm not much of a mother."

Scott Parris returned a crescent wrench to his toolbox. "Betty's your daughter?"

Still gazing upward, the parent nodded at a cobwebbed moth carcass. "She left this morning—and should've been back hours ago."

So that's what this is all about. Assuming his grumpy-bulldog expression, the chief of police was about to bark at the woman. At a cautionary look from Moon, Parris snapped his mouth and the toolbox lid shut. After drawing in a deep breath and counting slowly to six, he addressed the citizen in a dangerously smooth monotone. "Let me make sure I've got this straight, ma'am—you insisted on me and Charlie coming out here because your daughter is *a few hours late coming home*?"

Wanda Naranjo met his flinty gaze with an unflinching one of her own. "Yes, I did." Her dark eyes challenged the cop: *Do you have a problem with that?*

Parris's icy-blue orbs shot right back: *Damn right I do!*

Expecting a double explosion, Deputy Moon moved between the two to reach for a kitchen chair. He turned it so the back was up front and straddled it to face the feisty little lady. "Who's this Mike you mentioned?"

"Michael Kauffmann is my boy—" She grimaced. "My ex-boyfriend. I run the louse out of the house this morning." *I should've shot the bastard dead.*

Charlie Moon nodded as if he'd heard this story a hundred times before. He had. "When did your daughter leave?"

The Ute's voice had a calming effect, like a soft breeze in the pines. The woman cocked her head and strained to recover a clear memory of this morning's events. "Betty left after Mike drove away in his Jeep."

"How long after?"

"Just a little while." Wanda put her thumb on the table and attempted to rub a wrinkle out of the worn oilcloth. The greasy crinkle refused to be flattened. "Maybe ten or fifteen minutes."

Ol' Charlie sure knows how to talk to women. Resting his butt against the edge of the kitchen table, Scott Parris elbowed himself into the interrogation. "What was she driving?"

"My daughter doesn't have a car—or a driver's license. She was on foot."

Parris arched an eyebrow. "So where was she footing it to?"

"Betty was walking down to the commuter bus stop." The weary woman examined bulging veins on the backs of her hands. *I'm getting old before my time.*

Ever so gently, Charlie Moon pressed on. "Where was your daughter going on the bus?"

"To see her high school counselor—Dr. Whyte." The mother's eyes narrowed. "Betty *said* she had an appointment, but she must've been confused. I called and got a voice-mail message that said the doctor's office is closed on the second Friday of the month." She glanced at Parris. *I guess he ain't so bad as I thought.* "Did I mention that my daughter is eight and a half months pregnant?"

"No, ma'am." Parris exchanged a quick glance with his deputy. "How old is Betty?"

"Seventeen next January."

"Maybe . . ." Not knowing quite how to pose the sensitive question, Parris disguised his query as a suggestion. "Maybe she was going to visit the baby's father."

Mildly amused at his embarrassment, Wanda Naranjo appreciated the tough cop's clumsy attempt at delicacy. "Maybe she was."

She ain't making this easy. There was nothing to do but ask outright. "Who is the father of your daughter's unborn child, Mrs. Naranjo?"

The mother effected a nonchalant shrug. "Betty never told me."

The white policeman felt his face redden. "D'you have any idea who your daughter might've been . . . *close to*?"

"Some pimple-faced kid at school, I guess." Wanda had already considered the possibility the beefy chief of police was hinting at. "D'you figure she's run off with her boyfriend?"

"Maybe." Parris pretended to change the subject. "Speaking of boyfriends—and ex-boyfriends—could you tell me where I could find Mike Kauffmann?" Seeing the woman's eyes glint, he wondered whether she'd caught his drift and added quickly, "What I mean is—where does Mr. Kauffmann hang out when he's not here?"

Unconsciously, she assumed Moon's mossy-soft tone. "Mike's got a bedroom over at Mrs. Hawley's Boardinghouse."

"Thanks. I'll ask him a question or two." Parris jotted this information into his shirt-pocket notebook. "Maybe your daughter mentioned something to Mr. Kauffmann about her intentions."

"I doubt it, Betty never had much to say to Mike."

"I expect you're right, ma'am." Parris had picked up her

tattered phone book and was looking up Mrs. Hawley's number. "But he might know something that'd be helpful."

As Wanda watched the cop place the call to Hawley's Boardinghouse, the impact of his question finally dawned on her. *So that's what you think—that my boyfriend was messing around with my daughter!* That was crazy. For a dozen racing heartbeats, the angry mother glared at the cynical chief of police. But with every contraction of her left ventricle, Wanda's suspicions increased. *I wouldn't put anything beyond Mike.* And the timing was right. *Rat-face started hanging around my house about ten months ago.* She searched for some evidence in the ex-boyfriend's favor and found it. *Right before I went to work on the night shift at Snyder Memorial, Mike always kissed me good night and left for his bedroom at Mrs. Hawley's place.* But there was a "but": *But quite a few times, he was already here when I got home the next morning.* Her lazy boyfriend—who wasn't one to be up with the sun—had provided an explanation for his early presence. *Mike said he wanted to make sure he showed up by breakfast time.* Nevertheless, even a man who lied almost every time he opened his mouth deserved the benefit of the doubt. At the moment, doubt was a commodity in short supply. *When I left for my night shift, Mike could've gone two or three miles down the road, then come back and spent the whole night with Betty.* It was a sinister jigsaw puzzle that Wanda was assembling, and Rat-face was looking uglier with every piece that she fitted into place. As her slow simmer approached a boil, a significant subliminal memory bubbled up: *A few times last winter, when I got home from work in the morning, Mike's car had thick frost on the windshield—or even a skim of ice . . . like the old clunker had set outside my house all night.* The Prosecution rested, and bit her lip. *I'm an idiot.*

After exchanging a few words with Mrs. Hawley, Parris said goodbye and disconnected. He directed his remarks to his deputy. "Mr. Kauffmann left the boardinghouse early this morning, on his way over here I suppose. He returned to Mrs. Hawley's place about an hour or two later, cleaned his belongings out of the rented bedroom—and left without paying his bill."

"That's Mike at the top of his form." Wanda Naranjo snorted. "By now, he's long gone." She forced a brittle smile. "The bastard could be in Salt Lake or Kansas City by now—or maybe he's waltzed halfway across Texas."

One of the best poker players in six states was studying the woman's face, and Charlie Moon was thinking Scott Parris's thoughts virtually word-for-word: *She knows where Kauffmann's gone to, but she don't intend to tell us.*

True. And Mrs. Naranjo also knew what the lawmen were thinking.

Without doubt, a congregation of highly perceptive minds.

By contrast, the missing daughter does not perceive *anything*. Betty Naranjo has not the slightest awareness of what has happened, where she is, or of her very existence. One might reasonably conclude that the young woman is sleeping, and she is—in a macabre manner of speaking. Sadly, the girl's slumber is not of that kind which refreshes both body and mind.

Then does she dream?

No.

CHAPTER ELEVEN

THE LADY LIES THROUGH HER TEETH

And sharp teeth they were. But, unlike her daughter and ex-boyfriend, Wanda Naranjo practiced deception only when she deemed it absolutely necessary. Which was rarely more than two or three times a day. To assist in expelling the fabrication, Wanda Naranjo cleared her throat. "Before you ask me, I don't know where Mike might be headed." *But I've got a pretty good idea.* Jutting her chin, she narrowed her eyes to slits. "He could be anywhere." *And I know exactly where* anywhere *is.*

The lawmen continued to read the falsehoods her face could not conceal.

Scott Parris's eyes were also capable of narrowing to slits, and did. "If you happen to think of some place Mr. Kauffmann might have gone to—"

"I already told you I don't have any idea!" Wanda snapped.

Parris's face began to redden dangerously.

Wanda Naranjo's hands clenched into knotty fists.

Again, Charlie Moon intervened. "Did your daughter say when she'd return home?"

This gentle query snapped the tension like a rotten rubber band.

Wanda's hands relaxed as she shook her head. "But when

she goes to see Dr. Whyte, Betty's always back in a couple of hours. With his office closed, she should've been home sooner than that. She rides the little commuter bus, and it makes the circuit every half hour."

To keep her talking, the Ute asked another routine question: "Has Betty called home since she left?"

"No. And she's got a cell phone that I gave her for her sixteenth birthday."

"Sometimes cell phones don't work," Parris said grumpily. "Batteries can die."

"So can teenage girls," Wanda whispered. *And their babies.*

Charlie Moon had read her lips. "Your daughter might've decided to stop off somewhere. A friend's house, maybe."

"She don't have any friends." Wanda exhaled a down-and-out sigh. "The kid's what you might call . . . a loner." *Betty's a bitch and nobody likes her.*

Wearying of this interview, Scott Parris got right to the heart of the matter. "Officially, Mrs. Naranjo, it's way too early to treat your daughter as a missing person." Seeing a flash of anger in the mother's eyes, he added, "But I'll see what I can do."

Moon smiled at the distraught mother. "Do you have a recent photograph of Betty?"

Wanda shook her head, then had an afterthought. "But there's a picture in last year's high school yearbook." The lawmen followed her into the parlor, then into an unkempt bedroom where posters of scruffy punk-rock stars and fuzzy kittens were thumbtacked onto the yellowed plastered walls. The woman rummaged around in a pile of unused schoolbooks and tattered romance magazines until she found a volume with a white imitation-leather binding. She thumbed through it. "Here it is—sophomore class."

Scott Parris reached out.

Pointedly ignoring the ranking officer, Wanda gave the yearbook to Charlie Moon.

After taking a perfunctory look, the deputy passed the book to his boss.

Parris stared at the array of seventy-six smiling faces, then squinted at the list of names.

Wanda's painted fingernail touched the page, guiding his gaze to her daughter's face.

Parris stared at the big-eyed brunette who looked back at him over a bright smile. Betty Naranjo was easily the prettiest girl on the page. "Could I keep this for a few days?"

Wanda Naranjo nodded.

Charlie Moon had gotten barely a glance at Betty's image, but that was sufficient to ruin his day. Unlike his aged aunt Daisy, whose mind was attuned to a whole range of spooky things, the tribal investigator was a down-to-earth fellow who managed to get by on common sense and analytical thinking. Moon's secret curse was that nine times out of ten, he could look at a photograph and instantly know whether the face looking back at him was dead or alive. This one was alive, but only barely so—and Betty Naranjo had the look of someone who didn't have too many hours left in this world. Making a snap decision, Moon signaled his friend with a barely perceptible tilt of his chin.

While Wanda restacked Betty's pristine schoolbooks and well-used magazines, Scott Parris followed his deputy into the shabby parlor. "What's up, Charlie?" *Besides your antenna.*

Moon didn't meet his friend's earnest gaze. "This is starting to look serious."

The white cop felt a sudden chill. "So what should we do?"

"I wish I knew." The Ute tilted his face to take a thoughtful look at the rough-cut pine rafters. "Maybe check with that doctor the girl said she had an appointment with."

"Right." After consulting Mrs. Naranjo's telephone directory again, Parris placed a cell-phone call to Dr. Stuart

Whyte's residence office. There were seven rings before he heard the recorded voice that Wanda Naranjo had listened to hours earlier. It tailed off with; "If this is an emergency, please hang up and dial 911. If you wish to leave a message, you may begin after the beep." Immediately after the tone, he barked, "This is Scott Parris, Granite Creek Police Department. I need to speak to Dr. Whyte as soon as he has a spare minute. He can call me at—"

"Hello—this is Mrs. Lorna Whyte." The woman was out of breath, but her voice was loud enough for Charlie Moon to hear their conversation. "I just walked in the front door and heard the phone ringing in Stuart's office. May I be of any help?"

"I hope so." Parris scowled at the unseen person. "I don't suppose you're acquainted with your husband's work, but—"

"Oh, but I am—I serve as Stuart's receptionist." The spouse shifted to her professional tone: "Do you wish to make an appointment with the doctor?"

"Uh, not that kind." Parris blushed beet red. "This is official business."

"Regarding what?"

"One of his patients."

"Oh, I see. Is this an emergency?"

"I don't know. I sure hope not."

"Oh, dear." There was a nervous giggle from the psychologist's wife. "If you'd said 'yes,' I was going to suggest that you call 911."

"Yes, ma'am." Parris grinned. "I'm the chief of police, so the buck stops on my desk. Now, if I could just speak to Dr. Whyte—"

"I'm sorry, but the doctor is not in." A two-heartbeat pause. "He's away for the weekend."

"Where can I reach him?" Parris fumbled in his shirt pocket for the notebook.

"I'm sorry, but that isn't possible." Mrs. Whyte cleared her throat. "Stuart is on one of his retreats. On the second

Friday of the month, he goes on a camping trip. He camps in the mountains in a tent. No radio, no television, no telephone."

"Not even a cell?"

"Well . . . yes—but only for emergencies, like if his truck breaks down. Besides that, he keeps his mobile phone turned off."

"Sounds like a fine idea." The overworked public servant sighed at the thought of a few days' downtime with no phone ringing. "When do you expect him back?"

"Late on Monday morning. Stuart has no appointments scheduled until one thirty P.M."

"Okay. When the doc shows up, tell him I'll be dropping by about noon."

"That will be satisfactory. And the patient's name?"

"Sorry, ma'am—that's official police business."

"I see." The temperature dropped ten degrees. "When my husband shows up on Monday, may I at least tell him what the issue is?"

"Sure. Tell the doc that his patient is . . . well . . . kinda late in getting home. Her mother's worried."

"Oh." Silence. "I see."

Parris said his goodbye, disconnected, and said to his deputy, "So what d'you think?"

The tribal investigator murmured into the white man's ear so that the mother in the bedroom couldn't hear, "I don't think this missing girl's gonna be coming home." Moon's grim face resembled chiseled stone.

Chilled by his friend's haunted expression, Scott Parris realized that pessimism was infectious. Determined to avoid contagion, he attempted to shield himself with a mix of professionalism and wishful thinking. "You know the drill, Charlie—if the girl don't show up in forty-eight hours, I'll issue the usual bulletins." He clapped the slender Indian on the back. "Now stop worrying so much—this'll turn out okay."

The deputy had barely heard the hollow reassurance,

hardly felt the friendly pat; Parris's hand was like a feather, his voice faraway like the day before yesterday.

Realizing that he wasn't getting through, the chief of police assumed a flinty-edged tone: "Leave it alone. Okay?"

The deputy nodded, but Moon's mind's eye was focused on what he could not avert his gaze from—the pretty girl's face in the yearbook. His inner ear listened intently to the voice he could not bear to hear—Betty's curvaceous lips whispering, *Thanks for caring, mister . . . but it's too late.*

The Lady Makes a Decision

After her unnerving conversation with the chief of police, Lorna Whyte checked the messages on the office answering machine. There were only three, two sales pitches and a call from a worried mother. She played that one several times. Over and over, she listened to the woman's anxious voice:

"Uh . . . This is Wanda Naranjo. My daughter thought she had an eleven A.M. appointment with the doctor, but . . . I guess she must've been mixed up about what day it was for. Betty's awfully late getting home and I'm worried about her . . . but I guess I shouldn't be bothering you with my troubles. Sorry."

Lorna was about to place a call to her husband, but for obscure reasons of its own her right hand refused to touch the cordless telephone. And the lady had her own reasons for hesitating. *This isn't the first time the police have called about one of his patients.* In her husband's line of work, that was to be expected. Also . . . *Teenage kids go missing all the time, and almost all of them come home again.* There was, of necessity, a dark side to that shiny penny: *And a few of them don't.* Either way, in a few days this police business with Betty Naranjo would be old news. And not only that . . . *Stuart gave me strict instructions not to call him unless there was an emergency.* And this was not an actual emergency—not really. *Not yet.* She stared at her diffident hand, the long, slender fingers outstretched— and withdrew it. *I'll wait until he calls me on Monday morning.*

CHAPTER TWELVE

LATE ON FRIDAY NIGHT

A few minutes before midnight, Wanda Naranjo was in her four-poster, flat on her back and still as death itself. To enhance the macabre effect, the woman's face glowed with a sickly green luminescence, as if her taut skin were illuminated by a sinister source of inner twilight. Was the woman merely deceased . . . or was her fleshly presence suspended in a far worse state that does not bear even thinking about?

Neither.

The truth of the matter is disappointingly pedestrian. The lady's eerie olive pallor was produced by a pair of fluorescent nightlights plugged into electrical receptacles on either side of Wanda's sturdy bedstead.

Unaware of her lime-tinted complexion and the heart-stopping effect it would have on a nervous burglar, the lady turned onto her right side. Her fevered brain festered with the malignant seed the chief of police had planted there. *Likely as not, Mike's the father of my idiot daughter's baby.* Flopping back onto her back like a beached carp, the feisty little woman stared at the ceiling where whiskers of greenish cobwebs mimicked that parasitic growth that rolling stones do not gather. Her first assumption led to a second. *One way or another, he's responsible for Betty not coming home.* And the second a third. *So Mike knows where Betty is.* Why did this cause her lips to curl into a vicious grin?

Because Wanda knew where to find Mike. *Rat-face'll be holed up in that dumpy little camping trailer down south of town.* Rolling onto her left side, she doubted that Betty was with the lowlife. *Mike wouldn't want to have a pregnant teenager on his hands.* A clock in the parlor chimed twelve times. Back onto her back. *I don't know what I ever saw in that sorry excuse for a man.*

An interesting question, and one worthy of perhaps three seconds of thoughtful introspection, but not the burning issue of the moment—which was: what should she do about Michael Kauffmann?

Having mulled this over after Charlie Moon and Scott Parris had departed, Wanda Naranjo had come up with a plan. She was just itching to share her bold plot with an audience that could be counted on to keep a secret. Having neither fuzzy dog, standoffish cat, nor scaly goldfish to converse with, she whispered to the mossy growth of cobwebs hanging overhead, "I'll drive out to his trailer, kick the door in, and stick my pistol into his belly button, and if Mike don't tell me what's happened to Betty, I'll gut-shoot the worthless son of a bitch four times." (Do not jump to the conclusion that the woman is without mercy; she has saved a cartridge.) "After the miserable coward kicks and screams and rolls on the floor and begs me to put him out of his horrible misery and tells me everything he knows, I'll finish him off with one right between the eyes."

Despite these violent promises to herself, Wanda had never killed a human being—not even a sorry specimen like Michael Kauffmann. She supposed that it might take a couple of days to get up the gumption to carry the thing off.

We all know that lurid plots laid at blackest midnight are frequently tempered by the soothing glow of dawn's first light. So what was the likelihood that she would actually go through with the daring plan to encounter her ex-hairy-leg one last time with a cocked-and-loaded pistol in her hand? Somewhere between *very likely* and a *sure thing.* The moment the lady had made up her mind to go agunning for Mike, the robust young man was instantly burdened with what is known in the trade as a *disqualifying precondition*. Had the part-time carpenter carried a term-life policy, any insurance company *in the know* would have immediately downgraded the insured from so-so to extremely poor risk.

A serious dose of bad news for the part-time carpenter, but what's terminally toxic to the philandering gander can be delightfully agreeable to the vengeful goose. Was Betty's angry mother already feeling better? Yes indeed, and here's why: just as a nagging vacillation about how to deal with a vexing problem tends to feed insomnia, coming to a firm decision is often an effective soporific. It was on this occasion. After enjoying a soul-satisfying yawn, Wanda Naranjo smiled like a darling little girl cuddling an adorable kitten—and drifted off into a restful sleep.

Betty Naranjo's Singular Awakening

By one of those peculiar synchronicities that connect parents to their offspring, the daughter's journey commenced just as Wanda Naranjo was falling asleep. In contrast to her mother's swift transfer into that shadowy locale where pleasant dreams and hideous nightmares alike are fashioned, the girl not only was moving in the opposite direction—but her return to consciousness was to be an exceedingly gradual process.

The teenager's first vague sense of identity was not that she was—or ever had been—a living, breathing human being. In Miss Naranjo's murky dream-coma, she was an entity akin to that forgotten refuse of life that lies beneath the bright world where dazzling sunflowers burst into glorious bloom, exultant bluebirds sing, and flighty butterflies take to wing. Betty was twin sister to some dumb, unthinking thing . . . a waterlogged cypress trunk that had resided on the bottom of a dank, silty swamp for decades, centuries . . . perhaps millennia. The initial spark of awareness began somewhere just under her rough-bark skin, then penetrated sixteen growth rings deep into the very core of her wooden self.

Her not-quite-dead presence supposed that this drift toward semiconsciousness was due to that ordinary decay that causes corpses of animals to bloat and float to the surface. The process seemed quite natural; during their digestive and excretory processes, the concerted action of trillions of single-cell cannibal animalcules produce tiny bubbles of gas. As a result, the heavy life-form the creatures inhabit becomes slightly lighter than the liquid media it is immersed in . . . and is obliged by the laws of physics to rise.

But toward where?

Some pleasant interface between buoyant liquid and fresh, life-giving air?

Not in this instance.

Betty's destination was not a warm, welcome *light*. The youth was destined to encounter another kind of darkness entirely, and one far more terrifying than the dumb numbness of deep, endless sleep.

When the girl eventually opened her eyes—she blinked in surprise at the infinite, impenetrable blackness. It took a few faltering heartbeats for the question to form in her mind: *What's happened to me?* Her confused intellect came up with an answer. *I've gone stone blind.*

Under the circumstances, a plausible deduction. But . . .

Not so far away, a dim rectangle of gray was materializing in the darkness.

Oh—that looks like a window.

Perhaps so.

I think I can hear something.

Indeed, her eardrums and associated cochlear apparatus had begun to provide tantalizing whispers of information. Or was it *misinformation*? Hard to tell. But the data was duly processed by her increasingly functioning brain.

That sounds like rain. The girl closed her eyes and strained. *Rain falling on . . .*

Falling on what?

On a metal roof.

Betty opened her eyes again. Something seemed to be forming on the gray rectangle. Tiny dots. Pearly spots. *Those must be raindrops.* She tried to focus on the space directly above her face, and listened intently to the ploppity-plops of supposed raindrops. *The roof isn't too far away.*

But what was beneath her?

I'm on my back, laying on some kind of bed. A little cot, she thought, with a mattress that felt hard and lumpy. Along with these quasi-clues to her immediate environment, Betty was also becoming aware of a dullish collection of pains. Her spine and ribs ached. Summing up all this sensory input, her mind attempted to make up a story to account for her situation. *I've gotten hurt and somebody has taken me inside.* She sniffed. *It's dusty here.* And though she couldn't see the walls, some deep instinct assured her that the space she occupied was small. *I'm probably in a little shack, like the old shed behind our house where Momma stores old furniture and stuff.* The girl tried ever so hard to see through the blackness. *Or maybe I'm upstairs in a tiny loft, and it's raining on a steel roof.* Wherever she was . . . *I'm all by myself.*

Reasonable conclusions, given the totality of her prior assumptions: If it was rain that the girl heard. If there was a metal roof over her head.

If she *was* alone.

Betty Naranjo tried to move her right hand. That reluctant member refused to respond. As did her numb left hand. *What's happened to me?*

It occurred to her that she might be paralyzed from an injury. Or . . . *Maybe I'm strapped onto this hard bed.* Or both.

Terror's icy fingers stroked Betty's throbbing throat.

I'm hurt really bad and somebody has tied me down. The grim assumption led to a stark conclusion. *Unless somebody comes to help me, I'll die here!*

Fear feeds on itself and invites additional predators to

dine—sadistic Terror was immediately joined by her insane sister Hysteria. Their dark appetites now synergistically combined, the hideous siblings licked their lips in anticipation of devouring the teenager.

The *pregnant* teenager.

This most significant fact of Betty's existence suddenly flooded her consciousness.

As it did, she was distracted from the horror of her presumed predicament by the realization that the innocent child in her womb was also a victim. If Betty was about to slip away into that final, deepest of sleeps—so was the little one she had never seen.

Let it be noted that despite her several shortcomings, the girl was no whimpering sissy. Like her mother, father, and a thousand other hardy ancestors—the youth had steel in her backbone and a bushel of grit in her craw. Though unable to move her limbs, she could open her mouth and make use of her lungs, vocal cords, and lips. And so she did. Not loudly, though.

There would be no shrill screams from Wanda Naranjo's daughter.

Oh so softly, the expectant mother began to murmur a loving lullaby to that new soul inside her body. As she sang so sweetly—and forgot her miserable *self* so completely—the dismal center of Betty's soul was likewise born anew. Her transformation was ignited by the tiniest spark of light, but it is written that "An infinitesimal twinkling in God's eye outshines a supernova in the blackest sky." By and by, that heavenly radiance would blossom and grow into a purifying inferno—burning away all her inner darkness.

Forevermore.

CHAPTER THIRTEEN

Saturday Morning, Long Before Dawn

Excepting wide-eyed insomniacs, overcaffeinated long-haul truck drivers, and prowling police officers trawling for wary nightcrawlers—Colorado's citizenry was asleep. Each of them has an interesting story to tell, but we shall limit our attention to just one of these slumbering souls.

The Sleeper

Far to the south of Granite Creek and even farther from her nephew's vast cattle ranch, Daisy Perika is cuddled snug in her bed, a plump feather pillow under her head, a hand-stitched quilt pulled up to her chin. Doesn't she look like a *Saturday Evening Post* cover painted by Norman Rockwell's magic brush—the very image of wrinkled-granny innocence? Which illustrates why one must not judge a magazine by its cover; the most hard-boiled cynics among us would be shocked, stunned, and outraged to read what is written on the secret pages of Daisy's diary.

To avoid unnecessary scandal, we shall limit ourselves to the more benign aspects of our notorious subject's public life—what a tolerant soul might call her *charming foibles*.

Anyone who knows Charlie Moon's aunt is aware that Miss Daisy is a mite cranky before she's had her morning coffee, and waking the tribal elder in the middle of the night is like touching a flame to a short fuse on a stick of dynamite. According to Mr. Moon, the tribal elder's explosive temper led to that well-known Southern Ute proverb: "Unless the tipi is on fire, let sleeping aunties recline."

This sage advice (so Moon asserts) is the origin of several derivative "old sayings" such as: "Let sleeping jackals lie"; "Leave well enough alone"; and, "Don't go yanking on Superman's cape," but that is neither here nor there.

Yes, there is a point here and it is this: in the grand scheme of things, there must always be an exception that exists for the sole purpose of proving the rule. As Daisy Perika snores through both nostrils and her mouth, this exceptional personage is about to announce his extraordinary presence. While Daisy's uninvited guest is considering how best to effect his dramatic entrance, the sleeper—whose happy dreams are generally liberally provided with flora—finds herself in a setting reminiscent of the recent mountain-meadow production.

Her Dream

A mere wisp of a girl with the fresh breeze whipping her long black locks, a teenage Daisy rides a spotted pony bareback across a buffalo-grass prairie dotted with wildflowers of every color a human being's mind can reproduce from the wavelengths of sunlight, and a few impossible hues invented especially for this occasion. To enhance her experience, the vast dreamland pasture is inhabited with several species of agreeable mammals, including lovable bewhiskered mice, delightfully cute cottontails, and an innocent spotted fawn that has been recently orphaned. But the scene is not entirely one that would please Mr. Disney (God bless his soul). The unseemly blemish on an otherwise charming landscape is a hideous jackalope, bearing a pair of huge elk antlers that would look mighty fine mounted over Charlie Moon's mantelpiece. Those who are not familiar with the species might argue that an authentic jackalope would wear genuine antelope headgear but this is Daisy's dream, which is based upon genuine postcards she's seen.

When her piebald pony pauses to drink from a sparking stream where rainbow trout dart about, the willowy rider slips off her mount, kneels on the pebbled bank, and is about to quench her thirst, when—the horrid jackalope kicks her in the ribs!

This was not a friendly kick; the Ute girl feels like she's been hit by a brick.

A Singular Night Visitor

The impact had awakened Daisy Perika from her restful sleep—so abruptly that she turned her head to see what had kicked her and felt something pop in her neck bones. *Oh, my—that dream was so real!*

So real that her ribs still ached like all get-out from the jackalope's kick, which raised a dark suspicion in her mind.

The old woman blinked in the darkness. *Something really did hit me on the side.* But despite Daisy's rather broad-minded view of reality, she did not believe in such folk as kicking jackalopes, prissy English fairies, or green-hatted Irish leprechauns. She did believe that . . . *Something is right here in my bedroom.*

Something was. She could feel its presence.

I bet one of those fuzzy-faced masked buggers slipped into the house. The tribal elder knew for a fact that the Raccoon People were very clever. They could open tightly fitting trash-can lids, buckled lunch boxes, and latched gates. So why not locked windows or doors? It was not clear to her how a furry animal could manage that latter task, but . . . *Maybe they carry skeleton keys.* (Miss Daisy was still groggy. Also ready to put up a fight.) *I wish I had the 12-gauge shotgun here by my bed.*

The fact that she didn't should not encourage a burglar. When at home alone, Daisy keeps a well-honed butcher knife under her pillow. (Those citizens who wish to keep all their fingers firmly attached to their hands should not follow this practice in their own four-posters, or when sleeping out.) Ever so slowly, she moved her trusty right hand toward the wickedly sharp weapon. And had just gotten her fingers around the hickory handle when—

Her visitor addressed her with a greeting, the gist of which was that—it'd been way too long since he had enjoyed her company.

When he was of a mind to, the intruder could converse in passable English, Spanish, or the modern Ute dialect, but the words Daisy heard were uttered in an archaic version of her native tongue. The tribal elder sighed and let go of the butcher knife. "Oh, it's *you*."

Indeed it was—none other than that *alleged* knee-high dwarf who *supposedly* inhabits an abandoned badger den in *Cañón del Espíritu*. (The qualifiers are inserted because hardly anyone besides Daisy has ever seen the legendary personage. Sarah Frank believes she has seen approximately half of the *pitukupf,* and Scott Parris may have seen his miniature footprints in the snow.) Whatever the truth may be about his objective reality, the homely creature—who was real enough to Daisy—appeared clad in dirty buckskin britches, a green shirt that looked like it had *never* been washed, and a tattered straw hat that might have been discarded by a discerning hobo. Did we mention how his soiled toes protruded from a filthy pair of dilapidated doeskin moccasins? It was just as well; the effect was distinctly offputting. Which suggests that enough has been said on the matter. Except for the proverbial bottom line: in addition to his questionable taste in apparel and no doubt due to his disinterest in hygienic virtues, Daisy's visitor was—to state the case bluntly—noticeably malodorous.

The tribal elder put it more bluntly: *He stinks like something the dog likes to roll in.* She posed those natural questions that tend to arise in a tense social encounter such as the one at hand: "What're you doing standing on my bed at this hour—and why did you haul off and kick me in the ribs?"

Whilst affecting a convincing shiver, the *pitukupf* provided an answer.

She snorted at the Little Man's response. "Because you're *cold*?"

He certainly was. And so would Daisy be if she resided in a hole in the ground. It was not as if such rustic domiciles came equipped with central heating.

She rolled her eyes. "Why didn't you pitch some more sticks onto your fire?"

This impertinent query irked. *Because* he was out of firewood.

"So what d'you want from me?" Daisy thought she knew.

The shaman's elfish guest confirmed her suspicion by tugging at her quilt.

Charlie Moon's irritable auntie toyed with the notion of giving the cheeky little runt the old heave-ho, but all the fight had gone out of her. "Oh, all right." She rolled the quilt back. "Get in beside me."

He did. Resting his tiny head on the pillow beside Daisy's, the chilled *pitukupf* sighed with pleasure at the welcome warmth and pulled her handmade quilt up to his bristly chin.

"Be still now, so I can go back to sleep." The weary woman yawned. "I'm old as Moses great-grandmother and I need my rest."

Being of the male persuasion, the *pitukupf* could not resist the least opportunity to assert his superiority. He archly observed that he was ten times older than herself.

"I know that." *Nasty little braggart.* Another yawn. "Hush now."

To her dismay, the dwarf was in a talkative mood. The diminutive chatterbox began by filling Daisy in on what had been going on in *Cañón del Espíritu* and thereabouts since her last visit to that vast space between Three Sisters and Dogleg Mesas.

"Stop your yammering." She closed her eyes. "You can tell me all about it after the sun comes up."

Short of physical violence, it was virtually impossible to silence the little fellow once he had gotten up a good head of steam. Her companion continued with a brisk commentary on how wet it was for this time of year, his concerns about the large number of mule deer foraging in the canyon (they were bound to eat every sprig of grass), and how one of the human spirits (a Scottish silver prospector who had been murdered by Apaches in 1871) had recently been "taken up" by the *shining ones*—presumably to cross over and settle into a permanent home.

This reference to a familiar ghost proved to be an eye-opener. Literally. Daisy's eyes popped open to resemble a pair of poached quail eggs. "That reminds me of something I'd like to tell you about."

And so she did, eventually summing up her problem thusly: "And ever since that morning when Charlie and Sarah and Scott Parris were here for breakfast, I haven't been able to see a single one of those haunts in Spirit Canyon."

This astonishing admission aroused the *pitukupf*'s interest, and like menfolk of any tribe, the dwarf figured he knew what had happened and why and how to fix it. What it all boiled down to was that Daisy Perika had spent so much time away from her home and the canyon that she had *lost her touch*. What she needed was a stiff dose of huckleberry wine spiced with nutmeg, dandelion petals, castor oil, and minced mole whiskers.

The experienced pharmacist was aware of the efficacy of the prescription, but she disagreed with her guest's diagnosis. And told him why. Daisy advised the dwarf that she could still *hear* the spirits; their voices were just as clear as his.

It that case, the tribal elder was undoubtedly the victim of a curse.

This was a startling assertion. "D'you really think so?"

She felt the nod of his knotty little head on the pillow.

The Ute shaman had never considered such a possibility, but had to admit that the dwarf was probably right on the mark. *Some witch has cast a spell to rob me of my powers. Probably some Navajo I crossed years ago. Those Skin-Walkers never forget the least little insult.*

The dwarf assured his bedmate that if her recent misfortune was the result of a broad-spectrum bewitching, there might be no way to restore Daisy to good health. But, in a more hopeful vein, he suggested that the curse might be one that was effective only in the neighborhood. If the stricken woman was away from home, she might be able to see truckloads of ghosts.

"How far away?"

He told her.

"A long day's walk?" She requested a more specific metric.

The dwarf provided that information forthwith. Which was: twelve miles if the trek was by day or ninety-six furlongs if she walked during the dark hours between dusk and dawn.

Daisy was beginning to suspect that her sly little guest was making sport of her. But this was one of those occasions when she felt compelled to follow the *pitukupf*'s advice. "I know just what I'll do." She waited for him to ask "What?"

He did not.

Finally warm from toes to chin, the dwarf had fallen asleep quite suddenly—as those of his ilk are wont to do. Within a few beats of his plum-size heart, his eyelids started to flutter. The Little Man's tiny hands clenched into fists, then relaxed. His spindly little legs began to run.

No. Don't ask. What the Little Folk dream of is not a suitable subject for civilized discourse.

Now wide awake, Daisy Perika resented the dwarf's

sleep. *I won't get another wink for hours.* But after a little while, the senior citizen's lids began to grow heavy. After an even littler while, they could not have been pried open with a claw hammer. Indeed, Daisy dreamed that her tired old body was being prepared for burial; the miserly mortician had laid counterfeit, lead half-dollars over her eye sockets. After that, her dreams got really strange. Again, speculations are discouraged. Suffice it to say that while she slept and dreamed, the old woman's mind was not entirely occupied with fantastical trivia. Daisy's gray cells were also busy conjuring up an action plan to restore her shamanic powers. Several potential plots would have to be considered and rejected before she selected just the right approach. The creative processes cannot be hurried, so this would take awhile.

Watch the dancing minutes strut by; see firefly stars flit across the night sky.

About the time when morning's warm sunshine smiled on her leathery face, Daisy opened her eyes without the aid of any carpenter's tool. Pleased to see that her bedroom window was illumined by the golden glow of dawn, she decided to tell the *pitukupf* about the dandy plan that had *just come to her.* But the half-pint in bed beside her was . . . absent without leave.

Now, wasn't that just like a man who'd crawled into her bed only a few hours ago? Daisy was severely vexed. Where was a thousand-year-old dwarf when you needed him? *That pushy half-pint don't mind waking me up in the middle of the night and talking my ear off, but where's the gabby little rascal when I need somebody to talk to?* What was a woman to do?

What her mother had always done, that's what—which was to set her jaw, roll up her sleeves, and *make do* with available resources. Her supply of dwarves severely depleted, Daisy Perika was obliged to improvise.

She addressed the beamed ceiling above her bedroom: "I'll go miles and miles away and find me a great big cemetery that's bound to be loaded up to the gills with haunts." She grinned at an ear-shaped pine knot. "If all it takes to get my powers back is being a long way from *Cañón del Espíritu,* then I'll see more spirits than I can shake a hickory stick at!" But the opposite possibility lurked in the shadows—the shaman's ghost-eyes might remain blind no matter how far from home she went. What then? *Then I don't know what I'll do.*

Not true.

Daisy Perika knew what she would be *compelled* to do, and the thought grated like long fingernails scratching on a dusty blackboard. *I'll have to go see the Little Man and ask for his help.* She assured herself that this would not be quite so humiliating as last night's nightmare, in which she'd shown up at church on Sunday morning naked as a jaybird. Despite their occasional disagreements, the dwarf was a professional colleague. *It'll be more like two doctors consulting on a difficult case.* And like her momma had always said, "Two heads are twice as good as half as many." Though Daisy revered her mother's memory, she doubted this arithmetic result . . . *when one of the heads is about the size of a cracked teacup.* But these speculations were getting the tribal elder nowhere, which was not her preferred destination. *I need to get somebody to take me to a good-size cemetery.* The list of persons who provided Daisy with motorized transportation was a short one, and topping it off were Sarah Frank and Charlie Moon—both of whom resided on the Columbine. *And the nearest big graveyard to Charlie's ranch is the one in Granite Creek.*

This seemingly innocuous decision turned out to be the first firecracker in a Daisy-chain of explosive events that (in hindsight) she would recollect as a series of coincidences that were—from the tribal elder's peculiar point of view—fortuitous. Which circumstance might lead a few cynical observers to conclude that the whole business was slyly contrived.

CHAPTER FOURTEEN

AN UNSEEMLY INCIDENT AT GRANITE CREEK CEMETERY

Sunday, 2:10 A.M.

Despite meager wages, a soul-numbing loneliness, and occasional bouts of rheumatoid arthritis, cemetery custodian Morris Meusser considered himself a most fortunate man. And so he should. Mr. Meusser loved his work. Three times a day, he patrolled the verdant cemetery grounds in a battery-powered vehicle that was first cousin to a golf cart. During these quiet, dignified inspections he would nod respectfully at visitors who were there to pay respects to family members and friends who had passed over and occasionally pause to exchange a few words with some forlorn soul who had no one left to talk to. It was a pleasant, useful way to pass the daylight hours. When no one was looking, the whimsical fellow enjoyed tipping his billed cap to ducks and swans on the cemetery pond, which was somewhat larger than its counterpart nearby in U.S. Grant Park. The custodian had no disposable income for movies or meals in restaurants, but he did look forward to a weekend game of checkers with his best (and only) friend, Freddy Whitsun.

After a long day filled with honest labor, Meusser's quiet nights in the three-room custodian's residence were devoted to a book from the public library, a brief bedtime prayer, and as much sleep as his aching joints would allow. When his slumbers were interrupted by a throbbing pain, a troubling dream, or ordinary sleeplessness, he would sometimes divert himself by making an unscheduled nighttime inspection. These were the most peaceful hours of all, when the cemetery was truly asleep. On occasion, he might startle a big-eyed mule deer or frighten a cottontail into spontaneous flight. Just as often, the custodian would spot a young couple who had parked among the tombstones with amorous intent. Such romantics invariably withdrew when he turned on his five-cell flashlight.

On this particular evening, his sleep had not been interrupted by ache, nightmare, or insomnia. Morris Meusser had awakened shortly after two A.M. with the suspicion that something was amiss. For a full minute, he could not imagine what was troubling him. There were no unusual sounds, like last week when he was awakened by a throaty motorcycle rumbling through the cemetery's winding blacktop lanes. There was not even the yip-yipping call of a lonely coyote, or the tooting hoot of an owl. Even the light breeze rattling aspen leaves outside his window had fallen still. Oddest of all, the grandfather clock in the corner had ceased to tick and tock. *I'm sure I wound it before I hit the sack.* He smiled at his foolishness. *I don't know what's bothering me; a sensible man should be thankful for a quiet night.* He yawned, rolled over on his side, and—

As Meusser liked to say, the significance of the heavy silence *hit him.*

Of course. He pushed himself up on an elbow. *There's no sound because something out there ain't right and the animals all know it.* He listened again, and felt more than heard the throb of his heartbeat. It was as if all the creatures who occupied the cemetery were holding their collective breaths—waiting for Morris Meusser to do his duty. *Guess I'd better go take a look.* Without hurry, the patient man rolled out of bed and dressed himself as he did every morning—in a blue cotton work shirt, neatly pressed khaki slacks, and a tattered leather vest (to which, from long habit, he attached his treasured pocket watch). He pulled on a pair of white cotton socks and rawhide boots, and (figuring it would likely be shivery outside) donned his brown Carhartt billed hat and an oversized OshKosh B'Gosh denim jacket that swallowed him up.

Equipped with his trusty seventeen-inch Maglite flashlight and an unwavering faith in his ability to deal with whatever trouble he might encounter, he left the warm comfort of his cozy bungalow and stepped into the chill night. While several of the legal residents of the cemetery watched and waited expectantly for the biped to deal with this irksome matter, Morris Mcusser cocked his ear and listened intently.

The stillness persisted.

Beneath the silence, he heard something. A faint, faraway something. Someone (or some*thing*?) was making the sort of sounds that an edgy fellow doesn't want to hear late at night in a cemetery.

Scuff. Scuff. Scuff-scuff.

For a long string of the old man's irregular heartbeats, the scuff-scuffing would continue. Now and then, a pause. Beginning to feel distinctly uneasy, the man who was responsible for looking after the cemetery entertained a hopeful thought: *Probably just a hungry ol' porky-pine gnawin' on a cedar tree.* A man can sham himself when he wants to, but Meusser knew that such sounds were unlikely to be made by a quilled animal or any other of God's innocent creatures. The sound he had heard was disturbingly familiar—but the custodian did not want to think about *that* possibility. There had been no scuffing now for quite some time. *Well, whatever it was—seems like it's over and done with.* He drew in a deep breath and counted to twenty. *It ain't going to start up again, so I'll just go back inside and crawl under the quilt and—* No.

There it goes again.

Scuff. Scuff-scuff.

The elderly man knew what he had to do. *But I don't intend to walk.* Morris Mcusser mounted the cemetery's battery-operated cart and set off toward the sounds. Every so often, he would stop the cart and listen to get a better fix on the location where the sounds were originating. Some six minutes later, he topped a small ridge known as Pink Rose Knoll and stopped to listen.

Scuff-scuff. Scuff.

That's not fifty yards away. Taking care to make no noise, the custodian got off the cart. In the moonlight, he saw a dark form. And movement.

Meusser was about to switch on his five-cell flashlight, when the clouds parted for an instant to bathe the dusky nightscape in a misty flash of solar light reflected off the face of earth's pockmarked satellite. During this brief interlude of moonglow, he saw *what* the trespasser was up to. More or less. *But why would someone come out here in the middle of the night to do a thing like that?* And . . . *Why in that particular spot?*

It was the cemetery employee's responsibility to find out. *That's what I get paid minimum wage to do.* True. But from somewhere deep inside, a voice fairly screamed, *Get back on the cart, drive back to the house fast as you can, lock yourself inside, and call the police!* So what did he do?

You know.

One stealthy step at a time, Mr. Meusser approached the sinister malefactor.

CHAPTER FIFTEEN

A GRUESOME DISCOVERY ON THE CHRISTIAN SABBATH

8:15 A.M.

Morris Meusser's checker-playing buddy turned his battered blue panel truck off Copper Street and under the ornate iron arch beside the Granite Creek Cemetery sign. Freddy Whitsun drove slowly along a narrow blacktop lane that snaked its sinuous way through the verdant space that, for seven score years and more, had served as the resting place for hundreds of locals and not a few passers-through. Freddy Fixit (this was the sign painted on both sides of his venerable van) had not come to pay a respectful call on one of those citizens who slept beneath the sod. After passing by dozens of residents whose names and significant dates were chiseled into marble, granite—and even lowly limestone—he braked his vehicle to a stop in the graveled driveway of the only dwelling thereabouts that had been constructed to shelter the living.

The handyman got out of his truck and slammed the door. Hard enough, an observer might have concluded, to *wake the dead*—or for that matter, a cemetery custodian who might be sleeping in.

As regards an observer, there was one. What he may have concluded is unknown, but inside the cemetery custodian's modest residence, Morris Meusser did not take the hint.

Freddy Whitsun gazed at the modest bungalow's damaged front door with a scowl. *That sure looks like somebody pried on it.* An obvious enough conclusion, but the man who made his living mending broken things noticed something that most callers would have missed: the telephone line was not firmly connected to the terminal box on the west wall. Matter of fact, it was not connected at all. The limp section of cable was hanging from the electric-utility pole, a yard or two curled up on the grass like a skinny black viper. Morris Meusser's early-morning visitor picked it up and squinted at the broken end. *Why, that's been cut clean through!* He eyed the few inches of cable hanging from the terminal box on the cottage, which was, of course, also cleanly cut. *Now why would somebody do a thing like that?* He could imagine only two reasons. A mean-spirited misfit who enjoyed committing petty acts of vandalism had practiced his nastiness on Morris Meusser. Then, there was the more troubling possibility: *Somebody wanted to make sure Morris couldn't use his telephone.* Which thought immediately summoned up an ugly picture of an intruder bent on violence. Uncertain about how he ought to proceed, Morris Meusser's friend resorted to the nervous habit of flexing the fingers on his big, strong hands. *I don't want to go barging in.* Whitsun knew that he ought to call the cops right away, but . . . *Before I do that I guess I ought to tap on the door and find out if Morris is okay.* The edgy fellow rapped cautiously on the damaged facing. "Morris . . . you at home?"

If he was, the occupant did not stir.

Freddy Whitsun glanced nervously to his left and right. He was experiencing the skin-crawling sensation that . . . *Somebody's out there watching me.* Even those unfortunate paranoiacs among us are occasionally justified in their fears.

Somebody was.

From some thirty yards away behind a neatly trimmed hedge, a beady pair of unblinking eyes stared at the unexpected Sunday-morning visitor. *If that big bruiser had showed up five minutes earlier he'd have caught me inside and I'd be dead meat.* But the bad guy knew that the brawny man in the Mr. Fixit truck would be calling the cops pretty quickly, and it wouldn't take the boys in blue long to get to the cemetery. The slender felon's thin hand clenched the valuable he'd taken from the custodian. *I ought to throw this away so I don't get caught with it.* An eminently sensible plan. *Then I should walk over to the park and sit on a bench and wait for the cops to show up and ask me if I've seen any suspicious characters hanging around.* Also highly advisable. But the man's avaricious fingers refused to release the prize, and his lean legs fairly ached to run like a terrified gazelle pursued by a hungry lion. The malefactor pocketed the wages of his sin. *I guess I'd best make myself scarce and get out of town while the getting's good.*

Citizen Whitsun sucked in a deep breath. "Hey, Morris," the burly handyman bellowed. "It's me—Freddy." He frowned at the damaged door. "You okay?"

Nary a peep from the custodian.

Whitsun took the doorknob in hand, turned it gently, and pushed the door open just enough to poke his shaggy head into the inner twilight. "Is there somebody here?"

Some body was . . . somebody was not. What remained of Morris Meusser was the residue thereof.

Whitsun blinked at the man on the parlor couch and swallowed hard. *I sure hope Morris is asleep.* He approached for a better look at a purple bruise on the prone man's forehead. *He don't look like he's breathing.* The worried man pressed a thumb under his friend's jawbone. *Oh, Lordy—there ain't any pulse at all!* He took another look at Meusser's gray face. *I never saw anybody who looked deader than that.* At that very instant, Whitsun noticed a detail that startled and horrified him. To verify this disagreeable discovery, he leaned to squint at the dead man's chest. Sure enough . . . *Some lowlife thief has pinched Morris's pocket watch right off his vest!* Obviously, the same lowlife who had cut the phone line and pried the door open.

The way Freddy Whitsun saw it, a killing was one thing—in a fit of anger, fright, or self-defense, even a decent man might bop another fellow on the head without the least intention of doing him any serious harm. Whitsun had done this himself a time or two. But to steal from a corpse? That was miles over the line.

As the room began to spin slowly around him, the big man made a grab for an armchair. When the dizziness did not subside, he eased his bulk into the convenient seat. Thus stabilized, he began to absorb the enormity of what had happened. *I can't believe my old buddy is really dead.* A single tear coursed its way down his leathery cheek. *This is the awfulest thing that ever happened in my whole life.* Without warning, Whitsun's massive frame began to quake with a horrible shudder that shook every joint in his body and rattled his teeth. Overcome with grief, the big man began to wail and then to weep. As if to stop the flow, he pressed both hands over his eyes. It seemed this pathetic paroxysm might never end, but even the most violent thunderstorms have a way of passing quickly. After a few moans, his huge shoulders ceased to heave; his reddened eyes had no more tears to shed.

There were important things to do here, and Freddy Whitsun was the man on the spot. Cool as blue alpine ice, Yukon cucumbers, and November's frosty breath, Morris Meusser's outraged, grief-stricken friend got up from the armchair, marched out the front door, and made a beeline for his van. Freddy Whitsun got his mobile phone out of a plastic toolbox, leaned his butt on the truck, dialed the appropriate three-digit number, and provided a terse report to GCPD dispatcher Clara Tavishuts: "I just found my buddy Morris dead in his little house at the cemetery." Pause. "Yes'm—

Morris Meusser, the custodian." Shorter pause. "Yes'm, I'm sure he's dead." The caller responded to another query. "I'm Freddy Whitsun." A deep intake of breath. "Yes'm, I'll be here when the po-leece show up."

CHAPTER SIXTEEN

GCPD's TOP COP TAKES CHARGE

Sunday, 9:40 A.M.

The chief of police skidded his GCPD unit to a stop between its black-and-white twin and the Mr. Fixit van. Like a fighter pilot ejecting from the cockpit of a craft going down in flames, Scott Parris fairly exploded from his unit. Giving Freddy Whitsun a glance as he passed by, the beefy cop barreled into the custodian's quarters—and stopped on a dime when he saw the dead man on the parlor couch. Towering over GCPD Officer Alicia Martin, Parris glared accusingly at the corpse as if it had committed some particularly odious social offense. "State cops'll show up any time now, not to mention our favorite medical examiner. Before things get really noisy and confusing, gimme the essentials."

The petite blonde in the dark blue uniform began the recitation by advising her broad-shouldered boss that the victim was one Morris Meusser, who was—make that *had been*—custodian of the Granite Creek Cemetery for as long as she could remember. "Morris must've been in his midseventies." It was almost impossible to believe he was dead. "Nice old fella." She glanced at her wristwatch. "Body was discovered shortly after 8 A.M. by Freddy Whitsun, who stopped by for coffee and a game of checkers."

"I know Whitsun—and Meusser too," Parris said abruptly. "Those two've been buddies for a 'coon's age."

"I haven't got a written statement from Whitsun yet, but

he looked like he'd cried his eyes out." Martin wiped a speck from her left eye and cleared her throat as she pointed to a telephone on an end table by the couch. "If Meusser had tried to dial 911, he wouldn't have gotten the call through. Before the perp pried the front door open, he cut the phone line at of the terminal box on the outside wall."

Parris was mildly surprised at this unusual precaution. "This wasn't an ordinary dope-addict burglary that turned into a killing—this guy had homicide on his mind and he *thinks* about something before he does it." *Which puts our chances of arresting the sly bastard someplace between slim and none.*

Nodding her agreement to both the statement and the thought, Officer Martin took a deep breath. "We'll get the official word from Doc Simpson later on, but you can see that the victim's forehead has suffered trauma." She pointed her miniature laser flashlight at the corpse; the ruby dot jittered on the purple bruise. "Funny thing, though—the perp didn't take the victim's wallet." She waited for the boss to reach the obvious conclusion.

Parris did not disappoint. "Probably because his work was interrupted." The cop followed this train of thought. "The killer was probably here when Freddy Whitsun showed up." He blinked at Martin. "So what *did* he take?"

She knelt by the couch. The dead man's face was smiling, perhaps (she thought) at something amusing known only to the deceased. "Meusser always carried a Hamilton pocket watch. It's been ripped right off his vest—along with the chain and fob."

Parris was pleased to hear that the killer had taken something that would be easy to identify. "What kind of fob?"

"An old coin." Officer Martin tilted her chin to smile at the boss. "Five-dollar gold piece."

The chief of police grinned at the lady with the extraordinary memory for detail. "You absolutely sure about that?"

"Mm-hm." Miss Martin closed her blue eyes to recall the image of the custodian's treasure. "Half eagle." She opened her eyes. Both of them sparkled at the boss. "Minted in 1867." She dangled the bait. "Which was a memorable year."

"Sure." Parris made a wild guess: "That's when the Civil War was over."

With some delicacy, Officer Martin cleared her throat.

The man who couldn't recall what he'd had for supper last night glared at the show-off cop. "What?"

"Unless memory fails me, General Lee surrendered to General Grant at Appomattox Court House on April 9, 1865." *Please, please please ask the right question.* The cop crossed her fingers, wished upon a star, and so on and so forth.

Say what you like about absurd superstitions—it worked.

Parris grinned. "Okay, Little Miss Smart Britches— what's so special about 1867?"

Feigning surprise at such a question, Martin assumed her big-eyed expression of astonishment. "I'm sure it just slipped your mind, but that was the year when Mr. Samuel Clemens—known more widely as Mark Twain—made his famous steamboat trip to Europe and the Middle East. That journey was the basis for *Innocents Abroad,* for which he gained national acclaim."

"Oh, right." *Martin needs to find herself a man and get married and have a couple a kids.*

Matter of fact, that was precisely Miss Martin's aspiration. And she was looking the *man* right in the eye. Hardly a week went by when she didn't pause to daydream about how elegant MRS. ALICIA PARRIS would look on her personalized stationery.

Oblivious to either her amorous sentiments or matrimonial intents, the mildly myopic cop grunted his way into a painful squat and got a closer look at Morris Meusser's scuffed leather vest—where a buttonhole was torn through. *That's where the bastard ripped off the watch chain.* "Maybe we'll get lucky and the pocket watch with the gold half whatzit will show up in a Denver pawn shop." Parris scratched at a two-day growth of itchy, bristly stubble on his chin. "That gold coin on Meusser's watch chain—I wonder how valuable it was."

"That depends upon the quality, which I would judge as 'very fine.'" Officer Alicia Martin paused. "And of course on the number of half eagles minted in 1867."

"Go ahead, Martin—show off."

She blushed. "Just under seven thousand."

"Don't be so danged modest." The moderately overweight cop grunted his way up from the painful squat. "We both know you can do better than that."

The Lady Who Could raised her chin. "Six thousand nine hundred and twenty."

The boss nodded agreeably. "That sounds about right to me." His tongue-in cheek remark was interrupted by a literal sound. Eight rubber tires crunching gravel.

Parris and Martin went to the open doorway to see a sleek Colorado State Police Chevrolet follow the Granite Creek County medical examiner's van into the driveway. Reminding Officer Martin of a slightly tipsy Father Christmas, the merry old M.E. was laughing as he told his youthful driver a grisly joke. (The one about a couple of big-city elk hunters, an ill-advised rifle shot, and a startled country veterinarian. If you haven't heard it, be thankful.)

Like the late Mr. Morris Meusser, Doc Simpson loved his work.

While the medical examiner probed the corpse's various orifices with precision thermometers, fiber-optic viewers, and other instruments of his morbid profession, the chief of police turned his back on the unseemly spectacle and checked his wristwatch. *Charlie goes to the early service, so he ought to be getting out of church right about now.* Scott Parris placed a call to his sometimes deputy and caught the Southern Ute tribal investigator as Moon was pulling out of the St. Anthony's parking lot. After a mildly sarcastic "Good morning," the pale Caucasian cop gave his dark Indian friend a thumbnail sketch of the homicide, including the detail about the missing pocket watch and gold-coin fob.

Parris terminated the forty-second executive briefing by advising Mr. Moon that he was "on the time clock at your usual rate," and invited his part-time employee to ". . . please drop by the cemetery at your earliest convenience."

Which, since the Catholic church was not quite a mile away, was about three and a half minutes later.

CHAPTER SEVENTEEN

MR. FIXIT

It was a chilly Sunday morning, so to keep his companion warm Charlie Moon left the Expedition engine idling and the heater on. The young lady who was occupying the passenger seat had not uttered a word since Moon had taken the call from Scott Parris. One of Sarah Frank's many endearing traits was that the nineteen-year-old kept quiet when she didn't have anything to say. A corollary to this singular virtue was that she did not trouble Moon with pesky questions such as, "What's this all about?" But even a girl with tight lips cannot help what her big eyes say.

The skilled poker player was about to open the car door when he read the query under Sarah's arched brow. Grimly eyeing the winking lights of three squad cars and the ME's van, Moon replied, "Police business." Enough said.

Sarah winced as the heavy door slammed shut. "Well I could see *that.*"

Outfitted in his gray Sunday-go-to-meeting suit, the lean, lanky Ute pulled the matching gray Stetson tightly onto his head and adjusted the silver-veined lump of turquoise on his bolo tie. Feeling sufficiently spiffy for a dinner date with Patsy Poynter, he took several long strides toward the khaki-clad chief of police.

Breaking off his conversation with Freddy Whitsun,

Scott Parris waved at Moon. He also gave Sarah Frank a snappy salute.

"Can't stay more than a few minutes, Scott." Moon jerked his chin to indicate the Columbine flagship puffing exhaust. "I promised Sarah a breakfast at the Sugar Bowl."

"This won't take long." Parris nodded to indicate the man who had discovered the corpse. "Freddy's not exactly anxious to tell me all the gory details, so I asked him to wait till you got here from St. Anthony's—that way he won't have to do it twice." He turned an expectant gaze on the dead man's friend.

Whitsun sucked in a deep breath that puffed up his broad chest, and got right at it. "It was like this, y'see. I drove over this morning to see Morris . . ." He hesitated, then clamped his mouth shut.

Parris prodded by asking what he already knew: "About what time did you show up?"

"Oh, not long after eight o'clock." Knowing what was expected of him, Whitsun made a valiant attempt to tell the lawmen what they needed to know. And choked again.

Embarrassed for the witness, Charlie Moon turned his head to glance at the handyman's beat-up van.

Whitsun's eyes followed the Indian's gaze. He cleared his throat and tried again. "Most weekends I stop by to have some coffee with Morris, and we generally play a game or two of checkers. Ever' now and then, he'll have a little job of work for me to do."

The cattle rancher, who'd been through some hard times at the Columbine, felt sorry for the man. "Business a little slow, then?"

Whitsun nodded. "Some days, I don't get a single call."

Parris snorted. "You ought to drop by Wanda Naranjo's place."

The entrepreneur stared blankly at the town cop.

The chief of police explained, "Couple a days ago, Mrs. Naranjo called a plumber who didn't show. She appreciates men who turn up right on the dot and know how to stop leaks under her sink." Parris winked at Moon. "And there's lots of crumbly old pipes in her house that need fixing." He beamed a toothy smile at Freddy Fixit. "I expect she's got enough work to keep you busy for a month."

"Oh, I don't know." Whitsun licked his lips. "I mostly do carpenter work and roofing and painting and the like, but I never was much of a hand at fixing water pipes and such."

Charlie Moon steered the drifting conversation back on course. "So what'd you find when you showed up at Meusser's place this morning?"

Freddy Whitsun hesitated again. After exhaling a sigh, he began. "When I got here, I saw right off that his door was all busted up." The handyman pointed his chin at the custodian's cottage. "Right after that, I saw that the phone line had been cut. I hollered some but Morris didn't answer back, so I poked my head inside and there the poor fella was on the couch." Anger flashed in Whitsun's bleary eyes. "Some no-good thief had pinched his pocket watch and chain—the one with the gold piece on it." A pause. "And Morris was dead as a . . . I don't know. One a them ocean fish that dies soon's it's taken outta the water." He thought about it. "A mackerel."

Scott Parris posed the obvious query: "Did you notice anybody in the cemetery when you showed up this morning?"

Freddy Whitsun shook his shaggy head. "Not a living soul." While Moon maintained a poker face and Parris smiled, the superstitious witness shuddered. "And I'm glad to say, I didn't see no haunts." The handyman was tempted to mention his eerie sense that someone had been watching him as he stood at Morris Meusser's front door. *But that'd sound pretty silly.*

It's an Ill Wind That Blows No Good

Such as a stray twenty-dollar bill sailing down a ghost town's main street to hit the sole surviving member of the community smack in the face. Here's another one—a long, slow rain shower drifting onto a destitute rancher's thirstiest section of pasture. Or, in the current instance, a regular job and a comfortable place to hang his hat for a handyman who's down on his luck and more or less living out of his truck.

As is often the case, the Good arrived right on time and in a highly effective disguise.

The lawmen's conversation with the witness who had discovered Morris Meusser's corpse was abruptly terminated when a sleek black Lincoln came creeping along the cemetery lane at the posted limit of fifteen miles per hour, turned into the custodian's crowded driveway, and braked to a sedate stop behind Charlie Moon's Expedition. The driver, a nervous-looking little man in a black three-piece suit, emerged with the instinctive caution of a citizen who wears both a belt and suspenders. Spotting the threesome, he approached warily, regarding both the lawmen and the handyman with an expression of concern that might have been a mask. "Is it true?" he asked in a half whisper. "Is Mr. Meusser actually dead? And did someone really club him to death?"

Scott Parris's solemn nod assured the manager of Granite Creek Cemetery that he was correct on all counts.

George R. Hopper wiped a spotless linen handkerchief across his forehead. "This is absolutely terrible."

"It's pretty grim," the chief of police agreed.

"Oh, you don't know the *half* of it." Hopper flailed his spindly arms. "It will be a terrible scandal—a *dead* man found in our lovely cemetery!"

Charlie Moon turned his face away.

Scott Parris bit his lower lip.

Freddy Whitsun stared blankly at the stricken man.

As oblivious to the dark humor in his remark as Mr. Fixit was, the cemetery manager shook his head. "I'll have to submit to interviews with the newspaper and radio stations, maybe even cable TV. It will be a horrible disgrace!" But the canny capitalist could see a potential bright side to the calamity: *After all the fuss dies down, the publicity might drum up some business.* It was a matter of branding, and from now on Granite Creek Cemetery would be etched in the public's memory—a final location to be reckoned with. *We might even attract clients from Salida and Durango.* But there was a downside that could not be sugar-coated. "With Mr. Meusser absent, as it were—I'll have to hire a replacement custodian." Hopper glared at the lawmen as if Scott Parris and his part-time deputy were responsible for his troubles. "You have no idea how many hoops the federal and state governments make me jump through when I must hire someone—not to mention those tedious bureaucrats over at the county courthouse." He glared harder at Granite Creek's top cop, whom he considered a peripheral member of that clique of parasites.

The chief of police stopped biting his lip long enough to make a helpful suggestion: "You ought to hire yourself a temp, George."

"A what?"

"A temporary employee. All it takes is filling out a form C-122."

Hopper blinked. "That's all?"

"Practically. All you need is the mayor's signature on the bottom and you're good to go."

"Really?"

"Sure. And you can work a temp for up to eighteen months, only not full-time. Twenty hours a week, tops." Parris jerked a thumb at Moon. "That's how I got my first-rate deputy. And Charlie's hourly rate is so low it's downright embarrassing."

The Ute nodded to verify that this was so.

"Well . . . that does sound like a possible solution to my problem." George Hopper frowned. "But where would I find a person with even minimal skills who would be willing to work half-time for absurdly low wages?"

Scott Parris aimed his trusty forefinger at Freddy Whitsun.

The cemetery manager made no effort to conceal his doubts about this suspect recommendation.

The handyman took a long look at the custodian's cozy quarters. "Would I get to stay in Morris's little house?"

"If I should decide to hire you." Hopper looked the shabbily dressed man up and down. Down and up. Made a snap decision. "When could you move in?"

"Oh, I don't know. . . ." Whitsun shrugged like one having second thoughts.

Hopper pressed. "Soon as Doc Simpson hauls the body away?"

"It'll take a little longer than that." Parris's lip was sore from biting. "For a couple of days, Morris Meusser's former residence will be treated as an official crime scene."

"That's not a problem." Mr. Fixit nodded at his van. "I'm used to bunking in my truck."

A native of Iowa, Hopper appreciated a man who had even a smidgen of *get up and go.* "Very well. Pending the mayor's signature on form so-and-so, you may consider the job yours."

Leaving Freddy Whitsun and George Hopper to shake hands on the deal, Parris took Moon into the custodian's quarters. No matter how many dead bodies a lawman gets a gander at, it never gets any easier. This was a grim business.

Barely three minutes later, the Ute emerged from the modest bungalow, strode purposefully to his Expedition, got in, and eased his way through the collection of parked vehicles. Within a dozen of Sarah Frank's heartbeats and eight of Charlie Moon's, they were out of the cemetery.

The young lady held her silence. *When Charlie wants me to know he'll tell me.* But who knew when that might be?

Moon knew that his companion was just *aching* to ask, and he appreciated the Ute-Papago orphan's fortitude. And for that matter, her quiet initiative. It had not escaped the tribal investigator's attention that the clever girl had shut off the heater and engine. She had also lowered the passenger-side window just enough to overhear Freddy Whitsun's account of discovering his friend's corpse. As he aimed the big Ford Motor Company vehicle toward the Sugar Bowl, Scott Parris's poorly paid, part-time deputy rewarded Sarah's patience and resourcefulness by providing a summary of what she already knew, and a few things she did not. And that about sums up their Sunday morning.

For breakfast?

A poached egg on toast for the slender girl. And freshly squeezed orange juice.

For Charlie Moon, the Sugar Bowl's fabled Lumberjack Special—three fried eggs, a thick slab of maple-sugar-cured ham, a heaping helping of home-fried potatoes, and four hot-from-the-oven made-from-scratch biscuits, with sure-enough churned butter and homemade raspberry jam on the side. For the Sugar Bowl's favorite customer, a whole pot of New Mexico Piñon Coffee. And that wasn't all. From the Ute rancher's private stock, which was kept under lock and key in the chef's special pantry, a twenty-four-ounce jar of Tule Creek honey to sweeten the rich, dark brew.

No, *of course* he did not use all twenty-four ounces. Only a meager three tablespoons. Or . . . perhaps four.

Chapter Eighteen

Miss Daisy Seizes the Day

Sunday, 12:10 P.M.

But not before doing some serious thinking. *I can't just call up the ranch and say, "I want somebody to take me to the Granite Creek Cemetery so I can find out if I can see any dead people there."* That was likely to raise some eyebrows and quash the shaman's critical experiment. What Daisy Perika needed was a more mundane excuse to go cruising the tombstones, vaults, crypts, burial plots, and whatnot. But try as she might, the crafty old soul couldn't come up with a plan that didn't stink like last week's roadkill skunk. After staring at the cordless telephone in her hand until she was about to go cross-eyed, the woman who had lost her ability to see the haunts in Spirit Canyon finally placed a call to the Columbine. One ring. *I hope that Ute-Papago orphan answers.* Two rings. *If it's Charlie I'll say, "I want to talk to Sarah."* Three rings. *But then what'll I say to the girl?* Four rings. *I'll just play it by ear.* Five rings. *They must not be home from church yet.* A sigh. Six rings. *I'll hang up an' call back—*

"Hello!"

She sounds all out of breath. "Sarah—is that you?"

"Yes. Charlie and I just walked in the door and I heard the phone ringing so I ran across the parlor and picked it up and—"

"This is a long-distance call and silver dollars don't grow

on cottonwood trees so let me do the talking." To emphasize her annoyance, Daisy scowled.

Sarah smiled sweetly. "Okay."

"When you have time, maybe you could drive your little red pickup truck down here and haul my old carcass back to the Columbine."

"I could leave right away and be there in about—"

"There's no big hurry." The pessimistic old soul was not expecting a happy outcome to the experiment suggested by the *pitukupf.* "You can come in a few days—whenever you're not too busy with schoolwork."

Sarah Frank closed her eyes to consult her mental calendar. "How about Tuesday morning?"

"Day after tomorrow'll be fine." *I'll wait till then to mention a visit to the cemetery.*

"Oh, I almost forgot—you'll never guess what happened this morning right after me and Charlie left church."

Charlie Moon's aunt chuckled. "The big gourd-head finally pop the big question?"

"No!" Sarah's face burned like fire. "Charlie got a phone call from Mr. Parris, then took me over to Granite Creek Cemetery."

Cemetery? Such coincidences as this fairly made Daisy's skin crawl. "Why'd he take you *there*?"

The girl lowered her voice to a whisper. "A man got *killed* there last night!"

"Who was he?"

Sarah proceeded to tell the tribal elder all about Morris Meusser's murder, terminating her narrative with, "It'll probably be on the TV news this evening."

Daisy nodded. "I expect it will." The old woman had no doubt that this development was another case of Fate at work; whether on her behalf or not remained to be seen. But at the very least . . . *This might help me come up with a good excuse to get a ride to the Granite Creek boneyard.* And then, as it so often did, the answer *came to her.* "When we're passing through Granite Creek on Tuesday, let's stop and do a little shopping."

"Sure. That'd be nice."

Daisy took a deep breath, and expelled it with, "And if we have a little time left over, maybe we could drop by the cemetery."

Sarah Frank was not naturally distrustful, but the innocent had been lured into several of the unpredictable old woman's bizarre adventures. The girl's wary tone betrayed her suspicions. "The cemetery—what for?"

Daisy Perika told her *what for.*

After Sarah had listened intently to the blatant fabrication, there was an interlude of dead silence on the line. Then: "Could you really *do* that, Aunt Daisy—I mean figure out who killed Mr. Meusser by just visiting the scene of the crime?"

"Sure I could." The accomplished storyteller was beginning to believe her own work of fiction. "Why, you see it all the time on TV shows. Somebody gets shot four or five times right between the eyes and the cops can't figure out who pulled the trigger. Then, one of those blue-eyed *matukach* psychics goes into a trance and sees the whole crime happen, just like it was a scary picture-show. Miss Sees It All tells the police exactly where the shooter's hiding out. They go look in the ratty little shack in the cypress swamp behind the Do-Wa-Diddy Walmart and sure enough, there's the crazed killer with the big, black six-gun still smoking in his hand!"

Having seen several such startling documentaries on television, Sarah was nodding and holding her breath at the same time.

Certain that she had made the sell, Daisy smirked. "You can take it from me, young lady—anything a silly white person can do, a clever Ute elder can do *twice* as good!"

Like measles, mumps, and miscellaneous other maladies, the old woman's confidence was contagious.

"All right." Sarah's heart was racing with excitement. "I'll take you to the cemetery."

"You won't regret it—we'll have ourselves a fine old time." And they would. So far, so good. *Now I'll have to convince Sarah to keep mum about this so Charlie Moon don't find out about it and mess up all my plans.* Daisy took a deep breath, and was about to make her pitch, when—

Sarah said, "But I don't think we should tell Charlie what you intend to do—he might think it was kind of . . . *weird.*"

"Well, I don't know . . . that seems a little bit sneaky." A sly smile creased the aged conniver's wrinkled face. "But you're doing the driving, so I'll go along with whatever you say."

"Okay, Aunt Daisy." Sarah made a kissing sound. "See you on Tuesday."

As it turned out, quite a lot would happen between *now* and *then,* when Sarah and Daisy's excellent adventure began. Monday would be a remarkably eventful day.

CHAPTER NINETEEN

THE EARLY BIRD

Monday, 7:58 A.M.

Though he was arriving a few minutes ahead of schedule, the avian reference does not apply to Dr. Stuart Whyte and *getting the worm* was not at the top of his to-do list. That priority was to place a call to his wife. According to plan, the psychologist telephoned his missus as he passed the Granite Creek City Limits sign. "Hello, dear—how are you?"

"I could be better, Stuart."

This was not the upbeat greeting he had hoped for. *It'll be another bout of melancholy or one of Lorna's migraines . . . or both.* The hard-pressed husband barely suppressed a sigh. "What's the matter?"

"You had a Friday afternoon telephone message from Mrs. Naranjo."

The relaxed left hand on the steering wheel clenched into white-knuckle mode. "Betty's mother?"

"The very same." A significant pause. "The lady was worried because her teenager was late getting home."

He hesitated before asking the obvious question: "So why'd Mrs. Naranjo call *me*?"

"The woman was under the impression that her *pregnant* daughter had an eleven A.M. appointment with you."

"Really?" The psychologist slowed his pickup for a fat black cat that was crossing the street like a fuzzy bag of

Bad Luck that owned the right-of-way. "Did you tell her that my office is closed on second Fridays?"

"I did not speak to the lady, but that information is provided by the answering machine." Having set the mood, Lorna Whyte proceeded to unload the second installment of ill tidings: "Later on Friday, a man who identified himself as the local chief of police called. His name is Scott Parris."

Damn! "What'd he want?"

"All the tight-lipped constable divulged was that it concerned one of your patients—who was late in returning home. But given the telephone message from Mrs. Naranjo, it is apparent that the policeman wants to talk to you about Betty Naranjo." Having elicited no response from her husband, she continued. "I haven't seen anything about this matter in the newspaper, but if the girl had been found . . . that is to say, if she had returned home—I rather think that Mr. Parris would've called to let me know."

"Yes. I suppose so." What with all his attention focused on these unwelcome revelations, Dr. Whyte's big pickup might as well have been on autopilot.

Having laid the groundwork for imminent disaster, his wife dropped the bomb: "I hate to say this, Stu—but we mustn't entirely discount the possibility that you might be a suspect in the girl's disappearance."

"Well I hope you told the cop that I was away—"

"Well of course I did!" Discomfited by this minor outburst, the lady managed to calm herself. "I also told him that you'd return *late* this morning. Mr. Parris said he'd drop by at about noontime today." She paused to let that sink in.

It did. "Which gives us plenty of time to get our stories straight."

"Of course. But despite the circumstances, you needn't fret—"

"Brrraaaap!"

"Yikes!"

This rude interruption was very off-putting. "If I have

told you once, Stuart, I have told you a dozen times—burping is an infantile habit, and particularly unseemly for one of your profession." *He can be so annoying.* "And I do resent your yelping in my ear."

"I yelped because I was startled, dear." Dr. Whyte explained further: "And that burp was a siren."

"A siren?"

"That's what I said. A police car is right behind me."

"A police car?" When Lorna was flustered, she tended to repeat what her husband had said.

"Most certainly. The colored lights on its roof are flashing."

"Colored lights?"

"Red and blue. I believe the police-person wants to pull me over."

"Pull you over?" She waited for a response, which was not forthcoming. "It is probably about a minor traffic infraction." But Lorna had tons of womanly intuition and a city girl's natural suspicions. "If it's that nosy cop, don't say a word about the missing girl. If he probes, remind him about doctor-patient confidentiality and—"

"I need both hands to drive so I'd best hang up and—"

"Don't disconnect, Stuart!" She closed her eyes. "Where are you?"

"About two blocks from our house."

"I want you to drive all the way home."

"But the cop wants me to stop."

"Pretend not to notice the police car."

"What?" Whyte's forehead wrinkled into a scowl. "How do I not notice blinking lights and a damn siren you could hear miles away?"

"Now listen carefully, Stu—and do *exactly* as I say. If the policeman gets belligerent, pull over—and tell me precisely where you are. But don't disconnect—right this instant, lay the telephone on the passenger seat so that I can hear every word you say to the officer!"

Stuart Whyte, Ph.D. and certified henpeckee, made no

argument. But to demonstrate his manly independence, he did *not* put the communication device on the passenger seat. Very deliberately, he placed his mobile telephone in a cup holder on the console *between* the bucket seats. Following this flagrant act of rebellion—and another abbreviated burp from the GCPD black-and-white's siren—the psychologist pulled his truck over to the curb.

To maximize tension for the citizen, Scott Parris followed the standard procedure that applied to any pullover, ranging from (a) a sweet little old lady running a Stop sign at seven A.M. on a Sunday to (b) apprehending a prime suspect in a drive-by shooting at a nunnery. The chief of police remained in his unit while the GCPD dispatcher keyed the pickup's license plate number into her terminal, ran a background check on the registered owner for prior arrests and outstanding warrants—the whole ball of bureaucratic beeswax. Clara Tavishuts eventually reported what Parris already knew—that the license plate had been issued to a Dr. Stuart Whyte for installation on a two-year-old Ford F-250 pickup. She was advising him that the owner had two parking and three speeding violations over the past fifteen years (all out of state) when—"Oh, darn! The terminal has crashed again."

"Thanks, Clara—that's all I need to know." (It wasn't.) "It's a routine stop." (It wouldn't be.) Parris returned the microphone to its snug chrome cradle.

White-collar workers are loath to drip sweat, but Dr. Stuart Whyte was permitted to perspire and he did so. Thousands of salty little beads of perspiration erupted from an equal number of pores on his forehead, not to mention from his hairy armpits and at various other locations that need not be enumerated. The shrink kept his steely gaze fixed on the Ford pickup's door-mounted mirror. Every few seconds, he would update his spouse, who would respond with terse instructions ("Just sit tight.") and encouraging comments ("It won't be anything important—probably a faulty taillight.").

When the black-and-white's driver's door finally opened and the brawny man dressed in tan emerged, Mrs. Whyte's husband clenched his jaw and addressed the expectant mobile phone from the right side of his mouth. "Here he comes, Lorna." He surprised his wife by adding with manly authority, "Keep quiet."

"Very well," the mobile phone replied. "Remain calm, and all will be well."

Good advice. To compose himself, Dr. Whyte inhaled a deep helping of fresh air and expelled his carbon-dioxide-tainted breath with this whispered assurance: "Everything is fine as frog's hair. I'm cool as a frosty root beer, sharp as a brass carpet tack." He had a tad too much humility to add (aloud) what he was thinking: *And I have an IQ of 211.*

In a potentially perilous encounter with a tough, small-town cop who had—more than two score years ago—scored absurdly low on a Purdue Pegboard Test, there are bound to be significant advantages to being a brainy clinical psychologist.

As events unfold, perhaps we shall find out what they are.

CHAPTER TWENTY

A MODERATELY TENSE ENCOUNTER

Pretending not to notice the driver's pale face framed in the fender mirror, Scott Parris turned his head to peer through the aluminum camper cover's rear window. There was not much to see in the dusty interior. An extra spare tire, a couple of red plastic five-gallon gas containers strapped down with yellow bungee cords. Aside from a shiny new Coleman lantern, a surplus military folding shovel, and a U.S. Army cot—not a lot of camping gear. There was no sign of a tent.

Which makes sense, I guess. Parris scratched at the bristly stubble on his chin. *Why would a man with a nice camper shell on his pickup want to sleep in a tent? His wife must've gotten things mixed up.*

Figuring he'd given Dr. Whyte sufficient time to worry, the chief of police strode up to the cab to get a look at the driver—and was surprised. It was not that Scott Parris had expected to see a mere wisp of a man who wore horn-rimmed glasses. The psychologist's driver's license data, which he had perused the evening before, listed Stuart Whyte as having 20/20 vision (uncorrected), weighing in at 185 pounds, and topping out at six-two. But the cop did have his preconceptions about psychologists, and he expected Betty Naranjo's high school counselor to be of more or less run-of-the-mill physique.

Dr. Whyte was anything but. What Parris saw was a man with bulging biceps, a neck like a Broncos fullback, and a chest that bulged under his black T-shirt. *He looks like he could pull up a cottonwood sapling, roots and all.* As the driver stared back, the vain cop sucked in his gut. *When he ain't talking to his patients, the doc must work out with weights.* Parris, who usually wore a venerable felt fedora, tipped his official GCPD billed policeman's cap. "Good morning, sir—may I please see your operator's license and vehicle registration." This was the polite query required of all GCPD officers, but rank does have its privileges and Chief Parris was not obliged to include a question mark.

The driver produced the requested documents without a word.

Scott Parris inspected both, then shook his head. "Now don't this beat all?" He smiled genially at the citizen. "I woke up before the crack of dawn and couldn't get back to sleep, so I saddled up and decided I'd while away some time patrolling the neighborhood—protecting and serving, don'cha know. And who do I run into but the very gentleman I need to talk to. Matter of fact, I already told your missus that I'd drop by around noon." He leaned on the F-250 door, so close that Whyte could smell the coffee on his breath. "Now what would you call that, if not a first-rate coincidence?"

"A synchronicity," the Jungian said. Do not mess with a fellow whose IQ exceeds the atomic weight of lead.

Being one of those good ol' boys who detest five-syllable words, Parris ignored the remark. But not the cell phone in the cup holder. He pointed his prominent chin at the instrument. "From what looks like the glow of a little red light, I'd guess that your phone is turned on." He flashed his menacing toothy grin. "I wouldn't want you to run the battery down."

"I appreciate your kind concern." Whyte reflected the sharkish smile. "As it happens, the telephone comes with a convenient charger, which—should the need arise—I plug into a twelve-volt dashboard receptacle thoughtfully provided by Ford Motor Company engineers."

Parris's smile faded to half strength. *Smart-ass.* But two could play the game. "I also wouldn't want to run you downtown on a charge of chatting on a mobile telephone whilst operating a motor vehicle." After an effective pause, the cop added, "It is a serious offense."

Dr. Whyte's face had paled a notch. Score one for GCPD's top cop.

"Tell you what," Parris said. "After I go check out a thing or two, I'll come back and check out your mobile phone. If it's on and there's a party on the other end when I get it in my hand, I'll have to throw the whole book at you." He winked at the offending motorist. "If the phone's dead, you're off the hook."

About a block and a half away, Lorna Whyte discreetly disconnected.

The driver watched the big cop amble up to the front of the F-250. Like a man who might be in the market for a nice-looking, low-mileage pickup, Parris made a couple of halfhearted kicks at a tire.

The chief of police returned to the cab window, accepted the cell phone in his gloved hand, and gave it a once-over. "Sorry, sir—my mistake. That phone is definitely turned off." He returned the innocent instrument to Dr. Whyte. "The little red light ain't on—I guess I must've been seeing a reflection."

The grateful citizen slipped the instrument into a canvas pouch on his belt. "Thank you, Officer."

"You're welcome, Doctor."

"So—what did you want to talk to me about?" *Like I don't know.*

"One of your clients." *Like your wife ain't already told you.* Turning his expressively suspicious face away from the psychologist's frank gaze, Parris took a look up the sleepy residential street. Almost a block away, a tall, sturdy woman in a dark blue terry-cloth robe was striding along the sidewalk. Purposefully. Like an ardent bug hater stomping inoffensive beetles. Even at this distance, the cop could hear the distinct *pop-pop* of her flip-flops. "Looks like one of your patients has run away from home."

Whyte delivered his line deadpan: "No . . . that's my wife."

Scott Parris could not restrain a chuckle. *I'm beginning to like this guy.* Composing himself, he said, "I was making reference to a patient who went missing on Friday. A minor."

"A teenage runaway?"

Parris breathed a sorrowful sigh. "I hope so."

Betty Naranjo's counselor arched his left eyebrow. "You *hope* she's a runaway?"

"Sure." The cop's cold blue eyes glinted like ice in midwinter starlight. "I'd hate to think that a pregnant sixteen-year-old had met with foul play."

If Whyte had a response to that, it caught in his throat.

No. The small-town cop, who had deliberately avoided mentioning the gender of the missing patient, had not missed the psychologist's reference to a *she*. Which merely increased his suspicion that Dr. Whyte had been briefed by his wife. Speaking of whom . . .

Without glancing left or right, Lorna Whyte crossed a side street at a brisk trot. *I wonder what they're talking about.*

While retaining the approaching woman's image in his peripheral vision, Parris gazed at the psychologist's stony face, which was beginning to show a stress crack here and there. *I'd like to play a few hands of high-stakes poker with this joker.* "I know you can't provide me with any confidential information about one of your clients." A heartbeat. "Not without a court order, and all that rigmarole."

Dr. Whyte waited for the next big boot to drop.

It did, and with a heavy thud.

"Which is why I woke up DA Pug Bullet early this morning and asked him to get the paperwork started." Parris grinned again and the effect was that of a great white about to put the big bite on a cornered codfish. "Judge Meekins is highly responsive to certain sensitive social issues, such as preserving the lives of our youth. That being the case, I expect we'll have his honor's John Henry on the dotted line before suppertime." He used a horny thumbnail to scratch the remains of a moth carcass off the pickup's door-mounted mirror. "But it might not be necessary to serve the warrant if you felt comfortable about answering a few general questions about . . . let's say some *other* person who's similar to Betty Naranjo." Seeing not the least sign of surprise on Whyte's face at the mention of this name, Parris lost the remnants of his grin. No doubt about it . . . *His wife has told him.* "Let's call the young lady Jane Doe."

"Ah, a hypothetical patient." The defeated psychologist nodded. "And more to the point, a generic troubled youth."

Chapter Twenty-one

The Psychologist's Worthy Spouse

As the slapping of Mrs. Whyte's flip-flops began to sound like a pair of beached carps flopping on Mississippi River mud, both men paused to watch the agitated woman's approach. Parris murmured to the driver, "You want me to handle this?"

"Thank you kindly. But let me have a go at it."

These words were barely out of Whyte's mouth when his wife began rapping her knuckles on the passenger-side window.

Parris gawked at the woman, who was almost as well built as her husband. And not only that . . . *She looks enough like him to be his twin sister.*

Dr. Whyte pressed a button to lower the transparent barrier. "Good morning, dear."

"Stuart—what's happening?" She glared across the cab at the ruddy face framed in the opposite window. "Why has this police officer pulled you over?"

"We're having a discussion about one of my clients." Her husband smiled thinly. "A *private* discussion."

"Oh . . . of course. I see." The self-assured woman was clearly taken aback by this mild but unexpected rebuke. "Well then . . . if this involves confidential professional matters . . . I suppose I should withdraw."

"Just out of earshot will be fine." Parris offered her a

genial smile. "There's no need to go all the way back home—this'll only take a couple a minutes."

At a slight nod from her husband, Lorna Whyte took several brisk steps past the Ford's shiny front bumper. She paused under the shade of a convenient mulberry tree, whose leafy branches she made a pretense of taking an interest in.

"Now," Dr. Whyte said. "Where were we?"

"We were about to talk about a hypothetical Jane Doe." Parris shot a furtive glance at Mrs. Whyte. "Just for the sake of discussion, let's say she happens to be pregnant."

"As you like."

"I'm thinking Miss Doe might've told her high-school counselor the name of the unborn child's daddy."

"She *might* have." The psychologist observed the cop with more than clinical interest, and reminded himself not to underestimate his inferiors. "But that's not as likely as you might think. Let us assume that the hypothetical teenager was not only promiscuous—but also highly profligate in the dispensation of her sexual favors."

The lawman nodded. "So you figure our Jane Doe has several boyfriends?"

"If you don't object." Whyte allowed himself an amiable smile. "It does make our discussion rather more interesting."

"Okay, Doc—let's go with that."

"Thank you. *If* Miss Doe knew who the father was, she would be likely to keep such information to herself."

"Rats," Parris muttered.

"Yes, I'm afraid so." Whyte sighed. "I do wish I could be more helpful."

Yeah, I bet you do. But the stubborn cop was not ready to throw in the towel. "This make-believe patient of yours . . . if she told her mother she was going to see her psychologist on a Friday morning when his office was closed"—still no sign of surprise from Whyte—"then vanished like a snowball in Death Valley, what would you figure happened to her?"

"I am a clinical psychologist, not a Gypsy mind reader." Dr. Whyte paused to take thought. "That said, I prefer to believe that our generic Jane Doe is not suicidal. Neither is she the type to be concerned about worrying her mother." He drummed his long fingers on the steering wheel. "No, I expect that our hypothetical teenager would take a notion to run away somewhere. Perhaps to stay with a friend for a few days."

"Or with the father of her baby?"

"In Miss Doe's instance, I'd say . . . not likely." Whyte's gaze was pulled, magnetically it seemed, toward his wife. "But that possibility cannot be entirely discounted."

"Thanks, Doc." *For nothing.* Parris slapped his palm on the F-250 door. "I might want to talk to you again later on, but you might as well run along home now." He scowled at the relieved motorist. "But don't exceed the speed limit— and don't be talking to Mrs. Whyte on that mobile phone while you're operating a motor vehicle."

Again, I have underestimated the fellow. "I appreciate the sage advice, Chief Parris."

The cop didn't have his name on his jacket. "So you know who I am?"

"Of course—you're practically famous." The merest hint of a smirk played with Whyte's expressive lips. "But only in a strictly local sense."

Parris returned the grin. *I was right the first time. He's a first-class smart-ass.* But a likable smart-ass. He strode around the pickup to salute Lorna Whyte. "Sorry for the inconvenience, ma'am. But now you can ride home."

Her reply was an icy "Thank you."

"Don't mention it." Parris opened the door for the lady, and supported her arm as she got a flip-flop on the steel step mounted under the cab.

When she thanked him again, the ice was beginning to melt.

"My pleasure," said the ex-Chicago cop. *The lady has a*

biceps like a White Sox pinch hitter. After watching Mrs. Whyte buckle in, he closed the door.

Dr. Whyte pulled the F-250 away from the curb.

Charlie Moon's best friend watched them go. *The doc's doing about thirty-five in a twenty-five miles per hour zone.* And not only that. *He just ran a Stop sign without even slowing down.* Parris shook his head. *And the cocky bastard did it on purpose—just to show me he's no pushover.* The big, beefy cop reminded himself never to underestimate a man on account of his profession—or for that matter, a determined woman whose primary aim in life was to protect her husband.

CHAPTER TWENTY-TWO

BUSINESS IS TOO GOOD

Monday, 8:10 A.M.

As Scott Parris was watching Dr. and Mrs. Whyte depart in the snazzy F-250 pickup, the sole owner of the Columbine Land and Cattle Company was driving his Expedition through the Triple-W gate. No, not another central-Colorado ranch where beeves were bred, fed, and fattened for market. The WWW brand was affixed to the false front of a sprawling cinder-block structure that housed a furniture manufacturing and sales business. The prosperous enterprise, also known in Granite Creek as Wally Wordsworth's Woodworks, was where locals with ready cash could purchase maple dining tables, chairs of all descriptions, four-posters, chests of drawers, sturdy sideboards, knickknack shelves, and miscellaneous *special* merchandise. The latter category included an unadvertised product that was provided on an as-needed, made-to-fit basis.

Even though the small sign in the door informed potential customers that the establishment was open from eight A.M. till six P.M., Charlie Moon found the entrance firmly locked, latched, and *barred*. Really. As in "Katy-bar-the-door." The knob mechanism was key locked, the dead bolt securely latched, and when Scott Parris's part-time deputy peered though the glass, he could clearly see a varnished oak two-by-four barring any attempt to open the door. He also spied the owner-manager, who was perched on a three-legged stool whilst simultaneously sucking on a corncob pipe and humming "Morning Has Broken." (Wally was a notorious multitasker, and determined to enjoy his early-morning quiet time.) The Ute Indian was notoriously persistent, and determined to conduct some serious business. Moon pounded his fist on the door. "Open up!"

Eyeing the door, Wally recognized his favorite customer. Easing his plump bulk off the stool, the proprietor waddled forth to unbar, unlatch, unlock, and open the main entrance to his business. He removed the pipe stem from between stained teeth. "Good morning, Charlie—do you intend to make a purchase?"

The long, lean Ute eyed the chubby little munchkin. Even in the worthy pursuit of law, order, and justice—Moon could not tell a lie. "No."

"Is that a promise?"

The deputy nodded.

"Then you may come in."

Moon did, and Wally closed the door. He did not go so far as to replace the sturdy two-by-four, but he did throw the dead bolt. Returning to his stool, he explained, "Business has been too damn good, and I aim to discourage customers." He pointed to a month-old sign mounted prominently over the counter. "I also put that on my Web site."

Moon read the advertisement.

WWW'S PRODUCTS ARE **OVERPRICED**
OUR QUALITY JUST **SO-SO**
and
THE CUSTOMER IS ALWAYS WRONG!

He cocked his head at the proprietor. "That ought to do the trick."

"It oughta but it ain't so far." Wally sucked on his pipe. "All it has accomplished is make folks want to buy more

Wordsworth wooden products." He removed the pipe from his mouth and blew a perfect ring that floated up toward a slowly turning ceiling fan, where it was brutally mangled.

Knowing what was expected of him, Charlie Moon posed the obligatory query: "So what's so bad about business being brisk?"

For a long, thoughtful interlude, Mr. Wordsworth chewed on the tasty pipe stem. Then, the corncob bowl bobbled as he said, "I am just plain tired of working, Charlie. I can't shut the business down because I've got a half-dozen salt-of-the-earth employees who have families to support. They need the work, but I'd like to slack off some and go fishing."

"Sounds like a fine notion." The ardent angler seated himself in a comfortable armchair from Wordsworth's Oak Colonial Collection. *This feels pretty good. Maybe I should buy it for Aunt Daisy.*

Reading the satisfied expression almost word-for-word, Wally snapped at his guest, "Nothing doing. You promised not to make a purchase and every soul in Granite Creek County knows that if there's one thing a man can still count on hereabouts, it's Charlie Moon's word." He watched a tiny black wasp pass by his nose, then whine off to circle the silk shade on a maple table lamp. "So what brings you here—that business with Mrs. Naranjo's boyfriend leaving town without paying his rent?"

The deputy gave the businessman an admiring look. "You don't miss a trick."

"It don't take a genius to figure things out." Wally pointed his pipe stem at the telephone. "I got a call from Mrs. Hawley, who wanted to find out if she could garnishee Mike Kauffmann's wages for the three weeks' back rent he owes her." He paused for a refreshing puff of what was smoldering in the bowl, which was Prince Albert Tobacco plus some additional aromatic ingredients he'd prepared himself. "I told the landlady that wasn't a workable notion, and Mrs. Hawley said she'd 'see about that' and threatened to talk to a lawyer about doing the paperwork." The happy man chuckled. "I said 'Do whatever you're of a mind to, ma'am,' but I advised the lady not to waste her money. I pay Kauffmann at the end of every workday he puts in here, so unless he comes back looking for some work—which ain't all that likely under the present circumstances—there won't be a single greenback dollar for Mrs. Hawley to garnishee."

"And you figure I'm here because of Kauffmann's unpaid rent?"

"Nah. But everybody also knows that you're Scott Parris's best buddy and part-time deputy. So you've come to ask me what I know about Mike Kauffmann, who must be in some kinda serious trouble to skip town. Not that I'm hinting for you to tell me what the rascal's been up to." Another pipe pause that refreshed. "So I'll tell you what I can, which is not a helluva lot. Kauffmann's worked here on an as-needed basis for almost a year." This recitation was interrupted by a string of coughs. "Damn! If something else don't kill me first, smoking will." He blinked at the Ute. "Where was I?"

"You were about to tell me where Mr. Kauffmann hangs his hat when he's not bunking in Mrs. Hawley's Boardinghouse, or visiting Mrs. Naranjo's home."

"No I wasn't." After noisily clearing his throat, Wally spat into an antique brass spittoon. "I would if I could, Charlie—but I can't. He might be roosting in a buzzard's nest for all I know. All I can tell you about Kauffmann is that he generally drops by every once in a while and asks if I have any job of work for him to do." Pause. "You have any more penetrating questions?"

"No, you're doing fine without any help for me."

"Please ask me what kind of woodworking Kauffmann likes to do."

"Would that make your day?"

"You bet."

"Okay. What kind of woodworking does Mr. Kauffmann like to do?"

"Since you inquire so politely, I will give you a big, fat

hint. In addition to our so-so line of home and office furnishings, now and then we do a piece of work for one of several funeral homes who've been buying our product since fussy old dogs was frisky pups. These enterprises occasionally have a bereaved customer who requests a simple, inexpensive burial."

Moon's eyebrow arched about a half millimeter.

Gratified by this display of interest, Wally continued. "And when we get an order for a sturdy pine box, Mr. Kauffmann is the go-to guy. It's what you might call his preferred line of work."

A fellow who has Daisy Perika for an aunt is bound to be broadminded about other folks' peculiarities and as the Southern Ute tribal investigator turned this factoid over in his mind, he couldn't find anything particularly sinister in Kauffmann's leanings. *I guess we all have our small eccentricities.*

Yes, the *we* includes Charlie Moon, who is not without his own strange habits. It is whispered that in October, when the Moon of Dead Leaves Falling is plump and yellow as a county-fair pumpkin, the Ute rancher saddles up ol' Paducah and loads a side of prime beef onto a Tennessee pack mule whose given name is Elizabeth. Mr. Moon and his equine companions (so the rumormongers *say)* journey deep into the pristine spruce forests on the northern border of the Columbine, where they spend anywhere from five nights to a full week. No, despite his famous appetite, Charlie Moon does not consume an entire side of beef during these few days. And despite what you may've heard, almost all horses and mules are strict vegetarians. It is alleged that Moon goes to meet a dangerous recluse who is unbearably lonely. This large carnivore, who subsists primarily on elk and venison, looks forward to the delicious novelty of beefsteaks broiled over a campfire. It is said that while the golden disk rides high in the night sky, the Indian has long, thought-provoking conversations with the formidable creature who has been mistaken for a grizzly bear. But even if that improbable tale contains a grain or two of truth, it has nothing to do with the price of furniture.

Wally took a long pull on his pipe and exhaled a lungful of gray smoke with this challenge: "Bet you ten cents you can't guess what Mike Kauffmann's nickname is out in the shop."

In normal circumstances the habitual gambler would jump on any wager with both feet and an unashamed intent to win. In this instance Moon pretended not to have deduced the obvious truth. "Well . . . I'll make a run at it. How about . . . Mike Hammer?"

"No, but I like it." After chuckling his belly into a hilarious case of the shakes, Wally caught his breath long enough to say, "The boys in the shop call him Kauffmann the *Coffin Man*."

"No kidding?" Moon flipped the winner a shiny new dime.

Wally snatched it out of the air with the quickness of one who catches houseflies in flight. Anticipating the deputy's next question, he said, "Yes, if I think of anything else about Mr. Kauffmann—no matter how insignificant it might seem to be—I'll call you on the phone."

"I'd appreciate that." Moon got up from the armchair.

Wally pointed his pipe stem at the fine piece of furniture. "Please take that hunk of junk with you, Charlie—before somebody slips in here and buys it and boosts me into a higher tax bracket."

"You sure?"

Mr. Wallace Wordsworth nodded. "Give it to Aunt Daisy with my compliments." He grinned as only a bona fide member of the Munchkin Clan can. "And tell her the cushions are stuffed with dirty straw, which is contaminated with deer ticks, poisonous centipedes, and fleas collected from rabid coyotes."

"She'll be happy to hear that." Moon thanked the reluctant entrepreneur and departed with the gift chair in hand. As he loaded the furniture into the back of his SUV, a seemingly trifling matter nagged at him. He attempted to dismiss the thought, but it was as if some unseen presence continued to whisper *"Coffin Man"* into his ear.

From the instant when he'd realized what Wally was hinting at, the tribal investigator had been bothered by this descriptor. The sinister nickname would have been appropriate for several murderous hardcases the lawman had encountered over the years—every one of whom had filled more than one coffin with the residue of a human being. But it seemed a poor fit for part-time carpenter Michael Kauffmann. Charlie pulled an old woolen blanket over the gift chair and lowered the tailgate. *Even Mike Hammer is a stretch.*

As he eased the Expedition through the WWW gate, Charlie Moon upbraided himself. A man who allowed trivia to occupy his thoughts needed to get his mental battery charged. *What I need is to slip away for a while and do some serious fishing.*

But that happy day would have to wait. Deputy Moon was on his way to an appointment with his best friend.

CHAPTER TWENTY-THREE

THE LAWMEN COMPARE NOTES

Monday, 8:44 A.M.

It was a mite late in the morning to be enjoying a coffee break at Chicky's Daylight Doughnuts, which closed right on the dot at nine A.M.—or earlier if the megacalorie pastries sold out, which was the case more often than not.

The chief of police had arrived just in time to purchase the last of Chicky's scrumptious jelly doughnuts, and most of this plump sugar bomb was still on his platter. His deputy had purchased a matched pair of glazed doughnuts that (so the Ute claimed) were heavy enough to sink a nine-foot poplar-bark canoe.

What did they have to say about the murder in Granite Creek Cemetery and the mysterious disappearance of Miss Betty Naranjo? So far, not a word. By mutual unspoken agreement, when enjoying a morning renewal at Chicky's delightful eatery the sensible diners did not discuss business until the very last bite had been washed down with coffee strong enough to grow hair on a dead man's chest. Because Charlie Moon had gotten off to a head start, the final morsel was masticated by Scott Parris, who also drained a mug of java that would have satisfied a persnickety Seattle gourmand.

The wizard who performed the culinary magic materialized to swipe a damp dishcloth across the table. "How was things?"

Moon saluted the chef. "Like always—first rate."

"Great." To accentuate this heartfelt compliment, Parris burped.

Gratified, Chicky was transported to other tables, where he queried additional customers in a similar manner and was rewarded with due praise.

Scott Parris wiped his mouth with a pink paper napkin. "You want to hear my theory on the graveyard killing?"

"Not necessary," Moon said. "I already know what you're thinking."

This retort produced the expected snort. "No you don't."

"Bet you a nickel I do."

The overweight cop searched the change in his skin-tight pocket. "Don't think I have a nickel."

The skinny rancher shrugged under his denim jacket. "Bet you a dime."

The chief of police laid the specified coin on the greasy table.

Moon saw the wager with two shiny Jefferson facsimiles. "Okay, Chucky—tell me what I'm thinking."

"Well, for one thing, you're thinking this bet's a sure thing. When I tell you what your theory is about the Morris Meusser homicide, you'll say, 'That ain't quite right,' and grab the twenty-cent pot like a kid snatching a lemon lolli-pop."

"Now that hurts, Charlie." The man whose mind had been expertly read tried hard to work his face into an injured expression. "D'you really think I'd outright lie to beat you out of a couple of nickels?"

"Now that you put it that way, pardner—I guess not." Moon's grin flashed kilowatts. "But if the wager was for two bits, I'd hate to take the chance."

"Thank you." Parris returned a toothy smile. "So tell me what's written on my brain—so I can laugh out loud."

"It's like reading a Little Lulu comic book. But before I start turning pages, I need some liquid refreshment." Moon raised his mug, gesturing for a refill. The conversation was suspended while Chicky poured fresh-brewed Bishop's Blend into the aforesaid receptacle. As the proprietor departed, Moon took a sip and a sly glance at his companion. "You figure Morris heard someone prowling around the cemetery at night. Being a conscientious custodian, he naturally went to find out what was coming down. But Morris must've met somebody he couldn't scare off, and got chased all the way back to his bungalow by the seriously bad guy, and locked himself inside. Figuring the custodian was about to call the cops, the prowler cut the phone line off the terminal box. Then he busted the door open, went inside, and bonked Morris Meusser on the head until he was stone-cold deceased. After which the felon snatched the dead man's pocket watch and hit the road."

Parris's theory was that a crazed dope addict who fed his habit by burglarizing isolated dwellings had murdered the lonely old bachelor. He stared at the canny tribal investigator, who never failed to surprise him. "Just to humor me, tell me why I'd be thinking along those lines."

"Because you're clever and you notice things."

The clever chief of police was beginning to feel uneasy. "Such as?"

"Oh, little things. Like the story in the newspaper last month about somebody stealing an old tombstone from the historic section of the cemetery—and in the dead of night. And the fact that while Meusser's corpse was stretched out on his parlor couch, his bed had been slept in—which suggests something woke him up after he'd hit the sack. And the peculiar way his electric vehicle was parked."

"I noticed that the little electric truck was parked in the garage with Meusser's Volkswagen Bug, just like it always is."

"No you didn't."

"I didn't?"

"Mr. Meusser always parks his German motorcar and the

cart the same way: he *backs* them into the garage. What yo*u noticed* was that the cart was parked headfirst."

"Oh, right." Parris paused to cerebrate. *It takes longer to back the cart into the garage.* "Which suggests that Meusser was in a big hurry when he returned to his quarters."

"That's what it looks like, all right." But Moon was entertaining another notion entirely.

Parris assumed his bulldog-stubborn expression. "Maybe Meusser's bed hadn't been slept in on Saturday night, maybe he didn't make up his bed from the night before. And maybe he pulled the cemetery cart into the garage headfirst because—"

The Ute terminated the string of protests by raising his palm. "Pardner, I was telling you what *you're* thinking—it ain't my fault if you do an awful lot of supposing from some pretty shaky physical evidence."

The chief of police muttered a crude expletive under his breath.

Happily immune to this negative commentary, Charlie Moon eyed the twenty cents. "So?"

Parris glared at his impertinent deputy. "So *what*?"

"Was I close enough to take the pot?"

The chief of police shook his head.

"No?"

Parris pushed the dime and two nickels across the table. "But take it anyway."

As Charlie Moon pocketed his less-than-two-bit winnings, he thought it advisable to change the subject. "What've you heard from Mrs. Naranjo?"

"Not a peep. But Clara Tavishuts has been calling her twice a day to ask whether there's been any news about the missing daughter. There ain't." Scott Parris tied his pink paper napkin into a knot. "I guess I oughta drop by and see how the lady's doing." He shot a hopeful glance at his deputy. "You want to come along and see what needs fixing?"

"No way—unless you want to put me on a journeyman plumber's hourly pay."

"Hah! Fat chance."

Moon took a sip of coffee. "So tell me about your chat with Betty Naranjo's psychologist."

"Well . . ." Parris tied a second knot in the napkin. "Ever since I talked to Mrs. Whyte on Friday, I've had a hunch about that story about her husband camping out for the weekend, and him being so far out in the boonies that he couldn't be reached by his cell phone—that was all a bald-faced lie. I figured Dr. Whyte got a call from his wife right after I hung up." Tossing the knotted napkin aside, he helped himself to a wooden toothpick. "On Friday evening, I got the word out to cop shops in the closest six towns to Granite Creek—asking them to keep a lookout for a blue-and-white F-250 with Whyte's license plate—and to phone me the minute they spotted it. I got the call from Salida PD a few minutes past seven A.M. this morning, so I saddled up and intercepted the doc a few blocks from his residence." He provided a detailed account of his encounter with Dr. and Mrs. Whyte.

Charlie Moon enjoyed Parris's lively narrative, which was punctuated with pithy commentary on the couple. "Well, I can see why you've got some suspicions about the psychologist."

"It's more than just suspicions, Chucky—it's based on some actual police work." The ex-Chicago cop chomped the toothpick between his teeth. "Before he came to Granite Creek last year, Dr. Whyte practiced his honorable trade in Houston."

"Houston PD have anything on him?"

Parris shook his head. "But I talked to a contact in the public school system. Turns out Whyte has built himself somewhat of a rep."

Moon arched an eyebrow. "The counselor exhibits a preference for teenage female patients?"

"Mm-hm." Parris removed the chewed-on splinter of wood from his mouth. "There was some gossip about improper behavior, but nothing Dr. Whyte could be charged with."

"Could be the man's innocent of any serious wrong-doing."

"Maybe." *And maybe black bears don't steal honey from the bees.*

"But you figure him for a prime suspect in Betty Naranjo's disappearance."

Parris shrugged. "He could be her baby's father."

"If he is, the doc might've taken the girl someplace where she could deliver her child—and put it up for adoption."

Another snort. "More likely, he took Betty someplace for an abortion."

Neither lawman broached the subject that haunted them . . . *Desperate men are often driven to desperate actions.* If he had fathered Betty Naranjo's child, Dr. Whyte might decide that the safest course of action would be to make both mother and child vanish. Forever. And if he had committed a double homicide, Mrs. Whyte was probably at least suspicious of foul play. The wife might even be a willing coconspirator.

Parris grinned at Chicky's buxom waitress as she passed their table; the lady returned the compliment with a wink. The widower with the roving eye returned his attention to his deputy. "So tell me about your interview of Michael Kauffmann's curmudgeonly employer."

"It wasn't exactly what you'd call an interview." Charlie Moon described his one-sided conversation with the owner-manager of Wally Wordsworth's Woodworks—including the fact that Wanda Naranjo's part-time carpenter boyfriend specialized in making pine boxes that served as the final dwelling places of the dearly departed, and his nickname.

"Kauffmann the Coffin Man—that's pretty lame." Parris groaned.

"Yeah." Moon picked up a sticky plastic-bear dispenser and added a dab of honey to his coffee. "But almost every cowboy on the Columbine has a sillier nickname."

Making a big fist, the white cop studied his knuckles

with intense curiosity. "You figure Kauffmann might be responsible for Betty Naranjo's vanishing act?"

"The mother's boyfriend can't be crossed off our list." After a long draw of coffee, Moon feigned a thoughtful expression. "I mean . . . a guy with a handle like Coffin Man is a natural suspect."

Scott Parris had a great notion: "You want to make another wager?"

"Kauffmann against Whyte?"

The town cop nodded. "Let's say—a dollar."

"You got it, pard." The gambler who couldn't say no laid a dollar bill on the table.

As Parris saw it with a half-dollar and a pair of quarters, he had one of those nagging second thoughts: *Charlie jumped on that bet a little too fast.* He squinted at his part-time deputy. "You sure you want to risk a whole greenback on Kauffmann?"

"Sure." Moon returned an innocent look. "Unless *you* want Mrs. Naranjo's boyfriend. If you'd like to switch, I'll bet on Whyte."

Parris's squint narrowed to knife-edge slits. *Maybe Charlie's using what they call reverse psychology—setting me up so he can put his buck on Dr. Whyte and leave me with Coffin Man.* "Well, I don't know. . . ."

"Not a problem, pard. You pick which one you want, I'll take the leavings." Moon flashed the electric smile. "Hey, a dollar won or lost won't make or break me."

True enough. But this was not about money.

Charlie's up to something all right. But what? *Maybe it's a double-reverse psychology. Maybe he's trying to—*

"So what'll it be, pard?"

Confused to the core, Parris gave up. "You pick which suspect *you* want."

"Okay. I'll take Whyte."

I knew it! Parris was delighted with himself for rightly reading Moon's devious intentions.

The chief of police would have had less reason to be

pleased if he had noticed a minor detail in the tribal investigator's selection of suspects. It was what Mr. Moon had *not* said that was significant: "I'll take *Dr.* Whyte."

But we must allow Scott Parris a little slack. Granite Creek's top cop did not know that Charlie Moon had met Mrs. Whyte on two or three occasions, and that the formidable lady had made a considerable impression on the Ute.

As the proprietor generally did when the lawmen friends made a serious wager on the premises, Chicky agreed to hold the two-dollar pot. And often as not, bets between Charlie Moon and Scott Parris remained unresolved. To date, their informal banker was almost thirty bucks the better for the service provided.

CHAPTER TWENTY-FOUR

PISTOL PACKIN' MOMMA

Monday

Exhausted by her worries over the longest weekend of her life, Betty's mother had slept in. At about the time when Scott Parris and Charlie Moon were making their one-dollar wager at Chicky's Daylight Doughnuts, Wanda Naranjo awakened with an unshakable conviction: *My daughter's not coming home. Not this week, or next month . . . not ever.*

The horror of this dismal realization was magnified by her suspicion that—one way or another—her miserable excuse for a boyfriend was responsible for Betty's disappearance. On top of all that, she ached all over and her feet were swollen. An awful way to begin the day, but Wanda was determined to get well and get even.

First things first. The nurse's aide's self-prescription was a stiff dose of caffeine. Over her first cup of coffee, Wanda reviewed the plan she'd made on Friday night and could find no major fault with her audacious plot. During a nutritious brunch (a cold biscuit and a steaming bowl of green chili stew), she fine-tuned her scheme here and there. By mid-afternoon she had smoked a half pack of cigarettes and worked up the gumption to flat-out *do it*.

The determined woman stashed the firearm and a box of brass cartridges in her purse, locked the front door behind her, cranked up the trusty Toyota Tercel, and departed Granite Creek with blood in her eye and the sweet foretaste of revenge on the tip of her tongue. This was it—there would be no turning back; her decision final, the die cast.

The stimulation of physical action can be an excellent remedy for despair, and the feisty little lady was beginning to feel mighty fine. *Before the sun goes down, I'll have the bastard lined up in my sights!*

Excepting the citizen's murderous intent, her enthusiasm for the daring venture is admirable. But—and please pardon this merest hint of negativity—not every happy enterprise proceeds precisely according to plan.

Wanda used up most of an hour motoring to and fro in the unpopulated foothills south of town. Despite her clear memory of the spot, it was proving difficult to find the turnoff to the travel trailer where Mike Kauffmann had taken her on their first "date." *I'm sure it's around her somewhere. It's got to be.* The mildly myopic woman leaned forward to squint over the steering wheel. *I remember a Forest Service sign with a number that I thought I'd remember if I ever saw it again because it had something to do with how old I am, but—*

What was that by the side of the little creek that paralleled the road? Hard to tell. It was partially concealed by an overgrowth of willows.

Wanda saw it again and got a better look this time.

A sturdy cedar post with a pine plank nailed across the top.

She braked the Toyota to a halt, got out, and the trotted over to the post. Sure enough, there was the wooden sign she'd been searching for. Despite several bullet holes provided courtesy of the local chapter of the ADA (Armed Dimwits Association), she could make out the letters and numerals burned into the wood. Aha! Forest Road 1963. *That was the year John Kennedy was gunned down in Dallas by that nutcase in the School Book Depository—and also the year I was born.*

She walked a few yards down a dirt lane and crossed a bridge over the stream. A few paces farther, there was a low, mucky area where isolated little pools of water remained from the recent rains. She paused to take a look at several heavy tread marks in the mud. Mr. Kauffmann's former girlfriend had seen them often enough in her yard. *If those weren't made by Mike's Wagoneer, I'll eat my underwear!* When tracking down a treacherous ex-boyfriend, it is highly gratifying to discover a helpful clue to the scoundrel's whereabouts. But were the tire marks coming or going—or both? A satisfactory answer to this riddle was beyond her expertise. *I hope he hasn't skipped already and holed up someplace I don't know about.*

Wanda returned to her Japanese automobile, turned off the paved road and onto the rutted lane, and clattered over the wooden bridge. Startled by the noise that might alert her quarry, she shifted quickly to low gear and proceeded at a crawl through the muddy puddles, adding her tire prints to those so thoughtfully provided by Michael Kauffmann. The neighborhood began to look more familiar as she passed through a thickish forest of mature spruce and pine that was dotted with occasional clusters of aspen. As Wanda topped a slight rise, she slammed her foot on the brake pedal. There, barely two hundred yards away and nestled in a few acres of pasture, was the tiny stainless-steel trailer that she remembered from their initial tryst. A retired cattle rancher had (so Mike claimed) given him permission to crash in the modest lodgings whenever he was of a mind to. *More likely, the landowner don't know the lowlife has ever set foot on his property.* Wanda's hard eyes searched the picturesque landscape, but . . . *I don't see his old car.* Which didn't necessarily mean Mike wasn't home. *Rat-face probably parked it out of sight so nobody will know he's in the trailer.* The vengeful lady smiled wickedly. *Especially me!*

Wanda eased her Toyota off the lane and parked it in a clone of aspen that she hoped would conceal her automobile if her intended victim happened to drive by. Which was not likely, she thought. *If Mike's still here, he's probably dead drunk and snoring his fool head off.* After pulling on a pair of latex gloves she had "borrowed" from the hospital for washing dishes, the nurse's aide opened her purse long enough to check the .38 caliber revolver. *Betty's not likely to be there with him, but odds are Mike'll know where she is.* Getting out of her car, the lady felt light as a flitting butterfly, but the weapon was heavy in her hand. *Even if he tells me what's happened to my daughter—I'm going to stop his clock for good.* Her face, which might have been chipped from gray flint, was grim as Death itself. *After I shoot him, I'll find someplace to throw this gun away where nobody will find it in a thousand years.* Wanda Naranjo returned to the dirt lane and began what seemed to be the longest walk of her life. It was not. Her longest trek was yet to come.

All the way to the trailer, the armed-and-dangerous woman experienced the same eerie sensation that had unnerved Freddy Whitsun on Sunday morning, when the handyman had stood at the front door of Morris Meusser's cottage. Wanda Naranjo was haunted by the feeling that someone was watching her. With every third step, she assured herself that . . . *It's just my nerves.*

Not so, Mrs. N.

Someone *is* watching.

As Wanda approached the trailer, she kept an eye out for the old Wagoneer. *Mike's either gone somewhere or he's hid his car. I'll just knock on the trailer door and wait for him to show his ugly face and then I'll—*

She blinked.

It was unnecessary to knock. The metal door was unlatched and standing open a couple of inches. A warning bell began to ring deep within that lobe of Wanda's brain that warned of a sidewinder nestled just on the yonder side of the mossy log she was about to step over. *This smells like a trap.* Maybe so. But the woman was here to take care of business, and backing off was not an option. She set her jaw. *I'll walk in and take him by surprise and if Mike so much as blinks I'll shoot him right between the eyes.* After inhaling a deep breath, she pushed the door. The hinges barely creaked as she entered the twilight space and felt the rotting plywood floor give slightly under her weight. *If Mike's here, he must be in the bathroom or under the bed.* The intruder exhaled the stale air she had been holding, and felt a sudden pang of conscience. Cold-blooded murder could be justified, but somehow it did not seem polite to enter someone's home without at least announcing your presence. Even if you intend to dispatch the occupant with extreme prejudice and then dance around his warm corpse whilst singing "Salty Dog Blues." "Mike . . . are you here?"

He was not. The filthy space under the bed concealed not a single ex-boyfriend. Neither did the stinking little bathroom.

But someone was present to greet Wanda Naranjo—a field mouse perched on the tiny dining table. The famished rodent was nibbling at a saltine cracker. The furry creature paused long enough to give the intruder a churlish look, as if to say, *This is my soda cracker, sister—make a move for it and I'll bite your finger off!*

"Hiya, Mickey." She grinned at the impudent diner. "You seen Mr. Rat-face?"

The mouse, with a chunk of cracker in its mouth, scampered away to continue its feast behind a stained coffee cup.

Sniffing a peculiar odor, the armed woman took a look at the four-burner propane range. *The nitwit left a pot on a lighted burner and the water's all boiled off.* Wasn't that just like a man? Shaking her head at such folly, she reached for a greasy black knob and turned the blue ring of flame off. Wanda wrinkled her nose at the remains of what—judging from the red-and-white soup can sitting beside the pot—was intended to be a serving of Campbell's Bean with Bacon soup. *The big coward must've seen me coming and run away to hide in the woods.* She estimated how long it would take for a pot of soup over medium flame to reach this desiccated condition. *Twenty minutes, tops.*

What to do?

She considered sitting on the unmade bed and waiting for his return. *But Mike might stay in the brush for hours. Or even all night.*

Maybe I should leave him a note. She imagined what it might say:

> *Sorry about what happened on Friday.*
> *Drop by when you feel like it.*
>
> *—W*
>
> *PS: I'll have a surprise for you (something sweet)*

Her lips twisted into a smile. *A .38 caliber treat.*

Wanda sighed. *But I'd be stupid to leave a note inviting Mike to my home and then shoot him dead when he shows up.* Written invitations to murders (the amateur assassin imagined) had a way of showing up in the cops' grubby hands. *So what can I do?* It seemed that the frustrated lady had run out of semiclever notions. Which left her with only one choice—a strategic retreat. *I'll walk back to the car and go home.*

It can be so difficult to commit a capital crime. But had our plucky heroine given up? Certainly not.

While I'm driving back to Granite Creek, I'll put on my thinking cap and come up with another plan.

Which, as if to demonstrate the rewards of virtuous perseverance, she did right on the spot.

I know what I'll do!

Is she going to tell us? Of course.

I'll park up the road and wait in the brush by the bridge. Mike's probably scared now that I've showed up and he'll leave this dump tonight and go looking for another hideout. And when he does, I'll shoot him dead.

Her Longest Walk

Wanda Naranjo was making the hike back to her Toyota without admitting to a growing sense of unease. But not without looking over her shoulder a dozen times or more.

Someone was still watching.

The woman knew this for a fact. Not that she had anything to be afraid of; having a loaded Smith & Wesson in her hand was a great comfort. *Mike knows better than to mess with me!* Nevertheless, the certainty that a pair of eyeballs was focused on her was unnerving. As Wanda picked up her pace, her barely repressed fears exploded in a surge of nausea.

Things were about to go from bad to worse.

Zzzzmmmm. Ka-bam!

The source of the gunshot was almost a hundred yards away, but Wanda would have sworn that the shooter was close enough to spit on her—and the terrified woman was convinced that she heard the slug go spinning past her ear. She had.

Another buzzing hum of a lead bumblebee, another booming report.

Instinctively, the targeted woman turned toward the sound of the gunshots, squinted into the purpling sunset, and emptied her revolver. Bam-bam-bam-bam-bam!

Ha! That'll give the bastard something to think about.

It did.

Wanda didn't waste another second in self-congratulation; her instincts had initiated a hasty retreat. Barely aware that she was running for all she was worth, the alarmed woman had forgotten about the spent pistol in her hand. Mrs. Naranjo's highly focused mind was occupied with two thoughts: *If I can get back to the car before he shoots again, I'll be all right,* and . . . *I should've figured that slimy bastard would try to back-shoot me!*

By the time she saw her Toyota, the firearm was dead weight—an anchor dragging along, preventing her speedy escape. Betty's mother cranked up the cranky engine and got her trusty motor vehicle into gear. As she roared away toward the paved highway, knocking bushes and saplings left and right, Wanda's face was flushed, her blood pump going thumpity-thump in her chest, her lungs gasping for every breath. Scared to death?

Yes.

Chapter Twenty-five

All We Have to Fear Is—

Monday, An Hour After Sundown

Fear itself. (Thank you, President Franklin Delano Roosevelt.)

Like so many ambitious projects that are launched with enormous enthusiasm and boundless optimism, Wanda Naranjo's enterprise had suffered a jarring reverse. And don't blame her—it wasn't because she hadn't given it her best shot. But that is an unfortunate metaphor; let us say merely that the lady had "spared no effort" in her attempt to rid the world of Mr. Michael Kauffmann. And if there is a moral to be gleaned from this misadventure, the lesson learned might be that spicing a homicidal plot with malice aforethought and murderous intent does not necessarily guarantee its success.

But Wanda was not one to waste precious moments on thoughtful introspections; she was concerned about immediate practical issues, like staying alive. *I can't believe that lowlife actually took a couple of shots at me.* It occurred to her that Mike might have more steel in his spine than she had imagined. One such thought tends to spawn others of like kind . . . *Me shooting back at him probably made him mad.* And if so . . . *He probably intends to finish what he started.* This possibility made her heart leap. *Mike might be following me home.* Glancing in the rearview mirror, she was relieved to see no headlights glowing behind her.

Which don't necessarily mean he's not back there. She took another look. *The idiot might be driving without lights.* And the gunshots might start popping at any instant. *What'll I do if he starts shooting through my rear window?* Silly question. She ground her teeth. *I'll stop the car and shoot back!* Which reminded the willing combatant of a small problem; a mere technical detail. But one that must be dealt with forthwith.

About nine miles and ten minutes before she would pass the sign that identified the Granite Creek city limits, the tough little woman pulled over onto the grassy shoulder and reloaded her revolver. This preparation calmed her, and as Mrs. Naranjo got her Toyota back onto the two-lane, she shifted gears. *If and when Mike shows his ugly face, I'll deal with him. But for now I've got to get my mind off the lowlife.*

And she did, applying her intellect to ordinary everyday subjects. *Soon as I get a chance, I'll call the hospital and tell them I'll be back at work tomorrow.* The mere contemplation of returning to her routine tasks was soothing. Pleased with this consolation, Wanda tried for another, focusing her thoughts on what would be waiting for her when she got home. *The house will be nice and quiet.* Quiet was good. *I'll make me a nice cup of hot tea.* But not a dainty little-old-lady's china cup—this would a big honking crockery mug with two teabags. *I'll have some graham crackers and extra-crunchy peanut butter with the tea.* She could practically taste the imagined snack. *After that, I'll lay down on the couch and take a long, restful nap.* The world-weary woman almost smiled. So far, so good.

Couldn't last.

When she finally saw the lights of town, her hopeful thoughts began to take a dark turn. *Nothing good I plan on ever works out.* This afternoon's failed attempt at coldblooded murder was proof enough of that proposition. *My life is a bucket of stinking garbage and it ain't ever gonna get any better.* A sensation of self-pity almost overwhelmed the poor soul. *I'll be out of tea and down to one graham cracker and the peanut butter'll be moldy and when I lay down for a nap I won't be able to get a wink of sleep because there'll be rats gnawing in the walls.*

It was debatable whether such worrying might actually be worse than stark, wide-eyed terror of a real and present danger. Debilitating as the latter experience was, the threat of imminent death did tend to heighten one's sense of being alive—and enable the threatened mortal to do her utmost to remain firmly in that preferred state.

By the time the unsettled woman turned her motor vehicle into the long, dirt driveway to her ramshackle dwelling, she had finally accepted the fact that . . . *I'm in way over my head.* Wanda pulled the Toyota Tercel to an abrupt stop and blinked at a low-hanging juniper branch. Swaying in the breeze, the gaunt arm beckoned her to an empty house that could never be a real home again. *Not without my daughter.* The anemic headlight beams attempted with pathetic futility to illuminate the inky road that led to the end of the trail. *I can't handle this mess all by myself.* She opened her purse, found a pack of mint-flavored cigarettes, put one between her lips, and touched a lighter to its tip. *I need some help.* She inhaled a long breath of the carcinogenic vapors, then exhaled a puff of gray smoke to fog the windshield. *So what do I do?* She knew. Pass the buck where it belonged. *I'll tell the cops where Mike's trailer is and that when I went to ask him what he knew about Betty he took some shots at me.* Not such a bad notion, and not so far from the truth. Thus buoyed, her fertile imagination presented a romantic version of the outcome: *That tough white cop and the hard-eyed Ute will hunt Mike down and beat him with fists and blackjacks until he admits he tried to murder me and tells them what he's done with Betty.*

But contacting the legally constituted authority would be risky.

Wanda knew that once a person started talking to

the police . . . *The cops won't stop till they've wormed everything they want to know out of you.* And not only that . . . *Mike might tell them that I chased him off by shooting at him and then came to his trailer with a pistol in my hand.* Life was so terribly unfair, and making important decisions was extremely difficult. She took another puff. And another. *But if I don't call the cops right this minute, I'll chicken out.*

Which was just what she did.

As if to terminate her inner conversation, she stuffed the used-up cigarette butt into the Tercel's overfilled ashtray. Which freed up her right hand. Which is worth mentioning.

As it happened, Wanda's dominant hand feared nothing in all creation, and it also knew what to do. The spunky appendage reached into the open purse where her .38 revolver was nestled coldly inside, waiting for the mere touch of a finger on the trigger to snuff out a worthless life.

No. That was not what her hand had in mind.

Her clever fingers were looking for something else. And found it.

Wondering how the instrument had gotten into her hand, Wanda stared dumbly at the pink mobile telephone. Without waiting for an instruction from the semirational fraction of her brain, the hand's dexterous pointing finger punched in 911. She obediently pressed the instrument against her ear, just in time to hear Clara Tavishuts bark, "Granite Creek PD—what is the nature of your emergency?"

Wanda Naranjo opened her mouth. Nothing came out.

"Hello—is anyone there?"

"Yeah." The woman in the Toyota licked her lips. "I'm here."

"Please give me your name and location."

"I'm Wanda Naranjo and I'm in my car."

"What is the nature of your emergency?"

"I can't talk about it on the phone." Wanda felt her face blush.

Miss Tavishuts, who'd heard it all in her two decades as

a police dispatcher, didn't blink. "How may I help you, ma'am?"

"You can put the boss cop on the phone."

"Chief Parris?"

Wanda nodded.

"Hello? Are you there, Mrs. Naranjo?"

"Mm-hm." The citizen chewed her numb lower lip until she tasted the salty flavor of the crimson fluid that pulsed through her arteries. "I ain't going nowhere till I talk to your boss."

"I'm sorry, but Chief Parris isn't here. I'll ask the night-duty officer to speak to you—"

"Forget that." Another possibility occurred to her. "Get Charlie Moon on the phone."

"Are you the same lady who called last Friday, asking for—"

"Yes I am."

"Then you'll recall that Mr. Moon is a part-time deputy, ma'am. He doesn't take citizens' calls—"

"Then I'll talk to Parris."

"Could your inquiry wait until morn—"

"No it can't!" Wanda spat blood onto the steering wheel. "It's a matter of life and death." *Betty's probably already dead and my turn might come up any minute now.*

"Please hold on, ma'am—I'll see if I can locate the chief."

"Like I said, I ain't going nowhere." She switched off the Toyota's headlights and turned the ignition key to silence the idling engine. For a full minute, the distraught citizen with her ear to the mobile phone listened to classical music—courtesy of GCPD. Joseph Haydn. String Quartet Op. 64. No. 2, B minor. *Allegro spiritoso.* Your smallish Rocky Mountain cow-town cop shops are not without a touch of class. Or, if you prefer—a hint of pretension . . . a smidgen of affectation.

The soothing musical interlude was interrupted by the dispatcher's voice, less barkish this time: "Chief Parris is on his way, Mrs. Naranjo."

Relief rolled over her like a spring flood. "When'll he show up?"

"The chief didn't give me an ETA."

"Then gimme your best guess."

"Oh . . ." The distant dispatcher's shrug was perceptible. "I'd say just a few minutes."

"That'll be fine. G'bye." *I'll need a little while to get my thoughts together.* Wanda Naranjo restarted the engine, switched on the headlights, and drove the final quarter mile to her house in low gear.

An explanatory observation involving ethnic and regional concepts of time may prove helpful.

Here they are:

Like Charlie Moon, Clara Tavishuts is a full-blooded Southern Ute.

But unlike the tribal investigator, the GCPD dispatcher operates strictly on Indian Time.

Though Wanda Naranjo was half Picuris Pueblo Indian, she did not realize that Clara's *just a few minutes* might run anywhere from "pretty danged quick" to "as long as it takes Chief Parris to get there."

CHAPTER TWENTY-SIX

BETTER LATE THAN NEVER?

In this instance, the answer is—*no!*

The unfortunate incident commenced in the following manner:

After parking her automobile underneath a sickly elm that was still half garbed in last year's desiccated leaves, Wanda grabbed her purse, slammed the car door, trotted across the moonlit yard, hurried up the front porch steps, unlocked the door, stepped inside her parlor, slammed and latched the door—and let out the breath she'd been holding for so long that her eyes were about to pop. Inhaling deeply, she stood in the dark with the .38 caliber revolver in her trembling hand. It would not be excessively lurid to assert that "Fear's icy grip had begun to clutch at her heart again."

The clock on the parlor wall ticked.

I don't know why I'm so afraid.

And tocked.

I've got a loaded gun in my hand . . . and . . . That big blue-eyed cop will be here any minute now.

And tick-tocked. But ever more slowly, it seemed—as if Wanda Naranjo's quota of time was about to run out. When the edgy lady had aged about nineteen years, she heard the sound of an approaching motor vehicle. *Finally!* She switched on the porch light, and with the Smith & Wesson gripped tightly in her right hand, she used her left to pull back a tattered window curtain—100 percent certain that she would see the cop's car. Every life must have its share of disappointments. The motor vehicle that pulled up was not a GCPD black-and-white, but it was one that she recognized. Betty Naranjo's momma was wide-eyed with surprise. *Well would you look at that!*

She slipped the firearm into her coat pocket, unlocked the door a half inch, and peeked through the crack. The heel of her right hand resting lightly on the pistol's checkered walnut handle, Wanda sneered as she watched her visitor mount the steps onto the porch with typical masculine confidence. *Isn't that just like a man—the bastards figure they can drop by any old time they please and you'll be overjoyed to see them.* She opened the door wide.

The visitor's expression was—and there is no better way to put it—*sheepish.*

"Well, would you look at what the cat drug in."

The homely fellow removed his cap. "I come to fix that leak under your kitchen sink."

Wanda's tone was deceptively calm, not unlike the eye of a hurricane. "I called you on Friday."

Avoiding the homeowner's hard gaze, he turned the cap in his hands. "Uh . . . I run into a spot of trouble and couldn't make it."

The lady's upper lip curled to express her extreme distaste. "Well, you're three days late and a dollar short."

"I sure am sorry, ma'am." The hopeful man glanced toward his truck. "If you still want me to take a look at the leak, I'll go get my toolbox."

One does not wish to make excuses for those high-strung citizens who are prone to overreact. But this much must be said on behalf of Wanda Naranjo: the lady had already had a trying day. This latest outrage was a tad too much. Imagine that final straw being placed upon an already overloaded camel's back.

Something inside the woman simply *snapped*.

Wanda raised the pistol and pointed it at the startled craftsman's chest.

The sensible fellow departed without waiting for a verbal order. And speedily.

She took careful aim, and fired all five bullets at the ground, not very far behind the fleeing figure's heels, which encouraged the ungainly fellow to make some mighty high steps. When the cylinder was empty, she pocketed the weapon. *That'll teach the bum a good lesson!*

No doubt.

But Wanda Naranjo realized that her recent propensity for shooting in the general direction of annoying men was likely to become a habit, and one of dubious merit. She withdrew into the inner sanctum of her home, returned the weapon to her purse, sat down on the couch, kicked her shoes off—and wept. *I'm going crazy as a bedbug. If this keeps up, I'll end up in a lunatic asylum or in prison or dead.* Desirous of wiping her eyes, Wanda Naranjo reached for a handy Kleenex box. The dispenser of tissues was empty. She gnashed her teeth. *What I need is a long, quiet vacation. Some warm place where I can walk on a sandy beach and stick my toes into the salt water and*—

What was this? The woman noticed that her feet were damp. And she heard a sound not unlike the soothing whisper of surf. Was the power of suggestion conjuring up her hoped-for stroll on the beach's edge. Sadly, no.

The worn parlor carpet was soaking wet.

The surf sound effects—more like the spewing of an artesian spring—was originating in the kitchen.

Mystery solved.

It's another damn leak. The stunned woman stared unseeingly at the cracked-plaster wall. *That Ute Indian warned me about all those rusty pipes that need fixing.* She blinked.

And I just chased the three-days-late plumber away. Wanda Naranjo tried ever so hard to suppress an upsurging giggle. Mission impossible. The snigger just *had* to come out. Within a few irregular heartbeats, the lady was laughing loudly. Insanely.

CHAPTER TWENTY-SEVEN

MR. TOP COP ARRIVES

Some twenty minutes after Wanda Navajo had encouraged the repentant plumber's retreat with gunshots, Scott Parris arrived in his venerable red Volvo. The lawman, who was taking the call on personal time, was surprised not to see lights glowing in the windows of Mrs. Naranjo's house. Furthermore, the woman's Toyota was not parked in the yard. He could hardly believe the woman's insolence. *I've drove all the way out here to humor this crank and she's not even here.* It was not like he didn't have better things to do. *I could be in my living room, kicked back in my recliner with an ice-cold Coors in my fist, watching ESPN or HBO and not giving a minute's thought to this airhead or her runaway teenager.* But Parris figured it served him right. *I should've told Clara Tavishuts to send Officers Knox and Slocum out here.* The humiliated chief of police swallowed his pride and an incipient threat of heartburn.

He was about to make a U-turn and return home when it occurred to him that there was just the slightest chance that something bad had happened here. He tried to think of a "such as" that would fit the peculiar circumstances. The natural villain would be Kauffmann the Coffin Man. *Okay, the boyfriend shows up, shoots Wanda Naranjo dead, and hits the road again.* But that didn't explain the woman's absent Toyota. Not a big problem. *He comes back on foot, shoots her, then drives off in her Toyota.* This unlikely scenario and the fact that the chief of police already had an unhappy half hour invested in this alleged trouble call settled the matter. *I can't go back home without at least going through the motions of checking things out.* Emerging from the Volvo, Parris stomped across the littered yard just as sheet lightning illuminated the cloud-shrouded mountain peaks. An instant after that, a few drops of rain began to pitter-pat onto his felt hat. He mounted the four porch steps in two man-size strides and banged his gloved fist on the door.

No response.

"Hello inside!"

The rain was falling harder.

Cupping his hand by his mouth, he roared louder than a distant rumble of thunder, "Mrs. Naranjo—it's Chief Parris!"

The house creaked as a heavy gust of wind leaned against it. Hail shot out of the clouds like Heaven's buckshot, peppering the rusty steel roof.

Great. Though sheltered by the porch from rain and hail, Parris zipped up his jacket against the wind. *I'll get soaking wet before I make it back to my car.* On the other hand . . . *If I wait for a couple of minutes, maybe the worst of the storm will pass.* Being an energetic sort of fellow who can't stand around doing nothing at all, he tried the doorknob. When it turned easily, the cop pushed the door open. "Hello—anybody home?" *If folks would just remember to lock their homes, it'd cut burglaries by 42 percent.* The amateur statistician stepped inside, turned on a pocket flashlight, and bellowed, "Police answering a call—anybody here?"

The hollow echo of his voice was an eloquent answer.

After a routine check of several drab rooms, Parris shook his head, muttered a mild oath, and grumped, "Like all I got to do is respond to so-called urgent calls from citizens who don't even bother to be at home when I show up." He strode onto the porch, closing the door behind him. Hail was still hammering the metal roof but (he assured himself) not *quite* so hard now. Parris grinned at his attempt at self-delusion. *Not more than two tons a minute.* He tugged his hat brim down hard enough to shut off the circulation to his scalp. *And the lightning's getting closer with every strike.* As if to validate this observation, a deafening crack of thunder split the sky just as a long finger of crackling fire reached out to tickle the top of a towering poplar that stood not fifty yards away. *Hell's bells and red-hot tamales!* He turned up his jacket collar. *This storm could go on for half the night.* The stubborn man who was determined to go home eagerly eyed his Volvo. So near—yet so far. *If I go real fast maybe I won't get so wet.* He gritted his teeth and made a run for it.

Look at him go!

Sorry. What happened next serves to illustrate the folly of anticipating.

The beginning of his sprint was rudely terminated when the heavyset fellow stomped his way through one of the rotted porch steps. *Damn—I could've broke my ankle!*

Another lightning strike sizzled the brushy crest of a ponderosa, that tree not quite so nearby.

Parris glared at the threatening sky. *Well . . . if it kills me, then I'm dead.*

Oddly comforted by this empty truism, he limped across the muddy yard and eased his bulk into the familiar automobile. *Now, that's better.* The man behind the badge and the steering wheel roared off toward hearth and home with one thought uppermost in his mind: revenge against a thoughtless citizen. *I'll file a false-report charge against that dopey woman.* This satisfying threat was immediately trumped by a healthy dose of reality. *No I won't.* Why not? *It ain't worth all the heartburn.*

Speaking of which . . . the searing gastric acid had surged its way up to his throat.

The dyspeptic cop fumbled for and found the ever-present roll of Tums in his jacket pocket, bit off three of the white disks, crunched them like candy, and swallowed. *Ahhhh . . . that felt good goin' down.*

Which raised that ever-pertinent hypothetical question . . . *I wonder what's goin' down.*

The issue was, of course, not gastrointestinal. The lawman's inner query referred to Wanda Naranjo's unexplained absence. Despite his annoyance, Scott Parris could not dismiss the stubborn fact that . . . *Something about this business ain't quite kosher.* Teenage runaways happen all the time, but . . . *First the daughter goes missing—and now the mother ain't at home when she should be.* And after all . . . *The lady did place a 911 call and Clara said she sounded scared.* It occurred to him that Mrs. Naranjo's corpse might be somewhere nearby . . . or in the backseat of her car, wherever that vehicle was at the moment. But the frustrated public servant didn't know what he could do about that.

Moreover, the off-duty officer had a strong hankering for his easy chair, TV, and a cold brew and was in no mood for negative thinking. So Parris went for a more upbeat scenario: *Ten to one, the prodigal daughter came home ten minutes before I showed and her momma was so happy she forgot all about calling the cops. To celebrate, Mrs. Naranjo and Betty got into the Toyota and motored into town to kill the fatted calf and celebrate.* Which thought aroused his latent appetite. *They're probably in one of Granite Creek's fine restaurants right this minute, chowing down on a couple a prime Columbine T-bones and baked Idaho spuds and apple pie and ice cream and no telling what else.* His obliging imagination instantly produced a twelve-second video of the mother-daughter reunion in full color. Scott Parris watched the hopeful little drama play out right down to The End.

The entertainment terminated, the lonely bachelor squinted at the windshield, where busy wipers were furiously swiping away gallons of water. *I've got some glazed doughnuts in the breadbox.* His tense expression gradually

relaxed into a wistful smile. *I'll warm a couple of them puppies up in the microwave, and spread some butterlike goop
on 'em, and pour me a cold glass of skim milk and . . .* And
all would be right again.

Until the next time.

CHAPTER TWENTY-EIGHT

THEIR EXCELLENT ADVENTURE COMMENCES

Tuesday Afternoon

After the long drive from the tribal elder's home on the Southern Ute reservation, Sarah Frank and Daisy Perika arrived at the Granite Creek Cemetery at a propitious moment. The methodical examination of the crime site completed, GCPD officers Eddie Knox and E. C. "Piggy" Slocum were in the process of removing the final few yards of black-and-yellow POLICE—DO NOT ENTER tape from the residence formerly occupied by the recently deceased cemetery custodian. This official act, and the fact that Morris Meusser had been buried not fifty yards from his beloved little cottage on this very morning, put a definitive period at the end of his soul's seventy-year sentence on planet earth. Or so it seemed.

Cemetery Manager George R. Hopper, dressed in a natty three-piece gray suit, pale blue silk shirt, and red power tie, was overseeing acting custodian Freddy "Fixit" Whitsun, who was outfitted in oversize blue bib overalls. Meusser's replacement was carrying a cardboard box of personal property into the snug quarters where he was about to spend his first night.

As Sarah pulled her spiffy red F-150 to a stop beside Knox and Slocum's black-and-white Chevy, Hopper left Whitsun to move his meager belongings in without benefit of the boss's helpful instructions. In a much better mood than on the Sabbath morn when Mr. Meusser's pale corpse had been found inside the dwelling, the spare little man stepped sprightly across the lawn that his new hire had mowed barely an hour earlier. As he approached the pickup's passenger-side door, a perfunctory smile appeared under Hopper's meticulously trimmed mustache. "Good afternoon, ladies . . . how may I help you?" There was no mistaking the hint of reservation in this offer.

Believing that Daisy was here to find a spooky clue that would identify the custodian's murderer, Sarah discreetly deferred to the senior citizen beside her.

The Southern Ute tribal elder put on the friendliest face in her collection of amiable expressions, which was a mild scowl. "I'm wanting to look at some burial plots."

"Ah." Trading his salesman's smile for a mortician's sad face, Hopper nodded knowingly. "Preparing for that eventual day when one must shrug off this mortal coil and pass over, are we?"

"I don't know about you, sonny, but I'm older than Moses' great-grandmomma and I might kick the bucket any second now." As she spoke, Daisy was opening the truck door and fumbling with her oak walking stick. "I'll need some time to wander around and get a good look at your graveyard."

Somewhat nonplussed, Hopper attempted an explanation: "As it happens, ma'am, we won't be able to accommodate you until after—"

"The girl will drop me off here for an hour or so." As the nervous white man supported her elbow, Daisy grunted herself to the ground.

"Actually, the cemetery is closed to the public." Hopper was trying very hard to be nice. "If you would like to return in a day or two, I'd be happy to help you find just the right—"

"I ain't the *public*," Daisy snapped. The wrinkled Indian aimed her meanest beady-eyed look at the annoying *matukach*. "And you don't need to *help* me. I can take care of myself."

"I do appreciate your consideration of Granite Creek Cemetery for your final resting place, ma'am." Following this conciliatory preamble, the cemetery manager stiffened his spine, raised his smallish chin, and assumed the firm, no-nonsense tone that he used with his children when the freckle-faced imps would not listen to reason. "But we cannot help you today."

Daisy was beginning to get his drift. "Why not?"

Mr. Hopper helped himself to a deep breath. Thus refreshed, he launched into a detailed explanation about how the police were still searching the cemetery grounds for physical evidence that might lead to the identification, apprehension, and arrest of the person or persons responsible for the recent "deplorable homicide" at the custodian's residence. Interpreting the old woman's blank stare as an indication that she did not understand the importance of cooperating fully with the local constabulary, he added, "Despite my natural desire to assist you immediately in finding a suitable burial plot, my first responsibility is to provide every assistance to our fine police department. The villain who murdered Mr. Meusser must be apprehended." *And read his rights right on the spot and hung from the nearest cottonwood!*

Charlie Moon's closest living relative was tough as a two-dollar steak and stubborn as a starving bulldog pulling on the other end of a pork chop and any other worn-out metaphor you might want to dust off, but Aunt Daisy realized that she was up against one of those feisty little white men who was not going to budge. Was she defeated? Perish the very thought; giving up was not an option. Challenges such as this merely added spice to her life. It was a risky move, but the sly old gamester was feeling lucky. After all, the ploy had worked with Sarah and . . . *That Ute-Papago orphan's twice as smart as this fussy little upstart.* "You're right as rain—lawbreakers have to be caught and punished. That's why I've come to lend a hand."

Hopper stared at the other party in this opaque conversation. "Excuse me . . . I don't believe I understand."

"That's all right, sonny." Daisy patted her mark on the arm. "I'm going to explain it so you can." She got started just as Freddy Whitsun ambled up to find out what was going on. Both men listened attentively. As did Sarah Frank, who had remained in her pickup.

Hopper's bright blue eyes popped.

Whitsun's lantern jaw dropped.

The cemetery manager coughed, cleared his throat, and repeated Sarah Frank's Sunday question: "Can you really do that?"

"Sure." Daisy produced a wicked grin. "Easy as eating a piece of cake."

"Pie," Whitsun mumbled.

As she addressed Hopper, Daisy pointedly ignored the nitpicking handyman. "You must've seen people do it on TV."

"Well . . . yes. I suppose I have." The cemetery manager cocked his head as he regarded the elderly specimen. "But those were . . . well . . . *professional* psychics."

"What do you think I am, some slipshod amateur?"

"Actually, ma'am—I don't know who you are." *Much less what.* "We have not been properly introduced." He recovered the polite smile. "I am George Rogers Hopper. I have the honor of being the manager of Granite Creek Cemetery."

"I'm Daisy Perika, Your Honor."

Blank stares from the white men.

She fleshed out the introduction: "I'm Charlie Moon's aunt."

The significance of this claim gradually dawned on the cemetery manager and the replacement custodian.

"Ah, yes." Hopper nodded knowingly. "I believe I have heard of you—aren't you the Navajo woman who prepares herbal medications, casts spells and whatnot?"

"No!" Daisy said. And she meant every word of it.

"Aunt Daisy's a Southern Ute." Sarah Frank's voice from the pickup cab surprised everyone. "Like Charlie Moon."

"Oh, of course." Hopper's apology was all over his face. "And am I to understand that you can visit a homicide scene and pick up ethereal hints of what transpired during the final moments of the fatal event—possibly even identify the malefactor responsible for the horrid deed?"

"Well, I don't know about *that*—but if the dead man's spirit is still hanging around here, I could ask him what happened."

Deathly afraid of haunts, Freddy Whitsun shuddered at the thought of conversing with one. But he couldn't help wondering whether Morris knew who'd killed him.

"You could actually speak to the late Morris Meusser?" Hopper's eyes betrayed his doubts. "As in a conversation?"

"Sure," Daisy said. "If that dead man knows who did him in, he'll tell me." And the more the shaman made her pitch, the more it made sense. *Maybe I should've been doing this kind of thing all my life.* A person who could talk to ghosts might even be able to turn a nice profit. *I bet I could make a pile of cash money finding out who pulled the trigger.*

Hopper was not entirely convinced. *I am certainly tempted, but . . .* "I don't know. It is a somewhat unorthodox procedure." And could be the cause of further scandal for the cemetery.

"Maybe so, but it works almost every time." Daisy shook her walking stick at the hesitant white man. "And it won't cost you a copper dime." Seeing that Hopper was teetering right on the razor's edge of indecision, she gave him a push in the preferred direction. "Scott Parris won't be happy if you don't let me give it a try."

This was a new wrinkle. "You're a friend of Chief of Police Parris?"

Got him! "*Friend* don't get you halfway there." Daisy's eyes moistened. "I'm like a mother to Scotty."

"Oh." A half-dozen heartbeats. "I will consult with Chief Parris about this matter. If he is in favor of what you propose, then I suppose it might be all right." *And if things go sour, Parris can take all the heat.*

"Suit yourself." Daisy shrugged. "Call a meeting of the town council, appoint a committee to study about it, and write up a thousand-page report. But in a day or two the crime scene'll be cold as a brass well digger's . . . uh . . . behind."

"I beg your pardon?"

"Dead folks' ghosts don't hang around for weeks on end, just hoping somebody like me might show up to hear their account of what happened. Haunts have places to go, things to do. For all I know, Mr. Meusser might've already left." She made a pretense of climbing back into Sarah's F-150.

"Oh, I see. Wait a moment."

Daisy paused at the pickup door.

George Rogers Hopper made a snap decision. "Very well. I assume you would like to begin in the custodian's residence."

"Sure." The supposed psychic addressed Sarah: "You drive on over to the park and do your schoolwork, then come back and pick me up in about an hour."

Miss Frank promised to do just that.

Hopper and Whitsun watched the red pickup depart.

A Sinister Foreshadowing

Daisy Perika also watched the departure of Sarah's shiny F-150, but with a sudden and inexplicable trepidation that the girl was driving off into harm's way. *Oh my goodness— what's she about to do—wreck that little red truck?* The internal answer was an immediate and conclusive *no*.

The form of Sarah's trouble would be far more subtle than a pickup wrapped around a telephone pole—the peril would be disguised to please a young girl's eyes.

Well. Daisy knew what *that* meant. Trouble with a capital *T* would be a member of the gourd-head gender. But the hairy-leg would not be a Ute, or even one of those Arizona Papagos. The tribal elder, who disapproved of romantic liaisons between Native Americans and *matukach,* imagined some good-looking white boy spotting Sarah alone in the park and flirting with the pretty Indian girl. Having been young herself about a million years ago, she had not forgotten how one thing could lead to another. *But Sarah knows how to take care of herself.* She tried to comfort herself with the conviction that . . . *Charlie Moon's the only man that silly Ute-Papago orphan is interested in.* Maybe so. *But young women's interests have been known to change.* Poor Daisy—every attempt to suppress her anxieties seemed only to aggravate them.

But don't waste any pity on Charlie Moon's agitated auntie. When confronted by nagging worries about an imaginary future calamity, the feisty old lady knows just what to do: look for the first opportunity to make some *real* trouble *right now.* For someone else, of course. Some rascal who *has it coming.*

Reinforced by the knowledge that she had been born into Uncle Sam's fabled Land of Opportunity, Daisy Perika felt better right away.

CHAPTER TWENTY-NINE

DAISY FAKES IT

After Sarah Frank's pickup was out of sight, the cemetery manager escorted Miss Daisy into the little bungalow. Once inside, Hopper stood at a discreet distance as the aged Indian woman began her examination of the dead man's former home. Despite his natural reservations about such spooky goings-on, the straitlaced fellow found the process rather exciting. *I'd give a shiny silver dollar to know what the peculiar old crone is seeing . . . and thinking.*

The elderly Ute stood silently in the plain little parlor, giving the merest glance to the couch where Morris Meusser's corpse had been discovered on Sunday morning. She took a long, hard look at a detailed cemetery diagram that covered most of one parlor wall. *I didn't have any notion of how big this graveyard is—it must be over a hundred acres.* And best of all for her experiment . . . *There's no telling how many people are buried here, but it's got to be thousands.* She was fascinated by the map, which displayed every numbered plot in each section of the cemetery—from Rockefeller Estates with its spacious accommodations (*I bet a grave there'd cost an arm and a leg*) to Pine Haven, where tiny plots were crowded together like segments of a beehive (*That'll be where the poor folks are buried*). Last, Daisy noticed a line that neatly bisected the historic section of the cemetery. This was evidently a pathway that connected to U.S. Grant Park. *If I see some spirits right away, there won't be any need to hang around this over-sized graveyard for a whole hour—I could walk directly over to the park and find Sarah.* Having absorbed all the information she needed from this carefully planned township of the dead, the old recluse turned her attention to the dwelling where Mr. Meusser had spent the last few years of his quiet life. *This little house is fairly clean for a place where a man lived all by himself. But that ugly old leather couch looks lumpy as a sack of potatoes. If this was my home, I'd put some nice white curtains on the windows.* As she inspected the small bedroom and smaller kitchen, Daisy imagined additional feminine touches that would make the custodian's quarters more livable.

When the crafty old woman had completed her arcane task in a manner designed to impress the cemetery manager, Hopper dared not ask what she might have "picked up on," and followed her out of the front door.

Daisy leaned on her oak staff. "Now I'll go spend some time in the cemetery." Her old eyes twinkled with amusement at the white man's apparent unease. "It'll be interesting to see who I meet up with out there—and what they've got to say."

Hopper gestured to draw her attention to his freshly washed and waxed Buick. "I'll be delighted to take you on a tour."

"No, I don't want to ride." The tribal elder shook her head. "I'll have to do this all by myself."

As she ambled off, the men gazed at Aunt Daisy's back. Both wondered if she would go directly to the fresh grave where Morris Meusser's corpse had been laid to rest only hours ago. This was the obvious place to find and interview the murdered man.

Daisy, who had no idea where the custodian was buried, did not.

His doubts about this self-proclaimed psychic confirmed, George Hopper dismissed Charlie Moon's aunt as an elderly eccentric who would probably amuse herself by reading inscriptions on old tombstones. Whatever her obscure intentions might be, they were of no further interest to this busy man of business. The cemetery manager leaned toward Meusser's replacement and murmured from the corner of his mouth, "Follow her in the electric truck, Freddy. But remain at a discreet distance, so as not to interfere with her . . . ah . . . concentration. The poor old thing will probably get footsore after a while. When she does, you can provide her with transport."

"Yes sir."

As George Hopper's amiable employee eased his bulky form into the modified golf cart, Hopper assured himself that he had made the right decision. *Nothing will come of this, but what harm can it do to allow an old lady to wander around the cemetery for a little while?*

CHAPTER THIRTY

THE SHAMAN'S EXPERIMENT

George Hopper's skeptical assessment of the tribal elder's extrasensory powers was not without some justification. Daisy Perika's psychic engine was certainly not hitting on all eight cylinders. If she'd had the least inkling that the replacement custodian was tagging along behind her on the electric cart, the cranky old soul would have turned to confront Freddy Whitsun with all the ferocity of a cornered wolverine.

Secure in her presumed solitude, Daisy toddled off into the vast environs of Granite Creek Cemetery with considerable anticipation of success. *There are bound to be lots of haunts here.* And with a little bit of luck, at least a few of those lonesome souls would want to start up a conversation. That was the way it had always been in *Cañón del Espíritu*. Ask Daisy and she'll tell you—if dead people had one thing in common, it was wanting to talk to somebody whose flesh was still warm. Which reminded the sly deceiver of her cover story. *If I'm lucky enough to run into that cemetery employee who was killed over the weekend, I might learn something that'd help the police find out who did him in.* But it had been Daisy's experience that some folks who died violently either didn't know what had happened or couldn't explain it so it made any sense. *All they do is jibber-jabber a bunch of foolishness!* Dismissing all thoughts of Morris

Meusser's spirit, Daisy gripped her walking stick tightly and concentrated on her actual mission. *I sure hope I'll be able to see these dead people.* She heaved a melancholy sigh. *But if I don't . . .*

The old woman didn't want to go there; that was a dismal bridge to be crossed if and when the time came. For all her long and interesting life, Daisy had been a *special* person. The very thought of suddenly becoming ordinary was not at all appealing. But there was this consolation: *Even if I can't see the dead folks, I can still hear them.* And how many people could make that claim? About one in a million, she estimated. And not only that . . . *Nobody but me knows that I've gone stone blind to ghosts.* Except for the exception. *Well, the Little Man knows.* But who would the *pitukupf* tell? As far as Daisy knew, she was the only living human whom the dwarf communicated with. *After I'm dead and gone, the little runt'll be lonely.* She wondered whom he would talk to then. The answer seemed obvious enough. *He'll take up with Sarah.* A rueful smile wreathed the tribal elder's wrinkled face. *Unless she's too scared to talk to him.* Her smile gave way to a melancholy sigh. *When I die, it'll be like a whole age has come to an end.* Which thought provided some prideful satisfaction. *People in the tribe will talk about 'way back then when old Daisy used to talk to the* pitukupf.*'*

But enough of these self-centered musings. At any moment a polite white person's spirit was liable to rise up from a moldy grave and say, "Excuse me, ma'am. Could you spare a poor, lonely soul a moment of your precious time?" Daisy set her jaw resolutely. *What I need to do now is keep my eyes peeled for anybody who don't look too healthy.* And in case the haunt was behind her, to listen. At that very instant, the Ute shaman did hear something. What she heard was . . . a sort of low, *humming* sound.

What the devil is that? She glanced over her shoulder. *Oh, no—it's that big moron in the baggy bib overalls.* And Daisy knew what Freddy Whitsun was up to. *He's following me around like I was a little child that needed looking after.* In a rare exhibition of equanimity, she acknowledged that the hireling was merely doing his job, but . . . *That sissy little white man in the three-piece suit put him up to it.* As the cemetery manager was not present to suffer her wrath, Daisy turned to face the underling driving the offensive vehicle. When her hateful glare bounced right off Whitsun's deadpan face, she shook her walking stick at the hulking annoyance.

Believing the tired old lady was flagging him down, Freddy Whitsun braked the cart to a stop.

Evil looks and stick shaking having failed, she croaked, "Go away!"

The cemetery's stolid soldier did not retreat. And not merely because he hadn't heard what she had said. Once Mr. Whitsun took on a task, he always got the job done. No matter what. He had, of course, never taken on Miss Daisy.

And neither had the steely-eyed woman ever dealt with anyone as stubborn as she was. This was extremely vexing. *If I start walking, I bet he'll just start up again and follow me.*

She did and he did.

Daisy uttered an oath in the Ute tongue. A vile one, which shall not be translated.

Pausing, she heard the mousy squeak of the electric truck's brakes. This was simply intolerable. No spirit was going to speak to her, much less show her (or his) face while the oafish cemetery custodian was motoring along behind her. *But what can I do?* Daisy considered bashing Whitsun senseless with her oak walking stick, but the irate old warrior decided against this course of action because . . . *His skull is probably two inches thick.* The thing to do (she thought) was reason with the man. On second thought . . . *No, there's no use talking to a fat white man that wears bib overalls—once that kind gets his so-called mind set on something, he just won't let go.* It occurred to the tribal elder that she was at least ten times as smart as the new cemetery custodian. *Maybe I can think of a way to discourage him.* This was a civilized approach and quite in keeping with modern ways of solving problems, but she decided to give it a try anyway. Without turning around, Daisy waved her walking stick in a gesture that clearly conveyed the message: *Drive your ugly little truck on up here, you big half-wit.*

Whitsun grunted and mumbled to himself, "I guess the old girl's feet are gettin' sore and she wants a ride back to where she started." He proceeded at the maximum speed that the mechanical governor would allow—i.e., a blinding twenty-two miles per hour. Braking the vehicle to a stop beside the aged Indian woman, he set the hand brake. "You want a ride?"

Turning to gaze at her hopeful benefactor, she gave the man a close inspection. Tufts of hair sprouted from Freddy Whitsun's nostrils and ears, and his eyes presented the vacant expression of a fellow who has to take his shoes off to count to twenty. While she grudgingly admitted that a man could not be held accountable for what was in his blood, Daisy figured he was responsible for his attire. This one wore a dirty red bandanna around his sunburned neck, and his billed ABC Hardware cap (which was adjusted about two notches too small) perched high on his pointy head. Worst of all, the custodian's blue bib overalls were suspended precariously from his right shoulder. The left gallus (Daisy's singular for *galluses*) had slipped loose from the brass bib button to dangle along Whitsun's massive arm. This combination of filthy bandanna, goofy cap, and dangling gallus was enough to make the old woman's eyes ache. *This must be the granddaddy of all the Beverly Hillbillies.*

Jed Clampett's alleged ancestor repeated his offer: "So—d'you want to ride?"

"I don't know," Daisy said. "I never rode in anything like *that*." Leaning on her oak staff, the critic directed her disparaging gaze at the electric motor vehicle. There was plenty of room for a passenger on the bench seat beside Whitsun, and the rear section of miniature utility truck was stocked with such implements as a short-handled shovel, a hedge clipper, a galvanized steel toolbox, and an assortment of odds and ends. Several sturdy steel eyebolts and hooks were affixed to the side and rear of the truck bed. Daisy thought these must be for attaching items such as buckets of moldy grave dirt, Acme tombstone-repair putty, Jiffy quicklime, and whatever else cemetery employees were accustomed to toting around. She returned her beady gaze to Whitsun's innocent face. "Your little truck looks kinda dangerous to me."

The custodian was quick to offer encouragement to the hesitant passenger. "It's safe as can be, ma'am. There ain't no doors nor seat belts, but it don't go fast enough to catch up with a three-legged snail."

The old woman was not comforted by these well-meant assurances. "Does it have good brakes?"

"Sure." Whitsun patted the hand brake. "When this is set, the truck won't move an inch."

"How do you make it go?"

The patient man showed her the throttle control on the steering column. "Would you like to get in now, ma'am?"

"Well, I suppose so." Daisy took a tentative step toward the vehicle.

The relieved custodian dismounted, with the intent of giving her a helping hand, and—

The old woman stopped dead still, raised her nose in the air like a wary coyote, and sniffed. "What's that?"

Whitsun blinked. "What's *what*?"

"I smell something that stinks," the sniffer announced.

The driver inhaled a healthy whiff through his flared, hairy nostrils. Freddy Whitsun's brow furrowed into a puzzled frown. "I don't smell nothin'."

"You've lived in town so long, all you can smell is beer and pizza." Lowering her head, the Ute woman took another sniff. "I live way out in the wilderness where there's no exhaust fumes to pollute my nose. If the wind is right, I can smell field-mouse pee a mile away."

Duly impressed by this specious testimony, Mr. Whitsun followed Daisy to the rear of the vehicle.

"There." The alleged smeller of distant mouse urine pointed her trusty walking stick. "It's a dead animal—caught underneath your little truck."

"Lemme see." Whitsun dropped to his knees and peered under the electric vehicle. After a careful inspection, he said, "I don't see nothin' under here; everything looks all right to me— Aaaiiieeee!"

The tribal elder watched the ugly little truck take off like . . . well, like an ugly little truck with an oversize man bumping along behind it like a fattened hog tied to the backside. A fattened hog wearing brand-new bib overalls, whose loose left gallus had (somehow or other) gotten attached to one of several convenient steel hooks that protruded from the rear of the truck—whose hand brake had (somehow or other) slipped out of the Stop and into the Go position.

And look at him *go!*

Barely twelve miles per hour with the massive human anchor in tow, but this was a pretty good clip for Mr. Whitsun, who—every time he attempted to get onto his feet—fell back onto his butt, or his face, and continued to be dragged along like the largish specimen of porcine livestock referred to above.

Certain professors of mathematics who teach university courses labeled Statistics 101 will protest that the convergence at practically the same instant of three unlikely events (hooked left gallus, malfunctioning hand brake, and throttle lever accidentally slipped to the let-'er-rip position) must be described as mildly suspicious. At the very least.

Daisy Perika would call it a fortuitous coincidence, and remind those nitpicking critics that they (coincidences) do happen.

It is true that Charlie Moon's aunt had more important

things to do than watch such a pitiful spectacle, but she felt obliged to tarry long enough to observe the hasty departure of the annoying cemetery custodian. Though not prone to dwell upon the faults of others, she could not resist an observation: *People who drive motor vehicles should be more careful.* Daisy cringed as she watched the man bounce off a mossy granite tombstone and heard his alarming oath. Mr. Bib Overalls was a vulgar fellow who was unable to control his dirty mouth in the presence of a lady, but . . . *I hope he don't get hurt too bad.*

Violence is (so they say) deplorable, but Daisy Perika generally managed to find a bright side to other people's sufferings. In this instance, she comforted herself with the satisfying thought that Mr. Whitsun's experience would be educational. *That'll teach him not to bother elderly ladies who want to be left alone.*

Chapter Thirty-one

Alone at Last

But only in a limited sense. There were the haunts she hoped to encounter, and somewhere back there behind her was a flesh-and-blood cemetery custodian who might properly be described as "in distress." Or worse. Was the unfortunate Mr. Fixit still among the living? Don't bother to ask the tribal elder. One of her favorite sayings is: "Out of sight, out of mind," and by the time she had proceeded a few steps from the site of Freddy Whitsun's sudden and dramatic departure, the lady's entire attention was focused on the important business that had brought her to Granite Creek Cemetery in the first place. The Experiment.

Sad to say, though Daisy did her utmost to watch and to listen for the least hint of an appearance of one of the graveyard's permanent residents, the shaman had neither seen nor heard anything out of the ordinary. But she wasn't about to give up. Not right away.

Like an aged she-hound sniffing out the hint of jackrabbit scent, she kept doggedly at her task. For almost half an hour.

Very commendable for an admittedly impatient soul.

But sooner or later, the hard Truth must be faced up to and Daisy was eyeball-to-eyeball with that tough customer. The far-from-home research project suggested by the *pitukupf* was a dismal failure. *Not only don't I see any spirits—I can't even hear any of their voices.* In a cemetery of this size, a score of whispering wraiths was bound to be clustered around her, each intent on bending the old woman's ear. The conclusion was inescapable. *I'm worse off now than I was in Cañón del Espíritu; I've lost* all *of my powers.* She expelled a self-pitying sigh. *By this time next week I probably won't be able to smell fat bacon frying or see my own face in the mirror.* One depressing thought produced another. *Sarah will have to spoon-feed me with oatmeal and lead me to bed.* Things would only get worse. *After a while I'll end up in some old folks' home and after a visit or two from Charlie Moon and Sarah, they'll get busy with this and that and come to see me maybe once a month.* If that often. *It's not like I've always been nice to them.* Miss Daisy tried to recall the last time she'd said a kind word to either of those sweet souls. *Sometime last year?*

The heavy wages of sin are hard to bear and impossible to spend.

As the tribal elder seated herself on an uncomfortable cement bench thoughtfully provided in 1939 by the Daughters of the American Revolution, she knew that it was time to call a halt to the Experiment. But in light of the accident suffered by the careless cemetery employee, she thought it might be imprudent to return to the custodian's residence and wait for Sarah Frank to show up. *If I do, that little white man with the silly mustache might ask me if I know what happened to the big fat one in the bib overalls.* Loath to provide testimony on that delicate matter, Daisy decided to take a shortcut to U.S. Grant Park, where the Ute-Papago orphan was (presumably) involved in her homework assignment.

Encountering the Unexpected

As the sad old woman trudged along a worn brick path that wound its serpentine way through a cluster of small hills, her mind was entirely occupied with her troubles. Daisy took little notice of this old portion of the cemetery, which was gradually being restored to its former glory by the Granite Creek Historical Society. Her inattention was unfortunate, because there were several interesting and curious sights to see, and—

But wait. All of a sudden, Daisy P. has stopped on a half dime.

It appears that the elderly person hears something that has caught her attention.

She has.

Something eerie.

It might have been the breeze whispering in the spruce, but to the shaman it sounded like, *Oh, please stop and talk to me . . . I'm so awfully lonely.*

Bingo!

Charlie Moon's discouraged auntie felt a surge of hope. *That sounds like a dead woman's voice.* "Where are you, sweetie?"

Right here . . . please don't pass me by!

Daisy cocked her head. *She sounds awfully young.* Of course. Beside the bricked walkway, in the cool shade of a venerable walnut tree, she spotted the weatherworn limestone tombstone. With some squinting, she managed to make out the inscription that decades of wind, dust, and rain had almost eroded away.

MAUDE PLIMPTON
1869–1888

"Maude . . . is that you?"

Can you hear me . . . ?

"Sure I can." Now for the acid test. "Come out where I can *see* you."

Nothing.

"Don't be shy, Maude . . . just step right up here and let me get a good look at you."

Again, the voice: *I'm right in front of you . . . I could*

reach out and touch you. And she did! The gentle stroke of a cold, clammy hand on Daisy Perika's cheek was like a slap in the face. The result of the shaman's experiment was in.

A devastated Daisy heard herself mumble, "I'm sorry . . . I can't quite make you out." *And I'll never see a dead person again . . . not till I'm on the other side with the whole lot of them.*

The haunt was pleading now: *Oh, please help me . . . I'm afraid and it's so cold and I can't find my way home.*

Daisy had troubles enough of her own and was not in the mood to comfort a whining haunt. But credit shall be given where it is due. Despite her disappointment in this rock-solid confirmation that she could no longer see dead folk, the tribal elder did her best to soothe and advise the distraught young woman. "Here's the thing, Maude—you're dead as a doornail and have been for over a hundred years, so you might as well get used to it." There being no immediate response from the spirit, she continued to dish out the consolations. "This hole in the ground is your home, until an angel comes to take you across the Jordan or . . ." Daisy didn't have the heart to mention the other possibility. "I'm sure that before you died of TB or dropsy or whatnot that you were a good little girl, so sooner or later you'll go to heaven and be really happy there." The old woman raised her gaze to consult the sun, which was visibly descending toward the mountainous horizon even as she watched. "I'm sorry, Maude—but I've got to get over to U.S. Grant Park and find Sarah." As Daisy was turning away, she glanced back at the specter she couldn't see. "But soon as I can, I'll come back and plant a little rosebush on your grave and we'll talk about whatever's on your mind. In the meantime, there's no point in being lonely—see if you can make friends with another dead person." An afterthought: "You ought to introduce yourself to a man. But try to find a decent fellow that you've got something in common with—like a hobby." *I bet she collects postage stamps or pop-bottle caps.*

Not a peep from the spirit.

Maude's probably upset because I won't stay and talk to her.

Either that or the invisible presence was mulling over what she'd said.

This latter possibility provoked Daisy to provide additional advice: "And find something *useful* to do, dearie—don't spend the next thousand years moping around here feeling sorry for yourself." Hoping that Miss Plimpton was at least considering her sensible counsel, the old woman said, "Goodbye." Her stout walking stick click-clicking on the worn brick pathway, Daisy trudged away through the dark, dreary old section of the cemetery. It seemed as if the bright green of the park where Sarah waited was miles and worlds away.

To Clarify a Small Point

Had Daisy Perika *really* had a brief conversation with the restless soul of one Maude Plimpton, whose name she'd read on the old tombstone? No. That spirit had departed ages ago. But in light of the disembodied voice's proximity to Miss Plimpton's monument, the tribal elder's error was understandable—and one that would not have greatly surprised her. As Daisy had observed not an hour ago—*There are bound to be lots of haunts in a graveyard the size of this one.*

One Last Thing

The advice Daisy had offered the lonely spirit had been heard by *someone.* And it would have remarkable repercussions. Where and when? Right here in Granite Creek Cemetery—and before the sun rose again.

CHAPTER THIRTY-TWO

SARAH FRANK'S ACADEMIC RESEARCH
IN U.S. GRANT PARK

The aforesaid scholar was surprised to discover such tranquillity and soul-soothing peace in this charming little hideaway—and right in the center of the busy, bustling Granite Creek! The lissome young lady was seated on a comfortable bench that was quite unlike the concrete monstrosity Daisy had rested on in the cemetery. This sensuously curved construct of slender pine slats seemed custom-made to caressingly support her thighs and back. To top it all off, the girl's large, dark eyes were treated to the sight of an oval pond where stunningly gorgeous wood ducks and haughty black swans glided effortlessly on a glassy opalescent surface. Stately weeping willows and soaring spruce on the bank seemed altogether too perfect to be real.

In this captivating environment, it is understandable that Sarah had dismissed all pedestrian thoughts. It hardly crossed her mind that Aunt Daisy was taking a walking tour of the adjacent cemetery, presumably applying her formidable psychic powers to solve a brutal murder. Also filed under "for future reference" was the university student's assignment to interview homeless persons in a park that was reputedly a hangout for surly alcoholics, dangerous drug addicts, and just plain crazy folk.

Feeling as close as she had ever come to experiencing

true peace, Sarah took a deep breath and released it in a long nostalgic sigh that hinted at a remembrance of a long-lost Paradise where her soul had once been perfectly happy, infinitely content . . . and would be again.

Alas, her sweet sojourn in this delightful little simulation of Eden was to be interrupted by that curse of all such moments of unadulterated bliss—the uninvited guest.

Here he comes now.

No, not *that* slithery serpent whose head must be bruised.

The Passerby

Which, despite her assignment to do a three-thousand-word paper on Granite Creek County's homeless folk, is what Sarah Frank ardently hoped the presumably destitute man would do. (Pass-'er-by.) The middle-aged fellow had an insane glint in his left eye, and his right orb was milky white and blind as a polished orb of marble. At first, he seemed not to notice Sarah Frank.

Which suited her just fine. *Please don't look at me!*

As if he had heard her plea, his sinister eye caught a glimpse of the winsome lass on the park bench. He turned toward her slowly, his knobby knees peeking through holes in faded denim trousers. The bum wiped his runny nose on the sleeve of a corduroy jacket that had seen better days a half century ago. The left eye blinked. "Hullo."

Sarah gazed at her hands in her lap. *Oh, please go away.*

The half-wit grinned. "Nice day." He ambled up to the bench and eyed the girl's black leather handbag. "I ain't had a bite to eat since I found a bagel in the trash can behind the deli. Could you spare some change?"

"I'm sorry." Sarah had a twenty-dollar bill but not two pennies to jingle together.

The vagrant snorted and pointed at the purse. "I bet you've got plenty."

Sarah glared at the pathetic figure. "Go away!"

"Not till you let me see what's in your purse." The loathsome fellow came a step closer and leered as he reached toward her skirt. "I bet you've got pretty legs under—"

She sprang to her feet and showed him a tiny fist. "You lay a finger on me, I'll punch your *good* eye out!"

The idiot was taken aback but not intimidated by this wisp of a girl.

There they stood, eyeball-to-eyeballs. (One of his, two of hers.)

Sarah was wondering what she should do if he didn't back off, when—

Seemingly out of nowhere and just in the nick of time, the Cavalry arrived. So to speak . . . or literally?

Over the vagrant's shoulder, Sarah saw a slender young man who, but for his slight limp and the old-fashioned hooked cane he used, had the military bearing of an officer. Too dignified to scream, she tired desperately to catch her potential rescuer's eye.

Like the lowlife who had preceded him, the healthy stranger also seemed about to pass her by without so much as a glance. But then—

Oh, thank God—he's noticed me! Sarah let out a breath.

The new arrival paused to smile at the girl, and apparently understood the situation in an instant. He immediately approached her adversary from behind and reached out with his cane to tap the half-blind half-wit on the shoulder. Sarah's adversary turned, blinked his working eye—and stared vacantly as if puzzled about how to deal with this unforeseen development.

The helpful young man summed up the situation for him: "Leave, or I shall throttle you good!"

The disabled vagrant seemed deaf to the threat.

Sarah's savior used his walking cane to smack the slow-witted fellow a sound whack on the side of the head.

This got the pest's attention. He yelped, put his palm where the cane had raised a lump, and ambled off like a sad old dog that'd been kicked for no reason at all.

Sarah beamed on her rescuer. "Oh—thank you!"

"You are entirely welcome." Placing the cane over his shoulder like a rifle, the dashing young man made a smart two-fingered salute—and clicked the heels of his shiny new shoes together.

The girl was quite overwhelmed, and then distraught as her hero turned as if to depart.

"Wait."

He paused to cast her a quizzical glance.

"I'd like to talk to you." Sarah blushed at the stranger, who was dressed in an immaculate black suit. "Unless you're in a hurry to go somewhere."

"Not at all." He flashed a brief smile under a slim ginger mustache whose color matched his wavy hair. "I have all the time in the world." He pointed his cane at the bench. "May I sit?"

"Oh, please do." She sat down again and patted the redwood planks beside her. "I'm Sarah Frank."

Before seating himself, the man made a slight bow. "Captain Erasmus Boyle, at your service, ma'am."

Sarah was wide-eyed. "You're in the military?"

"Yes." The slim man eased himself onto the bench, which did not creak. "But I'm not on active duty."

"You've been injured?" *Well that was a dumb question.*

Boyle nodded, and leaned his cane on the bench. "But I have been dismissed from the hospital."

She studied his handsome profile. *I'm sure I've never seen him before.* "Do you live in Granite Creek?"

A transient smile flickered across his face, but Boyle did not respond.

"I'm sorry—I guess I'm asking too many questions." She took a deep, refreshing breath and expelled it with: "It's just that I'm a student at Rocky Mountain Polytechnic and I've got this assignment to do a paper on homeless people and—oh," her blush burned deeper, "I didn't mean to suggest that *you're* homeless or anything like that—"

"Don't give it a thought." Captain Boyle turned to gaze

directly at the inquisitive young lady. "I reside within the city limits"—the smile reappeared, wry this time—"in a well-established if somewhat seedy district." He cocked his head. "Are you familiar with the Walnut Hills community?"

Sarah shook her head.

"I thought not." His blue eyes sparkled merrily at the pretty girl. "But if you should happen to be strolling through the neighborhood sometime, you are welcome to call on me at 144 Hollybush."

She attempted to memorize the address. *One hundred and forty-four is twelve squared, which is a gross, and Hollybush is like Hollywood except for the wood, which is what a bush is made of and—*

"Please tell me about yourself, Miss Frank."

Sarah was pleased to comply with this request. She began with her birth and filled Captain Boyle in on her parents, her face clouding as she described how they had died and brightening again as she provided a heartwarming account of how Daisy Perika had taken her in after some troubles she'd had while living with her aunt in Tonopah Flats, Utah, and how Charlie Moon was looking after her nowadays.

While Sarah Frank was occupied with these personal revelations, Daisy Perika had completed her walk through the historic section of the cemetery and emerged into U.S. Grant Park. As the girl began to describe the Columbine Ranch, Charlie Moon's aunt was about fifty yards from the bench where the Indian girl sat chatting with the fascinating white man.

Daisy stopped in midstride, her eyes narrowing to thin slits. Eyelids have a way of dropping like window shades when we don't like what we see. To further restrict her view of the present unpleasantness, the old woman's pupils contracted. In addition to these autonomic physiological responses, a seed labeled Dark Suspicion was taking root in her suspicious mind. Within a few irregular heartbeats, a sinister plant had sprouted and bloomed. Daisy Perika shook her head at the awful realization. *I must be getting stupid.* She added in a raspy whisper, "I should've seen this coming."

Under the circumstances, an understandable self-recrimination. But undeserved. Daisy could not possibly have.

CHAPTER THIRTY-THREE
AN INNOCENT CONVERSATION

It is regrettable that, among its various official activities, the Southern Ute tribal government has not seen fit to include an intelligence-gathering function. If they should decide to remedy this oversight, we recommend Daisy Perika as their first recruit. The tribal elder, who has a natural gift for spying, would make a dandy secret agent. Neither Sarah Frank nor the person who represented himself as Captain Erasmus Boyle was aware of the old lady's attempt to overhear their conversation. Which was difficult at the moment, because not a word was passing between them.

As Sarah eyed her fascinating companion, Boyle watched a gray duck descend to the surface of the pond. The feathered aviator executed an expert touchdown, creating a barely visible ripple on the glassy surface. "Do you live nearby?"

The young woman was mildly startled by this query. "No, out west of town on the Columbine." Everyone in the county knew that the Columbine was the biggest and best cattle operation within a hundred miles, so she made this claim with understandable pride. Detecting no sign that her new friend was even slightly impressed, she added, "That's Charlie Moon's ranch."

"I cowboyed with a West Texas cattle operation one summer." There was a faraway look in Boyle's eyes, as if he was gazing over time's horizon.

"That must've been fun."

"It was educational." He shook his head at the memory. "And it was hotter than six kinds of—" The gentleman remembered that he was conversing with a young lady. "Six kinds of *Hades*."

He's so cute. "It must be lots nicer where you live now."

"In a way." Again, the fleeting smile. "It's quiet enough, and peaceful." His pale brow furrowed into a slight frown. "Or has been, until quite recently."

Sarah could not resist this opportunity to probe. "I suppose a noisy neighbor has moved in next door."

"Well, you're about half right. There is some noise, but"—Boyle lifted his finely chiseled chin in a gesture—"she has moved in *above* me."

"Oh, that's even worse." The girl who loved the solitude of the Columbine could imagine how unpleasant it would be to have a noisy woman upstairs, probably stomping around in hard-sole sandals with her TV turned up to full volume. "Maybe if you talked to her, she'd—"

"I've tried speaking to her, but it hasn't done any good." He sighed along with a whispering breeze that was tossing away last autumn's dead leaves. "Which is why I get outside often nowadays . . . and do a lot of walking."

Sarah wanted to reach out and touch his arm but dared not be so forward. "What kind of noise does she make?"

"Actually, it is not the young lady herself who disturbs my slumbers. All night long, her infant child cries." Boyle stared, unblinking, at the gathering of ducks and swans gliding on the picture-book pond. "It must be a sickly child."

Sarah's face drooped in sadness. "Poor little thing."

"And all night long, the poor girl tries to sing it to sleep."

"It sounds like the mother needs some sleep herself."

"I rather imagine that she does," he said dryly. "As do I."

"Maybe if you called a social worker at the county welfare office—"

"My rather spartan quarters are not equipped with a telephone." Boyle's smile was taut. Almost twisted.

"Then you should go talk to someone who can get something done."

He turned to face this young woman who overflowed with well-meant advice. "Like who?"

Sarah knew just the man. "Chief of Police Scott Parris. He's a friend of mine."

He laughed at this suggestion, as if it were the punch line to a hilarious joke.

Which response irked the perfectly serious girl.

"I'm sorry, Sarah. But folks around here are not much inclined to listen to my complaints." The amused man flashed a bright smile at his exuberant companion. "Excepting yourself, of course."

Annoyed at this flippantly dismissive attitude, Sarah scowled at the man. "You pay a call on Mr. Parris and tell him about the poor girl and her crying baby. I'm *sure* he'll do something about it."

"I rather doubt it."

"Yes he will!" She banged her fist on the bench.

Boyle seemed to think it over. "And if he doesn't?"

"Then I'll talk to him myself."

"Fair enough." Boyle eased himself up from the park bench. "I must be getting along now."

"When will I see you again?"

He arched an eyebrow. "Are you sure you want to?"

The girl blushed. "Well . . . yes."

"Very well, then." The charming man laughed. "Almost anytime you happen to visit the park, I'm likely to be passing by."

Sarah presented her prettiest smile. "When I'm here again, I'll watch for you."

"It has been a pleasure to talk to you, Miss Frank." Repeating the two-finger salute to the young lady, Captain Erasmus Boyle turned and walked away, his spine straight as a lodgepole pine. Or a ramrod.

Sarah Frank waved. *Oh, he is just so dreamy!*

"Who were you talking to?"

The girl looked over her shoulder to see Daisy Perika approaching. "A nice man who stopped for some conversation."

Daisy leaned on her stout oak staff. "So what'd he want to talk about?"

She shrugged at Charlie Moon's nosy aunt. "Oh, this and that."

"Does he have a name?"

Sarah was tempted to reply, *Very likely, I'd think—most people do.* But she was obliged to treat elder folk with due respect. "Erasmus Boyle."

"Hah—that sounds like a made-up name if I ever heard one."

Miffed, Sarah repeated the name, this time adding her new friend's rank.

"*Captain* Boyle, is it? Well la-di-da!" Daisy shook her walking stick at the foolish youth. "If he really *is* a soldier-boy, you'd better be twice as careful." The aged woman's wrinkled face softened and her eyes took on a glazed look that hinted of sweet nostalgia. "I met me some soldier-boys back during the big war."

"Really?" Sarah thought she knew *which* big war.

"You bet. Why, I could tell you some stories about high-flying airplane pilots, tough-as-nails U.S. Marines, and good-looking sailors in bell-bottom britches." *I sure had me some fine times.* "Stories that'd curl your hair and make your eyes pop right out of their sockets."

The girl could not imagine Charlie Moon's aged aunt as a reckless young woman who dated soldiers and sailors she would never see again. And the knowing smirk on Daisy's wrinkled face, which suggested that Sarah was about to do the same thing, was an affront. "Captain Boyle is a perfect gentleman."

"No man that walks the face of this earth is perfect at anything—except lying through his teeth!" The crotchety old woman wagged a warning finger at the girl. "You'd better be more careful about who you talk to. Men that seem innocent as woolly little lambs generally turn out to be *wolves*!"

The Ute-Papago orphan barely suppressed a girlish giggle. *Aunt Daisy is so old-fashioned.* Suddenly remembering the tribal elder's spooky mission in the cemetery, she asked, "So—did you find out who murdered Mr. Meusser?"

This query caught the old faker off guard. She stared blankly at the girl.

Seeing the confusion on Daisy's face, Sarah added, "The cemetery custodian who was found murdered in his house. You were going to use your psychic powers to find out who killed—"

"Maybe I did, and maybe I didn't," Daisy snapped. With a sly smile, she added, "That's for me to know and you to find out."

Thus endeth the conversation.

CHAPTER THIRTY-FOUR

HOMEWARD BOUND

On their way back to the Columbine in Sarah Frank's spiffy F-150, Daisy Perika's eyes closed at the City Limits sign. After a half-dozen miles had slipped under the red pickup, her chin fell onto her chest and every other breath was a slight snore.

The driver cast an affectionate glance at the sleeper. *Aunt Daisy has had a big day; she needs her rest.*

It was a blatant ruse. The crafty old crone was wide awake and plotting. *I came on a bit too strong back there in the park. The silly girl's probably just dying to tell me all about this Boyle character, and would have if I'd been smart enough to keep my mouth shut and act like I wasn't interested.* At a convenient bump in the road, Daisy awakened with a start, then simulated a yawn that was magically transmuted into the genuine article. Her sly black eyes darted a furtive glance at the driver. "I'm sorry I was so fussy when you were telling me about Sergeant Rastus Doyle. It's none of *my* business who your menfolk friends are."

Sarah was greatly taken aback at Daisy's second apology in the span of a year, and completely taken in by the old actress's performance. "That's all right." But getting his name and rank wrong was not. She cleared her throat. "*Captain Erasmus Boyle* is really very nice."

The tribal elder shrugged. "I'm sure he is." She said this

in the tone of one who has completely lost interest in the subject. Yawned again. And turned her head away to watch fence posts flash by the passenger-side window.

Daisy's nifty bit of playacting did the trick.

Hurt by this display of disinterest, Sarah proceeded to provide an account of her chance meeting with the "perfect gentleman."

When she omitted some small detail, Miss Daisy—with the air of one who is merely holding up her side of a boring conversation—would interject a remark to pry out the desired information. An illustrative example:

SARAH: "And he has this neighbor upstairs, a young lady with a tiny baby. They keep him awake and he has to leave his apartment just to find some peace and quiet."

DAISY: "He probably lives in one of them new high-rises they've put up over on Arlington Avenue. I hear they're awfully crowded, with walls thin as paper so you can hear every word your neighbor says."

SARAH (shaking her head): "Captain Boyle's apartment is on 144 Hollybush Street." Not that it mattered. *It's not like I'd ever go visit him.*

By the time Sarah turned the truck off the paved highway, under the arched Columbine gate, and onto the graveled lane that meandered for miles before terminating at the ranch headquarters, she had just about run out of steam on the subject of Captain Erasmus Boyle.

Having Sarah's welfare in mind, Daisy took a deep breath. "You ought to tell Charlie Moon about this nice soldier-boy."

This remark startled the youthful driver. "Why?"

The cagey old lady turned to smile at Sarah's tense profile. "Because it might make Charlie a little bit *jealous.*"

"Oh—that's a terrible thing to suggest!" And just the sort of insidious proposal one should expect from Aunt Daisy. But . . . *It just might work.* As she half pretended to be outraged, Sarah Frank's face burned with shame. "Why on earth would I want to make Charlie jealous of a man that I don't have the least interest in?"

This produced a snorting retort from her surly passenger. "If you really don't know, kiddo—I'd never be able to explain it to you." Nevertheless, after a pregnant silence Daisy gave it a shot: "You're already nineteen, going on twenty—and not getting any prettier." She paused again to let this barbed hint of approaching old-maid status sink in.

It did; penetrating deep enough to pierce the girl's tender heart.

Satisfied with the effect of her initial assault, the well-meaning but misguided old warrior let loose a second missile: "When I was your age, I'd already had me a husband for three years." This dart, tipped with the poison of bitter memories, made a tight U-turn—and returned to wound Daisy's flesh with a dose of her own medicine. *Ol' Hubert wasn't much to look at and he hardly ever brought a greenback dollar home and the lazy boozer drank like a fish and never took a bath except that Saturday night when he fell into the irrigation ditch and drowned.* The resentful old soul frowned at another particularly distasteful recollection: *Worst of all, he chewed tobacco and spit on the sandstone hearth and I never was able to scrub those ugly spots out—not with a wire brush!* Hardly a catch to brag about. *But when times are hard and pickings are slim, a young woman can't afford to be too choosy.*

CHAPTER THIRTY-FIVE

THREE TACITURN INDIANS

Though usually a cheerful time for hungry folk at a table laden with tasty victuals, suppertimes at the Columbine were as varied as the moods of the diners. Most evening meals were spiced with lively and upbeat conversation, but a few were quiet, introspective gatherings.

This evening's feast was of that latter category.

The long, lean man at the head of the table seemed to have all his attention focused on a mouthwatering platter of venison-and-cheese enchiladas, black-peppered pinto beans, and Aunt Daisy's homemade green-tomato salsa. Truth was, Mr. Moon was barely aware of what he was putting into his mouth. *Scott's probably right about the cemetery custodian being murdered by some out-of-towner who's a thousand miles away by now.* The tribal investigator scooped up a forkful of beans. *But on the off chance he's not, and the bad actor who bashed Morris Meusser's head in is still hanging around town*—he shoveled the succulent pintos past his lips—*we might have us some serious trouble to deal with.* At a suggestion from Moon's subconscious, his crafty right hand found the salt shaker and seasoned the beans with an abandon that would have horrified a card-holding member of the American Academy of Cardiologists. Scott Parris's occasional deputy shifted to another subject. *Then, there's this business with Wanda Naranjo's pregnant daughter who's gone missing.* Moon's left hand hooked two fingers into the loop on his favorite mug and lifted it to his lips, which took a sip that distracted the compartment of his brain that was mulling over police business. *Tasty, but it could use more sweetening.* His right hand promptly put the grab on a plastic dispenser of Tule Creek honey, applied a generous dose to the cup of steaming coffee, found a spoon, and stirred the sweetener in. *Betty Naranjo'll probably turn up anytime now and tell her mother that she and her seventeen-year-old boyfriend just blew in from Reno where they tied the knot and now they're ready to move in so Momma can start babysitting the new arrival soon as the newcomer sees the light of day.* His taste buds appreciated the honeyed java. *But if the daughter don't show in a couple of days, I expect I ought to ooze on over to the Naranjo residence and see what else the lady might tell me about her boyfriend.* Not that the carpenter was a likely suspect, but it was hard to dismiss a prospective kidnapper with a handle like Kauffmann the Coffin Man. Moon's right hand returned the stainless-steel fork to the platter for a heaping helping of enchilada. *What with all the hullabaloo over the killing in the cemetery, Scott don't have time to worry about a runaway girl, and it's a deputy's job to take care of routine matters.* When he was a uniformed cop on the Southern Ute Police Force, Moon had harbored ambitions of promotion, but the lawman was a little older and a lot wiser now—and deeply grateful that he was not the chief of tribal police. Being top cop was a thankless job, and Scott Parris was taking enough heat to give a man an overdose of heartburn. *All the local newspapers and radio and cable TV are talking about the cold-blooded cemetery killer that the local cops can't find. Scott has all he can handle just keeping the town council from marching out some night with sheets over their heads and torches in their hands and burning the GCPD station down.* Mr. Moon paused his mulling long enough to enjoy the excellent enchilada that Sarah Frank had made all by herself. *That girl is a dandy cook.*

Speaking of the aforesaid dandy cook . . .

Pecking at a minuscule helping of enchilada in a teacup saucer, slender little Sarah shot a glance at the apple pie of her eye. *Charlie doesn't even know I'm here.*

Aunt Daisy was well aware of the girl's presence and could read Sarah's thoughts in her expressive brown eyes. The old woman dinged a spoon against her coffee cup, got the lovesick girl's attention, and shot her a look that said (more or less), *What're you waiting for, Cow Eyes— Valentine's Day?*

The potential old maid (who wasn't going to be any prettier tomorrow morning) read the old busybody's message loud and clear. But after thinking things over, Sarah was having doubts about Aunt Daisy's suggestion that she should mention Captain Boyle in the hope of making Charlie jealous. The nineteen-year-old frowned at the wildly unlikely prospect of the unpredictable old soul having an idea that would actually work. *Nine times out of ten she comes up with crazy notions that end up getting me into trouble.* But thoughtful people generally have difficulty making their minds up. *But even if Aunt Daisy's wrong, it couldn't hurt to try to make Charlie just a little bit jealous.* As she watched Mr. Moon scarf down the venison enchilada without the least indication that he tasted the dish she'd slaved away on for two solid hours, Sarah was unaware of the scowl she was directing at her favorite man on earth. *I bet Charlie doesn't even know what he's eating.*

Suffering from a mild bout of dyspepsia, Daisy had barely touched the generous helping of enchilada Sarah had dished onto her plate. The tribal elder satisfied herself with a small bowl of soupy pinto beans, a warmed-over jalapeño corn muffin—and the happy thought that . . . *Sarah's primed and ready to stick her fork into Charlie Moon's neck.* Figuratively, of course. *If she don't tell him about that soldier-boy she met in the park right now, she never will*. But the optimistic senior citizen was firmly convinced that every problem had a solution. *All that silly Ute-Papago firecracker needs is for somebody to put a spark to her fuse*. As it happened, Miss Daisy always carried a flint-and-steel kit in her apron pocket.

Daisy Lights a Fire

But not in a dramatic manner, like a barge load of fireworks exploding in the sky on the fourth day of July. The tiny little spark Daisy Perika struck would have barely been visible to a great horned owl at beak length on a cloudy, moonless night. And she worked her way up to it gradually. "I found a nice new chair in my bedroom."

Charlie Moon's shrug could be translated: *Glad you like it*.

Daisy edged closer to the important business. "While I paid a visit to the cemetery this afternoon, Sarah went over to U.S. Grant Park and sat on a bench."

Moon's polite reply to this revelation ranged somewhere between a grunt and a "Hm." Aunt Daisy, who generally expected to die before the week was out, visited cemeteries and funeral homes on a regular basis.

The tribal elder gummed an almost toothless smile at the girl. "She met a young man in the park."

Embarrassed to the core, the girl picked up a teacup and took a gulp of Lipton Choicest Blend.

Daisy shifted her gaze to the disinterested nephew. "A nice-looking young man."

Sarah took a second hit of the orange pekoe and pekoe cut black.

As befitting one who sticks strictly to the facts, Auntie D. added, "Or so she tells me—I didn't get that good a look at him."

Realizing that some sort of response was expected,

Charlie Moon smiled at the girl who was like a daughter to him. "The young man anybody I know?"

"No." Sarah shook her head. "I don't think so." *I don't think Captain Boyle even knew about the Columbine.*

Daisy took a sip of 2 percent sweet milk that left a thin white ring around her mouth. *I know how to set her off.* "I expect Sergeant Doyle is an out-of-towner."

"Sergeant *Boyle.*" Sarah cringed. "I mean *Captain* Boyle."

Charlie Moon was frowning. Any man who'd made captain couldn't be all that young. *Sarah must be confused about his rank.* Either that or Boyle was lying.

"Now ain't that something." Daisy's dark eyes sparkled wickedly. "You just met the young fella this afternoon, and by suppertime he's already got himself a big promotion." She cackled with immense satisfaction. "I guess he's got what we used to call 'get-up-and-go'!"

The nineteen-year-old put her fork aside. Closed her eyes. Began to count to ten. By the shortcut. *Two—four—six . . .*

Moon had rarely seen Sarah so angry. *What's going on here?* The man of the house thought he'd best put a stop to what looked like an impending hen fight. "This Captain Boyle—what's his first name?"

"Rats-butt," Daisy snapped.

"It's *Erasmus.*" Sarah shot a look at Aunt Daisy that startled the old woman.

Well, Miss Milk-sop can get her dander up. "Oh, right. Corporal Erasmus."

Realizing that the situation was teetering right on the brink of explosive, Moon reached out and put his hand over Sarah's clenched fist. "So tell me all about this Captain Erasmus Boyle."

"Oh, he's . . ." His warm touch had drained all the anger out of her. Sarah's big brown eyes beamed adoration back at the man she'd set her cap for a long, long time ago, when she was little more than a toddler. Weary of Daisy's play with military titles, she provided Captain Boyle with an honorable discharge to civilian status. "Mr. Boyle is someone I met in Grant Park." She strained to make the next assertion. "He's not anybody important." Her expressive eyes said otherwise.

Moon shook his head sternly. "Any young man who makes a play for my Sarah is a few notches more than important." There was only the slightest hint of humor in Moon's tone, the merest sparkle of fun in his eye.

My Sarah was deaf and blind to both. "Would you really like to hear about him?"

"I won't eat another bite till I know the fella inside and out." The gallant man looked longingly at the venison enchilada cooling in his platter.

With Moon's big hand resting lightly on hers, Sarah's fist gradually unclenched, and once her tongue got started it wouldn't stop until she'd flat run out of things to say about Erasmus Boyle. She went on and on about how he had cowboyed down in Texas and how hot the weather was, and how he'd been injured in the military but wasn't on active duty now, his problem with the upstairs neighbor who didn't respond to his pleading for peace and quiet and how he went walking in the park to get away from the noise and, (after catching her breath), how Boyle had, with some reservation, agreed to Sarah's suggestion that he should make a complaint to the police. In hopes that Charlie Moon would exert some influence on Scott Parris, Sarah emphasized the fact that she had *assured* the sleepless man that the chief of police would be happy to send an officer to speak to the woman who sang lullabies to her little baby who cried night and day.

All the while she was chattering, Moon was listening, but not intently. He had only a moderate interest in the young man Sarah had encountered in the park—until she mentioned that Boyle's noisy neighbor was a young woman with an infant. It seemed unlikely that Betty Naranjo's baby had been born prematurely during the past two or three days—and an even longer shot that Sarah had happened to meet Betty's downstairs neighbor. But every once in a while Fate dealt a player a full house, and the longtime lawman couldn't shake the nagging hunch that this might be the big break in the missing-pregnant-teenager case. In the casual manner of one inquiring about the price of alfalfa hay, the rancher asked, "Does Captain Boyle live in Granite Creek?"

Sarah nodded. "At 144 Hollybush Street."

Moon thought about it. "Don't think I know that one."

"It's in the Walnut Hills part of town," she said. *Which must be within easy walking distance of the park.*

Being a cowboy who liked to play poker now and again with his friends, Charlie Moon had a face that was well-nigh impossible to read when he switched his expression to Blank Page. Which he had.

Sarah hadn't noticed a thing, but—

But Aunt Daisy (who had dealt a few aces and eights of her own over the decades) had seen her nephew's wooden-Indian face appear at the girl's mention of a young woman with a baby.

When Sarah's account of her encounter with Erasmus Boyle had finally run its course, Charlie Moon graciously allowed as how this young fellow wouldn't be the last in a long line of prospective beaus who'd be queuing up at the Columbine headquarters front door with flowers and candy and the like. Mistaking the disappointment that glazed her eyes for fatigue at the end of a busy day, he committed an even worse error with a well-meant offer: "Would you like to invite Captain Boyle to supper some evening?"

Unable to speak past the lump in her throat, Sarah shook her head. A few broken heartbeats later, she got up from her chair and hurried away before the tears came in a flood.

A mystified Charlie Moon watched the girl vanish into the hallway and heard Sarah's bedroom door shut softly behind her. The clueless detective eyed his aunt with a worried expression. "Something seems to have upset her." *Probably something she ate.*

Daisy Perika rolled her beady black eyes. *A minute don't pass that someplace in the world some jackass of a man is aggravating a poor woman.*

CHAPTER THIRTY-SIX

THE LONG SHOT

Tuesday Evening

It may be fairly said that understanding the tender gender is not the tall man's long suit. Where women were concerned, Charlie Moon was about as befuddled as the average hairy-leg. But when it comes to taking care of something in his line of work, Aunt Daisy's nephew is the man for the job—and he jumps on it *right now*.

One minute flat after Sarah had locked herself in her bedroom and fallen onto the bed to cry her brown eyes dry, the lawman she adored was upstairs in his office, getting ready to tend to some serious business. Was the tribal investigator strapping the heavy .357 Magnum revolver onto his waist and pinning the GCPD deputy's badge onto his rawhide vest?

No. Things hadn't yet come to that.

Charlie Moon was turning pages in the Granite Creek telephone directory. After checking the B surnames (no Boyles) and H-street listings (no Hollybush), he placed a call to his best friend.

Having just settled into his comfy recliner to watch something or other on cable TV, Scott Parris took a quick look at the caller-ID and answered on the second ring. "What's up, Chucky?"

"Beef prices, at about a nickel a pound."

"I'm always glad to hear good news." Still annoyed by the Monday-afternoon episode involving Wanda Naranjo, Parris gave his deputy an account of how "that crazy woman called 911 *again* and insisted on me coming to see her personally. But when I showed up, she wasn't even at home."

"That was about twenty-four hours ago, pard; has Mrs. Naranjo come home yet?"

"I don't know, Charlie—and frankly, I don't much give a damn." But the hard-nosed cop did, and he was mildly embarrassed by his unprofessional remark. "She's a nurse's aide over at Snyder Memorial. When I get around to it, I'll check to see if she's reported for work at the hospital." Parris preferred a less vexing subject of conversation. "So tell me what's on your mind."

The Ute provided a summary of Sarah's chance meeting with the man who called himself Captain Erasmus Boyle.

Like Moon, Parris was intrigued when he heard the part about the noisy neighbor who sang lullabies to her baby. "And this guy told Sarah he'd make a complaint at the police station." Parris mumbled this comment to himself.

"But don't hold your breath until he shows—I expect the fella was just humoring Sarah."

Scott Parris had not missed the hint of suspicion in his deputy's tone. "You figure this soldier for a wooden nickel—a Captain Bogus?"

"Well, there aren't any Boyles in the local phone book," Moon said. "If that's the fella's real name, he's probably from out of town." The rancher stared unseeingly at the Cattleman's Bank calendar on the wall over his desk. "And any way you slice it, the 144 Hollybush address is a phony."

Parris nodded at his unseen friend. "I know this little burg like the back of my hand and I can flat-out guarantee you that there ain't a Holly-anything in Granite Creek."

"So the guy's lying through his teeth." *But why?*

"You couldn't shoot a sawed-off shotgun in the Silver Mountain Hotel lobby without severely injuring a dozen liars." Parris grinned appreciatively at his paltry witticism.

"This so-called Boyle is probably a John Doe who's married to a Mrs. Jane Doe and they have a houseful of little Does." The town cop glanced at his hugely expensive wide-screen, high-definition, wall-mounted TV screen—which product of state-of-the-art technology was presenting an advertisement for a mouthwatering cheeseburger that topped five thousand calories *without* the heaping helping of honeyed fries. "But we both know you didn't call me at home about some lowlife who's hitting on our favorite kid."

Moon blinked at the prize Hereford bull pictured on the calendar. The magnificent creature returned a stolid bovine stare. "What do you think about the noisy neighbor with the crying baby?"

"Seems like a peculiar story for an out-of-town wolf to be pitching to a sweet young lady he's just met at a park bench." Parris, who shaved maybe every third day, scratched at the reddish stubble on his chin. "Could be the guy's a borderline loony."

That worrisome thought had already crossed Moon's mind. "He may be way yonder *across* the border." He heard an owl hoot in the spruce just outside his office window. "But whatever the state of Boyle's mental health, there's just an off chance that he lives in an apartment one floor down from where Betty Naranjo is hiding from her mother—and that he don't have a landline telephone."

His deputy's hypothesis for why Boyle wasn't in the phone book was reasonable enough, but it didn't explain the Hollybush address. Nevertheless, Scott Parris had learned to pay attention to his own hunches—and Charlie Moon had a keen instinct. The lawman thumbed his remote control to a baseball game. "I'll do some checking on the alleged Captain Erasmus Boyle who lives at an address that don't exist. Drop by my office when you have a few minutes."

"I'll be there tomorrow. Eleven A.M. sharp."

"First thing you hear'll be coffee perking. G'bye, Charlie."

"Good night."

* * *

For many, no doubt, this will be a good night, wherein all the day's cares are washed away by the soothing surf of peaceful slumbers. But sad to say, not for the wide-eyed individual who would gladly have traded a fine pair of eye-teeth for a mouthful of Zs.

No, the insomniac is not the character who calls himself Captain Boyle. During these few hours between dusk and dawn, the soldier's rest will not be disturbed by his neighbors.

The crying child has fallen silent.

The mother's plaintive lullaby is no longer heard.

Indeed, the night's hush is miles wide and leagues deep; a drowsy little mouse could hear her tiny heart beat.

Given this quiet interlude, one might reasonably conclude that mother and child have vacated the premises. Or have they been forcibly evicted—perhaps driven away by the downstairs tenant? Tempting as it is to speculate about such matters, let us concentrate on that wide-eyed citizen who would trade pointy teeth for a few hours' sleep. Who *is* this person, and why is the weary soul deprived of a restful siesta?

Stay tuned.

CHAPTER THIRTY-SEVEN
A FITTING END TO A TERRIBLE DAY

But for whom?

Certainly not for Charlie Moon, whose notion of a terrible day would be the bottom falling out of the market for beef on the hoof, all the ranch's quarter horses coming down with some mysterious equine illness, the new barn burning down, lightning striking a towering haystack, swarms of range worms and locusts ravaging the vast Columbine pastures—and waking up in his upstairs bedroom with an abscessed wisdom tooth just aching to be pulled and not being able to find a pair of rusty wire pliers anywhere in the house.

Not for Sarah, who was fast asleep in her bed at the Columbine, enjoying pleasant dreams about the man sleeping upstairs. But Charlie Moon was no longer the only man in her life. From time to time, a gallant Captain Erasmus Boyle in full dress uniform would drop by, kiss her delicate little hand, compliment her stunning good looks, and inquire whether she'd like to ride to downtown Dallas in his four-mule purple buckboard and take in a moving-picture show starring Chief Ouray, Tom Mix, and Marilyn Monroe.

Even Daisy Perika, who had determined without a doubt that she had lost her lifelong ability to see dead people, would not have described this as a *terrible* day. Like her upbeat, can-do nephew, Aunt Daisy wasted little time dwelling on life's disappointments. As she turned in her bed . . . *At least I can still* hear *the spirits, and talk to them.* And Daisy knew a lot more about her disability today than she had yesterday. Now she was certain that her powers had not simply vanished into nothingness like those Smoke People who can be seen walking on Navajo Lake at the first glow of dawn—only to evaporate into thin wisps of vaporous mist when the sun rises to warm the chill waters. Daisy's misfortune was more like losing her key ring. Such possessions didn't simply fade away—they have been dropped somewhere, misplaced in her purse, or stolen. By some hard thinking (*Where was I when I had it last?*), a little bit of luck (a metallic glint in a dark corner), brass keys and ghost-eyes can be recovered. The partially disabled shaman did not yet understand the details of *how* she had been deprived of her powers, and so had no idea about how she might reverse the process. Nevertheless, the hopeful old soul drifted off to sleep comforted by the firm conviction that the problem could be solved. And would be.

The Unfortunate Is Identified

The citizen who had suffered a truly terrible day was the badly bruised Freddy "Fixit" Whitsun. After extricating himself from the cemetery's electric cart (which had ended up upside down in an irrigation ditch), the late Morris Meusser's replacement had limped back to the custodian's quarters with some vague thoughts about resting and mending for a few hours. The injured employee had encountered an appalled George Hopper, who expressed more concern about the condition of the cemetery's "practically new electric utility vehicle" than of his new hire's health and well-being.

But darkness had finally fallen on Mr. Whitsun's terrible day, and he was about to spend his first night in the cemetery custodian's official residence. Groaning, he switched off the table lamp at his bedside, pulled the covers over his aching body, and exhaled a great sigh. *I feel like I've been run over by all the iron wheels on a railroad train with a big diesel engine, sixteen coaches, and a red caboose.* As he tried to settle in and enjoy the peaceful solitude of Morris Meusser's snug little bedroom, Hopper's dire warning was still ringing in his ears: "You must learn to be more careful with the cemetery's expensive property, Mr. Whitsun—wheeled transport does not grow on trees." And that was just for starters. Once Hopper had gotten his dander up, the man didn't stop until he had run out of hurtful words.

What Whitsun needed was a good night's rest, but as he drifted between periods of half-conscious wakefulness and brief interludes of fitful sleep, he was haunted by Hopper's off-the-wall metaphor. He could not shake the horrifying vision of thousands of miniature golf carts budding on the branches of every aspen, willow, and cottonwood within the boundaries of Granite Creek Cemetery. During these bizarre nightmares, the faithful custodian—under the critical eye of Mr. Hopper—would deftly pluck plump little wheeled vehicles from trees heavy with new birth, and carefully place each whining machine into its own minuscule wicker basket.

It was enough to drive a man stark raving mad.

After midwifing several dozen such unnatural infants, Freddy Whitsun finally made up his mind to stay wide awake all night. But when he made this decision, was the man actually awake? An interesting question, but at the moment one for which a trustworthy answer is not forthcoming. For days afterward Mr. Whitsun would ask himself, *Was that for real or was it just—*

—An Awful Nightmare?

With the noble intention of *lighting a small candle in the darkness,* the hopeful insomniac fumbled around in the unfamiliar space until his calloused fingers found the lamp, turned it on—and promptly knocked the appliance off the small table. As it crashed to the floor, the sixty-watt bulb exploded with a loud "pop!"

His darkness and dismay now complete, Freddy Whitsun concluded that this incident was merely the latest in a string of recent misfortunes that would never cease. *Sometimes, no matter how hard a fella tries to do his best, things just go from bad to worse.* But being the sort of man who yearned to understand the root causes of his troubles, Mr. Fixit attempted to reconstruct what had happened when he was searching for the dead animal whose stink the old Indian woman's sharp nose had detected.

When I was lookin' under the back of the truck, my loose overall gallus must've got snagged on the hook where Morris used to hang buckets and whatnot when he was alive. So far, so good. *But how did that fool machine get started up and drag me off?* He frowned like a frustrated nine-year-old attempting to fathom a mind-numbing "word-problem" in his arithmetic book. *I must've not got the hand brake set good, and it slipped and off I went like a big boar hog drug away by a tractor.* Not that the handyman had ever witnessed a farmer towing a fattened swine behind a fine Farmall machine, but drowsy men do tend to come up with oddball metaphors. But, to his credit, Freddy (who was not an advocate of Jungian synchronicity) harbored a slight doubt about the simultaneous concurrence of a hooked overall suspender and a slipped hand brake. Two bad breaks in the space of a couple of heartbeats seemed an unlikely coincidence, but far stranger things had occurred in the shaky relationship between man and machine.

All these troubles should have been sufficient for his day, but like the late Morris Meusser (who had lain in this very bed during the final hours of his life), the new cemetery employee was about to be plagued by strange sounds in the night.

No, not the scuff-scuffs that had alerted his checker-playing buddy to some funny business out there in the cemetery. Nor would Whitsun be alarmed by the mournful hooting of big-eyed owls, a lonely coyote's yipping howls, or antique plumbing that goes bumpity-rumpity-gurgle in the night. We are talking Strange with a capital *S*.

This man who feared disembodied spirits began to hear *voices*.

Initially, the vague vocalizations seemed to come from somewhere far away. Mr. Whitsun could not make out any words, but there were guttural mutterings. Eerie murmurings. Sinister whisperings. But as his heart went pumpity-bump under his bruised ribs, the muttering-murmuring-whisperings drew ever closer. One annoying botheration often leads to another, and by and by, Whitsun was convinced that he saw someone's *face* at the moonlit bedroom window. Worse still, the pale countenance was looking directly at him.

As if one some*one* was not sufficient to get the job done, there suddenly were *two* faces on the opposite side of the windowpane. Male and female. Moreover, the voices were now distinct and their purpose unmistakable.

The masculine specter—a rather grim-faced presence—asserted that Mr. Whitsun was a less-than-upstanding citizen. To support this indictment, his self-appointed accuser provided a lengthy list of misdeeds, starting with a four-year-old Freddy painting the snow-white family kitten a detestable shade of purple. After pausing to elaborate on a few recent offenses that particularly rankled, the prosecutor terminated with a lurid description of how the new hire had (through inexcusable criminal negligence!) seriously damaged an expensive cemetery vehicle.

When this vicious diatribe was complete, the feminine entity expressed pity for Mr. Whitsun—whom she characterized as a pathetic creature of limited intellect and the warped product of a dysfunctional family. The accused (his defender asserted) was undoubtedly doing the best he could under difficult circumstances, and allowances must be made for such unfortunates. After all, the pitiful fellow had not actually *intended* to commit any offenses—he didn't have sufficient imagination to plan a premeditated hurtful act. The counsel for the defense did not suggest that the haunted man should be excused—rather that he must be *forgiven*! And unconditionally.

Well. That was a furlong too much for the angry male presence, who sneered at such bleeding-heart sentiments. He insisted that Whitsun was an idiot bungler who couldn't hammer a ten-penny nail through a pine two-by-four without mashing his thumb a half-dozen times and bending the nail to boot. This so-called handyman (he said) ought to change his Freddy Fixit sign to read Freddy Foul-up.

Even a certified stained-glass saint can endure only so much mean-spirited bad-mouthing, and one could hardly have faulted this ordinary sinner if Mr. Whitsun had rolled out of the bed and rushed outside in a rage to deal harshly with his accuser and thank the kindly lady.

But, unlike the prior custodian, Morris Meusser's replacement had no intention of leaving the secure residence in the middle of the night to confront this ghostly pair. Not on your sweet life. It had already been an awful day and Freddy "Fixit" Whitsun simply wasn't up to it. The bruised, aching man pulled the quilt over his head; his massive body quivered with shivers and shudders.

Poor fellow.

CHAPTER THIRTY-EIGHT

THE LAWMEN SIZE UP THE SITUATION

Wednesday, 11:03 A.M.

After muttering insults at a gang of enthusiastic workmen who were happily jackhammering a perfectly serviceable section of Copper Street into a pile of unsightly asphalt rubble, Scott Parris slammed his office window shut against the racket. The chief of police plopped into the chair behind his desk and addressed his guest. "You want me to tell you what that's all about?" He pointed in the general direction of the destruction. "Graft, that's what!"

Settling into a battered county-issue armchair, Charlie Moon prepared himself for the expected lecture.

Parris did not disappoint. With considerable arm waving, growling, and scowling, the lawman alleged an unsavory connection between the mayor and the construction company that was low bidder on the lucrative contract—and by a "suspiciously narrow margin." He reminded the Ute that the scoundrel who owned the favored firm was the mayor's brother-in-law and District Attorney Pug Bullet's fishing buddy. The angry cop ended his familiar harangue by assuring Moon, "One of these days—and it won't be long—I'll find a way to bust the whole crooked lot of 'em!"

If you don't bust a blood vessel first. "I hope you do, pardner." Moon wondered whether Parris had checked on

Wanda Naranjo yet, but thought it best not to raise that sensitive subject.

Suddenly remembering why his best friend had dropped in, Parris glanced sheepishly at the rancher. "Uh . . . I've been doing my best to find out something about this fella Sarah met in the park." *What was his name?*

Moon read the question on his friend's face. "Erasmus Boyle."

"Uh . . . right." *How does Charlie do that?* "And before you ask, I'll tell you that Sarah's new friend hasn't shown up at GCPD to make a complaint about his noisy upstairs neighbors. Not that either one of us expected him to." The lawman shuffled through a disordered assortment of papers on his desk. "You may be interested to know that I got some assistance from your favorite librarian." *Charlie oughta pop the question to that blue-eyed little cutie-pie.*

Despite Moon's firm intention to maintain a straight face, his lips were determined to smile at this reference to pretty Patsy Poynter. "How's the lady doing?"

"Seems to be happy with her promotion to the reference desk." *Where is that damn printout?* "She helped me wade through a great big stack of old Granite Creek telephone books and I don't know how many reels of microfilm."

"And you found a bucketful of Boyles?"

"'Fraid not." Finding the computer printout that Patsy had provided, Parris squinted at it. "There was only one family of Boyles, and they moved away or died out more than twenty-five years ago." He glanced over the paperwork at his friend. "All except for a Miss Emily Boyle."

Moon was pleased to hear this news. "If the lady's still in town, she must have an unlisted telephone number."

"In a manner of speaking. Miss Boyle has a phone in her room, but you have to place a call to her through the switchboard." Parris reached for his coffee cup, which rattled on the desktop. *Damn jackhammers!* "Miss Emily is an in-mate at—" *No, that's not what they call the folks who live there. But what do they* . . . His big face brightened when he remembered the word. "She's a *resident* at the Pine Ridge Nursing Home."

The bluegrass banjo picker grinned. Along with "Soldier's Joy," "Pine Ridge" was one of Charlie Moon's all-time favorite tunes. "A senior citizen, then."

"Ninety-seven years and counting."

The Ute pictured a frail little old lady knitting woolen socks. "That's a lot of winters gone by."

"Yeah, and I ain't getting any younger myself." Parris lifted the coffee cup to his lips and spilled a dribble on his chin. "Dammit!" He shot an angry glance at the window. "This keeps up, they'll shake the whole building down around us."

"I don't feel the least vibration, pardner. And the jackhammers have shut down."

When Scott Parris cocked his right ear, all he could hear was the low hum of traffic. "So what're you saying—I can't take a drink of coffee without spilling it?"

Before Moon could respond, Parris's desk lamp went out.

The angry cop glared at the offending fixture. "The idiots probably stopped hammering because they cut an electric line!"

"I don't think so." Moon raised his chin to draw his friend's attention to the ceiling fan, which was spinning full-speed.

Parris's sunburned face deepened to a dangerous shade of red. "The lightbulb must've popped a filament."

As if to disprove this reasonable conjecture, the desk lamp came on again.

"Must be a bad connection in the socket." Parris glared at the healthy bright light. "Or a goofed-up lamp switch."

"Well . . . maybe." The playful Indian feigned an uneasy expression.

Parris bristled like a scalded bulldog. "Maybe *what?*"

"Oh, I don't think you'd want to know, pardner."

"Whatta you mean by that crack?"

"You're in a kinda testy mood, and I wouldn't want to upset you."

"Sure you would, Charlie." Parris jutted his chin. "Go ahead—take your best shot."

"Okay, but don't say I didn't warn you." Moon hesitated. "What with your coffee cup acting up and electric light goin' on and off—there's just the off chance that you might be dealing with . . . a feisty *poltergeist*."

"What the hell's that?"

"I'd rather not say." To conceal a smile, the merry Indian raised his mug to take a sip of so-so station-house coffee. "But if you was to ask Aunt Daisy, she might tell you it was an old Ute word that got picked up by the German immigrants and exported to Europe."

"So translate."

"It means 'noisy ghost.' "

"*Ghost my hind leg!*" *Silliest damn thing I ever heard.* But Parris's face had paled to that shade that crayon manufacturers label "Merely Sunburned."

Warming to his subject, Charlie Moon forged ahead. "Folks who claim to know about such things will tell you that ninety-nine percent of poltergeists are harmless; they get their kicks out of playing little tricks on edgy folk."

Parris's stony smile could have passed for a granite gargoyle's hideous grimace. "Go ahead, Charlie—have your fun. Tell me about the other one percent."

"Well . . ." Moon's face darkened. "From what I've heard—ever' now and again there's a dangerous poltergeist that causes serious trouble." He paused as if remembering something pertinent to the subject. "When I was about eleven years old, I read this creepy book about the Bell Witch, where some awful things happened to a nice farm family in Tennessee almost two hundred years ago. If I recollect correctly, the way that nasty business got started was with tin cups rattling in pewter saucers, the flames in kerosene lamps going off and then coming on again, and—"

The desk lamp went off. And immediately flashed on again.

"I don't want to hear another word about it," Parris snapped. "So let's drop the subject and get back to police business."

"Whatever you say." Moon saluted his buddy with the coffee mug.

The haunted man's brow furrowed. "What were we talking about?"

"The elderly lady in Pine Ridge Nursing Home." Moon placed the empty mug on Parris's desk. "With a little bit of luck, maybe Miss Emily Boyle has a young relative by the name of Erasmus. He might be renting a room right here in Granite Creek." A hopeful afterthought: "And maybe Captain Erasmus Boyle isn't in the phone book, because—like lots of young folks nowadays—he could be making all his calls on a mobile phone."

"That's a hatful of maybes and mights and could-bes." Parris raised his gaze to the ceiling fan, which was swinging back and forth. Ever so slightly. And ever so slowly. *Charlie's making that stuff up about noisy polter-ghosts.* The cop forced himself to focus his attention on the poker-faced Indian. "But even if this Erasmus that Sarah met in U.S. Grant Park turns out to be the old lady's relative—and he does hang his hat somewhere in Granite Creek—Emily Boyle probably wouldn't be able to tell us a thing about him. When I called Pine Ridge about an hour ago, the nurse at the front desk told me that 'Miss Em has some problems with her memory.'"

"Uh-oh."

"You said it." As his desk lamp flickered, Parris felt a sour coldness in the pit of his stomach. How sour and cold? Like he'd swallowed a pickle-juice ice cube whole. "On her good days, the poor old soul might be able recall her own name. On her bad days . . ." He didn't want to go there.

Moon was beginning to get the grim picture. "So which one of us lucky fellas has the privilege of paying a call on Miss Boyle?"

Parris's grin was weak as one-bag-to-the-gallon green tea. "You want to volunteer?"

The deputy did not. "Tell you what." The Ute produced a worn (lucky) 1992 quarter dollar from his watch pocket. "Call it, and you get to interview Miss Boyle." Before his friend could think of a reason to protest, Moon had flipped the disk.

Virtually mesmerized by the ascent of the coin, Parris watched as the two-bit piece seemed to rotate ever more slowly on its parabolic ascent. It was as if time itself had slowed to observe—or perhaps to fix—the outcome. "Tails," he heard his mouth say. *Be heads or be dead!* Clenching his teeth, the tough cop imagined himself biting the coin in half.

The silver-clad copper quarter reached its apex a hand's-breadth below the ceiling fan, paused for an infinitesimal instant, then began the journey down. Faster now, a twirling blur.

The coin of the realm plopped onto the chief of police's varnished desktop. Twirled like a spinning top. Then . . . *ker-plop!*

Moon and Parris gazed at George Washington's stern profile. The Man Who Would Not Be King seemed to disapprove of the lawman using his likeness for a frivolous wager.

Scott Parris grinned, as his paternal granddaddy would have said, "Like a hungry 'possum with a ripe pawpaw."

Charlie Moon managed to conceal his dismay. "Looks like I win." But it didn't seem fair. *Scott paid a call on Patsy Poynter and I get to interview Grandma Moses.* As he eased himself up from the armchair and turned to go, Parris's deputy paused to take a look at the penduluming ceiling fan. "You might want to consult with an expert."

Parris's uneasy gaze followed the Indian's. *Charlie's right. I should call an electrician.* "Got anybody in mind?"

"Well . . . you might try Mr. M. V. Ingram."

"Who's he?"

"Author of that scary book about the Bell Witch." With this parting shot, the Ute tipped his black Stetson and made a brisk exit.

CHAPTER THIRTY-NINE

ONE OF THOSE DODGY
SPUR-OF-THE-MOMENT NOTIONS

The germ of the idea infected Charlie Moon's mind about nine seconds after he'd pulled away from the curb at the Granite Creek Police Station. Did he take a microsecond to think it over? Of course not. He immediately braked on Copper Street, executed an illegal U-turn, and headed back the way he'd come.

What causes a generally sensible soul who's on his way to visit a little old lady in a nursing home to suddenly reverse course and rush pell-mell into the dark unknown?

Though this impulse seemed to have appeared out of nowhere, the lonely man's urge was almost certainly inspired by Scott Parris's mention minutes earlier of a certain reference librarian. It is also possible that the dogged pursuit of Mr. Moon by sweet little Sarah Frank was an underlying cause of his detour. Excess testosterone might be involved. Or perhaps this move had been brewing in his fevered brain for a long time and Right Now just happened to be the propitious moment. Whatever the combination of root causes might have been for this about-to-happen train wreck, Moon slowed the Expedition as he approached the Granite Creek Public Library, braked it to a halt by a big fat fire hydrant that was painted blood red and situated by a sign that shouted, NO PARKING! In a deadly serious monotone, this addendum: VEHICLES WILL BE TOWED AWAY AT OWNER'S EXPENSE.

Only old ladies and other rational folk pay attention to such warnings.

Exiting his trusty Ford Motor Company automobile, the fervent fellow sprinted to the entrance, barged through the front door—and stopped dead still. Even the bravest soldier will have second thoughts when rushing a machine-gun nest armed with a rusty bayonet. Moon considered a hasty retreat. *I don't have to do it right this minute.* True. There would always be another day. But that was not the Cowboy Way. Gathering all his considerable courage, our hero adjusted his Stetson to a jaunty angle, hooked his thumbs under his belt, and sauntered nonchalantly over to the reference desk.

The blonde, blue-eyed lady looked up and flashed a smile. "Well hello, Charlie." *I wonder what brings him here.* The red-hot girl singer in Charlie Moon's Columbine Grass bluegrass band thought it probable that the banjo picker wanted to talk to her about . . . *that new "Cripple Creek" arrangement he's been working on.* But on second thought . . . *It's more likely that he wants to follow up on the business that Chief Parris was nosing around about this morning.* "Are you looking for somebody named Boyle?"

"Yeah, but that's not why I'm here." Moon towered over her oak desk. "I've got something personal to ask you."

Her smile brightened to that dazzling kind that is featured in toothpaste advertisements. *He wants to take me to the big square dance down at Salida.*

Wrong again, Patsy P.

It's now or never. Feeling a little dizzy, Moon unhooked his thumbs from the belt and leaned to place both hands on Miss Poynter's desk. "Have you ever thought about . . ." The words stuck in his throat.

Experienced librarians are practiced multitaskers. Somehow, the lady managed to frown without losing her smile. "Thought about *what*?" *He's so cute.*

Moon heard his numb mouth say, "About living on a ranch."

"Oh, sure—ever since I was a little girl that's been my big dream." She laughed. "Do you have a little log cabin and a section of prime pasture you want to lease?"

As he shook his head, the stockman's face was beginning to burn.

She couldn't resist teasing him. "I bet you're tired of your own cooking and want to hire somebody to do it for you. Do you see me as a chef?"

"Uh . . . not exactly." *But you're getting warm.*

Patsy laughed again. "Then what do I have to do to live on a ranch?"

"Well . . ." Moon gulped. "You might think about marrying a rancher." *There. I said it.* Buoyed by this success, he added, "So what do you think about that?"

Patsy was wide-eyed with surprise—so much so that her mouth made an O. "Well . . . I can't really say." A shy, sly hesitation. "Not until some rancher asks me."

A sensible answer and a sweet invitation.

The tall, lean man nodded the black John B. Stetson that he habitually removed in the presence of a lady. *Well, here goes.* Charlie opened his mouth to finish the job. Couldn't get the words past his lips.

As her smile gradually slipped away, Patsy's big blue eyes asked, *Well?*

The man who'd faced down armed-to-the-teeth maniacs, a hungry cougar who'd had him pegged for lunch, and Aunt Daisy at her worst—choked. Literally. *I'm the rancher who's asking you* stuck in Moon's throat. He blinked at Miss Poynter like a man whose brain was out to lunch.

The pretty lady arched an exquisite eyebrow.

Remembering to take his hat off, Moon cleared his throat—and (manfully) tried again. Failed again.

This was a furlong or two beyond embarrassing.

What was a steely-eyed hombre to do?

Charlie Moon is about to show us.

Watch the tongue-tied feller turn on the heel of his left-most cowboy boot, don his black Stetson, and depart. The lifelong bachelor retreated with as much dignity as a man in his situation could muster, which wasn't overly much. The library exit loomed miles away as he pushed a heavy book cart aside and slogged his way toward the street door through a mucky alligator-infested swamp, two patches of skin tingling hotly on each side of his straight-as-an-arrow spine. Charlie Moon could feel Pretty Patsy's laser-blue eyes boring smoking holes into the back of his denim jacket.

When (days later) he emerged from the library, Mr. Moon was immensely invigorated by a whiff of fresh air and the heady sense of escape. Pulling away in his Expedition, he tried to focus on the sunny side of the mountain. *Well . . . that didn't turn out as bad as it might've.* No worse than getting bucked off a snorty bronc and landing in a cluster of prickly-pear cactus where a family of angry rattlesnakes was fighting for squatter's rights with a do-or-die colony of deadly poisonous foot-long scorpions. And while you're getting fanged and stang by the combined shebang of venomous vipers and oversize arachnids—the fun-loving iron-shod bronc saunters over to give you four or five friendly kicks in the head.

When it comes to self-administered over-the-counter medications, a spoonful of positive thinking can be moderately effective, and the same can be said for a smidgen of self-deception. But when a man's attempt to woo his favorite lady into a condition of permanent merger has turned into a first-class fiasco, there's nothing quite so restorative as getting himself a long way from the scene of the humiliation. Which is why the cowboy was hankering to saddle up and ride away to anyplace that was a fair piece from the Granite Creek Public Library. Such as Big Timber, Montana, or Linton, Indiana—or the Pine Ridge Nursing Home, where he would interview a little old lady who might not remember her own name, much less recall someone who called himself Captain Erasmus Boyle. That was fine with Charlie Moon; wasting a few minutes in a quiet, peaceful place seemed like just the remedy.

So Señor Luna headed thataway rightaway and *muy pronto*.

CHAPTER FORTY

ANOTHER BLUE-EYED LADY

The Pine Ridge Nursing Home was located in the county's much-ballyhooed Snyder Medical Complex. Charlie Moon turned his Expedition off Copper Street and onto Snyder Avenue, a tree-lined strip of blacktop that snaked around the sixteen acres wherein resided the Snyder Memorial Hospital, the Physician's Medical Arts Building, and the Nurse's Education Center, which was staffed by Rocky Mountain Polytechnic University faculty. At the farthest boundary from busy Copper Street and adjacent to a vast expanse of national forest, the single-story redbrick nursing home was situated appropriately on a low ridge, and nestled into a shady grove of pines, spruce, and aspens.

Still rattled by his encounter with Patsy Poynter, the lifelong bachelor parked his wheels under the quaking leaves of a teenage aspen and strode down a broad cemented walkway to the front entrance. *I guess I should have thought more about what I was going to say before I went into the library.* A sober afterthought. But deep down, Charlie Moon knew that if he'd resorted to cerebration, he would never have broached the delicate subject. It was, the veteran of a foreign war realized, much like jumping out of a low-flying airplane at night with a puny little parachute strapped to your back. *Some things just don't bear thinking about.* A man just gritted his teeth, said a prayer, and stepped into the abyss, hoping for the best. Maybe that was the problem. *I forget to pray.*

On a spruce branch barely a yard above the brim of his John B. Stetson lid, a cheerful tuft-eared squirrel chuckled derisively at the passing mortal.

His Visit with Miss Emily

The receptionist was busily repainting her pointy crimson fingernails a sickly shade of pond-slime green. The young lady blinked when she noticed the stranger making his way through a small forest of potted palms. *Well—I wonder who this long, tall cowboy's come to see?* A wistful sigh. *Wish it was me* . . . "How may I help you, sir?"

Charlie Moon doffed his fine black hat and smiled back at the pleasingly plump, prettyish woman who (for all he knew) might have been anywhere between eighteen and twenty-eight. The rectangle pinned to her blue smock advised those who didn't know that she was STEPHANIE. "I'm here to see Miss Emily Boyle."

The girl with eight green fingernails and two red ones cocked her head at this announcement. "You're not family."

The Indian admitted that he was not.

Stephanie tried again. "A friend?"

"I'd like to be."

"I'm sorry to be so nosy, but—"

"I'm here on official business." Parris's deputy placed a picture ID on her desk.

The myopic picked it up and squinted. "Charlie Moon . . . Oh, I've heard about *you*." *You're that Indian rancher who's also a cop.* Stephanie gave the dangerous-looking fellow a closer look. *A couple of years ago, he was mixed up in that awful crime spree where all those people at the hospital were murdered.* Satisfied, she passed the plasticized card back to him and flashed a smile that exposed the glint of a gold tooth with a tiny diamond set in it. "You plan to arrest Miss Em?"

Moon returned a grin. "Not unless she gets rough with me."

"Hah!"

"I promise not to be a bother."

"I'm sure you won't be. Miss Boyle's in B-105." The receptionist got up from an armless secretary's chair. "I'll take you back there—for all the good it'll do you."

The deputy followed the 140-pound young woman, who stepped along with a brisk, athletic gait. "Miss Boyle doesn't like visitors?"

"Miss Boyle doesn't like nothing or nobody," Stephanie replied over her shoulder. "And she's practically stone deaf—you'll have to yell at her."

"I'll turn up the volume some." *This'll turn out to be a sure-enough snipe hunt.* He watched the receptionist open the door to B-105 and poke her head in.

Stephanie turned to flash another smile at Moon. "Well, at least she's awake." When a pager on her belt buzzed and a computerized voice reported a minor emergency in A-122, she hurried away.

Hat in hand, Charlie Moon entered a room that was illuminated by a TV screen mounted on the wall. As his eyes adjusted to the inner twilight, he got his first look at the occupant. The aged woman seated in a black wheelchair was hunched forward as if engrossed in the decades-old *Flintstones* cartoon flickering on the high-definition screen. "Excuse me, ma'am . . ." No response. He raised his voice by about ten decibels. "Hello!"

The tiny, shrunken figure might have been an Egyptian mummy that a morbid prankster had propped in the wheeled chair.

As he came closer, Charlie Moon noticed that her gnarled hand was stretched forth, frozen in a reaching gesture. On the floor was a wadded-up piece of tissue paper. A viscous fluid dripped from Miss Boyle's nostrils. He shook his head. *Poor old soul.* The lawman knelt, picked up the tissue, and wiped the woman's nose.

She turned her head; the cool blue eyes examining the stranger with a frank disinterest. Her lips parted to exhale a whispered, "Thank you."

Unwilling to yell into the deaf woman's ear, Moon murmured, "You're welcome."

"I'm not quite so hard of hearing as they think, but don't you go telling anyone." The lips that had whispered curled into a mischievous smile. "Playing deaf is my way of avoiding annoying conversations—and finding out what people *really* think about me."

"Well, you had me fooled."

"Who are you?"

"Charlie Moon." The Ute squatted to get his eyes level with the lady's. "I'm here on police business."

"Do tell?" The aged lady looked hopeful. "Has someone in the nursing home committed a heinous felony?"

"Not so far as I know. But if you don't mind too much, I'd like to ask you a question or two."

"Go right ahead, copper." She snatched the tissue from his hand and gave her nose another wipe. "But I can't remember what I had for lunch, and that was just a few minutes ago."

"I bet you can remember a lot about your family."

"Oh, my." She arched a slender gristle of cartilage where an attractive eyebrow had once graced a lovely face. "Has one of my straitlaced relatives gotten crosswise of the law?"

"I hope not." On this occasion, Moon popped the critical question with ease: "Do you know a young man by the name of Erasmus Boyle?"

"Erasmus!" Miss Emily's back stiffened, her face froze. "I should have known *he'd* be in some kind of trouble."

Pay dirt! "Has he every been in the military?"

"Him? I should say *not*!" The old lady laughed. "My nephew has neither the desire nor character to pursue any kind of *honorable* profession."

"What kind of work does he do?"

The elderly woman turned her face toward the TV, where Fred and Barney were watching a cute pet dinosaur cavort about the cave.

The determined lawman pressed on. "Anything you could tell me about Erasmus would be very helpful—"

"No—it is out of the question!"

"Ma'am?"

"I'm sorry; you're a nice young man. I have already made it clear that Erasmus is the black sheep of the Boyle family." She raised her chin in a stubborn gesture. "I have nothing further to say about him."

"All I need to know is where he's living—"

"Good *day,* sir!"

And that was that.

Accepting defeat gracefully, the deputy unfolded his lanky form until he was erect. Standing tall again, Charlie Moon smiled down at the resolute face glaring at the TV. "Thank you, ma'am."

Miss Emily had reverted to her stone-deaf persona.

As he took his leave, it was inevitable that this visit would remind Charlie Moon of his recent encounter with Patsy Poynter. Which it did. It is said (by Those Who Know) that A Sensible Man Learns from His Failures. Aunt Daisy's nephew was no exception to this rule. After recalling any number of pithy old sayings that had nothing to do with anything in particular, and applying his keen intellect to several seconds of deep analytical thought, our philosopher came to an insightful conclusion that is far too erudite for a detailed exposition herein. But any cowboy cook worth his pepper and salt knows how to *bile that cabbage down* and Charlie Moon summed it up thisaway: *This hasn't been a good day for talking to blue-eyed ladies.*

CHAPTER FORTY-ONE

A BRIEF CONVERSATION

As he motored away from the nursing home, mulling over what he'd learned from Miss Emily Boyle, Charlie Moon's mobile phone played a few bars from one of Scott Parris's all-time favorite cowboy ballads ("O' Bury Me Not on the Lone Prairie").

His deputy took the call. "Hello, pardner."

"And a big howdy to you, Charlie." The chief of police cleared his throat and got right down to business. "Just had a chat with my contact at the hospital. Since Friday morning last week, nobody at Snyder Memorial has seen hide nor hair of Wanda Naranjo—and that feisty little nurse's aide is automatically sacked if she don't show up by five P.M. today. I'd give a day's pay to know where she's gone to ground." *One way or another, that woman's up to no good.* "Did you have time yet to interview Emily Boyle?"

"Yes I did."

"So what'd you find out?"

"About half as much as I wanted to." Moon slowed for a traffic light that had turned from green to yellow. "But it turns out that the Erasmus Boyle that Sarah met in U.S. Grant Park is Miss Boyle's nephew."

"That's great, Charlie." Parris's big voice boomed in his ear. "I figured the old lady would be a dead end."

"Well, that's all I got. Except that the senior citizen doesn't think too highly of her nephew."

"So where do we find Erasmus Boyle?"

"That's the half I *didn't* find out, pard. Maybe the old lady don't know where her relative hangs his hat, but if she does she wasn't about to tell me." Moon stopped at the red light. "Mr. Boyle is probably renting an apartment somewhere in Granite Creek—or somebody's spare bedroom."

"Wait a minute—did I hear you say *Mr.* Boyle?"

"You did. He's no captain. His aunt says he's never been in the military."

"When a young man meets an attractive young lady, a little bragging is understandable, Charlie. But a fellow that lies about being an officer in the United States armed services is not a suitable companion for Sarah."

"That's the way I see it." As the Ute watched the stoplight, a dot of red fire glinted in each eye.

"D'you suppose Sarah has any plans to see this rascal again?"

"I don't think so." Charlie Moon pulled away as the traffic light winked a green eye at him. "But she hasn't finished that university project to interview homeless folk in Grant Park. Maybe Miss Boyle's disreputable nephew plans to meet Sarah there."

Parris chuckled. "If he does, guess who else'll be there to say howdy to this counterfeit captain."

The Ute Indian presented a flinty grin. "You and me, pard."

Very commendable. And the combination of Charlie Moon and Scott Parris had proved formidable on any number of previous do-or-die run-ins with hardened felons. Even so, Erasmus Boyle was not a man to trifle with—and despite our best intentions, events have a way of getting ahead of us.

CHAPTER FORTY-TWO

TROUBLE IN PARADISE

The paradise referred to is not, of course, that idyllic realm with a capital *P*. The lesser version—though barely a dim shadow of the real McCoy—is nevertheless the one place on this earth that is most like heaven to Charlie Moon. Not that he plays a harp at all hours and whiles the day away with old friends who've passed away. Daisy Perika's nephew is a plucky banjo plucker who leans toward bluegrass, and though his voice is not unpleasant to hear, the lonely rancher whose range includes both baritone and bass generally confines his crooning to the privacy of the prairie or his shower. Speaking of the latter, he is just about ready to go upstairs and lather up. And would have except for one of those annoying circumstances that tends to occur at the most inconvenient of times—and on this occasion, served to remind the part-time deputy that he was a full-time rancher.

Pseudo-Trouble

Pete Bushman rapped his knobby knuckles on the kitchen door.

Charlie Moon opened the oak portal, but not quite wide enough to admit his fuzzy-faced foreman, who had a wad of Red Man chewing tobacco bulging in his left jaw.

"G'mornin'," Bushman said. His eyes darted about for a suitable place to deposit spittle.

Moon shook his head. *Spit on my fine redwood porch and you're dead.*

Receiving the message loud and clear, the foreman went to spit into the yard. Thus relieved, he returned to confront the tall Indian who blocked the doorway.

"So what's up, Pete?" *Like I don't know.*

Bushman consulted his pocket watch. "We was supposed to meet almost half an hour ago."

The Ute jutted his chin. "Who says so?"

Moon's ranking employee puffed up his meager chest, returned the ticking chronometer to his vest pocket, and glowered at the owner of the outfit. "Yesterday afternoon, I called and left a message on your phone and said we'd get together this morning at half past—"

"Not going to happen," Moon said.

The foreman's eyes popped. "What?"

"Don't 'what' me, Pete—you heard what I said."

Mr. Bushman blinked at this curt response from the generally amiable Indian. He was, to say the least—peeved. To say the most—nonplussed. "Well . . . when *do* you want to get together and talk about all the ranchin' problems we need to deal with?"

"If and when I do, I'll let you know."

"Could you at least give me some idea, so I can—"

"No."

The foreman's jaw dropped. "No?"

"Yes." Moon offered a genial smile. "Good day, Pete." *That wasn't any trouble at all.* The boss closed the door with a sense of soul-glowing gratification.

So what is about to turn sour in Mr. Moon's little slice of paradise? We are about to find out.

The Actual Trouble

Preferring to be served up somewhere between frozen solid and well done, Charlie Moon started his morning shower the same way every day, by running water from the tub faucet into his hand until the temperature was Too Blamed Hot, then mixing in some cold H_2O until the combo was Just Right. But something wasn't quite. Right, that is.

I don't like the feel of this. He cranked the hot-water valve wide open and waited with his fingers under the spout, hoping the temperature would eventually rise from tepid to steaming hot. It did not.

"Dang it!"

Yes, that's what the disappointed bather said. One morning when he was six years of age, little Charlie had repeated his father's favorite cuss word in his mother's presence and Momma had washed his mouth out with homemade lye soap. This hard lesson had made a lasting impression on the youth. Having reported and analyzed what he said out loud, we may proceed to what he thought:

Pilot light in the water heater must've gone out.

Without reason or rhyme, things like that do happen from time to time.

Five minutes later, dressed in faded denim jeans and down-at-the heels deerskin moccasins, Charlie Moon was downstairs. More specifically, he was in the tool room off the kitchen, where, in addition to a fascinating variety of hand and power tools, resided the Columbine headquarters' primary eighty-gallon propane water heater. Also the backup.

All he had to do to direct hot water to the upstairs bathroom was turn a couple of valves. Which he did. The backup tank was working fine and there was no big hurry to fix the one that was on the blink. But Mr. Moon was not the sort of mechanic who can walk away from a problem without at least checking things out. He got on his knees, removed the corroded metal cover from the bottom of the water heater, and got a gander at the main burner. "Aha!" *Just as I sus-pected.*

The pilot light was out on the main heater. It makes a fel-low feel good when his prediction turns out to be spot-on. Makes him feel even better to find a problem that is trivial to remedy. This one was straightforward.

I can take care of that in a jiffy.

He turned the control knob to Pilot.

Grabbed the charcoal lighter that was hanging on a nail conveniently near the water heater and switched on the blue butane flame.

Pressed the water-heater button that enabled gas to flow to the pilot light.

Heard the slight hiss of propane.

Touched the butane lighter to the pilot light nozzle.

Smiled to see the pilot fixture ignite.

Counted slowly to thirty while the pilot light heated the adjacent thermocouple assembly. For good measure, he added another twenty counts.

Then released the Bypass button.

Watched the pilot flame shrink . . . and go out.

That old thermocouple must be shot. Not a problem. *Next time I'm in town, I'll pick up a new one.*

Five minutes later, Charlie Moon was in the upstairs shower again, enjoying hot water from the backup tank. Also singing loudly. "Jack of Diamonds." (There's another man who sings it better, but Michael Martin Murphey was busy rehearsing for a gig down in Red River, New Mexico.)

Showers are not only good for singing, but there is something about the pleasant sting of hot water and the smell of soap that makes a man think.

About what?

All sorts of important matters.

What he'll have for breakfast. *Big slab of ham and three eggs.*

Going to check out the grass over on the east five sections. *A nice little thundershower passed over that pasture last night.*

How glad he is that he'll be able to fix the water heater without calling a plumber and his helper to come do the job and pay the plumber's bill, which wouldn't be peanuts considering that he'd have to drive all the way out to the ranch from town and then back again. *A hundred bucks minimum, and that's before they get the toolbox outta the truck.*

And, Wanda Naranjo. How so? Because . . . *When the lady had a little leak under her kitchen sink that she could've fixed herself if she'd known how, she had to call a plumber.* And is so often the case, the guy hadn't even shown up. *The fella was probably working on another job and it took longer than he thought it would.*

Charlie Moon toweled himself off and commenced to get dressed.

I wonder which one Mrs. Naranjo called?

Most folks had a favorite barber, auto mechanic, dentist—and plumber.

After pulling on his old, comfortable work boots, Moon stomped across the upstairs hallway to his office, where he found the Granite Creek telephone directory. He let his fingers walk through the Yellow Pages until he got to the *P*s. *There are five plumber shops in town. Nowadays, they called themselves "mechanical contractors."* The rancher reached for the cordless phone on his desk. Twelve minutes later, he'd talked to the boss or dispatcher in all five shops and asked every one of them the same question—and gotten precisely the same answer: "No."

CHAPTER FORTY-THREE

SOME THINGS TO THINK ABOUT

During a late-morning breakfast with the ladies, Charlie Moon pretended to listen while Aunt Daisy made enough petulant complaints to outdo quarrelsome foreman Pete Bushman on his best day. The amiable nephew "mmm-hmmed" at frequent intervals, but Daisy knew that his thoughts were faraway. *I might as well be talking to a cedar stump.*

After the meal, Charlie Moon helped a remarkably silent Sarah Frank wash the dishes. These duties duly attended to, the meditative man wandered away in what appeared to be a more or less aimless fashion. Inevitably, Moon ended up down at the riverbank—a solitary place where a fellow could do some thinking. Nothing earthshaking. The cowboy ruminated about ordinary matters. How tasty this morning's ham and eggs had been. When the gray rain clouds might drift over the Columbine again. How water heaters failed right when a man was primed and ready for a hot shower. And about plumbers who charged an arm and a leg for fixing a piddling little leak—assuming Mr. Pipewrench bothered to show up to do the job. *But these are hard times and a hard-working man don't miss a chance to make an extra dollar or dime.* Not without a good reason.

Which was enough to make a man think even harder.

And we all know how one thought tends to lead to another.

Before long, the Southern Ute tribal investigator was experiencing a thunderous brainstorm. As white-hot flashes of lightning illuminated hidden cerebral landscapes, and cold rain mixed with hail rattled on the roof, a dark wind began to blow in the scent of something sinister—the inklings of another hunch. Like his earlier gut feeling that Betty Naranjo and her brand-new baby might be living upstairs over Erasmus Boyle—Charlie Moon figured this one for another long shot. A gnat's eye at five hundred yards. Sorry, no 4X scope—we're talking iron sights. And a brisk crosswind.

The way Moon summed it up was: *I guess this notion stinks like something the cat drug in or the dog rolled in. Then again . . .*

And that's how thinking too much about mundane matters can disturb a man's precious peace of mind. But there's no way out—what a fellow *isn't* thinking about can cause him just as much trouble.

Here's a pertinent for-instance: the rancher hadn't given a thought to wagging tongues.

Gossip

Sarah Frank was in her Columbine bedroom when the cell phone in her purse began to play a snippet from her favorite cut from a limited edition (one hundred copies) of the Columbine Grass's only CD. Her favorite banjo plucker was playing his version of "Shady Grove" to Sarah on her sixteenth birthday. And Mr. Moon was singing that she was his *little lady*! The little lady unsnapped the small ostrich-leather purse Charlie had given her on the nineteenth anniversary of her birth and fumbled around until she found the instrument under a jumble of girlish necessities. She slipped the high-tech communications device under her long, black locks and just above a nugget of Hopi turquoise that dangled from the lobe of her right ear. "Hello."

"Hello Sarah it's me Junie and you simply won't *believe* what I picked up at the public library and you'll just *die* when I tell you." Junie "Bug" Vincent, whose major talent was speaking with minimal punctuation, took a break to suck in a gasp of air and wait for Sarah to ask what.

Sarah rolled her big brown eyes. "A book?"

"No, silly, what would I want with a dumb old book?" A sigh to express her exasperation. "I heard from Lillian who works part-time in the library to help with her tuition at RMP that Charlie Moon was in there yesterday and you won't *believe* who he was all cozied up to at her desk like they was two lovebirds in a nest!"

"Miss Poynter, I expect."

"Oh you already know all about it." Disappointment fairly dripped from Junie-Bug's pouty lips.

"Patsy Poynter is not a librarian twenty-four/seven," Sarah reminded Junie. "When she takes a notion to, she sings in the Columbine Grass—which is Charlie's blue-grass band."

"Well *everybody* knows that, silly—it's not like I was born yesterday!"

"Then everybody must know that from time to time, Charlie and Patsy talk about which new song she'll sing next time the band gets together."

"Well music wasn't what they was talking about when Charlie Moon dropped by the library." Junie paused to smirk. "Unless it was *wedding bells*."

The line seemed to go stone dead.

Junie listened to the barely audible hiss of static, then: "Hey, Sarah, are you still there or am I talking to air?"

Sarah was there, but feeling oddly detached from her body. "How would Lillian know about a thing like that?"

"Well she was surfing the Internet on a computer not ten feet away and she heard practically every word Charlie Moon said."

Sarah's hands were numb, her voice wooden: "Did he really ask Patsy to *marry* him?"

"Well not in so many words I guess but you know how men talk around things like that."

"No, I *don't* know."

"Well you ought to for heaven's sake! Anyway, after Charlie left, Miss Poynter was very nervous so she ran into the ladies' room and stayed in there a long time and when she came out Lillian said she looked like she'd been crying all night and right after that she left the library and Lillian found out later that she didn't come in again all day!" She surfaced for another gasp of air. "What do you think of that?"

"I think it's none of my business." *Or yours. Or Lillian's.*

"Well I'm sorry I bothered to call." Junie disconnected.

Sarah glared at the innocent telephone through tear-filled eyes. *Nasty little rumormonger!*

More Gossip

While Sarah was getting the bad news in her bedroom, Daisy Perika was sitting in the Columbine kitchen and watching the oven, where a dozen tasty apple turnovers were baking. She figured they should be just about done to a flaky, golden brown. *They'll make a breakfast that Charlie Moon and Sarah won't forget for a month of Mondays.* She lifted her nose to sniff the delectable aroma of made-from-scratch pastries. *I don't care what they say on those TV commercials, there ain't no turnovers made in a factory that smell like that.* Chef Daisy nodded to agree with herself. *Why, when I was a little girl my momma would've never let any of that junk into the house, much less fed it to her family.*

This happy journey down Nostalgia Lane was interrupted by the telephone's warble.

Comfortable where she sat, Daisy scowled at Mr. Bell's infernal invention. *I don't have the least intention of getting up and answering it.*

Another warble.

She grimaced. *Eeew . . . that sounds like a tom turkey choking on a baby bullfrog.*

You can look it up: in a free country, every citizen has a right to her (or his) favorite made-up metaphors.

The urgent summons continued.

Charlie Moon's annoyed aunt groaned as she used her oak walking stick to push herself up from the cushioned chair. Her right leg half asleep, the old lady toddled unsteadily to the wall-mounted telephone, yanked the handset off the cradle, and barked, "Emogene Hogleg's Cowboy Bar—Emogene speaking. What can I do for you?"

She heard a silly giggle, then:

"Daisy, you are such a *card*!"

"Hello, Louise-Marie." The old Joker rolled her eyes. "What a big surprise."

"Well it shouldn't be—this is same time I call you every week."

The tribal elder recalled what day it was, took a quick glance at the clock on the wall. "Well, so it is." She pulled the still-warm straight-back cushioned chair close to the wall and seated herself with a grunt. "So what's happening down in Ignacio?"

Her elderly French-Canadian friend proceeded to tell Daisy about a cheated-on wife who'd set fire to her husband's pickup and then (just for spite) run off with a gas-field worker, a tribal member who'd been arrested for stealing a neighbor's nanny goat, and how a mangy old stray dog had dug up "a half dozen of my best tulip bulbs!"

Daisy Perika didn't even try to hold back a yawn.

When Louise-Marie was just about to ask her Southern Ute friend what was happening up yonder on Charlie Moon's big cattle ranch, the purveyor of significant news was reminded of something she'd heard a few hours ago. "Oh, and while I was sitting on my front porch this morning shelling colored butterbeans a sweet young lady—I can't recall her name but she lives about a half-dozen houses down the street—well, it turns out she was visiting her husband's mother who lives at that nice nursing home in Granite Creek—and *guess* who she saw there."

"I don't know." The yawn escaped. *And I don't give a hoot.*

"Oh, try."

"Okay." Daisy smirked. "Grandma Moses' great-granddaddy."

"No, silly—my neighbor saw Charlie Moon at the nursing home."

"Well, I'm not surprised."

"You're not?" Louise-Marie's disappointment was of that character often described as *palpable*. "You knew he was there?"

"No. My nephew's all worn out from working this big ranch and he's thinking about moving someplace where he can kick back. Charlie don't intend to lift a hand unless there's a fork in it and prime beef and pinto beans on his plate."

"Oh, don't tease me so. I bet you don't know who Charlie visited while he was there."

"No, I don't." *And I don't care a nickel's worth.* Another yawn.

"Your nephew spent some time talking to Miss Emily Boyle."

That had a familiar ring to it. "Who?"

Louise-Marie repeated the name. "Miss Emily never married, but she's descended from the Virginia Boyles, who came west after the Civil War and settled in Granite Creek County. The Boyles lost most of their money during the conflict—but they were a very respectable family."

Daisy made the connection. *That young man Sarah met in the park was a Boyle.* She stared blankly at the paneled wall. *And now Charlie's paid a call on an old woman with the same last name.* There was no telling what her nephew might learn and what the consequences might be. *I'd better find out what's going on before—*

"Daisy—are you there?"

"I have to hang up, Louise-Marie—before my turnovers go up in smoke. Talk to you next week."

She hurried to remove the tasty apple pastries from the oven, and just as the crust had begun the transformation from flaky golden brown to cinder black. As soon as she put the tray of turnovers on top of the propane range to cool, Daisy went off to find Sarah Frank. *I'll ask that Ute-Papago girl to take me to the Pine Ridge Nursing Home.* But realizing that the girl was still miffed at her, Daisy would be nice. She put on a sweet smile and tapped gently on Sarah's bedroom door. "Open up, Orphan Annie!"

Sarah opened the door. "What is it?"

"I need to talk to you about something." *Her eyes look like she's been crying.* "You look like week-old roadkill—d'you feel all right?"

Sarah shrugged. *I feel like dying.* "I'm okay."

"I'm glad to hear it." The unfamiliar smile was making Daisy's face ache. "Then you can take me to Granite Creek."

Having ample reason to be suspicious of the old woman's sudden urgings, Sarah inquired politely about the purpose of the proposed visit.

Dismissing the sham smile, the sly old soul lowered her gaze. "It wouldn't be right to talk about it."

She's up to something. The girl set her chin in a manner that made it clear that she was not driving Miss Daisy anywhere until she had a full and honest explanation.

After a feigned hesitation, the tribal elder assumed a pious expression worthy of a stained-glass saint who would never even *think* of boasting about a good deed. "Well, if you *must* know—I made some apple turnovers to take to some poor old white folks that hardly ever have a visitor." Seeing the girl's puzzled frown, she added, "At the nursing home."

The old woman's ploy worked like a charm: Sarah was completely disarmed. *Aunt Daisy must have some friends there.* "Okay then. I'll take you to town tomorrow."

The pushy old woman was about to insist on going right now, when she sensed that this was not the time to press the Ute-Papago orphan.

Breathing a wistful sigh, Sarah Frank made a halfhearted swipe at a moist eye. "While you're at the nursing home, I'll go over to the university for my computer-science class." The girl wished that she had the nerve to make a stop at the public library and ask Patsy Poynter point-blank—*What's this I hear about you and Charlie Moon getting married?* But that would be a horribly brazen thing to do. *Whatever they're planning is none of my business and Patsy might tell me so to my face.*

But somewhere deep inside Miss Frank, a small voice was inclined to disagree . . . *anything that's going on between Charlie and that woman* is *your business.*

CHAPTER FORTY-FOUR

THE KILL

On the Following Morning

Like any respectable western cattle rancher, Teddy Truman was up and rarin' to go. And rightly so. An hour before daylight, the hairy-faced carnivore had wolfed down a breakfast of two fried eggs, a smoked pork chop soaked in red-eye gravy, three or four so-so sourdough biscuits he'd made himself, and enough black coffee to make his veined old hands tremble with what his late wife had referred to as "the caffeine palsy." Dawn hadn't quite broken but it was seriously bent and about to snap when Teddy turned his old pickup off the blacktop highway, rumbled over the ramshackle wooden structure that bridged the north fork of Sulpher Creek, and bounced along the bumpy dirt road like a man on urgent business.

It was all a sham.

The seventy-seven-year-old semiretired rancher had nowhere to go and nothing in particular to do when he got there. Mr. T.'s destination was an ellipse of about four sections of sandy ridges, which was encircled and defined by the north and south forks of Sulpher Creek. This remote piece of subprime real estate was in either one county or another, depending on which of several surveys was considered legal and binding. It had happened this way: in the late 1870s, the border between Todd and Granite Creek counties had been specified as running along Sulpher Creek for some thirty-eight miles, but about a decade after the original survey was made, that contrary creek had split into two pitiful little streams and then joined up again about three miles away. This process had isolated a smallish chunk of taxable real estate, which was inevitably claimed by both counties. The legal controversy persists to this very day.

The only dwelling on the "island" is a tiny trailer that Mr. and Mrs. Truman had used for a fishing camp until the old lady passed away. A widower for almost nine years now, Teddy visits his isolated holding once or twice a month to check on a few spindly Herefords he'd put there so he could come visit them. Like the lonely rancher, his gaunt whiteface cattle roamed these arid hills on Truman's Island year in and year out to eke out the best living that can be had on dirt where prickly pears and sage are more abundant than tough old buffalo grass.

The rancher would never have admitted to himself that his activities amounted to a hobby. Teddy Truman took his "business" seriously and didn't miss a trick when it came to watching over his on-the-hoof investment. And so it was on this morning. With the clarity that only those of the hawk-eyed clan can, the alert old man spotted something about a half mile ahead. He squinted through the pitted windshield at the despicable creatures circling lazily over yonder pines, evidently waiting their turn to dine. *I make it to be six. Or maybe seven.*

(It would help if he would be more specific. Six or maybe seven *what*?)

"Damned buzzards!" Teddy shook his gray head and the straw hat. "I'd bet a five-dollar bill to two bits, that big momma cougar has pulled down another one of my beeves." He was mad enough to *spit* and did. No, not on the floor. Out of the pickup window. Or would have, had it been open. Which made an awful mess and made the cranky ol' rancher even madder. "Why can't she feed on deer, like any normal mountain lion?" Having had no one to converse with since the old woman had passed, he was accustomed to answering his own questions. "Because a steer don't run fast as a deer, and once Ms. Cougar has got a taste of rare beef, venison ain't at the top of her grocery list."

(The stockman's conclusions, though rational and entirely consistent with his long experience, were based upon a false premise.)

"If I can get there before she sneaks off into the brush, I'll take a pop at that damn cat with my 30-30." Teddy's trusty rusty carbine was handy on the rack on the back window and his trigger finger fairly itched. He stepped on the gas. Watch him go! Forty-five miles per hour on a rutted dirt road that would dislocate the spine of a coal-mine mule attempting a trot. Bumpity-bump!

The combination of excessive speed and the distraction of circling buzzards very nearly proved fatal to the highly caffeinated motorist.

Running his 1992 Dodge pickup into a shallow ditch and barely missing a two-ton lichen-encrusted granite boulder, Mr. Truman shifted to Low and made a skidding recovery, all without batting a bushy eyelid over eyeballs that remained focused on those hateful birds of prey. He shifted up to Second, stomped his scuffed Roper boot on the gas pedal again, and within three minutes flat was on the spot, out of the truck, and popping shots from his carbine to chase a pair of coyotes away from the carcass and . . . *give those damn buzzards something to think about.* No, the expert marksman didn't injure either the canines or the vultures. Never intended to.

After he had emptied the carbine, Teddy Truman stared at the kill in astonished disbelief. *That ain't beef.* Neither was it a deceased mule deer. Or an elderly elk who had recently passed on. The crusty old sinner removed his straw hat and muttered a singular oath—to which he appended a three-word prayer: *God help us.*

The Call

As he generally did, Charlie Moon eventually got to feeling guilty about toying with Pete Bushman. To make amends, the rancher was in the Columbine headquarters kitchen, talking serious business with his ranch foreman when—wouldn't you just know it—the same telephone that had annoyed Aunt Daisy yesterday, warbled again today. The Ute was a man divided. The rancher considered letting his machine answer the call, but the part-time deputy and the sometimes tribal investigator combined to vote down the stockman's choice by two to one. "Excuse me, Pete." Moon got up from the table and lifted the cordless handset from its cradle on the wall. "Columbine Ranch."

Scott Parris's voice boomed in the Ute's right ear. "I just got a call from the Todd County Sheriff's office. Seems a rancher has found a corpse on his land."

Enough said.

Moon nodded at his distant friend. "Tell me where and when, Scott—and I'll meet you there."

"Soon as you can, here at the station. I'll drive you to the site."

"I'm on my way, pardner."

Pete Bushman shook his head. *If Charlie'd pay half as much attention to his cattle bidness as he does to helpin' that town cop, the Columbine might turn a decent profit more than one year out of four.*

Charlie Moon's foreman had a point, of course, but the report of a dead body tends to distract a lawman from any number of more mundane issues. Such as—what mischief might Aunt Daisy be up to while her nephew was off somewhere with Scott Parris, mulling over the corpus delicti?

CHAPTER FORTY-FIVE

DAISY'S CHARITABLE PROJECT

Sarah Frank had skipped breakfast so that she wouldn't have to look Charlie Moon in the eye—and perhaps hear the worst news of her life since the death of her parents. She waited until the man who *might* be engaged to Patsy Poynter had driven away in his Expedition on some unexplained errand. The moment he was out of sight, Sarah ushered Daisy out to her red pickup, buckled the old lady in, and headed off toward town at a pretty good clip. But not so fast as to catch up with Mr. Moon, who was fairly *carrying the mail*.

When Sarah braked her spiffy F-150 to a stop at the Pine Ridge Nursing Home main entrance, Scott Parris and Charlie Moon were already rolling along a long way south of town—the Ute a passenger in his friend's low-slung Chevrolet black-and-white. The young woman glanced at her Timex wristwatch. *My computer-science class begins in sixteen minutes, so maybe I can make it on time.* She aimed the glance at Daisy Perika, who had already opened the passenger-side door. With her walking stick in her right hand and a canvas bag in her left, she was tottering precariously like a drunk about to go headfirst into the gutter. *Oh no, she's going to fall!* "Don't get out; wait until I come around to—"

"I don't need any help." Even as she spoke, Daisy Perika dropped out of sight with a startled "Whoops!"

Cringing inwardly, a wide-eyed Sarah whispered, "Please, God—don't let her be hurt bad."

The tribal elder's dried-apple face popped up to smirk at the startled girl. "That last step was a long one, but I don't think I broke anything I can't do without."

Thank God. "Are you sure you're all right?"

"I haven't been all right since I was eighty-two." Daisy waved her stick in a dismissive gesture. "Now drive your truck over to that fancy school." *Where old fools teach young fools all the nonsense that's between the covers of big books written by bigger fools.*

"Okay." Sarah smiled at Charlie Moon's aunt. "I'll be back in about an hour and a half."

"I'll be waiting right here." Daisy slammed the door. As she watched the pickup depart, the tribal elder hitched a black canvas shopping bag over her shoulder and set her face resolutely toward the glass doors. *Before I leave this place, I'm going to know who this Erasmus Boyle yahoo is—and why he was talking to Sarah in the park.*

Her mission began hopefully enough. The walkway was lined with bushes of white and pink and lilacs taller than her head. Orange, violet, and yellow butterflies put on a fine performance, fluttering about gaily from bloom to bloom, presumably to taste every sweet offering. Furious hummingbirds performed dazzling aerial acrobatics, suggesting tiny fighter aircraft warring over precious nectar rights. Virtually unnoticed, humble honeybees droned along with infinite patience, getting the pollinating job done without making a big show of it.

The green rubber mat at the entrance was emblazoned with a bright red WELCOME and the glass doors opened automatically. As Daisy stepped inside, she crossed the boundary between a delightfully disorderly natural world and a highly organized state of confusion.

In the tiled foyer, a profusion of potted plastic geraniums and elegant palms created the impression that the visitor had entered a garden unlike any Nature had ever imagined. This jarring transformation was softened somewhat by the faint strains of a Chopin nocturne that evoked iridescent silver-winged moths fluttering over a moonlit meadow of multi-colored wildflowers. Sadly, this soothing masterpiece was intermittently punctuated with the braying bark of a young man's voice calling out bingo lingo.

A harried nurse at the front desk was too busy dealing with a recalcitrant senior citizen (who had lost a treasured pearl earring) to notice one more elderly lady sauntering by with a roguish look in her eye. Did the presumed rogue intend to ask a Pine Ridge employee where she might find Emily Boyle? Certainly not. The Ute elder had her own methods. Noting that the rooms had the occupant's photograph and name on the door, Daisy Perika opted to wander around until she found who she was looking for. Which took quite some time and provided the eccentric old soul with considerable entertainment.

The Intended Victim

Almost as if she had not moved since Charlie Moon's visit, Miss Emily Boyle was parked in her wheelchair, facing the television set. But on this occasion, there were two notable differences.

No *Flintstones* performance; the TV screen was dark.

And the oldest woman in the nursing home was enjoying her mid-morning nap. Until she felt the tap-tap on her knee.

Miss Em opened her eyes to see what appeared to be—a hideous apparition. She considered the possibilities with the calm detachment of one who no longer fears the bizarre events of an unpredictable world. *It's an old witch carrying a big stick.* The lady's mistake (charity obliges us to deem it an error) was understandable. Standing before the just-awakened resident was a very old hunched-over figure of a woman dressed head-to-toe in black, with an equally black sack looped over her shoulder. *I bet she's got a bag of poisoned apples and she'll polish one on her sleeve and offer it to me and say, "Have a taste of this, my pretty!"* Which lurid picture suggested another possibility. *Maybe this is the shape of Death that comes to old women.* This latter conjecture seemed far more likely. *Sure—she'll jerk my old soul right out of my body, stuff it in her bag, and haul me off to wherever.* The doomed woman sighed. *Oh, well. I might as well get it over with.* Emily addressed her sinister visitor. "So who're you, granny?"

"I'm a Good Samaritan."

Well. That would have been Emily Boyle's very last guess. She eyed her guest with all the suspicion a ninety-seven-year-old descendant of hardy pioneers could muster up, which was enough to wither several acres of Russian thistle or crabgrass. "The last time I checked, this wasn't Samaria."

Daisy Perika cackled appreciatively. "That's a good one." She nodded at an armchair near the wheelchair. "D'you mind if I set down?"

Emily Boyle ignored the query. "What're you doing in my room?" Before the Woman in Black could respond, she answered her own question. "I know. You're either a dotty new resident that wanders around disturbing us sensible folk—or you're one of those do-gooders that come around with a sack of rock-hard apples to pass out to people who don't have enough teeth to chew overcooked noodles."

"I'm a do-gooder." Daisy leaned her walking stick against the armchair, seated herself, and put the black canvas bag in her lap. "And you're not that far off about the apples."

Emily groaned and rolled her pale blue eyes. "I knew it!"

The Ute elder leaned closer to the white woman and held the bag under Miss Em's chin. "What I've got is homemade apple *turnovers*—fresh from the oven just yesterday."

Miss Em caught a whiff. *My, that does smell scrumptious.*

Daisy patted the bag as if it were her favorite fat puppy. "And that's not all I got."

Her interest stimulated, the nursing-home dweller gazed longingly at the canvas bag. But Pride trumped Curiosity. She could not make herself ask.

Her visitor read the longing in the blue eyes. "I've got a thermos of the best coffee you ever tasted and some red-ripe strawberries that're big as a bear's nose, and to go with those—a little plastic bowl of powdered sugar."

"Oh, my gracious." Emily sighed. *All the things I'd love to have but cannot.* "That's very sweet of you, but I'm on a very strict diet."

"I know." Daisy nodded sagely. "Soon as I laid eyes on you, I said to myself—they're starving that poor old *matukach* woman to death!" Before the fragile white lady could protest, the Ute healer shook her finger in a manner that commanded a respectful silence while Dr. Daisy's expert diagnosis was provided. "That's why you're so weak and woozy all the time, Emily—you don't get enough sugar. And your mind wouldn't be so foggy if you had a stiff dose of caffeine five or six times a day."

The perplexed resident blinked. "How do you come to know my name?"

"Us do-gooders have our ways of finding out what we need to know." She settled herself more comfortably in the armchair. "And before you ask again, I'm Daisy Perika."

"You're an Indian, aren't you?"

"I'm a lot more'n that, Emmy." Daisy announced with understandable pride, "I'm a Southern Ute—and I can trace my family all the way back to Chipeta."

"Chief Ouray's wife."

Daisy nodded. *This old white woman knows more than you'd think.* "I have a nice little house down on the reservation, but I come up here to Granite Creek County from time to time to visit my nephew." She noticed that Emily was eyeing the goodie bag harder than ever, had commenced to sniffing again, and was licking her lips like a hungry coyote.

Daisy pulled a brown plastic Smith's Supermarket bag from the canvas sack, removed a Saran-wrapped pastry from that, and offered it to her new acquaintance. "Take a bite, and tell me it ain't the best thing you've put in your mouth since the day you started choking down nursing-home oatmeal."

While the white woman nibbled at the apple turnover, Daisy produced the thermos, unscrewed the cup lid, and poured it half full of steaming black coffee. She passed the brackish beverage to Emily. "Wash it down with this."

Emily Boyle took a tentative sip. "My gracious! That's *awfully* strong."

"You bet it is," Daisy chuckled. "It'll put hair on your chest."

For the first time in twelve years, two months, and six days—Emily Boyle laughed out loud.

And so began a brand-new friendship.

The women commenced to gorge themselves on greasy turnovers and sugar-dusted strawberries.

CHAPTER FORTY-SIX

THE SECRET OF MISS DAISY'S STIMULUS PLAN IS REVEALED

In a word, *caffeine*.

We slow starters who get our early-morning jolt of get-up-and-go from a cup of Folgers or Maxwell House can attest to the fact that the minuscule trace of that substance in our home-perked brew provides a helpful stimulant.

Charlie Moon's aunt snorts with derision at our sissified beverage—why, a mere half-teaspoon dose of Dr. Perika's Famous Rejuvenating Elixir is (so her grateful patients claim) sufficiently potent to inspire a pharaoh mummified for millennia to leap from his dusty sarcophagus, make a grab for the nearest startled female, and engage the lady in a sprightly samba, foxtrot, or whatnot until museum guards come to the rescue. Like so many enthusiastic endorsements, this one is exaggerated—but only slightly so.

Observe the remarkable results below.

By the time she'd drained her first cup, Miss Em was as animated as a giggling teenager describing last night's date to her best friend. Whenever the nursing-home resident would pause to take another sip, Daisy helped things along by mentioning someone in her family. The white woman would respond in kind, by bragging about her saintly parents, her distinguished older brother, and any number of reputable aunts, uncles, and cousins. But halfway through cup number two, the normally reserved old woman was admitting to some less desirable kinfolk, most of whom were lowdown menfolk.

After listening patiently through several scathing accounts, Daisy's ears perked at the mention of a nephew—one Erasmus Boyle—who was "a nefarious, ne'er-do-well." Miss Emily's eyes sparkled with blue fire. "Erasmus is actually my *great*-nephew, but you will understand why I prefer to omit that descriptor."

"A regular bad apple, huh?"

"To the very core, Daisy. In spite of the fact that he was named after my dear brother—one of the finest men who ever walked the face of the earth—young Erasmus has gone to great lengths to distinguish himself as an out-and-out scoundrel." The accuser seemed about to reveal some sordid details, when she suddenly clamped her mouth shut like a sprung bear trap.

It seemed as if their conversation might be over, but Daisy Perika was more persistent at conducting interrogations than her nephew, "the big-shot tribal investigator." Watch the old pro do her stuff.

The best way to keep Emily talking about Erasmus is to tell her about one of my kin. "I guess we've all got some peculiar monkeys hanging from the branches of our family trees." She cocked her head as if recalling two or three of these. "Now take my cousin Gorman Sweetwater. You won't believe this, but just last month he—"

"Whatever your cousin has done, he could not *possibly* compete with young Erasmus." Emily passed the thermos lid back to the Good Samaritan. "My nephew is what the lurid media would term"—her mouth twisted in obvious distaste at the phrase—"a *confidence man*."

Enjoying her game immensely, Daisy shrugged to suggest indolent disinterest. "That ain't so bad. Why, in my family we've got a sheep thief and a politician and—"

"No. You don't understand." Miss Em produced a vigorous version of Daisy's earlier finger wag. "Erasmus makes his disreputable living by gaining the confidence of innocent young women." Three irregular heartbeats. "I'm sure you understand what I mean."

The tribal elder nodded knowingly. And waited to find out what the white woman was talking about. Daisy's guile was promptly rewarded.

"Like others who practice his shameful trade, young Erasmus is good-looking, and—so they say—a regular charmer. After his female victims have provided him with what he wants—and I'm not talking just about their *money*"—the white woman blushed pink—"he leaves them without even the courtesy of a goodbye."

"Young men who fool around like that are likely to wake up dead some fine morning."

"Not Erasmus, I daresay." She blinked her pale blue eyes. "He seems to lead a charmed life."

"I hope your nephew lives far enough away from Granite Creek that he don't cause you any problems." Daisy Perika popped a slightly tart strawberry into her mouth.

"Thankfully, he rarely visits—but he does call me on the telephone." A sigh. "Young Erasmus rang me last evening. Seems he has a gambling debt that simply *must* be paid—'or else,' as zoot-suited hoodlums in pulp novels put it."

"I hope you didn't give the youngster a thin dime."

"You may rest assured of it."

Daisy's chat with Emily Boyle was almost finished, but there was the matter of her great-nephew's military status. "Some boys don't seem able to grow up and be a man. What that kind needs to straighten him out is three or four years in Uncle Sam's army—or better still, the U.S. Marines."

Miss Em nodded her agreement. "Virtually all male members of the Boyle family for seven generations—young Erasmus being one of the exceptions—have served in the military services. There was a Boyle at Valley Forge, another with General Jackson in New Orleans, and Boyle twin brothers at Gettysburg—one fighting for the Confederacy, the other for those damnyankee sons of bitches that burned

Atlanta to the ground." The delicate old lady continued with a list of more recent relatives who had served honorably in various conflicts, including both world wars, Korea, Vietnam, Iraq, and Afghanistan.

As the narrative moved from the 1800s into her own century, Daisy listened with renewed interest. *I'd say that just about puts the icing on the cake.*

It wouldn't be long before Sarah showed up, so she slipped the thermos back into her black canvas bag. As she grunted and groaned her way up from the chair, the wily old Indian woman was pleased with her clever self. And rightly so. By means of tasty apple turnovers, sugared strawberries, an overdose of knock-your-socks-off coffee—and her talent for judiciously applied probing—the sly tribal elder had pried most of what she wanted to know from Emily Boyle. Only one critical piece of information remained unearthed, but despite her tendency to bull ahead, Daisy Perika knew it wouldn't be prudent to press the white woman too far. There were issues that can't even be hinted at without giving the game away—and there was still another inning to play.

Ever resilient and forward-looking, the crafty player was already planning her next move.

CHAPTER FORTY-SEVEN

DAISY'S HISTORICAL RESEARCH

Minutes after Sarah Frank had picked Charlie Moon's aunt up at the nursing home, she shot a sideways glance at her unpredictable passenger. "You want to stop *where*?"

"You heard me." Daisy Perika elevated her chin in a stubborn gesture. "It'll be fun to look at all the books and magazines and whatnot." Especially the *whatnot*.

Feeling uneasy about the old woman's sudden interest in reading, Sarah pulled her red F-150 into the Granite Creek Public Library parking lot. She eased the vehicle into a handicapped space near the front entrance. "I don't have a permit to park here, so after I help you get out I'll park in a regular spot and then—"

"I don't need any help." Daisy Perika had already opened the passenger-side door and was prodding the warm asphalt with the tip of her oak walking stick. "Just leave the motor running while I get down to the ground."

It was too late to argue the point, so Sarah clenched her hands on the steering wheel and prayed. *Please, God . . . please don't let her fall!*

Daisy was making her own request: *Take good care of me, Jesus—the last thing I need is a busted hip bone.*

The response to these urgent entreaties was immediate: Daisy's feet connected to terra firma without mishap.

The girl gave thanks for this happy outcome.

As with most of the blessings she received and felt entitled to, the tribal elder took this one in stride. *I'll be inside before she can find a parking place for her truck.*

Not so. As Daisy Perika was approaching the entrance of the public library, the slender girl appeared beside her. "I'll be glad to help you find whatever you're interested in."

"Don't put yourself to any bother," Daisy grumped. "I don't need a babysitter to hold me by the hand." Her plan was to wander around aimlessly until she found what she was interested in. *If that don't work, I'll ask some smart-looking kid to help me.* Youngsters nowadays seemed to know almost everything.

"All right, then." Sarah patted her companion's hunched, black-shawled back. "I'll stay out of your way." But she would not let Charlie Moon's closest living relative out of her sight.

As it happened, Patsy Poynter spotted the tribal elder within a minute. *My goodness—that's Charlie's aunt Daisy.* The old woman appeared to be mildly confused (which was unusual) and immensely irritated (which was not). *I wonder what the peculiar old soul is doing in the library.* Daisy was not reputed to be a lover of books. *And why is she here all by herself?* The reference librarian got up from her desk and hurried toward the befuddled senior citizen.

Cunningly concealed behind a shelf marked FANTASY, Sarah Frank peered through a slot she had contrived by removing a pair of thickish J. R. R. Tolkien novels. *Fine. Patsy will take good care of Aunt Daisy.* Her youthful brow came very near to making a frown. *Just like she'd like to take good care of Charlie.* But despite her jealousy, Sarah realized that Miss Poynter was a sweet lady and anyone with eyes could see that she was uncommonly pretty. Add to that the fact that Mr. Moon was far and away the most eligible bachelor in the county, and the inevitable lesson learned was . . . *I can't blame Patsy for wanting to get her hooks into Charlie.* The acutely dejected angle of the romantic triangle breathed a long, melancholy sigh. *I bet Charlie would pay me a lot more attention if I had curly blond hair and big blue eyes and was even* half *as good-looking as Patsy.*

Daisy Perika saw Patsy Poynter approaching at a rapid clip. *Uh-oh, here comes Blondie Blue-eyes. After she says hello Daisy how nice it is to see you, next thing she'll do is hug me.* The grumpy old woman groaned at the prospect. *I hate to be hugged!* But there was an upside: the clever *matukach* woman would help her find what she was looking for. *I guess I'll just have to grin and bear it.* She steeled herself for the ordeal.

"Oh, Daisy—I haven't seen you in ages. What a pleasant surprise!"

The Ute woman rolled her eyes. *Close enough.*

A head taller than Charlie Moon's aged aunt, Patsy leaned to give Daisy a hug.

The old woman cringed at the embrace. *I knew she'd do that.*

Patsy backed off to beam upon this unlikely client. "What brings you to the library?"

"Oh, I was in the neighborhood so I thought I'd just walk around and take a gander at things."

The reference librarian reacted instinctively. "Is there anything I can help you with?"

"Oh, I don't think so." Daisy feigned an afterthought. "Well . . . maybe. If you're not too busy."

"Wonderful!" Patsy clapped her hands. "What kind of information are you looking for?"

The tribal elder considered this question for a moment, then said, "Well, I guess it's what you might call *historical*."

"Something about the Southern Ute tribe?"

"No." Daisy shook her head. "I'd like to learn more about this nice little town."

Patsy's big eyes got bigger. "Granite Creek?"

No, Toots—Muddy Gap, Wyoming. Daisy faked a smile. "That's right."

"So what do you want to know?"

Daisy's counterfeit smile was transformed into a sly smirk that was the genuine article. "Oh, nothing in particular." This was a bald-faced lie. "Do you have some maps of Granite Creek?"

"Oh my, yes—drawers full." Patsy Poynter pointed her pretty nose in the direction of the map files. "Most are fairly recent, but some of the early survey charts go back to the 1840s."

"Why, I was just a kid then." Cackling a raspy laugh, Daisy Perika raised her walking stick in an enthusiastic gesture. "Let's go have a look at 'em."

Sarah had not moved from her lookout post; the girl was still peeking through the slot where she'd removed the hefty books. As the Ute-Papago spy peeked, she whispered, "So what's Aunt Daisy up to this time?"

Not an unreasonable query to pose. Particularly by a victim who had, on several prior occasions, suffered the disastrous consequences of Daisy's zany plots.

About half an hour later, Daisy Perika's research was completed and her effort had proved entirely successful. Indeed . . . *This turned out a lot better than I'd hoped for.* She said thank you and goodbye to the shapely *matukach* research librarian whom (Daisy assumed) her nephew lusted after. These obligatory social formalities completed, the Ute woman began to peg her way toward the library exit. There was no need, she knew, to look for Sarah Frank. *That silly girl will still be watching every move I make from behind that shelf of books, and she'll catch up with me before I get to the door.*

Which Sarah Frank was, of course—and did.

A Minor Change of Schedule

Despite Sarah's desire to bring the F-150 closer to the library entrance, Daisy insisted on walking to the pickup with her youthful chauffer. After she had assisted the aged woman into the cab, the girl hurried around to the driver's side, slipped under the steering wheel, and helped Daisy fasten her shoulder strap. "We'll be back to the ranch in time for an early-afternoon lunch."

"No we won't."

Sarah snapped Daisy's buckle shut. "We won't?"

Daisy shook her head. "We'll get us a big, greasy pork-sausage pizza." As she was settling into the seat, she advised her driver that . . . "After lunch, we'll stop at the park that's named after that thirsty Yankee general who drank buckets of rotgut whiskey like it was spring water." The soldier's critic helped herself to the dregs of coffee in the thermos. "Ugh—that tastes like goat—(*vulgar expletive deleted*)."

"Why do you want to go to the U.S. Grant Park?"

That's for me to know and you to find out. "It'll be a nice place to relax after our big lunch."

"I'll be going to the park tomorrow to do some work on my school project. Why don't we wait until then? You could come along with me and—"

"At my age, I can't afford to put things off." Daisy burped up brackish coffee fumes. "Tomorrow morning, I might wake up dead as an outhouse doornail." The expectant corpse waved her hand in an impatient gesture. "Now get this old box of bolts a-rolling toward the pizza joint!"

CHAPTER FORTY-EIGHT

A MINOR PROBLEM ASSOCIATED
WITH CHRONOLOGY

It would be helpful if the major movers and shakers in this carefully documented account of their comings and goings would refrain from conducting important business in a simultaneous fashion. But they will not. Therefore, in the interest of maintaining some semblance of clarity, it is necessary to stipulate that at about the time that Daisy Perika entered Miss Emily Boyle's private room at the Pine Ridge Nursing Home, Charlie Moon and Scott Parris were about halfway between Granite Creek and the location where Mr. Truman (long since withdrawn from the grisly scene) had discovered the corpse, chased off the hungry coyotes and buzzards, and called the sheriff, who—in light of the disputed jurisdiction and as a gesture of professional courtesy—had in turn called Scott Parris. It is tempting to skip over this on-the-road interlude, but the lawmen are in a gabby mood and it appears that one of them is about to say something of importance.

A Probable Homicide

That was the way Todd County sheriff Ben Crowder had described the situation to Scott Parris, who had not yet shared Crowder's observation with Charlie Moon. As the

GCPD black-and-white sped along south out of Granite Creek, the chief of police addressed his part-time deputy: "D'you know a rancher by the name of Theodore Truman?"

The Ute stockman nodded. "Teddy's a sure-enough old-timer."

Ol' Charlie Moon knows just about everybody around here. After all the years he had spent in Colorado, the ex-Chicago cop had never gotten over the impression that he was still an out-of-towner. "From what Ben Crowder told me on the phone, Mr. Truman found the corpse this morning on a section of land between the north and south forks of Sulpher Creek." *I can't remember what they call that place.* His brow furrowed. *Something like* Gilligan's Island?

"Truman's Island," Moon said.

The driver shot a sideways glance at the man who seemed to read his mind. "You know that chunk of land?"

"Like the back of my right hand." Moon drifted off to enjoy a happy childhood memory. "Dad used to take me to the island on fishing trips. We'd camp out for a week to ten days."

Scott Parris hadn't thought about his own daddy for at least an hour. "Sounds like you and your old man had some fine times."

"We'd eat all the rainbow trout we could catch along with canned baked beans and corn bread Dad made over an open fire." Moon could almost smell the fragrant juniper smoke and taste the simple food that was so delicious under the sky. "Once in a while, Teddy Truman would drop by and spin yarns about those good old days, when rustlers and bank robbers and other bad outlaws used to hide out on the island. Back when he was knee-high to a donkey, locals called the place No-Man's-Land."

Nostalgia tends to be contagious when like-minded souls start swapping stories, and Scott Parris was beginning to feel a little bit feverish. "Back in Indiana when I was about seven or eight, my dad took me camping on Pigeon Creek. We caught a string of little bluegill and jughead catfish." He treated himself to a manly sigh. "That's where I drank my first cuppa coffee." The grown-up boy chuckled. "Momma wasn't there to make me walk the line." Parris was about to tell about the time they got chased by a coal-black bull, but he remembered what the county was paying him for. The lawman cleared his throat of the temptation and got back to the business at hand. "Early this morning, when Mr. Truman showed up to check on his cattle, he saw buzzards circling. That was how he come to find the body." Parris waited for Moon to inquire about the significant details. Was the deceased male or female? What was the apparent cause of death—accident, suicide, or homicide? And what was Sheriff Crowder's educated guess about the approximate time of death?

Charlie Moon pushed his black Stetson back a notch. "So—Mike Kauffmann got himself shot dead last Monday."

The black-and-white's tires hit the grassy shoulder; the startled driver recovered quickly. "Dammit—I wish you wouldn't do that!"

The Ute was the picture of wide-eyed innocence. "Do *what,* pardner?"

"Show off when I'm doing seventy-five on a narrow two-lane with soft shoulders and deep ditches on both sides."

"Sorry."

"I don't see how you could *know* so damn much." Parris smirked. "Unless you popped Kauffmann yourself."

After considering this allegation for a while or maybe a mile (whichever came first), Moon offered his professional opinion: "It don't seem all that likely, pardner. But I suppose it's a possibility we can't absolutely rule out."

"Ha-ha!" *Ol' Charlie always makes me laugh!* "Tell me a more likely possibility."

"Give me a minute or two to think about it."

"I'll give you six seconds flat."

Satisfied with that, Charlie Moon counted off a half-dozen heartbeats. "I've come up with something, but it's gonna be pretty danged thin."

"Go ahead anyway."

"Alright, try this on for size. We already know that Mrs. Wanda Naranjo called 911 late on Monday and told the dispatcher she had to see the chief of police *right away*. But by the time you showed up, the edgy lady wasn't at home. And far as I know, she hasn't been seen hereabouts since then. First the pregnant daughter vanishes—now the mother disappears. Okay if I go way out on a limb and make a completely unjustifiable conjecture?"

"Sure." Parris's sour stomach was beginning to churn.

"I figure something really bad had happened on Monday afternoon—and Mrs. Naranjo called you because she was scared."

Parris blinked several times, like a sailor trying to see through a fog. "You figure Wanda Naranjo shot Mike Kauffmann?"

"Well, now that you mention it—I wouldn't be inclined to argue against it."

Five long miles of blacktop passed under the Chevy without a word being spoken.

It was inevitable that Parris's gruff voice would shatter the silence. "If Wanda killed her ex-boyfriend, then why would she call the police station and ask to talk to me?"

"You pose a good question." The Ute took a deep breath. "I can't imagine the lady making a voluntary confession to a homicide."

"Me neither." Parris eased up on the gas.

Moon let another mile and minute pass. "So Mrs. Naranjo must've had some other reason for wanting to bend your ear."

Charlie's reaching. But he got a good grip on the steering wheel. "Such as?"

"Such as she didn't know her boyfriend was dead—or

even wounded. She'd taken a shot, but didn't see him fall—and figured he might come gunning for her." Feeling good about his game, Moon went for the home run. "Which would explain why a gun was found with Mr. Kauffmann's corpse."

Dammit! This time, Parris kept his unit off the grassy shoulder. But just barely. "You want to describe the firearm?"

"I'll speculate that it was a handgun. If Kauffmann had've taken a shot at her with a rifle or carbine, Mrs. Naranjo probably wouldn't have lived to come home and make the 911 call." The happy Indian could not suppress a smile. "You want me to guess the caliber, make, and serial number of the shooting iron Sheriff Crowder found in Kauffmann's hand?"

"No!" Parris snapped. "You tell me any more, there won't be anything worth knowing to find out when we get there—we might as well turn around right now and go home." The gruff chief of police was, of course, as happy as his best buddy. How many other lawmen could boast a sidekick the likes of Charlie Moon?

You really want to know? Subtract three deputies from the cube root of twenty-seven second-bananas—*that's* how many.

CHAPTER FORTY-NINE

THE CORPSE

The Todd County sheriff was on the ridge with the dead man's remains, but Ben Crowder had his gaze focused on the hollow below. The lawman watched the GCPD black-and-white park in the dirt lane behind his own official vehicle. The smile that split his face when Scott Parris emerged from the driver's side morphed into a frown as it became apparent that Granite Creek's senior lawman was alone. *Well, shucks—I sure was looking forward to seeing Ol' Charlie Moon again.*

Parris huffed and puffed his overweight frame to the crest of the pine-studded hogback ridge. Shaking Crowder's rock-hard hand, he gasped, "I ain't as young as I'd like to be—or as spry."

"Neither am I." The older man laughed. "And we've both got too much belly to carry around." Following Parris's gaze, Crowder nodded at Exhibit A. "This is a nasty business, Scott."

As he got a look of the residue of the late Michael Kauffmann, and caught a whiff of days-old decaying human flesh, Scott Parris was not inclined to disagree. And since there wasn't a hint of a breeze, there was no way to get downwind of the stench. Ben Crowder seemed oblivious to the odor, so Parris felt obliged to suffer the stink without complaint. But it was not only his olfactory senses that were assaulted. The chief of police had seen more than his fair share of corpses, but what was left of this one after rancher Teddy Truman had chased the coyotes away was sufficient to ruin even a hardened lawman's day.

"Predators sure have made an awful mess of him— there ain't a lot left for the medical examiner to work with." Sheriff Crowder pointed a gnarled finger at the dead man's abdomen. "But if you look close, you can see there's bullet wound in his belly."

The gunshot wound wasn't as plain as the bulbous nose on Ben Crowder's face, but it was obvious that the little round hole had not been made by a natural predator. And the dead man's hand grasped a pistol. The weapon was a detail that Crowder had not mentioned during their telephone conversation. Parris shook his head. *Ol' Charlie Moon's done it again.*

The Todd County lawman knelt and aimed his forefinger at the .32 caliber Colt revolver. "There's two empty chambers, so it's likely he took a couple of shots at somebody or other."

"And it looks like somebody or other shot back." *Score one more for Charlie.*

"It was a shootout, all right. And it looks like it happened some time ago." The arthritic old cop grunted himself back to an erect position and brushed dry pine needles off his knees. "But I suppose I shouldn't go jumping to too many conclusions before the medical examiner gets a look at the remains." Several minutes passed with the help of small-town cop small talk before Crowder cocked his head at Granite Creek's top cop. "I thought you was gonna bring Charlie Moon along with you."

"I did." Parris waved his muscular arm in a vague gesture. "He got out of the car back at the bridge. Said he'd walk in."

Ben Crowder chuckled. "Charlie likes to get a look at the lay of the land." He shook his gray head at something he'd heard about the Ute tribal investigator years ago. "They say that Indian can track a field mouse across a mile of solid rock."

"Only if the rodent was wearing hobnailed hiking boots and dropped a trail of shiny dimes." Scott Parris had not provided this response, and Mr. Kauffmann was way beyond talking.

The startled lawmen turned to see the seven-foot-tall subject of their conversation, who seemed to have materialized right on the spot.

Crowder laughed. "Hey, Charlie—you sure know how to sneak up on a fella!"

Moon shook the extended hand. "Nice to see you again, Ben."

After the Ute and the Todd County lawman had exchanged a few pleasantries, Moon—who had brought an erratic east wind with him—edged around to the sunrise side of the corpse, where the breeze would be at his back. Squatting, the Indian took a long, thoughtful look at what was left of Michael Kauffmann.

The two older men also positioned themselves so that the refreshing gusts of air would carry the odor away from their nostrils.

Pushing back his sweat-stained rawhide cowboy hat, Crowder grimaced at the coyote-mutilated corpse. "I'm no expert, fellas—but it looks to me like this poor bastard's been dead for several days."

"Since Monday," Scott Parris said.

The sheriff turned a questioning look on the town cop. "Sounds like you know something I don't."

"Not me." The chief of police aimed a thumb at his buddy. "Charlie had it all figured out before we got here."

Crowder turned his wide-eyed look on the Indian. "Is that a fact?"

"I've made a few guesses." Moon eased himself up from the squat. "A couple that might pan out."

"Don't be so damned modest, Charlie." Parris grinned

at the sheriff. "Unless my deputy is wrong—and I wouldn't want to bet a greenback dollar against him—Mr. Kauffmann was shot to death on Monday by his ex-girlfriend."

Ben Crowder didn't blink. "I guess you'd better fill me in."

Parris provided the elder lawman with a summary of what he knew about Wanda Naranjo, her missing pregnant daughter, Betty—and Michael Kauffmann the Coffin Man. He summed up like this: "Charlie figures that Wanda showed up here on Monday looking for Kauffmann. When her ex took a shot at her, the lady fired back—but probably didn't know she'd killed him. She drove back to town and—this is what we know for sure—she put in a 911 call asking for me to come see her. But by the time I got to her house Wanda was gone—and we ain't seen hide nor hair of her since."

Sheriff Crowder thought about this for a while. "I guess it could've happened like that." He frowned at the Indian. "But it'd be nice to have some hard evidence to support Mr. Moon's interesting speculations."

Both of the older lawmen waited for a response from the self-assured young whippersnapper.

Charlie Moon jerked a thumb over his shoulder. "I found some flattened grass back by the north fork." He told his fellow lawmen how to find the location. "Somebody parked a car there a few days ago."

Parris was not surprised. "Wanda's Toyota?"

"Could've been." Moon jutted his chin at the dirt lane below. "Somebody with small feet walked from the car park to the trailer—and then back." He pointed his gloved finger at a bushy little tree not far from the Todd County sheriff's car. "On the return hike, the walker stopped down there by that lone piñon, then turned to face this direction."

"To shoot at Kauffmann," Crowder murmured.

"I expect so." Moon took a look at the pistol in the corpse's hand. "Probably because he'd just taken a shot at her."

"Two shots," Parris said.

"I might be way off base here," Moon admitted. "But I figure Mrs. Naranjo fired several times at Kauffmann—and got off one lucky shot that happened to hit the target."

Crowder's practiced eye measured the distance to the spot from where Wanda Naranjo had presumably dueled with her ex-boyfriend. *That's a good ninety-five yards.* "At this range, it'd take a world-class marksman to drop a skinny man with a single shot."

"I don't believe the lady knew she'd put Kauffmann out of action. I think she figured he'd be chasing her." Seeing the curiosity in the sheriff's eyes, Moon explained, "From the looks of her footprints, after returning fire she ran all the way back to her car." The expert tracker glanced toward the spot where Wanda Naranjo had concealed her Toyota. "And she kicked up lots of rocks and sod driving away."

Ben Crowder pulled a leather pouch and a corncob pipe from his jacket pocket. He put a pinch of aromatic home-made tobacco in the charred bowl and lighted it with a kitchen match. After a half-dozen restorative puffs, he paused. "Sounds like we got us a prime suspect."

"Lotta good that'll do us," Scott Parris grumped. "By now Wanda Naranjo could be anywhere."

The sheriff spat on the ground, not far from Kauffmann's left boot. "Even if we locate the suspect, there's no one left to testify against her. Despite Charlie's tracking skills, I doubt we could put her here when Kauffmann got killed—not so's it'd hold up in a court of law."

Parris knew where this was going, and helped it along. "Only chance for a conviction would be to get our hands on the pistol Mrs. Naranjo shot Kauffmann with, and then prove it'd fired the bullet that stopped his clock."

Ben Crowder pointed his pipe stem at the wound in the corpse's abdomen. "Assuming we find the slug that bored a hole through him."

Scott Parris nodded. "And hope that it ain't so bent out of

shape that it can't be compared to a test-fire from the suspect weapon—which we don't have yet."

The Todd County sheriff sighed. "And even if we proved that the lethal bullet was fired from the suspect's weapon, it's likely that she fired it *after* she was shot at—like Charlie figures." The world-weary lawman shook his head. "My momma told me I ought to find some other line of work, like delivering the mail or cuttin' hair—but I didn't listen."

Parris kicked at a sandstone pebble. "So what do you figure we should do, Ben?"

"I don't know about you fellas. Me, I've got about thirty-one vacation days in the bank." Crowder tapped his spent pipe against a lodgepole pine. "I'll go visit my brother in Dalhart. Harold was a U.S. Marshal till he got shot in the knee."

The chief of police could not suppress his envy. "I'd swap my new ostrich-hide boots for a whole month of vacation."

Charlie Moon hadn't had a week to himself in years. "Thirty-one days is a lot of time off."

"Oh, it'll pass fast enough for me'n my brother." Ben Crowder reflected the tall Indian's bright smile. "We'll sit on Harold's big front porch and sip at Irish coffee."

Scott Parris produced his usual snort. "That's all?"

The old lawman shook his head. "We'll watch the pretty girls stroll by and recollect good times gone by when the man behind the badge congratulated a woman who'd fired in self-defense, and . . ." He stuffed the corncob pipe into his jacket pocket. "And by hook or crook—he made damn sure the worst of the bad hombres never made it to a jury trial."

CHAPTER FIFTY

A PRIME SUSPECT'S ALIBI

At about the time when Sarah and Daisy were perusing tantalizing lunch menus at the Sunburst Pizza Restaurant, Charlie Moon and Scott Parris took their leave of Ben Crowder, leaving the Todd County sheriff in the unsavory company of Michael Kauffmann's earthly remains.

As the lawmen ambled down the rocky ridge, a semblance of serenity was returning to the neighborhood. In about the time it takes Judy Collins to sing "Amazing Grace," the pedestrians arrived at their destination, which was Scott Parris's sleek, supercharged Chevrolet. The faithful copmobile waited coolly in a lone aspen's soft shadows. Ripples of golden sunshine dappled the ground under and around the ivory-barked tree. Concealed on a lofty branch, an operatic mockingbird trilled away, flaunting her repertoire of a half-dozen popular songs. The flower-scented easterly breeze gently caressed thousands of tiny aspen leaves, each of which quivered with effervescent delight. Isn't that nice? And topping off all these blessings, the good friends were conveniently upwind of the mutilated corpse that was rotting on yonder rocky ridge like a determined finalist in the Stinker of the Year competition.

All things considered, it was one of those fine-and-dandy interludes when silence is preferable to either amiable conversation or carefree song. Evidently sensing this, the songbird ceased her chirruping. Upon such occasions, sensible souls take a break to contemplate the joys of life. In no hurry to say goodbye to Teddy Truman's isolated island, the beefy chief of police and his long, lean deputy leaned against the low-slung GCPD black-and-white.

Perfectly content in the quietude of this solitude, Charlie Moon entertained himself by watching a company of persistent buzzards who had returned to circle. The expectant diners were riding a thermal above the kill site.

Accustomed to constant activity, the more tightly wound lawman had a hard time doing *nothing*. Scott Parris fished around in various pockets until he found a filthy toothpick. He slipped the wooden sliver between his teeth and commenced to chew on it.

This peaceful interval continued for almost a half minute, when it was suddenly and rudely interrupted by the sound of bridge timbers rattling in the distance. This woody clatter was promptly followed by the pleasing hum of a well-tuned gasoline engine.

Moon cocked an ear and estimated eight cylinders. "That'll be the ME, come to collect the corpse." The hopeful gambler waited for his buddy to take the bait.

Parris nibbled promptly. "Just as likely to be the state police, here to provide whatever assistance they can to Sheriff Crowder."

"You might be right." Moon prepared to set the hook. "But I'll betcha two bits it's Todd County's version of our Doc Simpson."

"You're on, high roller."

Within a minute, the lawmen watched the Todd County medical examiner's black van turn off the lane onto a dusty cow path and approach the base of the pine-studded ridge where Ben Crowder was waving his cowboy hat.

The Caucasian cop flipped a Colorado quarter-dollar to his Indian friend.

Making the catch, Moon slipped the shiny disk into his watch pocket.

The town cop inhaled enough air to swell his barrel chest and released it with a sigh. "You figure we'll ever see Wanda Naranjo again—or her daughter?"

"I doubt it." The Ute's dark face was concealed in a darker shadow under the brim of his flat-black John B. Stetson hat. "When Mrs. Naranjo hears that her ex-boyfriend is dead, she'll slip on her silver high-heel slippers, grab some castanets, and do a happy fandango right down the middle of the avenue."

Scott Parris could see the performance plain as day. "With fire aflashin' in her pretty dark eyes and a long-stemmed red rose clamped between her pearly-white teeth."

"That's the lady, all right. But she's not dancing down Copper Street in Granite Creek—we'll never see her in *these* parts again."

"Which makes it unlikely we'll ever find out what happened to her daughter." Parris paused for a thoughtful moment. "Betty's probably with her momma."

"You might be right." But Charlie Moon didn't think so.

"That about wraps it up, then." Parris waited for a few heartbeats before dangling his own bait. "I guess we might as well scratch Dr. Whyte off our list of suspects."

"You sound pretty sure that the psychologist had nothing to do with Betty Naranjo's vanishing act."

"Sure enough to bet on it."

The tribal investigator's teeth flashed in the hat-brim shadow. "Can you afford to lose another twenty-five cents?"

"I just drew my paycheck—two bits is chipmunk food." Parris nibbled off a chunk of toothpick. "As they used to say in olden days, 'Name your poison, slicker.'"

The man who could not resist a wager eyed his friend with a hint of suspicion.

Scott Parris had put on his best poker face, which, if not in the same class as Mr. Moon's chiseled-from-granite mask, was a couple of notches above what your typical Reno card-sharp can manage. Charlie read it like a roadside billboard, and took pity on his companion. *I guess he deserves to win every once in a while.* "I got a crisp two-dollar bill that says you're blowin' smoke outta both ears."

A sudden attack of avarice will stagger the best of Adam's descendants. Parris's semiblank expression fell off like the last apple on the tree. "Lemme see the color of your money."

The deputy removed the donation from his wallet and showed his buddy the green. "Sure you can cover this?"

The chief of police searched his pockets until he found four half-dollars. "Do you prefer to suffer in ignorance until this nasty business is eventually settled, or should I tell you right this minute why Dr. Whyte *couldn't* have had anything to do with Betty Naranjo going missing?"

"Prolonged misery ain't one of my favorite pastimes, pard—lay the bad news on me and get it over with."

"Okay, but brace yourself. On the same Friday morning when Betty Naranjo walked away from home, the psychologist was over two hundred miles away. Not as the crow flies, but as the pickup truck rolls."

"Would you mind fleshing that out some?"

"If it'll make you happy, I'll fatten it up like a Christmas turkey. Right about the time the girl headed down the dirt lane to catch the little shuttle bus into town, Dr. Whyte was in Denver." Parris chewed on the remnants of the toothpick. "On the third floor of the Federal Building."

"Government business, huh?"

Parris nodded his daddy's 1940s' felt hat. "The unfortunate fellow was engaged in an earnest conversation with a stern-faced suit who has a Harvard Law degree hanging on the oak-paneled wall behind his desk." Having embroidered the imagined scene to his liking, the lawman effected a dramatic pause. "We're talking Department of Justice."

"Sounds serious."

"Gimme the two bucks and I'll tell you *how* serious."

"Dr. Whyte's got an ironclad alibi; that's all I need to know." Moon tendered the debt of honor.

"Thank you kindly." Parris stuffed Moon's two-dollar bill and his own half-dollars into his jacket pocket. "But when a man's all primed and ready to tell a good story, you shouldn't ought to discourage him."

"It's a matter of professional ethics, pard—I don't want to hear another word about the psychologist's problems with the fed."

"Okay, I'll give you a bodacious big hint." Parris spat the used-up toothpick at the aspen trunk. Missed it by a *whisker*. "Dr. Whyte is obliged to visit the DOJ attorney once a month—always on the second Friday."

Moon frowned. "You surely don't mean—"

"'Deed I do." Parris looked over his shoulder, then this way and that—as if a curious squirrel or fox might be cocking a fuzzy ear to pick up a juicy tidbit of cop gossip. "Our highly esteemed high-school counselor has already served six months of a three-to-five-year sentence in a respectable federal resort in Maryland—for tax evasion. Nowadays, Dr. Whyte can live in any of the fifty states he chooses, but he is required to meet monthly with his federal probation officer. After his mandatory meeting with the fed on Friday, the doc spent the weekend doing public-service work in the Denver metropolitan area." He vainly searched his pockets for another toothpick. "So even if Whyte's the father of Betty Naranjo's unborn child, he couldn't have had anything to do with her disappearance last Friday."

"No, I suppose not." Moon counted off six seconds. "Not *directly*."

Parris arched an eyebrow. "What does that mean?"

Charlie Moon shrugged. "Oh . . . nothing important."

"You're just trying to take my fun out of winning your two bucks, Charlie." He added, "Nobody likes a mean-spirited loser."

"Like I said—"

"Dr. Whyte is clean as a shiny tin whistle."

Moon feigned a hesitation. Then . . . "Whatever you say."

The town cop's blue eyes glared under his bushy brows.

Charlie sure knows how to give me heartburn. This was literally true: Parris's stomach was about to produce a bumper crop of acid. "You're just dying to tell me what's on your mind."

"No I'm not. It's hardly worth mentioning."

Parris snorted. "Don't give me that, Mr. Modest. You've come up with another one of your slick-as-snail-spit theories."

"It's not exactly a theory." Moon blinked at an empty sky. Evidently recognizing the competition, the buzzards had dispersed with the arrival of the ME's van. *How do they know?*

"A working hypothesis, then?"

"Not even a respectable supposition. I wouldn't go so far as to call it an educated guess." His dark eyes sparkled. "Let's just say a hunch."

"I don't care if it's a wild-eyed speculation—I don't want to hear a word of it." Parris's fingers fumbled in his pocket and found the ever-present package of Tums. "But go ahead, wise guy—ruin my day."

"Okay." Charlie Moon drew in a deep breath. "Well . . . I might've been thinking about *Mrs.* Whyte."

"What's the psychologist's missus got to do with the price of new potatoes?" Parris tore a spiral ring of wrapper off the antacid package.

"Not a thing."

"You don't fool me for a minute, Charlie—I know what you're thinking."

"So tell me."

"Okay, here goes: Mrs. Whyte is her husband's secretary, and she sets up all his appointments. You figure she could've arranged for Betty Naranjo to be on her way to Dr. Whyte's office on that Friday morning when he was in Denver, talking to the probation officer."

This is almost too easy. Moon gave his buddy a little push. "What would the lady's motive be?"

"Well that's simple as two plus two. Mrs. Whyte was worried that the pregnant girl was going to accuse Dr. Whyte of fathering her child. Even if he was innocent, the scandal would've ruined them. It would've seemed like a fine opportunity at the time—doing away with Betty while the doc was out of town." Despite himself, the chief of police was warming to the notion. "You're suggesting that Mrs. Whyte murdered the pregnant girl to protect her husband's reputation." He shot a worried glance at Moon. "That's what you're gettin' at, ain't it?' "

"Not me."

"Don't try to kid me, Charlie." Parris tried to assure himself that this time, Moon's innuendo was way over the top. But when an upsurge of searing acid burned in his throat the dyspeptic chief of police popped three Tums into his mouth and crunched them noisily between his molars. How noisily? As his Arkansas uncle would have put it, *Like a razorback hog chompin' on hard corn.*

Charlie Moon regarded his friend with genuine compassion. "You okay, pard?"

"I'm fine as frog hair and—" Parris's response was momentarily interrupted by a strangling cough. Recovering, he waved his hand. "Go ahead, convince me that Mrs. Whyte has committed a serious felony."

"I never said she did—that was entirely *your* notion" Moon assumed a righteous expression. "But since you're my best buddy and I don't want to embarrass you, I'll forget all about your wild-eyed speculations."

The town cop eyed the enigmatic Indian, his expression suggesting a mixture of frustration and confusion. "Then you *don't* suspect the psychologist's wife?"

Charlie Moon's shrug was annoyingly vague.

Well, it's my own fault—I asked him to ruin my day. Scott Parris set his jaw. "We're burning daylight. Let's head back to town."

CHAPTER FIFTY-ONE

CHARLIE MOON'S CONJECTURE

As Scott Parris's GCPD black-and-white rumbled over the Sulpher Creek bridge, the chief of police was determined to ignore Charlie Moon's hints that something was amiss—but he could not help wondering what his enigmatic deputy was thinking about. *Charlie is aching for me to ask him, but I won't do it. Not if he begs me. Not in a hundred thousand years!* But about four eye blinks later: "I know you're just bustin' a gut to tell me about this latest hunch you've got."

Moon's face assumed a puzzled expression. "Hunch . . . about what?"

Big smart aleck. "About who's responsible for Betty Naranjo being missing."

"Oh, that." The taciturn Ute was silent while they passed two mile markers. "I ought to warn you, it'll sound a lot more like fiction than fact."

Parris watched the speedometer jitter around sixty. "As long as it moves along at a pretty good clip, almost any kind of story works for me."

"You're easy to please, pardner." Moon smiled. "How about that popular genre known as True Crime?"

"I read 'em all the time." The driver shot his passenger a sideways glance. "So what's the felony—kidnapping?"

"Might be." *In a strictly technical sense.* "But for now,

let's just call it a fanciful mystery about a disappearing teen-ager who happens to be pregnant." The passenger settled in for the ride. "Since I'm disinclined to mention a Mrs. You-Know-Who who's married to a local psychologist, I'll need a suitable name for my main character."

This sounds like the game I played with Dr. Whyte. "How about 'Smith'?"

"I like it." Moon paused to organize his thoughts. "Let's say that it's Friday morning, and this Smith character—whose gender shall remain unspecified—is in the vicinity of the Naranjo residence."

"What for?"

"Oh, I don't know as I should speculate about that just yet." The storyteller smiled. "For now, let's just say that our potential suspect had a specific purpose in mind."

"Like what?"

"Let's suppose that Smith had a job to do."

"Could you be a little bit more specific?"

"I could, but since this is my fable, I'll stipulate that Smith's task was something of importance. I might even go so far as to call it *serious business.*"

"I'm practically on the edge of my seat." Parris pretended to stifle a yawn, but the cop's heart was drumming a brisk tattoo.

Desirous of enhancing his narrative, Charlie Moon offered a helpful suggestion: "Imagine you're watching when our hypothetical motorist drives along that long lane between Rodeo Road and Wanda Naranjo's house."

"Okay." Parris recollected the buzzards. "I'm a redtail hawk, circling over the scene of the crime that's about to happen."

"You're likely to get your feathers ruffled, pard. That noisy Friday-morning storm is rollin' off the mountains like five hundred freight trains loaded with dynamite."

"Not a problem." Parris hunched his broad shoulders. "I just landed on the downwind side of a big ponderosa." He squeezed the Chevy steering wheel until his knuckles were white as boiled hominy. "And I've got my talons fastened on to the branch so tight that a West Texas twister couldn't rip me off."

"Way to go, pard. Now keep your keen hawk eyes peeled. It's dark as the inside of a tar bucket."

"That's pretty dark—but I like scary stories with run-away trains, high explosives, and big honking storms." The triple dose of Tums was beginning to get the job done.

"It gets even scarier, pardner."

"Don't hold back, Charlie. I'm a full-grown man and not afraid of anything I can hide from or outrun."

"You're a hawk hanging on to a ponderosa limb."

"Oh, right."

"As Smith rolls along the Naranjos' long, muddy drive-way, Betty Naranjo hasn't had time to get to the highway, and . . . she won't make it there." Moon let this grim image hang in the air.

Never mind. Mr. Redtail Hawk was beginning to get a glimmer of the ugly picture. "The girl couldn't see the car coming—and Smith run her down."

Moon nodded. "But there wasn't a corpse in the road."

The chief of police squinted at the windshield. "So Smith must've hauled her away." The lawman could imagine two or three reasons why, and the possible outcomes—all of them dismal.

The ensuing silence was bereft of the least vestige of peace or joy.

Finally, Parris whispered, "So finish your story."

Mr. Moon sighed. "I'd rather not, pard—not right this minute."

"Why?"

"Don't want to ruin your supper."

"Don't let that cause you any botheration." The lonely bachelor's lips twisted into a bitter half smile. "Supper'll be a glass of watery skim milk and a three-hundred-calorie TV dinner that tastes like warmed-over cardboard."

"Not if you spend the night at the Columbine."

The hopeful diner brightened at this prospect. "What's for dinner?"

"Nothing fancy, pard. I'll broil us some prime Hereford steaks, bake a half-dozen potatoes, and brew a big pot of coffee to wash it down."

"Sounds like good eats to me." But Parris wasn't one to rush right in. "So what'll we have for dessert?"

"Week-old store-bought doughnuts that're stale as Granddaddy's jokes—unless we can sweet-talk Aunt Daisy into whippin' up one of her mouth-smackin'-good peach cobblers."

"That's way too good to pass up—I intend to belly up to the Columbine trough and gobble it down like a starved pig. So all the way to Granite Creek, let's keep the subject of conversation on light topics that don't have nothin' to do with any kind of crime. And I'm not excluding petty misdemeanors—if you saw a cute little kitty cat jaywalking across a bicycle path last week, I don't want to hear one word about it."

"Suits me."

"Good. So tell me something that's so brain-numbing dull that I'll have to prop my eyelids open with toothpicks just to keep from fallin' asleep at the wheel."

"That sure goes against the grain, pard—but I'll do most anything for the sake of public safety." The afternoon sun was glaring off the Chevy windshield. The tribal investigator pulled his Stetson brim down. "I recently had a plumbing problem at the Columbine."

"A really awful one that flooded the whole place?"

"No, it turned out to be manageable."

"Sorry to hear that—I enjoy hearing about other folks' serious misfortunes." The pale-faced *matukach* grinned. "But tell me about the plumbing problem anyway, and make it sound lots worse than it was."

"I'll do my dangedest." Moon counted four electric poles. "Way it started, I was all primed for a hot shower. But the main water heater was on the blink. Nothing coming out of the tap but lukewarm water."

"It'd be a better story if you'd got scalded to death by the steam. You know, like Ol' What's-His-Name, who never let go of Ol' Ninety-Seven's throttle as she roared down the mountain without a trace of brakes and flew off the rails and—"

"Sorry, pard, there was no chance of me getting scalded. But being in the shower without any hot water just about ruined my whole morning."

"Good. Now tell me how much trouble it caused."

"Not all that much. But when things start going wrong, you know how one thing leads to another. I ended up calling every danged plumber's shop in Granite Creek."

Parris chuckled. "And nobody would come all the way out to the ranch and fix your faulty water heater."

"I didn't need any hands-on assistance. What I wanted was some information."

"Seems to me that any run-of-the-mill wrench twister could've dealt with a simple matter like that."

"You'd think so. But nobody could tell me what I wanted to know." The Ute watched a tufted-ear squirrel scurry across the highway. "Either that, or somebody didn't *want* to tell me."

The driver swerved to spare the reckless rodent. And waited for a mile. Maybe more. Parris really didn't want to know. But the curious fellow could not help himself. "So what did you ask all those plumbers, Charlie?"

"Oh . . . I'll tell you after supper." Moon's mouth almost smiled. "I wouldn't want to impair your ravenous appetite."

Yeah, I bet you wouldn't. "If you don't mind telling me something before supper—was this apparently pointless conversation taking us anyplace in particular?"

"If you'd been playing close attention, pard—you'd know we're already there."

"There where?"

"You evidently didn't notice that dotted line painted across the highway about a half mile back. If you had, you'd know we've just entered the city limits of Conundrumville."

Parris swallowed another surge of heartburn. *Ol' Charlie's still playing his game with me.* What the driver needed was a pleasant diversion from this unnerving conversation. "How about I turn on the FM and we listen to some soothing classical music for a while?"

"Whatever pleases you is fine with me, pardner." Moon leaned toward Chopin, Debussy, and the Grand Ole Opry like it was way back when with Flatt and Scruggs, Minnie Pearl, Charlie Pride, and all that happy tribe.

The driver pressed a button on the radio—with a pleasing result. So much so that Scott Parris laughed and Charlie Moon grinned ear-to-ear.

So what'd they hear? Why, Mrs. Nelson's little boy, loud and clear. "Whiskey River"? Sorry, no cigar. "On the Road Again?" No again, but that's sure a good 'un. The bewhiskered crooner was advising other little boys' mommas that they shouldn't ought to let their male young'uns grow up to be slack-jawed cowboys that picked guitars, whooped it up at all-night honky-tonks, drove rusty old pickup trucks to dusty rodeos where they rode bronky buckin' horses and wildeyed Brahma bulls and romanced big-eyed cowgirls. Being natural men, Scott and Charlie couldn't help but join right in—and they bellowed loud enough to startle several creatures lurking in the forest on both sides of the road, including a snarling cougar, a pair of big black bears, and a seriously bad masked badger. They even drowned out ol' Willie, but he didn't mind a'tall—which is just what you'd expect from a sure-enough superstar.

CHAPTER FIFTY-TWO

MISS DAISY PLAYS IT BY EAR

U.S. Grant Park, 2:40 P.M.

Following Daisy Perika's fortuitous discovery at the Granite Creek Public Library and her tasty lunch at Sunburst Pizza with Sarah Frank, Charlie Moon's relative had a specific destination in mind—which was *not* U.S. Grant Park. That grassy refuge was a mere stop along the way. Those cynics among us who are inclined to view Daisy with a jaundiced eye will suspect that the tribal elder has maneuvered her youthful companion to this neutral location with an ulterior motive in mind. Their suspicions are justified. But we need not speculate about what devious plot Aunt Daisy has hatched; as she strains to keep up with the slender girl's brisk gait—the sly old soul is about to reveal her thoughts.

I don't want to take Sarah with me—if that girl tags along, there's no telling what she might see. The sight of several park benches gave her an idea. *If I sit down one and play like I'm taking a nap, maybe she'll get fidgety and wander off to feed the ducks.* A wry smile crinkled Daisy's wrinkled face. *That'd give me a chance to sneak away and go have a look at that place I found on the library map.* She realized that such a simple plan might not work. *But even if Sarah sticks to me like moss on a stump, sitting down for a spell will give me time to catch my breath—and think up another plan to give her the slip.*

(Daisy Perika needn't have fretted so much. As it happened, someone was about to provide the tribal elder with a helping hand that would expedite her plan to part company with Sarah Frank.)

At her elderly companion's suggestion, Sarah led Daisy to a bench that viewed the park's lovely pond. Yes, the very same bench where the youth had sat when she had met the charming man who had introduced himself as Captain Erasmus Boyle. The ladies seated themselves.

"Ow! That hurts my butt." The old woman shifted her behind. "It's like sitting on a pile of rusty horseshoes."

Sarah Frank smiled at her companion's complaint about a bench that the Ute-Papago girl found quite comfortable. In a moderately whimsical mood, she wondered whether Daisy was qualified by experience to make such a comparison. The youth pictured the old woman strolling down a dusty Granite Creek street a century or more ago. As the senior citizen approached a blacksmith's shop, Daisy spotted a pile of discarded U-shaped appliances that had formerly been used to shoe four-legged creatures of the equine persuasion. Having fantasized thus far, it took no great stretch of the young woman's fertile imagination to envision Daisy deciding to seat herself on the heap of cast-off cast iron. (It was not a great stretch. Though Sarah did not know it, the impetuous old woman had once tried on a coffin for size.)

But by and by, Sarah lost interest in the silly fantasy. It was impossible to sit on this bench and not recall what had happened on the very spot only so recently. The girl's gaze darted this way and that as she calculated the probability of an appearance by Captain Boyle. *He said he walked in the park practically every day, so he might show up.* The nineteen-year-old gripped her small beaded purse with both hands. *Not that I really care.* But . . . *I wouldn't mind if he happened to walk by.*

"My feet hurt and all that pizza I ate has made me sleepy." Having achieved some degree of posterior comfort, Daisy feigned a yawn—which by some mysterious cerebral manipulation was transformed into the genuine article. She blinked drowsily at her young companion. "If Private Doyle shows his face, wake me up so I can get a good look at the fellow." The vain woman was proud of her witticism, which worked on several levels.

Sarah opened her mouth to correct the name and rank attributed to her new friend, but, realizing that Daisy was baiting her again—she clamped it shut. *I'll behave as if I didn't hear a word she said.* Which is what she did.

Have caught a glimpse of the girl's mouth opening and closing, the irascible old soul smiled. Her petty purpose achieved, Daisy proceeded to compound her deceit. *I'll just shut my eyes except for a little crack. That way I can make like I'm asleep and still keep an eye on her.*

Nice try, Daisy.

But as with her counterfeit yawn, before a minute had passed her pretend snooze was producing raspy little snores that were as indisputably authentic as her remaining molars and bicuspids, most of which were now on intermittent display for any interested passerby gnat, horsefly, or moth to view. Of such winged creatures, there were not a few.

But on this afternoon in the park, there were not a great many bipeds passing by. The ebb and flow of human traffic is a mysterious phenomenon, and a subject that scientists with time to spare might consider doing some serious research on. In the present instance, the dearth of pedestrians might be attributed to the cool, damp breeze whispering gossip in the trees about meteorological trouble brewing over nearby peaks. Alternately, it might be that those who normally enjoyed a pleasant postluncheon stroll in U.S. Grant Park had been discouraged by the cluster of gray storm clouds thundering over the mountains like a herd of celestial bison. Or perhaps sensible locals had better things to do during this particular P.M. than amble around in a picturesque wooded acreage named for a highly distinguished general of the U.S. Army who became a not-so-memorable U.S. president. For whatever reason, Sarah and Daisy remained mostly alone in the park.

The exceptions included a very large and obese man who was being pulled along by a tiny mouse-gray Chihuahua who was fastened to her burden by a red leather leash that glittered with rhinestones. (To Sarah, the sight suggested a tiny tugboat towing an unwieldy aircraft carrier.) The dog paused long enough to turn its disproportionately large head and gaze at the human females parked on the park bench, blink its protruding brown eyes curiously, and prick a pair of pointed ears as if attempting to pick up a snatch of conversation passing between them. Evidently satisfied that neither Sarah nor Daisy was of any interest, the petite canine proceeded to haul its overweight master toward the corner of Mulberry Avenue and Copper Street, where an old man with a hot-dog stand habitually offered the tiny dog a few puffs of buttered popcorn.

The few other sober citizens and domesticated chattel who passed by did not offer these significant women in Charlie Moon's life the merest glance, and so shall not be remembered here. Only the briefest mention will be made of the coarse fellow who had made a threatening appearance during Sarah's previous visit to this picturesque location. The one-eyed vagrant gave the girl a startled look of recognition and hurried on his way, no doubt to commit a loathsome misdeed in some more-favorable venue.

Are any of these passersby significant to current events? No. They are mentioned only to demonstrate how perfectly ordinary this afternoon was . . . *so far*.

The very soul of patience, Sarah Frank waited hopefully for Captain Boyle to appear. She wondered what horrid thing Aunt Daisy might say or do to offend her newly acquired friend. It was an inarguable fact that snoring old women rarely did any harm, but in Daisy's case, one could not be too careful. *If I see Captain Boyle, I'll just slip away and let her sleep.*

Daisy continued to doze, dreaming of her darling little brother who had gone to heaven so many decades ago.

All the while, the garrulous breeze continued to whisper delectable secrets and other half-truths amongst the deeply rooted community of spruce, cottonwood, and pine.

One cannot resist the temptation to assert that on Time's river, minutes glided by like snow-white swans, finally fading to silvery gray, then vanishing on shimmering wings of memory.

Very well. Perhaps one should have.

But as if to prove that marvelous coincidences and stunning synchronicities do occur now and again, an *actual* snow-white swan has just settled onto the park's bijou pond. Moreover, it glides with haughty grace across the glassy surface, and—

But forget haughty swans and fairy-tale ponds and whatnot—what is this?

Aha! Sarah has spotted the young man she'd hoped to see.

Or believes that she has.

The girl's back stiffened as she stared intently across the pond at a greenly oxidized copper sundial standing at the center of a circle of blue and yellow tiles. *I was sure I saw Captain Boyle, but there's no one there now.* But wait. Over there, behind that cluster of lilac bushes—*I'm sure that's him!* She popped off the park bench like a jill-in-the-box. *Where did he go?*

The mysterious fellow who wasn't there a moment ago, isn't there *again.*

Maybe it wasn't him. Whoever it was (she thought) was certainly behaving oddly. *If it was Captain Boyle, he didn't see me.* The logic behind the young lady's deduction? *If he had realized that I was sitting on the bench, he would have come over to speak to me and Aunt Daisy would have woke up and said something rude to him and I would've just* died *of embarrassment*. Sarah put her plan into action. *I'll leave without waking Aunt Daisy and hurry over there and find him before he gets away.* With nary a thought about the old woman napping peacefully on the bench, the winsome lass marched off smartly to a mossy cobbled pathway that encircled the pond.

She did her level best to catch up with the good-looking man.

From time to time, Sarah thought she caught a glimpse of her quarry here—and sometimes there—but though she tripped lightly along, the agile nineteen-year-old seemed always to be at least twenty paces behind him.

Trying to catch up with Captain Boyle was (for those who had attempted it) like chasing that fabled will-o'-the-wisp across a Mississippi swamp at midnight. And Sarah was beginning to doubt that she had actually seen the man who now competed with Charlie Moon for walk-on appearances in her dreams.

But her luck was bound to change, and it did. Sarah got a clear look at the fellow as he turned onto a red-bricked pathway that was hedged in on both sides by all sorts of bushes. It definitely *was* Captain Boyle, and the limping man was carrying the familiar cane. Tossing any thought of ladylike dignity aside, Sarah modified her gait from brisk strides to a trot. She did not call to mind a gazelle making a desperate dash across an African savanna to elude a hungry lion. Hers was a light, ladylike jog such as one might witness on the boulevard when Madam is chasing her favorite hat, which perky little lid has departed on the wings of the west wind.

It would be gratifying to report that this admirable effort produced the desired result.

It would also be gratifying to report that while she dozed, Charlie Moon's aunt Daisy was transformed into a loving, selfless old soul who was destined to be elevated to sainthood within a year after her demise.

Sarah Frank's graceful sprint slowed to a hesitant walk. *Where did he go?* Puzzled, she peered this way and that.

The fellow had certainly not sprouted wings and flown out of the park. Which (she theorized) left only one possibility: Captain Boyle had concealed himself in the brushy undergrowth that lined the bricked pathway.

But why would he do that?

The possibility that the charming young man might be luring her into some unseemly rendezvous never crossed the innocent's mind. It did occur to Sarah that . . . *Maybe he knows I'm following him, and he's slipped away.* The very thought of such a hurtful insult made the sensitive young lady's face burn with shame—and produced a surge of prideful anger. *If he's deliberately avoiding me, I certainly don't have a word to say to him!* Her embarrassing predicament called for a facesaving withdrawal. *I'll go back to the park and tell Aunt Daisy that it's time we headed for home.* A prudent strategy, but Sarah's intrepid feet had another plan.

Shh . . . Listen.

Plip-clop. Plop-clip.

(The sound of footwear slapping the pathway's worn bricks.)

Clip-plop. Plop-plip.

And so on and so forth as Sarah's sandals sallied forth.

CHAPTER FIFTY-THREE

SARAH'S SUDDEN AND UNEXPECTED ENCOUNTER WITH—

But that would be giving too much away; let events unfold as they may. We shall merely follow the winsome lass and see what happens.

After treading along for about a hundred yards, even Sarah Frank's feet were beginning to have second thoughts about pursuing a man she barely knew through a deserted section of the park. And not only that . . . *If I find Captain Boyle, what'll I say?* It would be necessary to admit to the truth: *"I thought I recognized you back by the duck pond, so I decided to follow you like a hound tracking down a fox."* But that did not sound very ladylike, and the dignified young woman was trying to think of a better way to explain her hurried pursuit—when she noticed several crumbling, moss-encrusted grave markers on either side of the red-bricked pathway. Sarah deduced (correctly) that she had crossed the unmarked boundary that separated U.S. Grant Park from Granite Creek Cemetery, and that she was now in the so-called historic section of that latter property. Much as little Dorothy might have done had she realized where the Yellow Brick Road was leading her, her adorable dog Toto, and their trio of oddball companions—Sarah stopped dead still to decide whether or not to proceed.

But the comparison is of limited utility. Unlike Dorothy,

Sarah Frank knew what lay ahead. Or thought she did. *It's only a little way to the modern section of the cemetery, where I left Daisy a few days ago.* From somewhere far behind her, there was a rumbling drumroll of midsummer thunder. *Right after that, I drove over to the park and sat down on the bench and met Captain Boyle and had a nice chat with him.* But now Aunt Daisy was in the park and she was among the tombstones. Be they historic or modern, Sarah had no burning interest in cemeteries. The sensible option that presented itself was to ignore her wanderlust feet, turn around, and return to the bench where Aunt Daisy was either still dozing peacefully or rubbing her sleepy eyes, looking around and wondering, *Where in the world has the flighty girl gone?*

And Sarah would have given up the chase except for two minor occurrences.

First, a thought: *This must be the same path that Aunt Daisy used last week to walk from the cemetery over to the park.*

Second, a sound. Or, more precisely, a series of sounds. *Scuff. Clink. Scuff-scuff. Scuff-clink.*

That sounds like someone digging. With a hand trowel, she imagined, in rocky soil. *But where?* The young woman cocked her head to ascertain the direction from which the various scuffs and clinks were originating. *Over there, to my left.* Digging in the modern section of the cemetery where there were still plots to sell was surely a commonplace enough event. But this historic section had (she supposed) been fully populated many decades ago; the recently deceased need not apply for space. *I bet someone is sprucing up one of the historic grave sites.*

Our scholar's conclusion was sufficiently correct to merit a grade of A. (But not an A+, which is reserved for those deductions that are the very essence of perfection.)

Sarah Frank peered through an opening in the undergrowth. No, she did not see Captain Boyle. What she did observe was the tombstone that Daisy Perika had paused to inspect last week (Maude Plimpton, 1869–1888). Yes, this was the very spot where the tribal elder had held a conversation with a female spirit who was—to Daisy's intense disappointment—invisible.

Sarah didn't get the least glimmer of a ghost of any description or gender. What the girl did behold, a yard or two beyond the Plimpton tombstone, was a battered little vehicle that (to the imaginative girl) suggested the hybrid offspring of a pigmy pickup truck and a golf cart. *It looks like it's been in a wreck.* The banged-up cemetery cart had also been recently painted. Within a few paces of the vehicle, she spotted a large man in brand-new blue bib overalls. He had a purple bruise on his cheek and an ACE bandage around his forearm. This flesh-and-blood person was on his hands and knees, tidying up a small patch of earth with a trowel. *Oh, I remember him.* As Sarah watched, Freddy Whitsun placed a small bouquet of white roses on the grave.

Isn't that sweet. Stepping through the hedge, the sentimental girl wiped a tear from her eye.

Freddy Whitsun got up slowly, the painful progress of his ascent punctuated with guttural grunts and moaning groans. The unfortunate had begun to wonder if he would ever fully recover from the humiliating accident wherein he had been attached to the runaway electric vehicle.

As he turned to present his homely face, Sarah smiled. "Hello, Mr. Whitsun."

The cemetery custodian who had replaced the recently deceased Morris Meusser blinked bleary, bloodshot eyes at the semifamiliar face. "Do I know you, miss?"

Sarah reminded him that she had been with Charlie Moon when Chief Parris's deputy had been called to the cemetery on Sunday morning, when Mr. Meusser's body had been discovered in his quarters. And that she was the person who had transported Charlie Moon's aunt Daisy to the cemetery on Tuesday. In a Ford pickup. A red F-150.

As the significance of this information dawned on him, Whitsun nodded slowly. "Oh, yeah." *You brought that old*

*Indian woman who I was following when my overall sus-
pender got hooked to the cart and I was drug halfway across
the cemetery.* Aunt Daisy's latest victim exhaled a melancholy sigh and tipped the bill of his ABC Hardware gimme
cap. "How're you doin', young lady?"

"Oh, fine." Which reminded Sarah why she had been
treading along the bricked pathway. "Have you seen a man
pass by in the last minute or so?" Her dark face blushed in-
visibly as she regretted her query, but in for a dime, in for a
dollar. The girl pointed toward where she had come from. "I
was over in the park and I saw someone I know, but before I
could say hello he walked away and . . . well, I was trying to
catch up with him, but he must have . . ." Her words petered
off like the end of a cold trail.

"No, ma'am, I ain't seen nobody around here but you."
Freddy Whitsun grunted again as he leaned to pick a coil of
yellow nylon rope off the ground. "But when I'm busy I don't
pay much attention to nothing but my work, so I guess anybody could've come by here without me noticing."

"He walks in the park quite often, so I suppose he might
come over here from time to time." She had a hopeful
thought. "Maybe you know him."

"I know almost everybody in Granite Creek County."
The cemetery custodian stuck the trowel into his hip pocket.
"What's this fella's name?"

"Erasmus Boyle," she said. "Actually, it's *Captain* Erasmus Boyle."

Whitsun's face went blank as a chalkboard slate that'd
just been wiped clean with a damp rag.

Sarah's expressive countenance mirrored her disappointment. "You've never heard of him?"

The custodian hesitated. "That name's a familiar one."

The happy girl flashed a pretty smile. "Do you know
where I could find him?"

Turning as if to avert his face from her gaze, Whitsun
nodded. After another, longer hesitation, the custodian muttered, "But I don't think he'd want me to tell you."

"Oh." This revelation was acutely embarrassing. "Well . . . it wasn't all that important; please just forget that I asked." As Sarah turned to depart, her gaze was pulled to the custodian, who was looping the end of the rope through a sturdy eyebolt on the cemetery utility cart. If being given the brush-off by Captain Boyle "wasn't all that important," then why was she so interested in such a mundane matter as Freddy Whitsun and his yellow nylon rope? Because, by means of some deep warning instinct, she was certain that something important was about to happen. Sarah Frank couldn't imagine what.

The Sleeper Awakens

Just as Sarah Frank had imagined, Daisy Perika did awaken and rub her sleepy eyes. Moreover, she looked around with an inquisitive expression. It would be gratifying to report that she wondered, *Where in the world has the flighty girl gone?* but Daisy's cooperation has its limits. Her actual thoughts were, *Good, that silly Ute-Papago orphan has gone off to toss popcorn at the ducks or annoy some poor homeless person. This is my chance to slip away and find it!*

Find what?

It would appear that Charlie Moon's aunt is not ready to reveal that piece of information.

CHAPTER FIFTY-FOUR

A LYNCHING

As Freddy Whitsun was tying the nylon rope onto the electric cart's steel eyebolt, a worrisome thought occurred to the custodian. He gave Sarah Frank a wary look. "I expect Cap'n Boyle brought you here to see me."

Sarah was at a loss for words at such a peculiar suggestion. But not thoughts. *Mr. Whitsun might be right.* His speculation certainly fit the facts. Had the enigmatic young man been—in a literal sense—leading her down the garden path?

"I guess I ought'n to be surprised." After grimacing thoughtfully at a stout cottonwood limb that stretched out about six feet over his head, Freddy Whitsun tossed the free end of the rope over the branch and grabbed it as it fell. The big man gave the nylon rope a hard tug and seemed satisfied. "Boyle's just one more person hereabouts who's mad at me. I did my best to apologize and make amends, but I guess he means to stir up all the trouble he can. I expect he knows what I'm fixing to do and wanted you to come and be a witness."

"I don't understand what you mean—" Sarah watched in horror as the custodian's dexterous fingers began to fashion a noose in the rope. She heard her mouth ask, "What are you doing, Mr. Whitsun?"

"You'd best leave now, young lady."

"You aren't actually planning to . . ." She could not get the awful phrase past her lips.

"Yes ma'am, I am." Whitsun stepped onto a stubby pine stump. "You run along now."

"No!" She stamped her sandaled foot on the ground. "You mustn't do that!"

The big man took his ABC Hardware cap off and slipped the noose over his shaggy head. "And why not?"

This stopped her cold. But not for long. "Because it's *wrong*."

"Say's who?"

"Say's *God*!" Her voice was steady now. "Suicide is a mortal sin."

A man can't spit around here without hitting a Catholic. But the fervent Christian's assertion had gotten his attention. The mortal who was about to embark on a one-way journey to an uncertain destination paused to explain, "I don't have no choice—I *have* to do it."

Sarah stepped past the Maude Plimpton tombstone. "No you don't."

"Yes I do."

She approached the stump and looked up. "Why?"

"Because all I do is mess up." Whitsun sighed. "If I go on living, I'm bound to keep on causing all kinds of trouble. But once I'm dead as a rusty doornail, that's the end of it."

Sarah shook her head. "No it's not."

"You're just a kid—what do you know?"

The little trooper straightened her back like a West Point cadet. "I know that anybody who doesn't face up to the hard things in life is a . . . a *coward*!" There.

The noosed man snorted. "What've *you* ever faced up to, Little Miss Goody Two-shoes?"

A fair question, and Miss Frank told him more than a thing or two. Which recitation included the violent death of her parents when she was a tot, and how she almost got sent to jail for a murder over in Utah and would have if Charlie Moon hadn't come to her rescue, and how she'd had to fight off a coyote down on the Southern Ute reservation who intended to eat Mr. Zig-Zag, and —

"Who the heck is Mr. Zig-Zag?"

"My cat."

"Oh." That struck a chord. *I had me a black kitty when I was five years old.* Whitsun's brow furrowed as he tried to remember the fuzzy little creature. *What was his name?*

"And that's not all." Sarah seated herself on a rectangular slab of weathered limestone that Whitsun had pushed aside from the grave he'd put the flowers on. She took a deep breath and told this virtual stranger what she'd never said out loud to a single soul in the whole wide world: "And more than anything, I want to be Charlie Moon's wife—but he hardly knows I'm alive. And he's going to marry someone else."

Despite his pressing personal problems, Mr. Whitsun was beginning to get interested. "Who?"

Sarah looked up at the massive figure looming above her like an overalled bear. "What?"

"Who's ol' Charlie Moon going to marry?"

"Patsy Poynter. She works over at the public library."

From time to time, the handyman checked out volumes by Zane Grey and Louis L'Amour. The reader breathed a low whistle. "That little blue-eyed blonde's sure a looker."

"Thanks a lot."

"Sorry, kid." Freddy Whitsun realized that some kind of compliment was called for. "You're cute as a spotted puppy under a red wagon."

Sarah glared at the peculiar man. "Now take that silly noose off your neck and get off the stump."

As Whitsun shook his head, the yellow rope scratched his sunburned neck.

Remembering how TV-show police dealt with jumpers and hostage-takers and the like, Sarah thought she might as well give that a try. *If I can just keep him talking long enough, maybe he'll lose interest in killing himself.* "You wouldn't want to die without making a confession."

The self-condemned man astonished his softhearted, would-be savior with this reply: "I hadn't thought about it, but I guess you're right." But a difficulty occurred to the non-Catholic. "Don't you need a priest to do that?"

"Not in extenuating circumstances." Sarah summoned up all her courage. "You can confess to me."

The potential confessee arched a doubtful brow. "And you wouldn't tell a soul about my sins?"

Her head bobbed in an earnest nod. "Cross my heart and hope to *die!*"

Reassured by this sacred oath, Freddy Whitsun proceeded to tell the girl about his many messings-up. The man on the stump started off with some bad things he'd done in grade school (dipping a red-headed girl's pigtail in purple ink), and proceeded with a long, seemingly endless list of failures that sounded more like dumb mistakes than sins to Sarah, who was pleased that her ploy to delay the suicidal man was working so well. So far.

Skipping some unseemly incidents that were too graphic for a young lady's ears, the repentant sinner finally worked his way up to his most recent troubles. "Everything I've done has come back to haunt me." Whitsun proceeded to provide a lurid account of the pair of "spirits" that had appeared at his bedroom window during the wee hours.

"When you say spirits, do you mean . . . ghosts?"

The haunted man groaned and nodded his head.

I bet he's been reading some scary ghost stories. Or watching them on TV. Sarah remembered those terrifying apparitions who'd haunted Scrooge. "Ghosts like in 'A Christmas Carol'?"

This reference produced a puzzled expression.

Sarah explained the gist of Mr. Dickens's plot, dwelling for quite some time on the scene where Marley's ghost appears at the miserable miser's bedside. She was about to move on to the Sprits of Christmas Past, etc., when Freddy Whitsun halted her narrative with an impatient gesture.

"I can't stand on this damned stump all day listening to fairy tales—my back is starting to ache." Sensing that he had hurt the storyteller's feelings, Whitsun admitted that he vaguely recalled the tale, and agreed that his experience was much like that. Except in his story, there were only two haunts and they always appeared together. "One of them reminds me of my worst sins and tells me how much trouble I've caused and how I ain't fit to live. The other one says— more or less—I ain't so much a sinner as a halfwit who's to be pitied." *I don't know which one of 'em aggravates me the most.* "They show up a few hours after the sun goes down and don't leave me alone till dawn—I don't hardly get a wink of sleep." The defeated man seemed about to burst into tears. "I just can't take it anymore."

Knowing that she was losing control of the potential suicide, Sarah took another tack. "Your ghost story sounds like a tall tale." She assumed a doubtful expression. "Are you making all this up?"

The noosed man shook his head. "If I'm lyin', I'm dyin'." *Which, come to think about it, is kinda funny.* "There, I've had my say—the confession's done with—end of story." Freddy "Fixit" Whitsun jabbed a thumb in the direction Sarah had come from. "Now you run along home so's I can get on with what I need to do."

The girl had opened her mouth to protest when her conversation with the cemetery custodian was abruptly interrupted—

"Leave this bozo to me, Sarah—I'll deal with him."

CHAPTER FIFTY-FIVE

ENTER THE HANGWOMAN

Sarah Frank got up from her uncomfortable seat on the old limestone tombstone and turned to gape in amazement at Daisy Perika. *How did she know where to find me?*

The young woman's question was based upon a false premise; the tribal elder had not gone looking for Sarah. Even so, she was not entirely surprised to find the girl in this spot—which was Daisy's *destination*. Like Freddy Whitsun, the old woman assumed that Erasmus Boyle must have brought Sarah here—and that possibility suggested all sorts of sinister business. But that wrinkle in Daisy's plot could be mulled over later on, when dark nights and chill winter winds kept an old lady close to the fireplace. At the moment, Charlie Moon's aunt had urgent business to tend to.

Pegging along on her sturdy oak staff, she left the bricked walkway and made her way to the stump that served as Mr. Whitsun's going-away platform. After a glance at the bouquet of white roses he'd placed on the freshly sodded ground, Daisy focused her hard black eyes on the person atop the stump. "I've probably seen more winters than any of the big trees in this cemetery, and I never heard a grown man admit to so much foolishness in my whole life."

Reeling like a massive statue about to topple off its pedestal, Whitsun glared down at the black-garbed old eavesdropper who'd heard his secret confession. Her abrupt appearance suggested a wicked witch who had materialized right on the spot. For the first time, it occurred to the cemetery custodian that this spiteful creature was probably responsible for his accident. *I bet she put a curse on that machine and made it drag me off.* This reasonable surmise led to another one: *Cap'n Boyle must've sent her here to torment me.* "So what's the plan, Granny—you aim to set me afire before I can hang myself?"

"Don't tempt me, Sonny." Turning to Sarah, Daisy pointed her walking stick toward the bricked pathway. "Go wait over there while I deal with this dimwit!"

Having about played out her hand with Whitsun, and hopeful that the resourceful old woman might know how to deter the potential suicide, the girl withdrew without protest.

When she was satisfied that Sarah was out of earshot, Daisy approached the foot of the stump and looked up at the massive man who loomed above her. "That was the sorriest confession I ever heard in my entire life."

"How would you know?" Whitsun managed a snort. "You don't look nothin' like a priest to me."

"For the problem you've got, I'm better than a priest." Daisy poked the butt of her walking stick at Whitsun's belly and was pleased to see him cringe. "I'm the only person in Granite Creek County who can solve all of your problems— why I've chased more haunts away than you've got hairs sprouting out of your ears."

The man's expression betrayed his apprehension. "You're some kinda witch, ain't you?"

The old crone cackled. "D'you want my help, or don't you?"

Resigned to whatever fate awaited him, the hopeless man shrugged. "I guess it couldn't hurt."

Daisy suppressed a smile. *Don't be so sure about that.*

He eyed his unlikely benefactor with frank suspicion. "What d'you want in return—all my hard cash?"

"No. I've got so many greenbacks that I bale it like hay."

Maybe so, but Freddy Whitsun knew that witches don't work pro bono. *She's bound to want something.* "So what do I hafta do?"

Lowering her voice to a hoarse whisper, Daisy told him, "Tell me what you *didn't* tell Sarah."

Her victim did not immediately consent to the tribal elder's terms; even the most upright cemetery custodian you'll ever meet has a few secrets he'd prefer to take to his grave. But the outcome was never in doubt. The haunted man was desperate for some peace of mind before he expired, and this doubtful opportunity seemed to be his last chance. He agreed to fill in the blank pages of his confession—but only on the condition that the presumed witch treat his revelation as Top Secret—For Her Ears Only. Daisy agreed.

About ten paces away, Sarah could barely catch a word now and then and only from the cemetery custodian's lips. *I wonder what Aunt Daisy's up to?*

From time to time, so does Charlie Moon, saintly priests, and heads of state. They shudder at the possibilities.

After Mr. Whitsun had kept his part of the bargain, Daisy pointed her staff at the rope. "You call yourself Mr. Fixit, and don't even know how to hang yourself proper."

The skilled handyman was *up to here* with self-appointed critics. "What d'you mean by that crack?"

The old woman's throat rattled with a derisive laugh. "Why that's nothing but a cheap old cotton clothesline rope—if a man of half your weight stepped off that stump, it'd snap just like that." To demonstrate, she snapped finger and thumb.

The prideful jack-of-all-trades puffed up his barrel chest. "I'll have you know, that's a brand-new nylon towrope that's rated for two tons. I bought it this morning at the A-1 Auto Parts store."

"Well those slickers sure saw *you* coming." Daisy eyed

the section of rope tied to the cemetery cart. "What'd you pay for it?"

The flustered consumer tried to remember. "Nineteen ninety-nine, I think." *Or was it twenty-nine ninety-nine? Prices went up so fast that it was hard to keep track of expenditures.*

Daisy approached the miniature truck and examined the rope. "Well, when I'm wrong, I'm wrong—that's nylon, all right." She gave it a light jerk. "And it oughta get the job done. But . . . well, I guess it's not any of *my* business."

Freddy Whitsun tried to look over his shoulder. "What's the matter?"

"You didn't give yourself quite enough slack." The old woman shook her head and sighed. "When you step off the stump, you'll just hang there like a silly jackass and strangle to death while your face turns blue and your eyes bug out and your tongue swells up and sticks out of your mouth like you was trying to swallow a purple squash." She examined the knot. "If you want me to, I'll untie this thing and give you a little extra rope. Then, when you take that final step, your neck'll snap like a dry stick."

"Well . . . okay." He swallowed hard. *In all my born days, I never met such a cold-blooded old woman.*

Leaning her walking stick against the electric vehicle, Daisy unlooped the heavy purse from her shoulder and placed it on the ground.

Sarah Frank was beginning to get fidgety. "Aunt Daisy—what are you doing?"

The Ute elder turned to yell at the troublesome girl, "I'm taking care of the job you started and couldn't finish." She waved impatiently. "Now back off and keep your mouth shut, or I'll knock him off the stump with my walking stick and put an end to this silly business!"

Not daring to interfere with any effort that might prevent a self-murder, Sarah backed up another two paces. She was delighted when the senior citizen began untying the knot on the eyebolt. *Aunt Daisy has talked Mr. Whitsun out of hanging himself!*

The optimist's joy was premature.

Daisy allowed about four inches of additional slack, then retied the sturdy rope tightly to the eyebolt.

Sarah was puzzled by this reversal. *What's she up to?* She considered several possibilities before settling on . . . *Aunt Daisy's playing for time until she can think of something to do.*

Grateful for the slight looseness at the business end of the rope, Freddy Whitsun watched from the corner of one bloodshot eye as the morbid old woman added a granny knot for good measure.

Like any skilled craftsman who takes pride in her work, Daisy fussed for some final touches. She gave the rope a stiff jerk that startled the about-to-be-hanged man, made sure the steel eyebolt was securely attached to the cart, eyed the knot, and whatnot. When she was satisfied that everything was in perfect order, Charlie Moon's auntie retrieved her purse and walking stick and toddled back to the stump. In a voice too low for Sarah to hear, she politely asked the aspiring rope-dancer for a small favor. Would Mr. Whitsun mind delaying his execution until she had time to find a better vantage point? Daisy explained that she had not witnessed a lynching since she was six years old, and wanted to get a good look at his final performance.

The condemned man nodded his agreement to this reasonable request, and Daisy turned her back and walked away.

The Ute-Papago girl was beyond puzzled. *Something doesn't look right about this.*

When Daisy Perika had withdrawn to the desired position, which was far enough away to avoid injury when the cemetery custodian stepped off the stump, she raised her oak walking stick and yelled, "Me and this Ute-Papago orphan have better things to do than stand around here all afternoon while you try to get your nerve up—let's get this show going!"

Sarah could not believe her ears. Surely, even Aunt Daisy would not urge a man to commit suicide.

The doomed Caucasian had his pride and he was tired of being bossed around by every know-it-all Indian who happened by. "Don't hurry me—I aim to do this right." Whitsun set his jaw in the same stubborn expression he'd used when he was three years old and in no mood to eat another spoonful of goopy spinach.

"You just need a little help." Daisy smiled sweetly. "I'll start counting—when I get to five, you can take your swan dive." The old crone raised her staff again and croaked, "One."

Sarah screamed, "No!"

"Two," saith the stolid tribal elder.

The tender girl closed her eyes. *This can't be happening.* It could and was and would.

Impatient with the proceedings, Daisy raised her voice and boomed like the crack of doom, "Three—four—*five!*"

Well, here goes nothin'. Freddy Whitsun closed his eyes tightly. Said a quick prayer. *Now I lay me down to sleep.* Took that final step.

Down he came.

When his boot soles were about eighteen inches above the ground, the stout rope went taught, the sturdy cottonwood limb bent like a drawn bow—but it did not break.

Something else did. The cracking *snap* was horrifying.

The ill-fated man hit the ground like a 260-pound sack of potatoes.

As she hurried toward Daisy's victim, Sarah shouted loud enough to wake the dead, "Oh, *no!*"

Flat on his back and still wearing the noose, Whitsun opened his eyes. He blinked a bleary-eyed gaze at the cloudy sky. "I think I sprained my ankle."

This was beyond amazing. "What happened?" The answer to Sarah's question was provided forthwith. The yellow rope had slipped over the tree limb and fallen with Whitsun. Several yards of yellow cord were draped over the overalled man. "But how . . ." She turned her wide-eyed gaze on the cemetery cart. A few inches of the nylon rope hung from the eyebolt, where it was still securely tied. "The rope snapped." She turned to Daisy. "It's a miracle!"

The worldly old reprobate snorted at this pious suggestion. "One broke rope, that's just a piece of good luck that could happen to any silly sad sack." Ever cheerful, Daisy Perika tapped Whitsun's swelling left ankle with her walking stick and chuckled as he winced. "How about having a few more go's at it, Freddy?" As the befuddled man pushed himself up to a sitting position, she presented a hideously wicked grin. "If that rope was to break, say six times out of seven—that'd be a sure-enough miracle."

A cruel old woman? Some might say so, but at grave risk of being uncharitable.

As if to demonstrate that she had his best interests at heart, Daisy leaned and whispered some advice into Mr. Whitsun's ear. Wise counsel that Sarah Frank could not hear. Was this the only evidence of Daisy's good intentions toward the sorrowful soul? No. Even as she whispered, Charlie Moon's mischievous auntie was slipping something back into her purse. A Baby Butterbean.

What in the world would Daisy be doing with something like *that*?

Well. What a question. Why, any freckle-faced Kentucky lad who ever peeled a red apple or skinned a jughead catfish will tell you that a Baby Butterbean is a smallish Case folding knife with two razor-sharp blades—either of which can slice through a yellow nylon rope like it was warm butter. Or, when a softhearted old sinner is obliged to produce a counterfeit miracle right on the spot—about 96 percent of the way through.

CHAPTER FIFTY-SIX

SUPPERTIME AT THE COLUMBINE

This evening's meal at the ranch headquarters was much like dozens of others Scott Parris had enjoyed since that turning point in Charlie Moon life, when—literally overnight—the hardworking, underpaid, uniformed Southern Ute police officer was suddenly transformed into the proud owner of one of the finest cattle ranches in Colorado. Moon has never revealed precisely how this highly unlikely transformation occurred, not even to his closest friend. And for good reasons. But that peculiar transaction had happened quite some time ago, not long after Daisy had told a skeptical little girl a tall-ish tale about Grandmother Spider. Such bizarre episodes are best left buried in the past.

As it happens, Mr. Moon is not the only person seated at the headquarters dining table who has a bizarre secret.

When Scott Parris was a Chicago police officer whose regular beat was South Halstead Street, the mostly straight-as-an-arrow cop cut a corner now and then. No, he'd never accepted a thin dime in the form of a bribe. Parris's occasional corner cutting involved protecting innocent citizens from seriously dangerous felons who were beyond the reach of legal justice.

Even Sarah Frank has done a few things she is ashamed of, such as knocking a Tonapah, Utah sheriff flat on his back with a baseball bat. Not that she had the least intent to injure a sworn officer of the law—the fellow with the badge on his shirt had snuck up quietly and *scared* her. And Sarah has another secret that she is obliged to take to her grave—the solemn promise she made to suicidal cemetery custodian Freddy Whitsun to treat his confession with all the discretion of a Catholic priest.

Does Daisy Perika have dark secrets? (Is water wet?) To put it more quantitatively: sufficient to fill every square inch in the Granite Creek telephone book. Including the Yellow Pages. With small print that can be read only through a magnifying glass. Enough said.

Or perhaps not . . . Scott Parris is about to say something.

"Please pass me the biscuits."

Daisy passed them. "D'you want the butter too?"

He did. And as the chief of police used a serrated steak knife to slice a made-from-scratch biscuit neatly into halves, he cast an innocent glance at Sarah Frank. "So how's your schoolwork coming along?"

The university student shrugged. "Okay, I guess."

As he buttered his hot biscuit, Parris aimed another kind of glance at Charlie Moon—who got the message loud and clear.

The rancher stirred a spoonful of Tulia, Texas honey into his coffee. "You still interviewing those homeless folks?"

Sarah nodded. After taking a sip of iced tea, she added, "When I get a chance."

Parris pretended to recall a small detail. "Let's see—when did you say you were going back to Grant Park to talk to that Boyle fella?"

"I never said." Whilst using a three-tined fork to roll a green pea across her plate, the pretty girl batted her eyelashes at Moon. "I have no interest in seeing Captain Boyle again." Sarah waited for Charlie to ask *why*. She might as well have waited for the grandfather clock to strike thirteen.

"Sorry to hear it," Moon said. "I was hoping he'd accept an invite to the ranch." The rancher sliced a sizable chunk off his steak. "If I do say so myself, this is mighty fine prime beef."

After enjoying a helping of his own T-bone, biscuit, baked Idaho spud, and some private thoughts, Parris pointed a greasy fork at Sarah. "I sure wish you'd reconsider."

She stared at the cop. "What?"

"Hanging out in U.S. Grant Park to talk to poor homeless folk." Parris took the final bite of buttered biscuit, then lifted his cup for a long drink of black coffee. "Ah, that was good."

Sarah was still staring. "Why?"

In a buck-passing mood, Parris aimed the fork again—this time at his best friend. "You tell her, Charlie."

Knowing his buddy's game plan, Mr. Moon proved to be a reluctant receiver. "Tell her what, pardner?"

Charlie ain't no help at all. "That a young lady is well-advised to stay clear of insane vagrants, pickpockets, drunks, drug addicts, and all the other lowlife that drifts around in the park."

Sarah smiled at the white cop. "I appreciate your concern for my safety."

Parris grunted. "But you won't pay any attention to a word I've said."

"On the contrary." Having lost interest in the insipid green pea, she set her fork aside. "From time to time, I'll probably visit the park to enjoy the trees and grass and the duck pond. But I don't intend to continue my class project there. Tomorrow, I'll speak to my RMP adviser. With Professor Armstrong's permission, I'll move my interviews to safer places. Like the Salvation Army homeless shelter. And the Lutheran soup kitchen."

The chief of police blinked at the girl in disbelief. "Really—and just because of my advice?"

The girl nodded. *And because I don't ever want to see Captain Boyle again.*

Well, I guess there has to be a first time for everything. Was the hardened old cop deeply moved? Yes indeed. Coincidentally, there was something in the corner of Parris's left eye that needed rubbing away with his knuckle. Most likely, a stray gnat that had landed there to take a quick sip from a tear duct.

Elderly ladies find their entertainment where they can. Daisy Perika, who was enjoying scrambled eggs and white Wonder Bread for supper, had also enjoyed the small drama. And Charlie Moon's irascible aunt was feeling more than a little smug. *If that silly Ute-Papago girl knew one-tenth of what I do, she'd never set foot in that park again as long as she lived.*

After Sarah served up heaping helpings of Daisy's peach cobbler to the men, the tribal elder waited just long enough to receive their well-deserved compliments before withdrawing to the headquarters front-porch swing.

CHAPTER FIFTY-SEVEN
THE OLD WOMAN WHO KNEW TOO MUCH

Not that knowing ten times more about the recent crimes than Charlie Moon and Scott Parris combined could be characterized as excessive. On the contrary, having this edge on the lawmen was the delightful stuff that Daisy Perika's happiest daydreams were made of—but only when she had an opportunity to gloat. And high-quality gloating couldn't be had unless she told Charlie and Scott what she'd found out just by paying attention. In this instance, the shameless old braggart would be denied that delicious pleasure. She had agreed to Freddy Whitsun's condition that the second installment of his confession be treated with the same confidence as the admissions he'd made to Sarah, and . . . *Once you've given your word, you have to do what you promised to.* Her secret knowledge must be taken to the grave.

Aside from Daisy's solemn promise to the suicidal handyman, there were personal reasons for concealing what she'd found out. Not the least of these was protecting the more sinister secrets of her arcane profession. *I always intended to teach Sarah how to cure sores and stop bleeding and heal a bad cough.* These tricks of Daisy's trade were useful skills for the shaman's probable successor to learn. *But there are some dangerous things that the girl ought not to know— like how to steal another person's power.* Daisy supposed that Sarah's theft was unintentional, merely an unintended consequence of a playful, almost childish prank. Nevertheless, the tribal elder harbored an uneasy suspicion that Sarah's whimsical action might have been driven by some dark inner ambition that the girl was not aware of. It was just possible that . . . *Deep down inside, something in her is yearning for the Power.* If it was, that Something's appetite must not be satisfied—and Sarah Frank must never realize what she had accomplished.

There was still another reason why Daisy was compelled to conceal what she knew: *If Charlie Moon finds out that Freddy Whitsun was about to hang himself, he's bound to start asking questions.* And when her determined nephew made up his mind to "look into a matter," Charlie didn't stop digging until he'd gotten to the bottom of it.

As she sat on the front-porch swing, kicking herself gently to and fro, the tribal elder mulled over what she had to do. *I'll keep a close eye on that girl until Charlie forgets about Erasmus Boyle and Betty Naranjo's vanishing act is last month's news.* Mr. Fixit was another matter. *Freddy Whitsun knows where Sarah's friend is—and he knows why Boyle was complaining about being kept awake nights by some young woman and her crying baby. But what Freddy* don't *know is—* Daisy was momentarily distracted when she sensed a presence in the yard, where twilight was gradually giving ground to inky darkness. The old lady stopped swinging and craned her neck. *I don't see a thing out there.* Daisy concluded that it was probably one of Charlie Moon's cowboys lurking around. *What was I thinking about?* Oh, right. *What Freddy Whitsun* don't *know is how to keep his mouth shut—not even when his worthless life depends on it!*

She hoped that Mr. Whitsun had taken her whispered advice and left town. *But that don't mean that Mr. Fixit won't get picked up somewhere for running a Stop sign and start flapping his tongue about how haunts chased him out of Colorado.* Daisy closed her tired eyes and sighed. She had done her best. *But no matter how hard a person tries to make things right, there's a hundred ways they can still go wrong.* Especially with the legendary Southern Ute tribal investigator poking around. *Without any help from me or Sarah or Mr. Fixit or anyone else—Charlie Moon has his ways of figuring out what's been going on.* This assertion was truer than she knew.

Bewildered by the complexity of her difficulties, the frustrated problem solver resumed her swinging. She also shifted gears to consider a matter of some practical importance: *First thing I need to do is straighten out this problem with Sarah.* Daisy was wrapped so tightly in her thoughts that she didn't hear the screened door open with a slight creak and shut softly. Neither did her ears pick up the muted padding of store-bought moccasins on the redwood porch. She did feel the weight on the swing as the subject of her musings seated herself beside her.

Sarah Frank looped a slender arm around the old woman's hunched shoulders. "Mind some company?"

The tribal elder shook her head.

Having interrupted the rhythmic motion of the porch swing, the willowy girl used her right heel to apply a slight push that was perfectly synchronized with her companion's listless kick. "It sure gets dark quick."

Not inclined toward small talk, Daisy played the silent Indian. The senior citizen had a subject that she wanted to bring up, but did not know how to do it. *Not without telling this silly girl things she oughtn't to know.*

"Oh!" Sarah dragged her foot on the floor and pointed. "What's that?"

Annoyed to have her hundred-ton train of thought derailed by this mere slip of a girl, Daisy glared at the place where her companion was aiming her finger. "What's *what*? I don't see anything." Which, as it happened, was precisely the point.

"It looks like . . . a person." Sarah shivered.

"Your eyes are playing tricks on you." Daisy recalled her recent impression that someone was out there in the shadows, watching her. "Or it's one of Charlie's dumb cowboys spying on us."

"No, it's somebody with feathers on his head."

"Big Bird from the TV show?" The old woman cackled at her jest.

Sarah shook her head, brushing Daisy's cheek with a black braid. "It's an Indian!"

The tribal elder rolled her eyes. "So this is what the world's come to—a Ute-Papago girl who's afraid of redskins!" She elbowed Sarah. "You figure it's a 'Pache come to scalp us?"

The startled girl did not say a word.

"Physician, Heal Thyself."

The old woman turned her wrinkled face to stare into the moonlight-dappled darkness. *There* is *something out there.* She sniffed. *I can smell its stink.* Cocked her ear. *And I can hear it mumbling something.* But Daisy could not *see* it. Suddenly understanding, the Ute shaman seized this opportunity by the neck. "What you see is a dead person—an old spirit who probably lived in this valley ages ago."

"I know." Sarah clenched her hands into knobby little fists.

Assuming her best bedside manner, Dr. Daisy addressed her patient in a soft but knowing tone. "How long has this been going on?"

"I don't know. Not long." Sarah shrugged. "A week or two, I guess."

Daisy reached out to touch the girl's trembling shoulder. "Are you scared?"

"Yes." Relieved to tell someone about her fears, Sarah sucked in a deep breath. "Sometimes I'm afraid to go out at night." She closed her eyes. "I guess I ought to talk to a psychologist . . . or a psychiatrist."

"Oh, there's no need for that." The old woman held her smile inside. "I can help you."

Opening her eyes, Sarah turned to focus her gaze on the aged woman's shrunken profile. "You can?"

"Sure." Daisy had not missed the hint of doubt in the girl's question. "It's like singing warts away or curing stomach cramps with a cold stone from the river." *I'll tell the girl what she wants to hear.* "There's no magic to it—all it takes is what those know-it-all *matukach* doctors call 'suggestion.'"

"Really—it's that easy?"

Professionals have their pride. The shaman's face stiffened. "It's easy for those of us that *know how*."

"Can you do it right now?"

"I could if I had the right things to do it with."

"What do you need?"

"Well, a buffalo-hide drum would help. And a duck's-head flute made from a north-pointing branch of a cedar." Even in the twilight, she saw a shadow fall over the stricken girl's face. "But in an emergency, I might get by with—oh, I don't know . . . maybe a little feather."

Sarah blinked. "I have a feather!"

"Do you, now?"

Her head bobbed in a nod. "It's in my hatband." She hesitated. "Actually, it's *your* feather."

"My feather?" Daisy feigned a puzzled expression. "What're you talking about?"

Sarah proceeded to tell Charlie Moon's manipulative aunt how she'd found the feather in Daisy's closet, and reminded the forgetful old soul that she had flicked the feather across her closed eyelids and that Daisy had awakened from her nap with a start and—

"Oh, *that* feather."

"I'll go get it." Sarah ejected herself from the swing like a fighter pilot whose engine has flamed out.

Pad-pad-pad-pad-pad go the girl's soft doeskin moccasins.

Creak-bang goes the screened door.

Daisy let the smile out. *For years, I've wondered what'd happened to my special owl feather—and all that time it was in the bedroom closet.*

Special, indeed. The night-fowl in question had suffered the singular misfortune of being perched on the branch of a tall ponderosa when that tree was struck by a bolt of summer lightning. Daisy Perika had witnessed the fortuitous incident and—determined to take advantage of this once-in-a-lifetime opportunity—she had rushed to the burning tree and found the bird's charred corpse on the ground. After a close inspection of the warm carcass, the shaman had removed a single tail feather. The feather of a lightning-killed owl was potentially so powerful that the tribal elder had decided to conceal her prize until a critical occasion occurred that would justify its use. Alas, as so often happens, only a few weeks passed before the old woman forgot where she had squirreled her treasure away.

Sarah Frank is returning.

Creak-bang goes the screened door.

Pad-pad-pad-pad-pad go her moccasins across the red-wood porch floor.

She plops onto the swing. "Here it is."

Daisy accepted the offering. "This won't take a minute." She pointed with the feather. "Can you still see Mr. Feather-head in the yard?"

Forcing herself to take a quick glance, Sarah nodded.

"Okay, now close your eyes."

The girl didn't have to be told twice.

The shaman touched Sarah's left lid, and muttered an incantation in an archaic version of the Ute tongue that the *pitukupf* would have understood, but not this Ute-Papago college girl. Daisy repeated the treatment on Sarah's right eyelid, once again uttering the ancient words. The recitation was a piece of theater intended to enhance the drama. (Rough translation: "Rabbit stew is good for you.") The placebo effect is powerful therapy. Particularly when combined with the tail feather of a lightning-scorched owl.

"Now you can open your eyes."

The patient hesitated.

"Go ahead," Daisy said confidently. "There'll be no spirit to see; you're cured as you can be." Even while making the confident assertion, the self-taught physician crossed the fingers of her left hand.

Sarah opened one eye. Then the other. "Oh—he's gone!"

"Hah—what'd I tell you!" *But he's still there.*

How did the old woman know this? For the first time since that morning when Sarah had wiped the feather across her closed eyes, Daisy Perika could see dead people. Thus restored, the shaman felt like her old self again. How happy was she? Enough to cackle a raspy laugh, weep tears of joy that coursed down her leathery cheeks, and come very near losing control of her bladder. But she didn't; Daisy's victory was not quite complete. As if attempting to live up to her reputation, the alleged "meanest Ute woman ever to draw a breath" made a rude but meaningful gesture at the offensive specter. Sarah did not see the vulgar display of "sign language" but the Anasazi spirit evidently did. The offended haunt withdrew to the bank of Too Late Creek, concealing his humiliated presence in a cluster of trees.

Immensely pleased with her clever self, Daisy pocketed the owl feather. *Well, that turned out just fine.*

The delighted girl clapped her hands. "It worked—I really am cured."

"Sure you are." *And so am I!* Daisy puffed up like a toad. "And when I cure folks, they *stay* that way!"

The tribal elder's boast was not entirely reassuring. Moreover, the instant result seemed too good to be true. Doubt's cold breath began whispering misgivings in Sarah's ear. She frowned at her proud benefactor. "But what if the suggestion wears off . . . what if I wake up in the middle of the night and see a ghost in my bedroom?"

"Don't worry about it. You'll be having a nightmare."

"But—"

"Nightmare ghosts are all growl and bluff—just spit in Mr. Booger-man's big, bloodshot eyeball and he'll take off like a scalded hog." The miffed healer rolled her beady little eyes again. *Dumb kid.*

"But what if it isn't a dream and I really *do* see another ghost, what should I—"

"Take two aspirins and call me in the morning!"

Chapter Fifty-eight
Yet Another Uninvited Guest

Sarah Frank had withdrawn into the sanctuary of the Columbine headquarters (where haunts were rarely encountered), leaving Daisy Perika queen of the swing. Despite a sudden sense of loneliness, the aged monarch was determined to enjoy the restoration of her shamanish insight, the serene silence of the balmy night—and the smug recollection of how she'd dismissed the troublesome spirit that had frightened Sarah. For the first time since the girl had stroked the owl feather across her eyelids, Miss Daisy was at peace—and very near to being happy. This blissful interlude had lasted for almost a minute, when . . .

A big and bony Something commenced to bumpity-bumping under the porch.

The old woman sighed. *Soon as I get rid of one aggravation, up pops another to take its place.*

Emerging from his dark hideaway, the odorous descendant of wolves lurched up the porch steps to shuffle along the redwood planks and plop down by Daisy's feet. For some reason or other, Sidewinder was fond of Charlie Moon's grumpy aunt.

The arrival of the Columbine hound made the old woman feel lonelier than ever, the animal's presence serving only to emphasize the absence of human company. The tribal elder could have followed the nineteen-year-old girl into the big log house and found all the human companionship that a person of Daisy's irritable disposition could stomach, but . . . *Sarah would sit up all night talking my leg off about ghosts and goblins and whatnot.* And her nephew? *Charlie Moon would wonder what was bothering me. He wouldn't go to bed until he made sure I was okay.* Which reminded her of Scott Parris's presence. The combination of two inquisitive lawmen was more than she cared to deal with. What it added up to was that being lonesome was the least of the evils she had to choose from. And it wasn't like Daisy didn't have something pleasant to contemplate in her solitude. Putting one over on the Ute-Papago orphan with the very same owl feather that Sarah had used to steal her ghost-eyes was enormously gratifying, and Daisy was delighted to be her *old self* again. But the original problem remained. She was in the frustrating position of an angler who had just landed a twelve-pound trout but had no envious fishing buddy to show it to—or hear about the awful fight the rascal had put up. *I need to tell somebody how I figured things out.*

Shifting to a more comfortable position on the porch floor, Sidewinder laid his heavy head on Daisy's left foot.

She glared at the presumptuous animal. "That's all I'm good for—a pillow for an ugly jackrabbit chaser." This observation raised a pertinent question: "What're *you* good for, you hairy old bag of dog bones?"

The one so described rolled his big, brown eyes at the crotchety old biped. Almost as if to say, *What's the problem, Granny?* Almost.

Another interpretation of Sidewinder's highly evocative canine expression occurred to Daisy: *"You need somebody to talk to, fuss-pot—and I'm all ears and all you've got."* She frowned thoughtfully at the hound. *I guess that's why people keep a dog around—you can say whatever you want to a mutt, and they might whine or bark or growl but they don't actually talk back.* And more important than that . . . *A dog never repeats a word you say.*

Charlie Moon's aunt pulled her foot from under Sidewinder's jaw, which dropped with a thump. Pushing herself up from the swing with the oak staff, she leaned on the sturdy support and smiled slyly at the dog. "I've got something to say, Lassie—so listen up."

No offense was taken at the gender-bender designation. By the hound's reckoning, a Sidewinder by any other name was just as noble a creature.

Daisy addressed her companion in a distinctly upbeat tone. "I've got a notion that'll do us both a world of good."

Such an utterance from the tribal elder's crafty lips was sufficient to make strong men shudder, but the floppy-eared creature did not flinch. Deprived of his comfortable muzzle rest, the Columbine hound was open to interesting suggestions.

She prodded his rump with her oak staff. "Let's you and me go for a walk."

Though Sidewinder's English vocabulary was limited, the dog did get the gist of about a dozen vile curses and a few happy phrases ("go for a walk") that would cause his big ears to elevate just a smidgen and his tail to thump on whatever was beneath it.

And so they did. (Go for a walk.)

CHAPTER FIFTY-NINE

THE LAWMEN DELIBERATE

After helping Sarah Frank wash and dry the supper dishes, Charlie Moon and Scott Parris had withdrawn to the rancher's upstairs office.

While his host stood peering though a window, the overfed chief of police was reviewing the culinary treats. *Columbine prime beef is tender as roast turkey and Daisy's peach pie is strictly world-class.* And a fine feast like that made a man feel pleasantly lethargic. Never one to contend with the gentle tug of sleep, Parris stretched out on the rancher's leather couch. *This is just what the doctor ordered.* He pulled the brim of his felt hat down to shade his blue eyes from the ceiling light's glare, then clasped his fingers behind his head. "If you don't mind, I'll enjoy a short after-supper siesta."

Moon switched off the lights.

"Thank you kindly." Like Daisy on the park bench, Parris feigned a yawn that triggered the genuine article.

One might reasonably assume that the rancher, who is the very spirit of hospitality, has flipped the wall switch for the comfort of his drowsy guest. Not so. Charlie Moon darkened the room for his own convenience. As he peers through the window, the Ute's pupils dilate, enabling his vision to penetrate the murky depths of the moonlit darkness. *I thought so.*

He assured himself that this development was nothing to be particularly concerned about. *But just to be on the safe side . . .*

Little Butch Cassidy was in the bunkhouse. Like Scott Parris, Charlie Moon's employee was horizontal. In this case, flat on his back in the sack. But the scrappy cowboy was not hankering for a nap. Butch was reading a signed first edition of B. E. Denton's *A Two-gun Cyclone*. Just when he got into a hair-raising true account of what would surely turn out to be a sure-enough Wild West shootout—Dr. Cassidy's mobile phone began to play a few of his favorite phrases from Gustav Mahler's *Der Titan*. That's right—*Dr.* Cassidy. The Columbine cow-pie kicker had more graduate degrees than the dean of Rocky Mountain Polytechnic University. The cowboy-scholar pressed the communications device against his rightmost ear. "Cassidy here."

Charlie Moon's voice boomed from the tiny telephone, "Daisy's out for a walk."

"Right." The Columbine employee who was assigned to keep an eye on the boss's aunt already had his boots on the hardwood floor. "Which way's she headed?" Cassidy listened to Moon's reply. "I'm right on top of it."

Wide awake now, Scott Parris chuckled in the darkness. "So what d'you figure your elderly relative's up to this time?"

"Just an after-supper stroll. She'll be alright." *Unless she slips and falls into the river. Or picks a fight with a bobcat. Or . . .* Moon smiled at himself. *I'm getting to be a first-rate worrier.* Which defect needed amending. Shifting gears, he addressed his guest. "Would you like to talk about what I *didn't* find out when I called all the local plumbers?"

"No thank you." The dyspeptic cop rolled onto his left side. "This couch is comfortable as a wagonload of baby-duck feathers. If it's all the same to you, I'll sleep right here tonight."

"Anywhere you like, pardner."

Moon watched a flat-black Butch Cassidy cutout slip out

of the back door of the bunkhouse and blend with the other nighttime shadows. *With Butch on the job, Daisy'll be safe as a baby in its mother's arms.*

The darkness was just right for a snooze, the couch comfy-cozy, Moon's office dead quiet. And Scott Parris was wide awake as a ten-year-old boy who'd drunk a quart of cowboy coffee. *I might as well get this over with.* He groaned. "Go ahead. Ruin my nap."

"You remember how Wanda Naranjo told us she'd called a plumber to fix that leak under her kitchen sink?"

"Sure I do. But the guy never showed and you ended up doing the job yourself. So what?"

"Well, I got to wondering which plumber she'd called."

"Why?"

"Just curious."

And I'm just suspicious. "So what'd you find out?"

"None of the mechanical contractors in Granite Creek admitted to getting a trouble call from Mrs. Naranjo to fix a leak—or for any other plumbing problem you can think of. Not on the Friday morning when her daughter disappeared, or anytime before or after that."

"Big surprise." Parris snorted. "The one that took the call didn't want to admit to being a few days overdue."

"I expect you're right about that." Moon turned to gaze out the office window, filling his eyes with darkness. "But when a plumber don't answer a trouble call, there's got to be a reason."

"No there don't," Parris grumped. "Plumbers are like cops; they don't need any reason at all to be somewhere else when you need 'em." He grinned. "Maybe he stopped at a doughnut shop."

The Indian's silence was an eloquent response.

"Dammit, Charlie!" There was a creak from the couch as Parris grunted himself into a seated position, a double-clunk as his Roper boot heels hit the hardwood floor. "So the plumber didn't show—*so what*? Mix-ups like that happen every day of the week."

Moon turned on the lights.

The lawmen exchanged squints.

The rancher seated himself behind his desk. "Maybe the plumber *almost* showed up."

"What does that mean?"

"Let's say he turned off the paved road into that long dirt lane that dead-ends at Mrs. Naranjo's residence—but he never got as far as her home." Three heartbeats. "It was getting dark about the time Betty Naranjo left the house. That big thunderstorm was rolling off the mountains and a fella might run his truck smack into a careless coyote or a startled mule deer . . . or a sixteen-year-old girl . . . without knowing what he'd hit."

"Hell's bells." Parris gazed at his scuffed boots. "But if the plumber run Betty Naranjo down on the lane, why didn't we find her there—" He blinked. "Oh, right. He hauled her away."

"It would explain everything, pard."

The white cop aimed a doubtful gaze at the Ute's dark face. "What do you mean . . . *everything*?"

"The girl walked away on a Friday morning. I don't think it's a coincidence that the cemetery custodian was found dead in his residence on the following Sunday morning."

Parris strained to make some sense of what his inscrutable Indian friend was saying. When the epiphany occurred, it was like a hard slap in the face. *Ohmygosh.* "You telling me the plumber—or somebody—was burying Betty Naranjo in the cemetery on Saturday night and that Morris Meusser heard something and . . ."

"It fits. Somebody's busy concealing a fresh corpse under the sod, Mr. Meusser hears something, goes to find out what's going down—and gets killed for his trouble."

The chief of police nodded his balding head. "Just for the sake of aggravating me, let's assume you're right. After the no-show plumber murders Meusser, he takes his body back to the custodian's quarters and . . . But how does he manage that?" A furrowed brow. "I'd sure hate to have a rasslin' match with the hardcase who could throw Meusser over his shoulder and carry him all the way back to his house."

Moon had already considered that objection. "Try this on for size: Meusser shows up on his electric utility truck. The guy who whacks him uses that convenient motorized transport to haul Meusser's body back to the custodian's residence."

Parris was beginning to see the sense in Moon's hypothesis. "He took the dead man home so the police wouldn't find out where the crime had occurred—and where Betty Naranjo's body was buried."

"That's the way I figure it, pard. He'd arrange things so it would look like Meusser had been murdered during a burglary. Laying the cemetery custodian's corpse out on the couch made it look like the man had been caught napping and got bludgeoned to death. Then the killer takes the dead man's pocket watch and cuts the phone line. After that, he probably walked back to the grave site and finished the burial Meusser had interrupted."

"Yeah." The white cop's stomach was beginning to churn. "And he'd do his best to make the new grave look like undisturbed ground." Scott Parris got to his feet and began to pace back and forth across Moon's upstairs office. "But who is this guy? We must have at least a dozen plumbers in Granite Creek."

"There are five mechanical contractors listed in the Yellow Pages," Moon said. "And most of those licensed plumbers have two or three employees who handle the small jobs."

"We could interview all of 'em, but nobody who's guilty of two homicides is going to admit to anything." Parris paused to direct a hopeful look at his deputy. "With a little luck, there might be a paper trail, like a work order."

"There might." The Ute shook his head. "But I wouldn't lay a two-bit bet on it."

Moon's best friend shook his head and began pacing

again. "If it went down like you say, we've got a hundred-acre cemetery to search for signs a recent unauthorized burial."

"That's about the size of it." Charlie Moon added, "And maybe twenty acres of that hundred are the old cemetery."

"Which is a Colorado historical site that's protected by state law," Parris grumbled. Not being an accomplished multitasker, the lawman paused his pacing to scratch at an itchy bristle of beard sprouting on his chin. "Without some solid evidence to support your theory, there's no way our gutless DA would get me a court order to dig anywhere I want to in Granite Creek Cemetery."

Charlie Moon wasn't about to give up. "Before you ask for permission to excavate, we could use dogs to search for a fresh burial site." On more than one occasion, Side-winder had sniffed out a corpse. "There's bound to be some clothing in Betty Naranjo's bedroom for the blood-hounds to sniff."

"Sure. But unless Wanda comes home and gives us permission, getting samples of her daughter's clothes would also require a warrant, which I *might* be able to get if I could convince Pug there's a good chance you're onto something—and that he'll look like a prize dope if he don't help." Parris jammed his big hands into his jacket pockets. The public servant figured most of his county-employee colleagues for grafters, parasites, and other lower forms of life, but the district attorney was the worst of the lot. *Pug Bullet ought to be strung up to the nearest cottonwood till he's stone-cold dead, shot six times in the head just to make sure—and then run outta town.* He restarted his pacing. "I don't know. From a strictly legal-beagle point of view, this whole notion of yours seems pretty thin."

"I'm inclined to agree." Moon leaned back in his chair. "But seeing as how I'm just a lowly paid part-time deputy, the decision to act on it ain't up to me."

"I'm sorry, Charlie. If there was just something more to go on . . ."

Moon's left eye twinkled. "How about the identity of the no-show plumber?"

The chief of police stopped in his tracks. "You're kidding me."

The jokester—who was notorious for having fun with his best friend—denied this frivolous charge.

"Okay, wise guy—tell me Mr. Pipe-wrench's name."

"I'd rather give you a hint." Moon paused for dramatic effect. "After I fixed that leak for Mrs. Naranjo, d'you recall what the grateful señorita said to me?"

"Not offhand." Parris produced a snort of the derisive sort. "But I'll bet *you* do."

"A man tends to treasure the occasional compliment he gets from the ladies." The Ute grinned. "She said . . . 'You're a *sure enough* handyman.'"

Scott Parris stared at his part-time deputy with a tinge of envy. *Ol' Charlie Moon don't miss a trick.* "Wanda can't afford a licensed plumber, so she called somebody who'd do the job on the cheap."

The tribal investigator's face was set like flint. "And we know who *that* was."

Chapter Sixty

Daisy Walks the Dog

There they go—Charlie Moon's aged auntie stepping sprightly like a lady who knows where she's going and aims to get there *right now*—Sidewinder zigzagging a circuitous route to sniff out any appalling delicacy that might appeal to a canine's inquisitive nose. Let it be duly noted that this was not a night for fainthearted folk to be out and strolling about; the darkness seemed filled to the brim with nameless horrors. Passing unscathed through malignant shadows where they barely escaped being snatched by a gruesome twosome of hideous stump-hobgoblins, the pair was immediately embraced in the suffocating night shade cast by long, leafy arms slyly posing as innocent cottonwood branches. Gnarled woody fingers reached out to entangle and strangle the warm-blooded creatures—and suck their veins dry to the *last drop*!

A bit overdone, but an impressive horror show for a production improvised right on the spot by an ambitious company of local thespians. It seems a pity that neither Daisy nor Sidewinder took the least notice of the lurid drama.

The woman stopped a few paces short of the junction where Too Late Creek spilled over a cluster of granite boulders to join forces with the rocky river that was the pride and lifeblood of the Columbine. Having arrived at the pebbled riverbank, the hound looked back expectantly, hoping that the elderly human biped would wade the water to the yonder side. For what possible purpose would Daisy do such a thing? Why, to climb Pine Knob to the top, throw her head back—and howl at the moon.

Reading only the "wade the water" portion of the message in the dog's shining eyes, Daisy explained, "The river's thirty degrees too cold and I'm forty years too old." Nevertheless, the far bank did call to the weary old soul. The eldest member of her tribe knew that before many more winters had passed, she would be obliged to cross that ultimate River. But that day would come when it may; what concerned her now was the business at hand. *I might as well start telling my secrets to this floppy-eared mutt.*

Talking to the Dog

We know that practically everyone speaks to animals whenever the opportunity arises and Daisy Perika was not an exception. During her long and fascinating life, the woman had conversed with almost every living creature she'd come across, from A to Z—which is to say from pronghorn Antelopes (which are exceedingly taciturn) to *Zenaida asiatica* (which are white-winged doves). For one of such immense experience, talking to a dog would be as easy as falling off a slippery log. Buoyed by these advantages, the storyteller warmed up her audience by telling Charlie Moon's dour hound a joke that everyone knows—that old rib-tickler about a Ute child, a Navaho elder, and an Apache medicine man—all fishing from the same canoe for channel catfish. (For those who may have forgotten, the funny part had to do with their choice of baits.) Alas, during Daisy's expert build-up, Sidewinder's attention was diverted by the fragrant odor of a specimen of day-old bear scat. That was bad enough, but just as she delivered the hilarious punch line, the dog opened his mouth wide and—yawned.

Was Daisy Perika dismayed? At the very least. Despite

her best efforts, the stand-up comic had learned that directing a lively monolog to a dog is not all that it's cracked up to be. Is she about to give up the effort? Perish the negative thought. Far from tossing in the towel, Miss Daisy has decided to try a different approach. She will conduct a conversation with the rude beast.

Yes, a *conversation*. The frustrated raconteur has a tale that is just *aching* be told, and to an audience who will respond with encouraging comments and well-deserved praise. How will she manage a stimulating verbal exchange with an animal who does not qualify even as a polite listener? Why, by *imagining* Sidewinder's likely responses—were the ungainly beast equipped with a human voice and a brain bigger than a baby midget's fist.

Daisy may come up with an odd notion now and again, but the lady is no quitter.

Before getting to the heart of her narrative, she commenced with a short story that might appropriately be titled "Sarah Frank and the Owl Feather," with the somewhat wordy subtitle "How the Silly Ute-Papago Orphan Stole Daisy's Ghost-Eyes a Couple of Weeks Ago, and How—Not Half an Hour Ago—the Clever Tribal Elder Reversed the Process and Recovered Her Ability to See Dead People."

She wound up the self-aggrandizing yarn by addressing her canine companion in this manner: "I told you about that owl-feather business because it's all tangled up with what's been going on in Granite Creek Cemetery."

Sidewinder: *Very interesting.* It was apparent from this remark and the inquisitive glint in his eyes that the official Columbine hound was eager to hear more.

Just as eager to tell him, Daisy described the gist of Sarah Frank's encounter with the fellow who called himself Captain Erasmus Boyle, and the ensuing mystery about the man's actual identity—and his intentions.

Sidewinder spoke without moving his lips. *That's a real head scratcher—wondering how it'll all turn out is likely to keep me awake all night.*

"That was just for starters, fuzz-face." Daisy Perika's mouth curled into a self-satisfied smirk. "The really *good* stuff'll make your floppy ears stand straight up and your droopy old tail twist into a corkscrew!"

If the hound harbored any disdain for the shameless utterance of such blatant hyperbole, his somber expression did not—

(To be continued following some fast-breaking news.)

CHAPTER SIXTY-ONE

THE FAST-BREAKING NEWS

Scott Parris was not 100 percent convinced that Charlie Moon was on the right track. But Professor Experience was the teacher Parris leaned on, and the lesson he'd learned was not to dismiss the tribal investigator's hunches lightly. *When ol' Charlie takes a shot in the dark, he generally nails the bull's-eye dead center.* The white cop plopped onto the leather couch and heaved a heavy sigh. "Okay, Chucky. Just to make you happy, I'll drop by and see the potential suspect tomorrow morning." *And if Mr. Fixit has had a hand in this awful mess, I'll damn well find out.*

"Do whatever pleases you, pardner." Whatever the outcome, Charlie Moon would not be pleased. It always hurts to be proven wrong, but even if his theory turned out to be dead-on, there was a downside. He liked Freddy Whitsun and hated the thought of the hardworking craftsman spending a long stretch behind the walls. Even if the handyman was guilty of two homicides, there must've been extenuating circumstances. The instance of Betty Naranjo was easy enough to figure: even the most cautious driver might run someone down in a blinding rainstorm. *But not many would haul the victim away and bury her body in the cemetery.* The killing of Morris Meusser was another matter. Moon found it hard to imagine easygoing Freddy Whitsun committing a cold-blooded murder—particularly when the victim was his checker-playing buddy. *But when a fella's caught red-handed concealing the corpse of a missing teenage girl, and another killing looks like his only way out—the desperate man is liable to take desperate measures.* The kindhearted Ute hoped that Whitsun had been surprised by Meusser in the darkness, and did not realize whom he'd bludgeoned until after the violent deed was done. But we do waste a lot of precious time in pointless speculations. Within a few minutes, Moon would conclude that his musings about Whitsun were irrelevant.

As things turned out, Scott Parris would *not* go looking for Freddy Whitsun tomorrow morning. Even if he had, the town cop would have found the cemetery custodian's quarters vacant—and Mr. Fixit's van long gone. The suicidal custodian had taken Daisy Perika's parting advice, which was reminiscent of the classic Old West sheriff's directive to an undesirable element: "You get outta town before the sun goes down—and don't ever show your ape-ugly face in these here parts again!" Freddy had hit the road shortly after his *miraculous* deliverance from a self-inflicted lynching.

But where is the missing Mr. Whitsun, and what are his plans?

He is Seeking Greener Pastures

Upon arriving in Raton, New Mexico, the enthusiastic tourist had traded his Mr. Fixit van and a spare battery-operated DeWalt drill motor to an undocumented Panamanian migrant for a dandy Dodge pickup with Utah plates, a powerful Cummins diesel engine, and a shiny aluminum camper shell. As soon as that hasty transaction was completed, Mr. Whitsun had transferred the tools of his trade to the replacement vehicle and headed in a southeasterly direction.

Eager to put the "haunts" far behind him, the handyman has already passed through Clayton and is currently rolling along Route 87 toward Texline. Forever cured of his suicidal tendencies by Dr. Daisy Perika's no-nonsense shock therapy, he is about to say adios to the Land of Enchantment and howdy to the Lone Star State. After that crossing, Freddy doesn't know where he will eventually end up. But the former cemetery custodian is already giving the matter some thought.

I might keep right on going toward Oklahoma. A flash of sheet lightning illuminated a leaden sky. *Or I could head south through Texas and cross over into Old Mexico.* Somewhere far behind him, thunder rumbled a warning. *Maybe I'll go all the way down to Yucatán and get a look at some of those old limestone pyramids.* A big, fat bug splattered on the spiffy pickup's pitted windshield. *I'll make up my mind when I get to Dalhart.* A brighter flash of lightning. *Or maybe Dumas.*

He has troubles enough, but unlike so many of us, Mr. Whitsun is not the least concerned about finding employment. *Anywhere I decide to set up shop, folks'll need a handyman.*

Two Telephone Calls

The first was a routine communication.

Charlie Moon's mobile phone warbled unpleasantly. Before pressing the instrument against his ear, he checked the caller-ID. "What's up, Butch?"

"Nothing much, boss. Just wanted to let you know that your aunt's okay. She's down by the river with Sidewinder."

Why is he telling me this? "So where're you?"

"In the hayloft over the horse barn."

"That's a fine lookout." *I don't want to hurt his feelings.* "Unless Daisy gets into some mischief, you don't need to call me again."

"Yes sir."

"Good night." Just as Moon was slipping the telephone back into his pocket, Scott Parris's communications device sounded off with a three-note chime that identified the caller. The chief of police addressed his hardworking dispatcher. "H'lo, Clara—what's up?"

Miss Tavishuts told the boss what was up. And then some.

As Parris listened intently, his sunburned brow gradually furrowed into a frown. After almost a minute: "Got it. Thanks." Disconnecting, he fixed his gaze on Charlie Moon. "Ol' buddy, I'm sorry to be the one to have to tell you this."

For some reason or another, the tribal investigator doubted the sincerity of this declaration. Perhaps because the white man's blue eyes were sparkling merrily. "I'm listening."

The New Wrinkle

"As far as the cemetery custodian's death is concerned, you can forget all about your handyman–plumber theory."

"Tell me why, pardner."

"Because the Wyoming State Police have arrested a thief in Laramie—one Maximillian Schilling. The habitual criminal—who is wanted in five states besides Colorado—broke into an upstanding Wyoming citizen's trailer home, where he murdered the occupant. He also stole the victim's Browning automatic shotgun and eighty-some dollars in cash money. But I get ahead of myself. Before he broke in—are you ready for this?"

"No, but go ahead and completely ruin my day."

"Before he broke in, Max cut the phone line."

Moon made the expected protest. "That similarity to our cemetery-custodian homicide is interesting, but I don't think any jury in the land would convict him of killing Morris Meusser on something that slim."

"Well of course not, but—" Parris pretended to be momentarily confused. "Did I forget to tell you that when he was arrested, the dangerous felon had Morris Meusser's pocket watch in his possession—and Meusser's five-dollar-gold-coin watch fob?"

Charlie Moon's fine poker face concealed his dismay at this news. "Before you string me along any further, I'll make a wild guess—Mr. Maximillian Schilling confessed to murdering Mr. Meusser."

"We should be so lucky." The Granite Creek chief of police allowed himself a vinegar-bitter grin. "The suspect claims he peeked through the window and saw Meusser napping on the couch. Doing what just comes naturally, Max cut the phone line, and when he was about to apply his handy pry bar to the latch, he was surprised to find the door to the cemetery custodian's residence unlocked. After he got inside, he discovered that Meusser was banged-up some, but he told the Wyoming authorities he figured the man had been in a bar brawl and come home seriously intoxicated to crash on the couch. Max felt sorry for the bunged-up old drunk, but not wanting to leave empty-handed, he ripped off the custodian's watch and gold-coin fob." Parris added a chuckle to the sardonic grin. "Probably for mementos. Max claims he was about to check out Meusser's wallet when some guy drove up in a truck."

"Freddy Whitsun."

"The very same. We know this is so, because the thief remembered the Mr. Fixit logo."

"Well, at least *that* part of his story was true." Charlie Moon didn't feel the least bit like smiling. "So he insists that he left with the pocket watch, without having the least notion that Morris Meusser was dead."

"That's what he said." Parris pretended to recall a minor detail. "Oh, and one other thing."

"I kinda figured there would be."

"Max also told the Wyoming cops that he never laid a hand on the victim in Wyoming—he had a simple explanation for the bloody baseball bat they caught him red-handed with. The burglar just happened to notice the bat in the dead man's closet when he was stealing the shotgun, and ever since Max was knee-high to a day-old beagle puppy, he's had a hankering for a genuine Louisville Slugger."

"That just about wraps it up, then." Moon could not suppress a melancholy sigh. "Well, there goes my dandy handyman theory—down the well-known drain."

"Hey, don't be a Gloomy Gus—look on the sunny side of the creek. Our hardworking brother coppers in Wyoming have arrested Morris Meusser's killer. And since you were way off base blaming our upstanding Mr. Fixit for murdering his buddy, odds are you were also dead wrong about Betty Naranjo being dead and buried in our fine cemetery. Chances are, she'll turn up in a month or two with a brand-new bouncing baby of one gender or the other. What it all boils down to is that you and me can kick back and relax." Ready to commence with his portion of that leisure activity, Parris leaned back on the couch and closed his eyes. "Don't feel so bad, Charlie. You gave it a good try, and I like your made-up story a whole lot better than what actually happened."

This compliment provided little consolation to Deputy Moon. For a man who takes pride in being able to *figure things out,* giving up on a great notion is like pulling a sound molar with wire pliers—and the tribal investigator's simple solution to the mystery of the missing girl *and* the cemetery murder had seemed so promising. But there was another reason for his discomfort: Charlie Moon had noticed that Scott Parris's crocodile grin was getting wider with every tick-tock of the clock and displaying . . . *about two dozen more teeth than a normal man ought to have in his mouth.*

(Charlie Moon's quasi-orthodontic observation concludes the fast-breaking news.)

Chapter Sixty-two

We Return Now to Our Scheduled Program (The Interrupted Daisy–Dog Dialogue)

. . . Sidewinder spoke without moving his lips: *That's a real head scratcher—wondering how it'll all turn out is likely to keep me awake all night.*

"That was just for starters, fuzz-face." Daisy Perika's mouth curled into a self-satisfied smirk. "The really *good* stuff'll make your floppy ears stand straight up and your droopy old tail twist into a corkscrew!"

If the hound harbored any disdain for the shameless utterance of such blatant hyperbole, his somber expression did not reveal it.

Daisy launched into a revelation of Freddy Whitsun's confidential pre-lynching confession, which (though she didn't know it) entirely justified her nephew's suspicions. Daisy's gripping narrative provided a blow-by-blow account of how the handyman had responded to Wanda Naranjo's leaky-plumbing call, accidentally run down the woman's pregnant daughter in the rainstorm, loaded the injured girl into his Mr. Fixit van, and did his level best to keep her alive. "And then, after nursing Betty along all of Friday night and into Saturday—"

Sidewinder cleared his throat.

The narrator glared at the bad-mannered animal. "What?"

Why didn't Mr. Whitsun take the girl to the hospital?

"Well that's a dumb question!" But realizing that the dog expected an explanation, she drew in a deep breath and let it out with: "Freddy has already had some troubles with the police. He's been arrested in other states for killing deer out of season and selling pigs that wasn't his and hitting an elk with his truck while he was drunk and tooting on a brass trumpet. You can imagine what a judge would do if he was to be charged with running down a human being—"

Or worse still, a dog.

"Hush!" Daisy detested these unseemly interruptions. "That's why Freddy was afraid to take the girl to see a doctor."

Sidewinder: *He should've taken her directly to a competent veterinarian. There's an excellent practitioner over on Second Street who provides complimentary liver-flavored doggy biscuits and just last month she cured me of a bad case of bloated—*

"This is serious business." The tribal elder shook her walking stick at the impertinent creature. "D'you want to hear the rest of the story, or would you rather have a big lump on your noggin?"

After thinking it over for six milliseconds, the hound opted for the former.

When the somewhat deflated storyteller got back into the groove, she provided a heartrending account of Betty's subsequent death on Saturday evening and Freddy Whitsun's fateful decision to bury her corpse in the old section of the cemetery that night—a dismal procedure that was interrupted by the sudden appearance of a shadowy figure who got banged on the head by a startled, shovel-wielding Freddy Whitsun.

As Daisy pausing for a refreshing breath of air, Sidewinder posted another question: *So did he bury both of them in the same hole?*

"No, he did *not*." *Having a sensible conversation with this smart-aleck dog ain't as easy as I thought it'd be.* "Mr.

Meusser was still alive and Freddy was awfully surprised when he found out he'd knocked his best friend cold as a Popsicle. He hauled the unconscious man away on the same little electric truck that Meusser had rode in on. Soon as he got Meusser inside his little cemetery house, Freddy laid him out on the couch. He figured his buddy would wake up later with a bad headache, and wonder what'd happened to him and who did it and how he'd gotten all the way back home on his own. Freddy hurried back to where he'd already buried Betty and spent quite some time fixing the ground so there'd be no trace of a new-dug grave." Daisy paused to sigh about how—despite our best intentions, careful plans, and hard work—things have a way of going wrong. "When Freddy came back to check on Meusser not long after daylight, he found the poor fellow dead as a petrified polecat— and not only that   some rascal had stolen the dead man's watch!"

The dog was visibly impressed. *And Mr. Whitsun confessed all of this to you?*

"Of course he did."

Why would he do a thing like that?

"Because I'm easy to talk to, that's why! Now what do you want—a sharp stick jabbed in your eye or would you rather hear about the peculiar man our sweet little Sarah met in the park—a smooth-talking stranger who might turn out to be dangerous?"

Sidewinder decided on the latter—and within four milliseconds flat of the threat being made.

Daisy proceeded to describe Sarah's meeting with Erasmus Boyle, terminating with: "This young fellow told Sarah he was being kept awake all night by some young woman who was singing songs to her crying baby. Sarah thought the girl and her child was upstairs, above Boyle's apartment." She baited the hook: "And he gave her his address—144 Hollybush."

Sidewinder swallowed it whole. *So we know where to find this suspicious character and put the bite on him!*

"We would—except there ain't no Hollybush Street in Granite Creek—never was."

So why'd he lie about his address?

"He didn't lie about that." *Or about his name and military rank.* Foreseeing another vexing question, Daisy raised her palm to forestall the pushy dog. "I'll explain about that later, but before I do I'll tell you what I found out from Miss Emily Boyle over at the nursing home—and after that at the public library." Which Daisy proceeded to do. "The most important thing I learned from that old white woman was that her nephew had called her the day before and asked for money."

Why's that so important?

"Because . . ." Daisy paused. "Unless no-account dead men make phone calls to their aunties and hit them up for a few bucks—the old woman's nephew is still among the living."

Sorry—I seemed to have missed something here.

Sidewinder had. And Charlie Moon's aunt was about to fill in the blank space.

CHAPTER SIXTY-THREE

FINALLY, THE GOOD STUFF

Daisy leaned to impale the hound with her patented beady-eye gaze. "That day when I walked from the cemetery over to the park and found Sarah sitting on a bench—she was talking to a fellow who *wasn't there*."

Sidewinder: *Like on that creepy old radio show—The Invisible Man?*

"Yes," Daisy said. "Well, more or less. I already knew I couldn't see dead people anymore—but that was when I found out that Sarah *could* see them. She was talking to a spirit that very minute."

But wouldn't she have been scared by a ghost?

"I'm glad you asked." She leaned to pat the homely hound's head, then straightened up with a grunt. "From time to time, Sarah has seen some spooky things, but mostly at night—but the girl ain't used to seeing dead people walking around in broad daylight." A passing night cloud exposed the earth's pockmarked satellite, which bathed Daisy's wrinkled face in a faint glow of moonlight. "That girl didn't have the least notion she was talking to a dead man." Pausing to inhale a bracing breath of icy night air, she shuddered with a sudden chill. Recovering, she continued. "When I saw her talking to empty space, I realized right away that the girl must've stolen my ghost-eyes. It took me a little while longer to figure out *how* she'd done it and how I might put things right—but you already know all about that."

Right. So tell me more about this ghost Sarah was talking to. If he didn't lie about his street address—how come it was bogus as a plastic chew bone?

"First of all, because it wasn't a street address." Daisy paused to watch moonlight ripple eerily along the river like thousands of slivering silver snakes wriggling in a viperous mating dance. "An old cemetery map and a burial list I found in the library was a big help. Turns out that in 1917 a Captain Erasmus Boyle was buried in the *old* graveyard—which in those bygone days was called Walnut Hills Cemetery. He was laid to rest in the Hollybush Section, plot number 144."

Aha! The address he gave Sarah. Hounds can frown and this one did. *But an Erasmus Boyle who was buried way back then must've been—*

"Sure he was—Sarah had been talking to Miss Emily Boyle's elder brother—and in the park that bordered the county cemetery. I figured that wherever Captain Boyle was buried, the girl singing to her baby was planted somewhere close-by—probably right over his coffin. And that dead girl *had* to be Betty Naranjo." Daisy waited for a congratulation.

A simple "good for you" would have sufficed, but the dog outdid himself: *That is way beyond amazing, Daisy. Why, if word gets out about how clever you are at figuring out who killed who and where the bodies are buried, Scott Parris will pin a deputy's badge on you and tell Charlie Moon to stick to raising stinky old cows!*

Though gratified by this well-deserved praise (she couldn't have put it better herself), the old woman shrugged and replied with the humility of a medieval saint, "Oh, it wasn't all that much."

Sidewinder seemed to be highly impressed by the old woman's self-effacing protest, but his apparent concentration was a brazen canine sham. Though he stared at Daisy's left knee as if hanging on every word she uttered, the hound could hardly have cared less about her self-congratulatory narrative—

But wait. The animal's intense doggish gaze is *not* focused on the arthritic joint between Daisy Perika's femur and shinbone. His keen eyes are peering beyond his human companion's leg, at something or other *behind* the puffed-up storyteller. Like others of his ilk, this descendants of wolves occasionally exhibits peculiar behavior.

Her appetite for admiration whetted, the tribal elder was about to brag about an incident she'd skipped over earlier. "I bet you'd enjoy hearing what I did to keep half-wit Whitsun from stringing himself up."

Perhaps Sidewinder would have, but the dog was entirely focused on another, more urgent issue. Like a well-trained pointer who had just spotted a scaled quail under a tumbleweed, the hound was standing stock-still, his nose aimed at . . . Aha—there it is! Something in the undergrowth along Too Late Creek.

The vain storyteller had become aware of the canine's interest in something other than the center of her smallish universe. "What're you gawking at, you old goofball?"

Sidewinder responded to her question in honest doggish lingo—the bristly quills on his neck prickling porcupine-style, a low growl rumbling in his throat.

Charlie Moon's mystified aunt watched the peculiar animal stalk off toward the brushy tree line along the creek bank.

Daisy's stalwart escort, who viewed her as a child in his charge, was determined to defend his human companion with all the self-sacrificing instinct of any domesticated wolf who might accompany you during your midnight stroll along Lonely Street. Despite his deadly serious intent, the four-legged creature approached this particular menace with deliberate prudence. Was Sidewinder afraid? Certainly not. The intelligent animal advanced slowly and with due caution because he needed time to think. Think about *what*? Why, about how to deal with this atypical opponent—an adversary who could not be harmed by a dozen mouthfuls of pointy hound's teeth.

The old woman peered into the darkness—her so-called ghost-eyes now working fine—and she perceived the presence not twenty paces away. Yes. It was the very same feather-headed specter that had frightened Sarah earlier in the evening. The shaman had no doubt that the nosy Anasazi haunt had crept close with the ulterior intent of overhearing what she was saying to the dog. She was just as certain that it was a futile attempt: this ancient soul could not understand a word of English, Ute, Spanish, Spanglish, pig Latin, or any other major modern language listed in Daisy's repertoire. But that was quite beside the point; there was an issue of Principle involved. Though proud of her expertise in the subtle art of eavesdropping, the old woman valued her own privacy and was prepared to severely punish those who dared invade it. Miss Daisy stooped to pick up a hefty, smoothish rock. After taking careful aim, she tossed it at the spirit. Did her missile connect? You know it did!

There was a startled yelp.

One might reasonably conclude that feather-headed haunts have feelings, too, and do not appreciate being stoned. But commonsensical as a startled ghost-yelp might seem, there is another possibility that cannot be dismissed out-of-hand.

CHAPTER SIXTY-FOUR

THAT FINAL STRAW

Listening to the latest telephone report, Charlie Moon could hardly believe his ears. "She did *what*?"

Little Butch Cassidy was pleased to repeat himself. "The old lady pitched a rock at Sidewinder." He added with a snicker, "Hit 'im too."

"Well that tears it." Moon disconnected. With Parris at his heels, the rancher stomped out of his office, along the long hallway, down the stairs into the parlor, and outside onto the west porch. Hearing the thumping commotion of heavy boots in locomotion, a curious Sarah Frank hurried forth to serve as a caboose. Sidewinder was already at the door, hankering for some show of sympathy. Whining pitifully, the offended hound leaned against the boss's lean leg and looked up at Moon with big, soulful eyes.

"Poor *thing*!" Sarah stooped to hug the animal and murmur in his ear. "What's wrong?"

Daisy Perika came trudging across the yard, muttering angry expletives under her breath.

Mr. Moon's stern face did not soften as he helped the aged woman up the porch steps. "What've you been up to?"

"Nothing that'd interest you." She scowled at the annoying dog. "My throwing arm ain't what it used to be, and that big fleabag got in the way." Daisy pointed her walking stick in the direction of Too Late Creek. "But if I see old Feather-head again, I'll set the rascal ablaze with a blowtorch—and when he dances and hollers for mercy I'll give him a gallon of kerosene to put the fire out!"

Feather-head? Knowing the futility of asking for a clarification, Charlie Moon let the matter drop.

Knowing precisely whom Daisy was referring to, Sarah kept mum and hugged the hound all the harder.

Scott Parris, who hadn't had so much fun in weeks, was doing his best not to laugh too loudly but his braying was heard inside the bunkhouse by half-a-dozen wide-eyed cowboys and Butch to boot, who was making his way down from the barn loft.

Daisy scowled hatefully at Sidewinder, who—presumably fearing another unprovoked missile attack—had positioned himself behind Moon.

Aside from Parris's hilarity, the electrified atmosphere fairly crackled with tension.

But pent-up anxieties fade away after a few minutes; the important issue is: was the tribal elder displeased with the outcome of her somewhat one-sided contrived conversation with Sidewinder?

Not in the least.

Having unburdened herself to the hound, Daisy Perika was now free to enjoy the full recovery of her "ghost-eyes." She had already made up her mind to return to her home on the morrow and was looking forward (so to speak) to seeing dozens of her deceased friends, acquaintances, and enemies again. To give the crafty old soul due credit, Daisy was also pleased to know that Sarah Frank would be spared the discomfort of seeing every haunt who happened by—such as that dapper young officer Sarah had shared the park bench with.

Which, at least for some of us, raises a nagging question: was Daisy Perika correct in her bold assertion that the spook who'd chatted with Sarah was the long-dead brother of Miss Emily Boyle? The answer is: perhaps. One cannot be certain about such murky issues. But Daisy was definitely right in her educated guess about a related matter.

Freddy Whitsun did indeed deposit Betty Naranjo's earthly remains above an old oaken coffin wherein moldered the bones of the distinguished old soldier. The testimony to this fact that can be faintly seen on the limestone grave marker that Sarah had seated herself on whilst conversing with the suicidal Mr. Whitsun.

CPT. ERASMUS BOYLE—U.S. ARMY
1888–1917

The terse epitaph demands an addendum. We take chisel and hammer in hand.

HERE LIETH THE
GENUINE COFFIN MAN

And here endeth the account.
Almost.

EPILOGUE
All's Well That Ends

The Handyman Does Not Escape Justice

The dual morals of this sad vignette shall be provided right up front.

"Homicide, even when unintentional, leaves the victims just as dead."

And: "Never trust an undocumented Panamanian who offers a dandy Dodge pickup in trade for an over-the-hill handyman van."

That's right. The pickup with Utah plates had been stolen in Provo—and from an assistant DA, no less. Freddy Whitsun was apprised of this jarring fact when he attempted to register the tainted motor vehicle in the Lone Star State. Needless to say, the authorities did not buy his story about having traded his van for the misappropriated pickup. "Pure fiction" was the verdict. Moreover, the pickup's rightful owner was determined to see the presumed thief charged with grand theft auto, be declared guilty by a jury of his peers, and sentenced to umpteen years in the well-known slammer.

Freddie's ensuing trials and tribulations—which may be deemed due reward for committing two inadvertent homicides in Granite Creek, Colorado—shall not be described in detail. Except to note that he might not have beaten the bad rap except for a resourceful young Nacogdoches attorney who acquired written and video depositions from a pair of trustworthy witnesses, which proved that at the *very moment* when the Dodge pickup was being pilfered in Provo, the accused handyman was in the historic section of the Granite Creek Cemetery, dealing with some business of an intensely personal nature. (The embarrassing matter of suicide by hanging did not come up.) The witnesses were, of course, Daisy Perika and Sarah Frank—who did not reveal the fact of their testimony to either Charlie Moon or Scott Parris.

But that was not quite the end of Freddie's story.

Where Did Mr. Whitsun End Up
After All His Troubles?

Make that the *former* Mr. Whitsun. Both his business and person are currently identified by the new sign painted on both doors of a lime-green Ford E-250 van: FOX'S SMALL ENGINE REPAIR

As to *where*, Freddy Fox has settled into the mostly peaceful East Texas hill country and the gratifying mechanical profession of repairing lawnmowers, motorcycles, and outboard motors. He tends to a few other tasks for favorite customers, concentrating on small-job carpentry. But the former Mr. Fixit has traded his pipe wrench for a spirit level; he refuses all calls from locals who are suffering from troublesome plumbing.

And things are going tolerably well.

Nowadays, his slumbers are not disturbed by the Morris Meusser–Betty Naranjo twosome. Maybe they haven't located him yet, but Freddy hopes that his testy accuser has forgiven his checker-playing buddy for whacking him with a shovel. Which gratifying change of heart would make it unnecessary for Betty's ghost to appear and defend the hapless handyman who accidentally ran her down and buried her corpse over Captain Boyle's coffin.

Happily, the recent immigrant to the largest state in the lower forty-eight is not bothered by haunts of any description. But just to be on the safe side, the cautious fellow resides in a modest rented cottage that is twenty-nine miles from the nearest cemetery.

Mrs. Wanda Naranjo

Though Betty's mother has been designated a *person of interest* in the violent death of Michael Kauffmann, this interesting person has not been located. This, in spite of the fact that Wanda has allegedly been spotted in Washington (Richland), Texas (San Antonio), Kentucky (La Grange), Missouri (O'Fallon), and Arkansas (St. Joe). One of the few communities where there has been no report of her presence is worthy of mention.

The curiosity of a long-haul trucker who lives in Granite Creek was piqued when his order for chicken-fried steak, mashed spuds with brown gravy, and a cup of black coffee was taken by a spunky little waitress in Waycross, Georgia. The alert fellow wasn't taken in by Wanda Naranjo's dying her hair a bright red, wearing blue contact lenses over her brown irises, and assuming an overdone southern drawl.

So why didn't the trucker notify the legally constituted authorities?

One can only speculate.

It might have helped that Wanda winked at the lonely widower and addressed him as "honey-babe." Plus the fact that the dyspeptic diner had no stomach for assisting in the arrest and punishment of a gun-toting momma who—according to the Todd County Sheriff's Office bulletin—was suspected of shooting her boyfriend stone-cold dead. Experienced truckers are nobody's fools and this one had stayed alive during his career by exercising a measure of caution. *For all I know Wanda has a derringer stashed in her apron pocket.*

But the combination of the waitress's mild flirtation and the diner's instinct for self-preservation were not the sole factors in his decision to leave well enough alone. *Mike Kauffmann owed me twenty bucks and the welcher should've paid up before he took a bullet.*

He gave the lady a knowing wink, a thumbs-up—and left a five-dollar tip.

Regarding the Father of Betty
Naranjo's Unborn Child

There were, all told, five candidates. A sizable field of likely suspects, but Betty had not known who the daddy was—or given the matter much thought.

Why was she going to see Dr. Whyte on that fateful Friday morning? To extort a wad of cash money from the most prosperous of the potential fathers. The pregnant girl figured the psychologist was good for a hundred bucks.

A Final Matter

We recall that Sarah Frank had advised Captain E. Boyle to take his grievance concerning a lullaby-singing young woman and her crying baby to the chief of police, and that he had agreed to do so. We also know that an officer is a gentleman, and that a gentleman keeps his promises. Which raises the pressing issue: was the frustrated complainant responsible for the presumed poltergeist activity in Scott Parris's office? Did Miss Emily's distinguished brother jiggle Parris's coffee cup, make the cop's desk lamp go on and off—and create the ceiling fan's peculiar pendular motion? We simply do not know; the question shall be filed in that thickish folder marked UNRESOLVED.

Whatever mischief our limping soldier might have been up to in Parris's workplace, may Captain Boyle's weary soul and all others rest in peaceful sleep.

Speaking of which—a warm bed beckons, as does the dawn of a brighter, better day.

Good night.

Read on for an excerpt from

THE OLD GRAY WOLF

—the next Charlie Moon mystery by James D. Doss,
available soon in hardcover from Minotaur Books:

PROLOGUE

HESTER "TOADIE" TILLMAN

No; please do not ask. It would be less than charitable to
explain how the unfortunate old soul got tagged with a nickname which suggests frogish features. Ninety-year-old ladies are not without vanity, and are entitled to their privacy.

But that polite designation might be misleading. In the
interest of trustworthy reporting, it shall be noted that not
everyone in La Plata County who has encountered Mrs.
Tillman would characterize her a bona fide *lady*. Probably
not one in ten of them. Perhaps not one. Truth be told, the
mean-spirited old crone is believed by more than a working
quorum of duly registered voters to be a black-hearted, spell-
casting witch—of which dubious craft there is no over-
whelming market for in south-central Colorado. Yes, this
does sound like deliberately titillating gossip, and so it may
be—but maliciously disseminated rumors, barefaced hear-
say, and silly tittle-tattle are occasionally relevant to a significant current event, as is the case at this very instant,
about a mile and a minute north of the Ignacio city limits on
Route 172. Which is not a nice place to be if one is either
trapped inside a severely damaged automobile or attempting
to console the mortally injured citizen. Which unhappy duty
has fallen upon one . . .

Officer Danny Bignight

The aforementioned constable is a respected employee of the Southern Ute Police Department and a reputable (if displaced) member of Taos Pueblo, which venerable New Mexico community boasts the largest continually occupied apartment building in the United States of America and (as far as we know) the vast entirety of the Western Hemisphere. But that advertisement is an aside for which remuneration is unlikely, so let us get right to the grisly business at hand—which is an unforeseen and jarring encounter between Hester "Toadie" Tillman and Danny Bignight, which follows a far more jarring encounter between the sturdy motor vehicle Ms. Tillman was a passenger in and a medium-size ponderosa pine. No contest.

Even as we speak, the elderly reputed witch is about to be pried from a wrecked Dodge pickup—the very same conveyance that her granddaughter was driving when a bald front tire (the one on the passenger side) meandered onto the shoulder to roll over a pointy chunk of gravel and pop (*ka-boom!*) like a pricked balloon. For the record, the driver will depart in the first of two waiting ambulances which will (sirens screaming, emergency lights flashing) roar away speedily toward Durango's Mercy Regional Medical Center. Therein, she will be expertly treated in the ER and survive with a one-inch scar to cleft her chin. This mark will serve as a lifelong memento of the accident and a reminder not to use the rear-view mirror for applying shocking-pink lip gloss whilst exceeding the posted speed limit.

But enough about the granddaughter; back to Hester "T" Tillman.

As a brawny state trooper applies the hydraulic Jaws of Life spreader-cutters to the crushed vehicle's roof, Officer Danny Bignight is doing his level best to comfort the old woman *whom he is deathly afraid of.* Mrs. Tillman has a few words to say to this latter-day Good Samaritan who would have just as well "passed her by" if underpaid SUPD cops had the same options as Bible-time priests and scribes. Happily, the attending police officer is not the immediate object of her dreadful declaration; Bignight is merely Toadie's intended messenger. The alleged brewer of sinister potions and caster of evil spells has a menacing communication for one Daisy Perika, who shall be introduced in due time. But let it be said right up front that compared to Miss Daisy P., Hester T. is a sweet, purring, furry little pussycat.

This so-called pussycat, still trapped in the crunched-up Dodge pickup, hissed at the public servant: "Now listen to me, Danny Bignight—you pass what I've got to say on to Daisy *word-for-word*, or my curse'll fall on you and all of your family down at Taos Pueblo."

"Yes ma'am." As the cop listened to the message for Daisy Perika, he broke into a cold sweat, his soulful eyes bulged like big, brown bubbles in the white of an over fried egg and his stomach churned sourly. As one might expect, Danny Bignight also swallowed hard.

Following her final declaration, Toadie cackled a crackly laugh, hiccupped—and drew her last breath. Or—as old folks long ago used to say on dark nights in the flickering yellow light cast by kerosene lamps—she *gave up the ghost*. Where a particular given-up ghost goes and what it does when it gets there remains an open question—and one that is relevant to a forthcoming unnerving event which will create no small disturbance.

By the time the state trooper and an EMT had pulled the aged woman's warm corpse from the totaled pickup and loaded it into the second ambulance, which was perhaps six minutes after Toadie's final hiccup, Danny Bignight had retreated into the sanctuary of his SUPD unit, and locked the door. As he wiped perspiration from his forehead, the Southern Ute police officer knew what Job One was: *I'll go see Aunt Daisy right away!*

No, Daisy Perika is not Danny Bignight's aunt. As it happens, every Southern Ute on the res and most of the Hispanics and Anglos who reside in and around Ignacio apply the title Aunt to the crotchety tribal elder, who is more-or-less infamous in her little corner of the world, and mighty proud of it. If you were to ask Daisy, she'd tell you that if those do-nothing bureaucrats in Washington D.C. were really on the ball, that honorary first name (Aunt) would be printed in US Government ink onto her ragged old Social Security Card, but they are not (on the ball) and it is not (printed there).

Please—don't get Aunt Daisy started on the subject of government. Wild-eyed anarchists everywhere tremble at her heartfelt threats against all shapes and forms of authority—and her stated intent to: ". . . push on the pillars till I bring the temple down on all those #%$*! parasites." (Including those wild-eyed anarchists, who—seen through Daisy's gimlet eyes—are merely hopeful bureaucrats in disguise.)

CHAPTER I

THE UTE ELDER'S WILDERNESS HIDEAWAY

Imagine yourself miles away from the nearest human settlement, hiking along a dusty trail. All cares forgotten, you are whiling away a balmy autumn day in a wilderness which is both picturesque and forbidding. To the north, a slight blue haze shimmers over round-shouldered mountains. From those ancient peaks, miles-long brown mesas stretch out like a fallen giant's fingers, clutching at a crumbling earth. Between the steep sandstone cliffs of those flattened heights, the patient forces of nature have worked for hundreds of millennia to shape the landscape that you see today. Gurgling little springtime streams, gray winter rains freezing in sandstone cracks, and howling grit-laden winds—all of those relentless forces have combined to carve out deep canyons, wherein are multitudes of secluded, shady glades where direct sunlight has never beamed an incandescent ray on lichen, moss or fern, nor shall it ever. Away to the south, beyond the mesa's grasping fingertips, the sun-drenched topography is gradually transformed into a jumble of rugged hills, isolated buttes, rolling arid prairie and huge patches of nasty badlands that provide suitable habitat for those scaly, slithering serpents who will (when they are of a mind to) hiss, rattle—and then fang you.

But let us not be overly concerned about where we are stepping. (That coiled object half-concealed in the dead grass is probably a discarded hank of manila rope. Or so we hope.)

This image is etched indelibly on your consciousness? Good.

While distracted by the panoramic Big Picture, you have passed right by the most important feature of this remote landscape. We refer to the well-known residence of that notable citizen who—excepting a few fleshless exceptions to be described in a moment—is the only human soul who has a settled homestead within the vast neighborhood already described, which comprises approximately forty-four square miles of the Southern Ute Reservation.

But do not fault yourself for this understandable oversight. Just so you'll know where to look should you ever pass this way again, Aunt Daisy's home is situated *right over there*. Yes, on the sunny side of that low ridge and near (very nearly *in*) the yawning mouth of *Cañon del Espiritu*, wherein (so the tribal elder assures us) dozens of ghostly presences lurk. (We refer to the aforementioned "few fleshless exceptions.") Not only do these spirits *lurk*, they also (so Daisy claims) often appear to her in more-or-less bodily form. Why are they drawn to the cantankerous old woman? There is no one-size-fits-all answer. As each year of our lives is recalled by unique events and distinguishable seasons, so the spirits have their various and sundry reasons for rubbing elbows with Daisy. But, that said, the lonely souls of the long-dead reveal themselves to the Ute shaman primarily for the purpose of conversing with a warm-blooded human being. And the oftentimes cold-blooded Daisy Perika is, in a somewhat twisted sense, what a roving poker player might call "the only game in town." Way out here at the mouth of Spirit Canyon, the Southern Ute tribal elder is simply the only person around.

Except when she has company.

Which Daisy does at the moment. Which fortuitous circumstance enables us to focus our attention on three more of the four primary participants in the forthcoming adventure—which has already begun (only they don't know it.) Namely . . .

Charlie Moon, Scott Parris, and Sarah Frank

By way of introduction to those who have not yet been formally introduced to the citizens listed above, they are (respectively):

The amiable nephew of the notoriously cranky Southern Ute tribal elder. Charlie is that long, lean, lanky fellow who is toting Daisy's circa-1935 leather suitcase from her front door to his Ford Expedition. Mr. Moon is a former SUPD officer, a part-time tribal investigator, current owner of the Columbine Ranch in Granite Creek County—and sometimes deputy to Scott Parris, a tough ex-Chicago cop who is chief of Granite Creek Police.

The aforesaid tough cop has opened the rear hatch of the SUV and is pushing a cardboard box in between a heavy toolbox and a gallon jug of well-water. What's in the cardboard box? Four quarts of Daisy's homemade peach preserves, two loaves of m'lady's baked-in-her-oven rye bread, three pints of green-tomato relish, some leftover walnut fudge, and miscellaneous other delectables to spice up the meals at Charlie's ranch. Parris has the enviable distinction of being one of the few Caucasians (*matukach*) whom Dais Perika is fond of, which means that she does not spit in ' eye just for the fun of it. Speaking of eyes and distincti the blue-eyed lawman is also the only paleface wh seen physical evidence of that legendary dwarf wh sumably resides in the shadowy inner sanctum c Canyon. (Several years ago, the white man spied s footprints in the snow.) Gently suggest to Daisy might have been the paw prints of an adult racc will very likely knock your block off and then the road for a furlong or two.

Sarah Frank is that lissome youth who the front door of Daisy's house, and is now automobile to help the tribal elder into her customary seat behind the driver, i.e., Charlie Moon. Speaking of whom, the twenty-one-year-old Ute-Papago orphan (Sarah) lives in the continual distress of being deeply and passionately in love with Mr. Moon, who—when he bothers to reflect on the pretty, willowy young lady at all—thinks of Miss Frank as his semi-adopted daughter.

These cursory introductions complete, we return to the action already underway—which has to do with Hester "Toadie" Tillman's designated messenger, who is on his way to deliver the alleged witch's threat to Aunt Daisy. Will Officer Bignight arrive after they are long gone? Hard to say. We hope not. If Danny doesn't take care of business today, there's no telling what the consequences might be. (The tension is almost palpable.)

But wait a minute . . . about a quarter-mile away to the east-NE, isn't that a puff of dust on the lane? Yes, it is.

CHAPTER 2

SUPD OFFICER DANNY BIGNIGHT ARRIVES AT DAISY PERIKA'S DOMICILE

Which visit was, in itself, sufficient to annoy the edgy old woman—who was eager to depart with Charlie Moon, Scott Parris and Sarah Frank for a month-long stay at the Columbine Ranch. Daisy was, in fact, already settled into the backseat of Charlie's Expedition beside the Ute-Papago girl and waiting impatiently for the men to get in, close the front doors and "Get this big bucket of bolts rolling north!" when Bignight's SUPD unit pulled up and lurched to a neck-jerking stop.

Daisy scowled with understandable suspicion. *This'll be about some kind of trouble.* In her long experience, swo[r]n officers of the law rarely came calling to bring the glad [t]id[d]ings that a penny-pinching old woman who'd bought a [one-]dollar ticket in Someone or Other's Annual Fund [-]Raffle had won First Prize (a brand-new, dark-bl[ue] pickup). Or even Twentieth Prize (a two-pound b[ox of old-]fashioned cherry chocolates which you hardly e[ver see in] the store anymore, and which sugary treats D[aisy was] fairly watered for.)

Officer Bignight emerged from the offic[ial vehi]cle, hitched up his heavy black leather [belt over his] slightly bulging belly, and waved a fond s[alute to his] Southern Ute Police Force comrade.

Well aware that his aunt was anxio[us]

Charlie Moon ambled over to meet and greet his old friend. "Hello, Danny."

"Hey, Charlie." Having noticed the old woman hunched in the backseat of Moon's big SUV, Bignight recognized a welcome opportunity for passing the well-known buck. "Uh, I can see you folks are about to leave, so I'll just let you deliver a message from Hester Tillman to Aunt Daisy." He cleared his throat. "It was Hester's last words before she . . . passed on."

"I'm sorry to hear that, Danny." The devout Catholic Christian closed his eyes, crossed himself, and murmured a prayer for the sad old woman's soul. This done, Moon made the standard inquiry: "How'd she die?"

The SUPD cop described the pickup accident.

The world-class poker player had no difficulty reading the fear in Bignight's eyes. "What was Mrs. Tillman's message to Aunt Daisy?" Some kind last words to terminate their lifelong feud, the lawman hoped.

Bignight provided Moon with a brief summary.

Having no intention of passing on such a silly threat to his elderly relative, a disappointed Charlie Moon passed the buck right back to its rightful owner. "I think you'd bet- er tell Daisy yourself." One of the few Southern Utes who ʼn't believe in witchcraft explained without even the hint ʼ smile: "Hester might not like it if you used me as an ʼnediary."

ʼs reminder had the hoped-for effect. *Charlie's right— ʼ witch told me to tell Daisy myself.* Danny Bignight deep breath that swelled his barrel chest. *I might ʼthis over with.* Hitching up his sagging gun belt ʼroached the Columbine SUV with a tip of his ʼ window where Daisy sat, and mumbled the ʼeting: "How are you?"

ʼog's hair," Daisy snapped back. "Now tell ʼ so-called mind so I can get away from

amphibian reference only served to

elevate Bignight's anxiety. *I'd better get this right—Ol' Toadie is probably floating around somewhere close by, listening to every word I say.* Leaning close to the open car window, the reluctant messenger enlarged on what he'd told Charlie Moon about Hester Tillman's untimely death. "Then she said: 'Now listen to me, Danny—you pass what I've got to say on to Daisy Perika *word-for-word*, or my curse'll fall on you and all of your family down at Taos Pueblo. You tell that mean old Indian woman that if she don't show up at my funeral and shed some salty tears on my account—I'll come back and haunt her to death!'"

Expecting a vile expletive or at least a throaty oath, the bearer of bad news backed away from the Expedition. "I'm sorry, Daisy—you know I don't think you're mean, but I felt like it was my bounden duty to come out here and tell you exactly what Toad—what Hester had to say."

The old woman waved this apology off as if it were a black housefly buzzing about her wrinkled ear. "Don't worry about it, Danny—Toadie always was a big windbag, and one who had to get the last word in."

Oh, I hope she didn't hear that! After glancing right and left, Bignight leaned nervously from one booted foot to the other. "So . . . are you gonna go to Mrs. Tillman's funeral?"

"Maybe. If I have the time." Charlie Moon's a shrugged. "I might go to her burial too, and hang aroun after both of the hired mourners are gone and the wor have shoved dirt over the six-foot-deep hole in the and made a nice, smooth mound."

The worried cop sighed with relief. "That'd nice of you."

"Yes it would." Daisy grinned wickedly. *fun.*

Officer Bignight knew that he shouldn' *something awful.* Without a doubt. But l presented with a plump cricket, Danny resist the clever old angler's bait. "Fur

"Sure." Daisy Perika's black eyes sparkled wickedly at the cop. "It'd be great fun *to spit on Toadie's grave.*"

An optimistic citizen might assume that the irascible old soul was merely making a tasteless jest. (The same optimist might also draw to an inside straight.) But whether Daisy's vulgar threat is to be taken literally—or is merely an attempt to tweak an already nervous Officer Bignight—only time and opportunity will tell.

In the meantime, more urgent matters demand our attention. Indeed, the malignant seed of the oncoming calamity is about to be planted in one of those salt-of-the-earth Rocky Mountain municipalities where the thin air is so wonderfully exhilarating and down-right *nutritious* that a hardworking man who breathes it can live on nine hundred calories of beef and beans per day, and a lean longhorn can get along on about two dozen mouthfuls of alfalfa hay. (Or so they say.) Yes, we'd all like to go there and stay. Directions? Well, this particular All-American high-altitude community is positioned along the final 50-mile lap of the drive from Aunt Daisy's wilderness home on the Southern Ute reservation to Charlie Moon's vast cattle ranch.

If you're not sure that you can navigate your way there, do ot fret—we'll take you to this fine example of a wholesome stern cow town, and show up just as the unseemly hos- s are about to commence.